P9-CFE-315

DATE DUE

GREAT LIVES

American Literature

Doris Faber
and Harold Faber

Atheneum Books for Young Readers

Atheneum Books for Young Readers
An imprint of Simon & Schuster Children's Publishing Division
1230 Avenue of the Americas
New York, New York 10020

First edition   10 9 8 7 6 5 4 3 2 1
Printed in the United States of America

Library of Congress Cataloging-in-Publication Data
Faber, Doris.
    Great lives : American literature / Doris Faber and Harold Faber.   — 1st ed.
        p.   cm.   Includes bibliographical references and index.
    ISBN 0-684-19448-1
1. Authors, American—Biography—Juvenile literature.
2. American literature—History and criticism—Juvenile literature.
[1. Authors, American. 2. American literature—History and criticism.]
I. Faber, Harold.   II. Title.
PS129.F25   1995   810.9—dc20   [B]   94–10866
Summary: A collective biography of thirty great figures in American literature.

Contents

Foreword

One question is bound to strike anybody who picks up this book: On what basis did we select the thirty American writers whose life stories are told here?

The answer must start with the fact that we had only a limited number of pages available to us, so there was no way we could include every notable literary figure from the early days of the United States up until the present.

Since literary reputations are famously unstable, with the verdict of an author's own era often reversed after his or her death, we felt that the soundest way to simplify our selection process would be to declare *all* current contenders out of the running. In short, no writer now alive is listed in our table of contents. While choosing a specific cutoff point did not prove practical, in effect we have restricted our coverage to literary figures whose major work was completed before 1960.

But if this policy did a lot to solve one sort of problem, it magnified another. Since 1960 the emergence of many gifted writers who are women and/or members of various minority groups has much enriched American literature. As just one important example, if the novelist Toni Morrison had begun writing a few decades earlier, almost certainly she would have been the subject of one of our chapters.

Still, a book of this kind cannot change history; it is undeniable that most of the best American writing throughout most of the past two centuries was the work of white males. Indeed our restriction to a mere thirty short biographies has forced us to leave out even some mainstream literary men who were extremely eminent in their own day—among them the poet William Cullen Bryant, as well as the influential editor and novelist William Dean Howells.

Regretfully we also found it necessary to omit Bret Harte despite our own fondness for his verses and short stories. Crossing off Upton Sinclair from our list was much easier because his fame early in the twentieth century was founded more on his social-reformist fervor than his literary ability.

Part of the pressure we felt to keep paring away at our roster of possibilities arose, we should point out, from another policy decision: that all American recipients of the Nobel Prize in literature should be included. Nevertheless, in the case of the 1976 winner Saul Bellow, who has continued to publish new work since then, we sadly decided that we could not sow confusion by making him our sole living subject.

Perhaps we should also mention that, at the outset of this project, its editor gently expressed the wish that we feature a varied company of literary practitioners, including essayists, playwrights, and a few writers of children's books. As a result, the number of novelists and poets we could include was really closer to twenty than thirty.

Surely more than half of the names that do appear in our table of contents would appear on practically any list of outstanding American literary figures. As to the rest, no doubt we have done a certain amount of playing favorites—and why not? This is our list, inevitably affected by our own literary outlook. Even if yours might be somewhat different, there can hardly be any controversy about our underlying aim: to stir interest in the adventure of reading.

Frankly, though, most literary lives are not, on the surface, adventurous. Writers, by the very nature of their calling, spend a lot of time sitting alone facing empty sheets of paper. While their struggles to fill page after page may involve much inner conflict, outwardly only a few of them experience much high drama.

Yet the kind of adventure we hope our book will stimulate is enormously varied—and exciting. To us the best part of this project was its requirement that we read or reread so much marvelous literature. Although some of it might not seem at all appealing to young readers, jumping to such conclusions can be unjustified.

For even Henry James, who turned increasingly ponderous during his old age, wrote the best of his earlier works with a lighter touch. These are listed, along with examples of similarly accessible writings by our other subjects, in a separate section: Suggested Further Reading, page 301.

And now we warmly wish you long years of happy reading!

—D. F. and H. F.

PART I
Early Days

James Fenimore Cooper

1789–1851   The first successful American novelist

One evening when James Fenimore Cooper was nearing the age of thirty, he sat comfortably at home with his wife. He read aloud to her, as was their custom, from a newly imported novel from England. After a chapter or two, he threw it aside.

"I could write you a better book myself," he said confidently. His wife laughed. Her husband disliked writing even a letter, and the idea of his writing a whole book seemed absurd.

But Cooper persevered. He took out a quill pen, ink, and paper, and immediately started to write the first pages of a story.

"He soon became interested," his daughter Susan would later recall, "and, amused at the undertaking, drew a regular plot, talked over the details with our mother, and resolved to imitate the tone and character of an English tale of the ordinary type."

By writing several chapters, Cooper proved to himself that he could do as well as most authors. He was ready then to cease working on the manuscript and go on to other matters. His wife, however, was so impressed by his talent for storytelling that she urged him to finish the book. He did.

Called *Precaution*, it was published the following year. Despite its being a rather lifeless tale about English country society, a subject that Cooper knew only from his reading, it achieved a mild success in its day; in 1820, books by American authors were still a rarity. But it is largely and justly forgotten today.

It changed Cooper's life, though. He

set to work tirelessly with his pen, producing a book a year for the next thirty years. In his lifetime, he earned a reputation in the United States and abroad as this country's first successful novelist. Today some of his books are remembered not only because of their historical importance, but also because they are good stories.

At the time *Precaution* came out, Cooper was a well-off gentleman farmer with a total lack of literary experience—and quite a variety of other experiences. He had traveled widely in the wilderness of upstate New York, gone to sea as a sailor, served as an officer in the United States Navy, and managed large rural estates capably. Everywhere he went, he had listened carefully to the stories of older men who remembered the American Revolution and the founding of the nation.

Cooper himself had been born in Burlington, New Jersey, on September 15, 1789, the year that George Washington took the oath of office as the first president of the United States. His parents were William Cooper, a wealthy land speculator, and Elizabeth Fenimore Cooper, a gentle woman who, in her quiet way, had strong opinions.

Before the future author's first birthday, his father made up his mind to move his family to a new settlement he was establishing in the wilderness at the foot of Lake Otsego in upstate New York. But his wife refused to leave her accustomed surroundings. She went on a sit-down strike in an armchair while wagons were being loaded with furniture. Her husband solved the problem by picking up the chair with her in it and carrying it to a waiting wagon.

Young James was the eleventh in a family of twelve children. He grew up as one of the rather spoiled sons of the lordly founder of Cooperstown. A gray-eyed, ruddy boy with light hair, he swam, skated, rowed, used a sailboat, and played in the forests around Lake Otsego. After learning his ABCs from an older sister, he went to schools in Cooperstown and Albany and then entered Yale College at the age of thirteen, which was not unusual in those days.

Cooper was expelled from Yale, however, during his third year there. Although the college records do not show why he was sent home, family legend blames a prank involving the fastening of a small donkey to the chair of an unpopular teacher.

Back in Cooperstown, Cooper discussed career possibilities with his father. Even though his boating experience had been limited to sailing on Lake Otsego, he thought the navy would be a good place for him. Yet it seemed sensible for him to get familiar with life on the water first. So in 1806, when he was seventeen, he signed up as a sailor on a merchant ship, the *Sterling*, whose home port was Wiscasset, Maine.

Big and strong, Cooper made a good seaman, learning the ropes of a sailor. Some of the events he observed made a lasting impression on him, and later would be described in his novels: the boarding of the *Sterling* by an English officer who forcibly took off several seamen to serve in the Royal Navy; a chase by pirates in the Mediterranean; the rescue of a fellow sailor who fell overboard.

Two years later, in 1808, Cooper received a commission in the American navy as a midshipman. He served on small vessels on Lake Champlain and Lake Ontario with some of the nation's outstanding officers, among them Captain James Lawrence, who would become a great hero during the War of 1812. Cooper loved the navy life, and this feeling is reflected in many of his novels, but he saw no prospects for advancement in the peacetime service.

Two other factors influenced his decision to leave the navy. His father died in 1809, leaving him and his brothers relatively rich men. And, on furlough from the navy, he met and fell in love with Susan De Lancey, the daughter of a prominent and wealthy New York family.

In 1811 they were married; he was twenty-one at the time, his bride just eighteen. The young Mrs. Cooper did not relish being the wife of a naval officer who would frequently be away on long trips. As a result, Cooper resigned from the navy.

During the next several years the Coopers divided their time between Cooperstown and a farm near the De Lanceys, close to New York City. At both places, Cooper kept busy supervising the planting of crops. In the evenings, he and his wife played chess or he read aloud to her—leading to his becoming an author.

Even before *Precaution* appeared in print, Cooper began a second novel, *The Spy*. This time he turned to an American theme, writing about events during the Revolutionary War in an area he knew well, Westchester County, just north of New York City. It was then a "neutral ground" between the British army to the south and the American army in the Hudson Valley, with local residents torn between conflicting interests.

In *The Spy*, Cooper used the physical landscape as an important element of his plot, a technique he followed in most of his later books as well. In the no-man's-land between the two armies, families were divided and people were not what they seemed to be on the surface. As a prime example, Cooper created a memorable character, Harvey Birch, widely believed to be a British agent. But Birch really was General Washington's most efficient spy.

A fast writer, Cooper began to write as soon as he conceived an idea for a book. His daughter Susan later described his method of operation: "He first adopted some general leading idea, sketched vaguely in his mind a few of the more prominent characters, and then immediately began his work in final shape, leaving the details to suggest and develop themselves during the progress of the volume."

It was no wonder, then, that his grammar was sometimes faulty and his language stilted, that some of his characters were wooden, and that his style was somewhat careless. Still, Cooper mastered the technique of dramatizing his ideas and making them seem exciting— and he also managed to create some heroic characters.

The public responded favorably. Published in 1821, *The Spy* scored an immediate success in America and later that year in England. A dramatic version appeared on the New York stage within a few months. It was translated into several languages in Europe.

Cooper's most famous character— Natty Bumppo, also called Leatherstocking, the Deerslayer, and Hawkeye—appeared for the first time in his next book, *The Pioneers*, published in 1823. Cooper set the scene around Lake Otsego, near his Cooperstown home, back when white settlers were first establishing themselves in the area. The book's conflict is between Judge Temple, a fair-minded agent of the law, and Bumppo, the hunter who had roamed the land undisturbed for forty years.

To most readers, Natty Bumppo is a heroic figure, the original of the strong, silent man of the West familiar to today's readers, television watchers, and moviegoers. A crack shot, he is strong, able to cope with evil, respectful of women, and independent. In *The Pioneers*, though, Natty Bumppo stands in the way of advancing civilization and the many settlers who come, building farms and houses—and making laws restricting, for example, the hunting of deer, upon which Bumppo lives.

In this novel Cooper sets a theme that he would repeat over and over. As much as he admires Natty Bumppo's skill and independence, he strongly supports law and order as the basis of modern society. "Society cannot exist without wholesome restraints," Judge Temple says, and Cooper agrees.

Natty Bumppo had no recourse except to move on. As Cooper put it in the last sentence of the novel: "He had gone far toward the setting sun—the foremost in that band of pioneers who are

James Fenimore Cooper in his home at Cooperstown. *Engraving from the portrait by Chappel. New York Public Library.*

opening the way for the march of the nation across the continent."

But Natty Bumppo did not disappear. He became the central character in Cooper's most famous five novels, grouped together as the Leatherstocking Tales: *The Last of the Mohicans, The Prairie, The Pathfinder,* and *The Deerslayer,* as well as *The Pioneers.* Cooper interrupted the Leatherstocking series, though, to go off in a completely different direction.

At dinner one day in New York City, a friend of his praised the Scottish writer Walter Scott's new novel, *The Pirate.* To Cooper, however, this was the work of a landsman who had studied sea matters and language but obviously lacked firsthand knowledge. That night he turned to his wife and told her he had to write a sea tale "to show what can be done in this way by a sailor."

Cooper's *The Pilot* became, in effect, the model for a whole new category of fiction, the sea story. Such tales became widely popular in the next hundred years. His own first sea story took place during the American Revolution on a ship about to raid the coast of England. Besides relating exciting adventures, it also examines such issues as the necessity at sea for loyalty and obedience to the captain. Published in 1824, *The Pilot* further increased Cooper's literary reputation on both sides of the Atlantic.

Indeed, his early novels made Cooper an important character in the emerging American literary scene. He founded the Bread and Cheese Club in New York City, where writers gathered; he received an honorary degree from Columbia University; and he served on the committee that welcomed the Marquis de Lafayette on a return trip to the United States.

He also received an appointment as the American consul in Lyons, France, an honorary post that involved no duty or pay. It allowed him to take his family to Europe and travel widely, starting in 1826. The Coopers were happy in London, Paris, and Florence, living in fashionable areas, keeping their own carriage, and entertaining their friends.

Cooper found himself world-famous, known everywhere he went. His books were translated into numerous languages, including Turkish and Persian as well as French, Spanish, Italian, German, and Russian.

Despite all of his traveling, Cooper continued to write one after another new novel about the sea or about European life. But he discovered, as many travelers do, that Europeans had many misconceptions about life in America. So, in 1828, he wrote *Notions of the Americans,* aiming to provide a more accurate picture for foreign readers.

After seven years abroad, Cooper, at

the age of forty-four, returned to the United States in 1833. When he came back, he found that both he and the country had changed. What he noticed most was the disappearing wilderness, a rise in commerce, and an increasing lack of respect for the rights of property holders. A man with a strong sense of patriotism, he set out to write a new series of novels setting forth his own views about the true principles of American democracy.

However, these high-minded books attracted few readers, and they are remembered today only by literary historians.

A firm believer in private property, Cooper became involved in a quarrel with neighbors about a piece of land in Cooperstown. He also began a series of libel suits against newspapers that he claimed had made false statements about him. Although he won these cases, they spread the impression that he had a quarrelsome nature.

No matter that Cooper had to interrupt his work constantly, he still kept on writing. First, he finished a solid historical effort about a subject that he loved: the sea. His two-volume *The History of the Navy of the United States* was published in 1839. Then another navy book, *Lives of Distinguished Naval Officers*, came in 1846.

In this period Cooper lived in Coop-

erstown with his wife, four daughters, and a son. Even though he kept getting involved in disputes with his neighbors about land rights, he remained a respected man in the community, repeatedly invited to deliver the main address at the village's Fourth of July ceremonies.

He was "very domestic" in all his habits, according to his daughter Susan; she had a literary bent, too, and kept a journal that would later be published, providing many details about Cooper's family life. Susan noted that on sunny afternoons her father loved to go rowing on Lake Otsego with his wife. As he grew older and rowing became too strenuous, the afternoon excursions were usually horse-drawn–carriage rides around the countryside.

"Even while writing in his library," Susan wrote, "the door was often open, while the family were moving about in the adjoining hall; and very frequently he would leave an unfinished page for half an hour and join his wife and children for a little chat, or a game of backgammon or chess, of both of which he was very fond."

Throughout this later period, Cooper continued to finish a new novel almost every year. Most of these books are now forgotten, but literary experts say that some of them are worth remembering and reading.

Otsego Hall, James Fenimore Cooper's home in Cooperstown. *Culver Pictures, Inc.*

In the best novel of his old age, *The Two Admirals,* Cooper turned to the sea again and to one of his favorite themes, divided loyalty. The setting is the British navy before the American Revolution. Admiral Bluewater squarely faces the issue: Should he serve the king, his commander, or transfer his loyalty to another contender for the throne, whose claim he feels is rightful?

Cooper also wrote three novels about an important development in American history, the anti-rent wars in New York. In the mid-1840s, tenant farmers who did not have the right to own the land on which generations of their family had worked rose up in revolt against the landowners. To Cooper, a landowner himself, but also a firm believer in a democratic society, this was a disturbing development.

In *Satanstoe,* the best of the series, Cooper defends the legal position of the landlords. He argues that they are more likely to maintain a just society than the emerging commercial class. No matter that his point of view would find few defenders today, a leading contemporary critic has called *Satanstoe* "one of the most distinguished of American historical novels."

With the publication in 1850 of *The Ways of the Hour,* a murder mystery ending in a jury trial, Cooper's work came to an end. He died in Cooperstown on September 14, 1851, at the age of sixty-two.

Cooper had a realistic view of his own place in American literary history. Writing a preface to a new edition of one of his books, he had asserted: "If anything from the pen of the writer of these romances is at all to outlive himself, it is unquestionably the series of the Leatherstocking Tales."

He was right. Natty Bumppo remains alive for readers today—more than a hundred and fifty years after his creation by Cooper.

Ralph Waldo Emerson

1803–1882   The most eminent American literary figure of the
Nineteenth Century

In Europe as well as his own country, during the 1800s Ralph Waldo Emerson was considered the deepest thinker the United States had yet produced. His philosophic essays about moral and religious issues gave him a towering reputation. Even today, he is widely regarded as the most important writer of his century.

Over the years since Emerson's death, however, his fame has become increasingly hard to explain. Not merely the complicated thoughts he expressed, but also his austere personality, make it difficult for many modern readers to admire him. Still, the story of his life contains much more human drama than his solemn portraits suggest.

The background of America's first great intellectual leader could hardly have been more fitting. On both sides of his family, his ancestors were among New England's original settlers and many of the menfolk became preachers, a position that put them on the top rung of the colonial social ladder. In effect Emerson was born into the new land's equivalent of the Old World aristocracy.

But when tensions between the colonists and their rulers erupted into outright rebellion, his relatives unhesitatingly supported the cause of liberty. Indeed, his Emerson grandfather, a clergyman barred from fighting, cheered from an upstairs window of his residence—overlooking a soon-to-be celebrated little bridge in the Massachusetts village of Concord—when the local militia beat back British redcoats

11

Ralph Waldo Emerson at the age of fifty-four in an engraving by W. B. Closson from a crayon drawing by Samuel Rowse. *Joanne F. Polster.*

during one of the opening battles of the American Revolution.

Although Concord would acquire a good deal of additional distinction as the home of Ralph Waldo Emerson, he was actually born twenty miles away in Boston. On May 25, 1803, his father noted the arrival of his third son in his diary. "Mrs. E. well," he added tersely before listing the various meetings that the increase in his family had not prevented his attending.

Strictly upright, but more concerned with his many civic activities than with domestic matters, the Reverend William Emerson never developed a close relationship with the boy he named after his wife's seafaring brother and also after a distant connection of his own. The infant's mother, Ruth Haskins Emerson, was pious and dutiful, but almost as lacking in warmth as her husband.

No wonder then that Ralph grew into a standoffish sort of child. Nor did he show any early signs of being particularly bright. His father, a man of rigid rules and high expectations, complained to a relative a week before his son's third birthday that "Ralph does not read very well yet."

Altogether, his parents would have six sons and two daughters, but both of the girls died young, and so did one of the boys. One other son proved to be mentally retarded. Ralph's remaining three brothers—one older, two younger—all struck their parents as more promising than he was because they earned outstanding grades at school, while his were only mediocre.

Among the many thousands of words that Emerson would later write, hardly any touch on his youthful feelings. Once, though, he did say he had had an "unpleasing" boyhood, leading some people years afterward to compare him with the fabled ugly duckling who eventually turned into a beautiful swan. Yet Ralph did not suffer quite the same lonely isolation because he and his brothers forged a strong, affectionate bond.

The Boston of their day, with a population of only around twenty thousand, was just beginning to resemble the modern picture of a major city. Not far from its busy docks, the yellow-frame manse where the minister of its First Unitarian Church lived with his family was located on what still looked like a country lane. About three acres of gardens and fruit trees surrounded the dwelling; behind a brick wall, Ralph and his brothers whirled tops or otherwise amused themselves during their limited periods of leisure.

They were not allowed to associate with the "rude boys" who roamed the streets outside. Even at school, where their fellow pupils came from similar families, Ralph could not mingle easily, so he relied on his brothers for companionship. His solitary tendency was reinforced by a series of upheavals, starting with his father's death from the dreaded disease tuberculosis in 1811, when this very sensitive son was just eight years old.

Besides the emotional pain of losing his father without ever having succeeded in pleasing him, Emerson from then onward had no real home throughout the rest of his boyhood. Prominent as the Reverend William Emerson had been, he left no money to support his wife and six young children. Thus they were obliged to depend on help from relatives, along with the charity of church members. After Emerson's mother no longer had any infants requiring constant care, she began earning small sums by taking in boarders.

Forced to move frequently because of one crisis or another, she might have faltered in her efforts to bring up her sons respectably if not for her husband's extremely strong-minded unmarried sister. Aunt Mary Moody Emerson insisted that these boys had been "born to be educated." By the time Emerson was ten, she was already prodding him with letters that did much to inspire his future career.

"Scorn trifles, lift your aims," Aunt Mary urged him. Emerson must have hated having to share an overcoat with his brother Edward—during cold weather, they took turns wearing it to the Boston Latin School, where the sons of the city's leading families were prepared to enter Harvard College. Yet he buried whatever misery he felt beneath a confident air of superiority, which did not endear him to his fellow students.

When he was eleven, one of his uncles asked him a thoughtful question: "How is it, Ralph, that all of the boys dislike you and quarrel with you, whilst the grown people are fond of you?" What he replied did not get recorded.

With various kinds of assistance, including being excused from paying some student expenses in exchange for carrying the college president's private messages, Emerson entered Harvard in 1817. Only fourteen then, he was the youngest member of his class; similarly youthful applicants were admitted fairly often in those days, though, if they managed to pass the stiff entrance exams.

During his four years at Harvard, Emerson achieved only middling grades, and his standoffish manner won him few friends. He mostly occupied himself with reading widely on his own. Yet he made two notable decisions in this period, one of them somewhat mysterious: For reasons he never explained, he asked his family and everybody else who knew him well to start calling him

Waldo instead of Ralph. It can only be guessed that he thought his middle name sounded more impressive.

The second and far more significant step he took at college was to begin keeping a daily record of his thoughts. On January 25, 1820, at the age of seventeen, he made the first entry in the remarkable journal that he would continue compiling for more than fifty years. In itself a major contribution to American literature, filling ten large volumes when it was finally published decades after Emerson's death, it marked the birth of his serious effort to fulfill his dreams of greatness.

As an eighteen-year-old Harvard senior, he displayed his inner feelings frankly when he wrote in his journal, "I find myself often idle, vagrant, stupid & hollow. This is somewhat appalling & if I do not discipline myself with diligent care I shall suffer severely from remorse & the sense of inferiority hereafter. All around me are industrious & will be great [while] I am indolent & shall be insignificant. Avert it heaven! Avert it virtue! I need excitement."

Still, he could not but realize that he was expected to follow his family's pattern by becoming a minister. How this career might win him the distinction he craved was a matter that occupied his mind often while he spent the next few years teaching at a small school for young ladies in order to save enough money to pay for further religious training.

When Emerson was twenty-two, he enrolled at Harvard's divinity school and, in keeping with the era's prevailing practice, two years later he began delivering sermons at various Unitarian churches as a sort of apprenticeship. While he was temporarily assigned to preach in the New Hampshire town of Concord, he met the sixteen-year-old sister of one of his Harvard classmates.

Ellen Tucker, a beautiful and very religious girl with a bent for poetry, stirred the most powerful emotion Emerson had ever felt. The following year he went to see her again, and soon they were writing each other high-minded love poems. Although she, like her mother and sister, was afflicted with tuberculosis, her health seemed to improve marvelously upon becoming engaged to her tall, solemn suitor.

On September 30, 1829, when Emerson was twenty-six and Ellen eighteen, they were married. During the next several months he experienced a sublime happiness, but with the onset of a blustery Boston winter, the symptoms of his wife's disease returned alarmingly. Less than a year and a half after their wedding, on February 8, 1831, Ellen died.

"My angel is gone to heaven this morning & I am alone in the world," Emerson wrote to a relative. Although he appeared resigned to her departure, he showed the intensity of his sense of loss in his journal: "Shall I ever again be able to connect the face of outward nature, the mists of the morn, the star of eve, the flowers, & all poetry with the heart and life of an enchanting friend? No. There is one birth & one baptism & one first love & the affections cannot keep their youth any more than men."

As he had predicted, Emerson never again achieved the happiness he had known with Ellen. By the time he lost her, though, he had already become the pastor of Boston's Second Unitarian Church. Despite several other tragedies afflicting his immediate family—within a few more years he and his oldest brother, William, practicing law in New York City, would be their mother's only surviving offspring—his own success at carrying on the Emersons' ministerial tradition seemed assured.

But less than a year after the death of his young wife, Emerson resigned his church position. Whether he would have done the deep soul-searching that led him to this decision if she had lived is a question that can never be answered, but in one way his new status certainly made following the dictates of his conscience easier. For Ellen had received a modest fortune as a result of other deaths in her family, and from her he inherited enough to keep himself at least in frugal style without ever having to preach another sermon.

Not that Emerson disliked preaching. With a wonderfully resonant voice as well as a temperament that took naturally to composing sermons, he liked nothing better than standing in a pulpit proclaiming opinions he had worked hard to express in highly polished sentences. But he felt very uncomfortable performing the routine clerical duties of officiating at weddings and funerals. More importantly, he had come to feel that he could not continue presiding over his church's sacred Last Supper ceremony because he no longer accepted its significance.

Emerson did not abandon his religious faith, nor did he even cease being a clergyman, when he quit his Boston post. Indeed, he still delivered occasional sermons at other churches in the vicinity. Yet his resignation freed him from having to follow any prescribed mode of belief—in effect, it was his own declaration of spiritual independence.

Because Ralph Waldo Emerson would go on to brilliantly assert the supremacy of every individual's inner spirit, he achieved a rare sort of fame. Among serious thinkers on both sides of the Atlantic, what he wrote and the example he set were seen as a uniquely American contribution in the realm of philosophy, something like Thomas Jefferson's contribution in the realm of political science.

But the magnitude of his eventual impact was certainly not apparent right away. Already, Emerson had written some poetry destined to be regarded as outstanding, most particularly a kind of hymn to nature entitled "Good-bye, Proud World!" And he had also published a few scholarly articles in religious periodicals. Still, approaching the age of thirty, when he set off on a tour of Europe a few months after resigning his church position he appeared to be just an ordinary American traveler seeking a taste of Old World culture.

Thanks to his Boston connections, though, Emerson carried letters of introduction to some of Europe's leading writers. Unknown as he was, the scope of his interests in "all of the great questions" about human life and conduct made him a welcome visitor. Britain's eminent Thomas Carlyle found this young Bostonian's conversation so stimulating that their meeting brought the start of a literary letter-writing relationship lasting more than forty years.

On returning home late in 1833, Emerson took two major steps. He decided to settle, with his mother, in the Massachusetts village of Concord, long associated with his family. And he began taking part in one of the most popular features of American life during this era,

when practically every city and town had its own "lyceum" where lectures were regularly given. These talks on all sorts of topics—a century before the invention of radio or television—drew large audiences of local citizens desiring to broaden their minds.

Thus, it was as a lyceum lecturer that Ralph Waldo Emerson first emerged into prominence. The opportunity to deliver inspirational sermons, without the restrictions involved in speaking from a church's pulpit, suited him perfectly. What's more, he soon developed an ideal system, allowing him to compose over a hundred different lectures during the next few decades, deliver them on tours around the country, and also preserve polished versions of them permanently.

To do all this, Emerson used his private journal as his "savings bank." Whenever the occasion arose for him to prepare a new lecture, he culled out his thoughts on subjects like heroism or friendship or history and merely strung them together. After further reflection, he would painstakingly revise the material and eventually publish it in the form of an essay.

The brilliance of Emerson's literary style, as well as of his intellect, is beyond dispute: Numerous words of his appear in every modern collection of familiar quotations. Here are just a few of the

Emerson with his son Edward and second daughter, Edith. *Journals of Ralph Waldo Emerson, 1909.*

often-repeated phrases from his essay "Self-Reliance," probably his best-known work:

"Whoso would be a man must be a nonconformist."

"A foolish consistency is the hobgoblin of little minds."

"To be great is to be misunderstood."

Despite the clarity of his sentences, however, Emerson's paragraphs are often confusing, and sometimes the meaning of entire pages defies the understanding of most readers. Even so, following the publication of his first short book of essays in 1836, his stature as a great man became firmly established—and some of

his most fervent admirers began treating him the way believers in various modern cults treat their gurus.

Among these disciples none looked up to him more than his second wife. At the age of thirty-three, Emerson married a suitable but rather dour woman named Lydia Jackson, eight months his senior. Lydian, as he insisted on calling her because he liked the sound of it better, might have made him much happier, besides being more cheerful herself, if he could have ceased always comparing her unfavorably with the saintly Ellen who had been his first love. Despite their domestic difficulties, though, Lydian gave him four children, whom he doted on, and also did her best to appreciate his "transcendental" genius.

That multisyllabic word became indelibly associated with Emerson because of his frequent references to the transcendent spirit within every individual. As a result, he and his followers were tagged transcendentalists, and the term sometimes held undertones of ridicule because the Sage of Concord struck some observers as more than slightly ridiculous. Nevertheless, the verdict of history would amply confirm the admiration of his disciples.

One of these deserves special notice. Henry David Thoreau, a young neighbor of Emerson's, was immeasurably influenced by him on his own path to

Ralph Waldo Emerson's residence in Concord, Massachusetts. *Culver Pictures, Inc.*

fame—but their connection will be described more fully in the separate chapter on Thoreau's life. Here it is sufficient to say that Emerson encouraged Thoreau in many ways, and mourned his early death movingly: "The country knows not yet, or in the least part, how great a son it has lost."

As Emerson himself advanced toward old age, he continued diligently lecturing and writing. The respectful attention he received during his occasional trips abroad reinforced American pride in having produced an internationally admired intellectual figure. But some of his own countrymen joked about going to hear him lecture just to bask in his wisdom, even though everything he said went way over their heads.

At least a few of his words were simple enough, though, to be memorized by generations of schoolchildren. Upon the completion of Concord's monument to the Revolutionary War minutemen who had fought there, Emerson was asked to compose a suitable hymn— and, since then, pupils in countless classrooms have recited:

By the rude bridge that arched the flood,
　Their flag to April's breeze unfurled,
Here once the embattled farmers stood,
　And fired the shot heard round the
　　world.

Despite the many honors heaped on Emerson, his private life remained emotionally unsatisfying, especially after the death of his adored first son. Although he had two daughters, as well as another son, he never ceased mourning the boy named after him, who had died at the age of five in 1842.

Still, Emerson kept active throughout the next several decades, even taking an adventurous lecture trip all the way to California in 1871, when he was sixty-eight. The following year, however, a fire broke out at his Concord home, and in the excitement of trying to rescue his books and papers, he suffered a slight stroke. After that he became more and more forgetful.

Despite his failing memory he was such an impressive-looking old man that a noted sculptor who came to make a statue of him told a friend, "I think it is very seldom that a face combines such vigor and strength."

A month before he would have celebrated his seventy-ninth birthday, on April 27, 1882, Emerson died at his home in Concord. Over a century later he is still regarded as a key figure in this country's literary history.

Nathaniel Hawthorne

1804–1864   The novelist of old New England

Nathaniel Hawthorne was born on July 4, 1804, in Salem, Massachusetts, then one of the leading seaports in the United States. He grew up, lived, and worked in and around Salem, which became the geographic centerpiece of his tales and novels. He was so intimately connected with its history—of witchcraft trials and of maritime prosperity—that a recent biographer of Hawthorne called his book *Salem Is My Dwelling Place.*

Many of the writer's ancestors went to sea, following the Salem tradition of trading with far-off places. He scarcely knew his father, a sea captain also named Nathaniel Hawthorne, who had been on the high seas returning from a trading trip to the Far East when he was born. But he knew a lot about his family's role in the history of Salem.

Among its first settlers was William Hathorne (the spelling would later be changed to Hawthorne), who arrived in Massachusetts in 1630. He became a prominent citizen, a major in the Salem militia. His son John, Nathaniel's great-grandfather, sat as one of the judges at the trials that condemned nineteen women to hang as witches in 1692.

As the son of a mariner often away from home on long voyages, Nathaniel grew up in a house of women. He lived in a modest home not far from the wharves with his grandmother; his mother, the former Elizabeth Clarke Manning; and two sisters—one older than he was, the other younger.

Their father died of yellow fever in South America in 1808, when Nathaniel was four years old. Left all but penniless, the widowed Mrs. Hawthorne and her three children went to live with her parents. A prosperous family of merchants, the Mannings welcomed young Nathaniel and his sisters.

He had a normal boyhood, going to school, fighting sometimes with other boys, and caring for a pet monkey a relative brought back from some distant voyage. When Nathaniel was nine years old, he injured his foot while playing ball. Forced to use crutches in order to get around, he spent most of his time lying on the floor reading. Because of his accident, he was kept out of school for almost two years, until February of 1816.

That summer, the Hawthornes moved temporarily to a Manning cottage on Sebago Lake in Maine—and stayed there for three years. "I lived in Maine like a bird in the air, so perfect was the freedom that I enjoyed," he later wrote to a friend. He added a negative recollection too: "It was there that I first got my cursed habit of solitude." By himself he roamed in the woods, hunted, and fished. On rainy days, though, Nathaniel read—the plays of Shakespeare, Bunyan's *The Pilgrim's Progress*, and "any poetry or light books within my reach."

He returned to Salem in 1819, at the age of fifteen, and began preparing to go to college while working as a bookkeeper in the office of the Manning stagecoach business. For a brief time, helped by his sister Louisa, he wrote and published a hand-lettered family newspaper, *The Spectator*, filled with news, gossip, poetry, and essays. It was his first attempt at writing.

He soon gave it up, telling his sister Elizabeth that "no man can be a poet and a bookkeeper at the same time." Although he had not yet decided on a career, he informed his mother that being a minister was out of the question, that there were too many lawyers already, and that he did not like the idea of becoming a physician.

"Oh, that I was rich enough to live without a profession!" he wrote to her up in Maine. "What do you think of my becoming an author, and relying for support on my pen? I think the illegibility of my pen is very author-like." Even though his tone was humorous, it seemed that Hawthorne at the age of sixteen was mulling over the idea of becoming a writer.

In September of 1821, when he was seventeen, Hawthorne climbed into a stagecoach for a trip to Brunswick, Maine, where he enrolled at Bowdoin College. In the coach he met a fellow student, Franklin Pierce, who would be his lifelong friend—and also president of the United States.

At college Hawthorne was an average student, devoting much of his time to walking in the woods and to reading books he enjoyed instead of studying. Even so, he excelled in Latin and English composition; but he detested mathematics.

Hawthorne joined a group that called itself the Pot-8-0 Club, in joking tribute to Maine's principal crop, the potato. It met weekly at Ward's Tavern, located on the edge of the campus. There its members recited poetry, discussed topics in the news, drank, and ate good dinners.

Despite the college's rules against gambling, Hawthorne and several other students played cards for money. He wrote to his mother during his second year: "All the card-players in college have been found out—my unfortunate self among the number. One has been dismissed from the college, two suspended, and the rest, with myself, fined fifty cents each."

After graduation Hawthorne returned to Salem unsure of his future. "It was my fortune or misfortune to have some slender means of supporting myself," he wrote later, "and so on leaving college in 1825, instead of immediately studying a profession, I sat myself down to consider what pursuit in life I was best fit for. . . . And year after year I kept considering what I was fit for, and time and destiny decided that I was to be the writer that I am."

For ten years Hawthorne lived in what he called his "long seclusion," in a small chamber under the eaves of an upstairs room in his mother's house. But he was not a hermit. Every summer, he traveled—to Vermont, to New Hampshire, on Lake Champlain, and along the Erie Canal. A good listener, he put into his journals his observations of people and landscapes, a practice he continued throughout his life.

In that period, he also began to write what he called tales—today, we would call them short stories—about the clash of ideas in the New England of his Puritan ancestors. After several years he put together a book of seven of his tales, but he could not find a publisher for them. In despair, he burned the manuscript.

Hawthorne also wrote a novel, *Fanshawe,* set at a remote college in Maine, similar to Bowdoin, about two students in love with the same woman. In 1828, he paid a Boston publisher one hundred dollars to issue it. Although his first book received some kind reviews, he himself felt dissatisfied by it and he burned the copy he had given to his sister Elizabeth.

Nevertheless, *Fanshawe* caught the attention of another Boston publisher, Samuel G. Goodrich, who wrote to Hawthorne asking if he had anything else ready for print. Hawthorne sent him some tales and brief sketches, which appeared starting in 1830. Even

A portrait of Nathaniel Hawthorne by Emmanuel Lentle. *New York Public Library*.

though these works appeared anonymously, Hawthorne began to be regarded as a promising writer in Boston's literary circles.

In 1836 he moved to Boston to become editor of Goodrich's *American Magazine of Useful and Entertaining Knowledge.* At the age of thirty-two he had a job for the first time in his life. But it was drudgery filling the magazine every month, and the pay was low. So Hawthorne soon returned to Salem. Before leaving, however, he submitted to Goodrich a collection of eighteen stories he called *Twice-Told Tales.*

This was issued the following year. Unknown to Hawthorne, it appeared only because of the intervention of a college classmate and friend, who had guaranteed the publisher against any financial loss if the book did not sell well. Although it received some very favorable reviews, it sold poorly and earned only a meager amount of money for its author.

Still, that year of 1837 was a turning point in his life. Not only was *Twice-Told Tales* a critical success, but also it led to his meeting the three talented Peabody sisters of Salem. Elizabeth Peabody, the eldest, perceived in Hawthorne an eligible bachelor who was a rising literary star, so she invited him, as well as his sisters, for a visit.

When Lizzie Peabody opened her front door she was struck, as she later wrote, by "the splendor of his young beauty." For he was then a very handsome man of thirty-three, with a massive head, heavy eyebrows, and dark hair. His eyes were particularly noticeable, seeming at times like blue-gray sapphires.

Lizzie ran upstairs to tell her sister Sophia, who had gone to bed with a headache, "Mr. Hawthorne and his sisters have come, and you never saw anything so splendid—he is handsomer than Lord Byron. You must get up and dress and come down."

Sophia refused. "If he has come once, he will come again," she said. The youngest of the Peabody sisters, Sophia was twenty-eight then. Soft-spoken, she was the artist in this family of gifted women who wrote and taught.

Hawthorne did visit again. That time Sophia came down the stairs, dressed in white. He sprang to his feet—and they looked at each other silently. Later they would both say they had fallen in love at first sight.

But their romance had to overcome many obstacles. Her family regarded Sophia as an invalid who needed to be protected in all sorts of ways. For her to marry a man without a good and steady income seemed out of the question. So Hawthorne realized that, one way or another, he must prove he could support a wife comfortably.

Although moody at times, he was a hard worker. He took up editing another magazine in Boston, wrote several books for children, and even tried to gain the position of historian on an exploration trip to the Antarctic. Finally in 1839, through the influence of friends, he was appointed to a minor post in the Boston Customs House, measuring and counting loads of coal and salt coming into the harbor.

Efficient in his work, Hawthorne found it impossible to write while busy in "an occupation so alien to literature." So he was not unhappy when he lost his job because of a change in political administrations in Washington. By then he and Sophia were formally engaged to be married, and they agreed that they would join Brook Farm, a high-minded experiment in communal living being organized by some of the leaders of the idealistic transcendental movement.

Hawthorne went first, investing some of his savings from his job in Boston. On a visit, Sophia was impressed by the beauty of the rural Massachusetts countryside but warned Hawthorne against working too hard at community chores. A few months later he decided not to join Brook Farm permanently, after all, because communal living no longer seemed very appealing. There was no time to write, either.

But 1842 was another turning point for Hawthorne. A new edition of *Twice-Told Tales*, containing twenty-one additional stories, appeared to favorable reviews. And he wrote several more children's books. Furthermore, he and Sophia were finally married; he was thirty-eight then, and she was thirty-three.

They moved into a house in the pleasant village of Concord, about fifteen miles from Boston. Called the Old Manse, it had been built as a parsonage by Ralph Waldo Emerson's grandfather. Emerson himself was the most influential American writer of the era, and as a welcoming gesture he had his young friend Henry David Thoreau plant a vegetable garden for the newlyweds.

At the Old Manse, Nathaniel had a studio in which to write, and just below it Sophia had her own studio for painting. After seven weeks of marriage, Hawthorne wrote in his journal that he had "rather be on earth than in the seventh Heaven just now." Sophia wrote to her mother, "Say what you will, there never was such a husband to enrich the world since it sprang out of chaos. I feel precisely like an Eve in Paradise."

Hawthorne and his wife wrote a joint journal, he fished, he worked in the garden, he took walks with his friend Emerson—and he wrote stories for various newspapers and magazines. But even though he published twenty pieces during his years at the Old Manse, his income was scarcely enough for the couple after they had their first child, a daughter they named Una.

Three years later, in 1845, the Hawthorne family returned to Salem. His second collection of tales and essays, called *Mosses from an Old Manse,* published in 1846, was a critical success, but it earned him little money. That year, through the intervention of friends with political connections, President Polk appointed Hawthorne to a supervisory post in the Salem Customs House. The job temporarily eased his financial burdens.

His work at the Customs House left no time for writing, though. Again, he felt somewhat relieved to be dismissed after the next election, and he took up his pen once more. Closeted in his study, working furiously both in the mornings and afternoons, Hawthorne wrote *The Scarlet Letter,* a powerful story of public shame and private guilt in the early days of Puritan Salem, with an unforgettable heroine, Hester Prynne.

When the noted publisher James T. Fields visited Salem, Hawthorne showed him an unfinished version of *The Scarlet Letter.* The author said, "It is either very good or very bad, I don't know which." Fields thought it was very good.

Not only was it very good, it was the best novel Hawthorne ever wrote—and it has even been described by some literary pundits as the best American novel ever written. Along with its examination of deep moral issues, it contains some intensely dramatic scenes, for instance the one depicting Hester's public punishment for the sin of adultery. To other readers Hawthorne's portrait of the guilty minister Arthur Dimmesdale stands out most memorably.

Published in 1850, *The Scarlet Letter* was greeted with high praise. It firmly established Hawthorne as one of the outstanding literary figures of his era.

Eager to leave Salem after his ouster from the Customs House, the Hawthornes moved to the scenic village of Lenox in the Berkshire Mountains of western Massachusetts. There, he and a younger writer, Herman Melville, then working on *Moby-Dick,* became so friendly that Melville later dedicated his masterpiece to Hawthorne.

In Lenox Hawthorne settled down to write a novel that he called *The House of the Seven Gables.* Published in 1851, it is a brooding story of a great, gray mansion in Salem that cast a spell over the people who lived in it or coveted it. Hawthorne himself thought it was a better book than *The Scarlet Letter,* but hardly anybody else has ever agreed with him.

An engraving of Nathaniel Hawthorne reading to his family. *The Bettmann Archive.*

The following year the Hawthorne family moved back to the Boston area. Their third child was born at a temporary home in West Newton, where Hawthorne himself completed his third novel in three years, *The Blithedale Romance.* The only one of his books with a contemporary theme, it was a thinly disguised story of Brook Farm, the experimental community in which he had lived briefly a decade earlier.

In 1852, around the time *The* *Blithedale Romance* was published, the Hawthornes moved again. They bought a house in Concord called The Wayside, which became their permanent home. Hawthorne's first literary project there was a campaign biography he wrote for his college classmate and friend Franklin Pierce, who had just been nominated for the presidency.

After Pierce's election, Hawthorne was rewarded with a well-paying job. He became the American consul in Liverpool, one of the major ports in England for ships sailing to the United States. In 1853, when he was nearly fifty years old, Hawthorne embarked with his family on his first trip to Europe. He remained there for seven years.

Along with his literary gifts, Hawthorne was an efficient administrator, who faithfully performed his duties as consul in Liverpool. However, these left him little time for writing, as had been the case during previous periods of official employment. When a new president of the opposing party, James Buchanan, entered the White House in 1857, Hawthorne was happy to do what was expected of political appointees by resigning his post.

Free by then of financial worries, he and his wife set off to travel through England, France, and Italy. They walked together through Roman ruins with their old friend, former President Pierce. Hawthorne was particularly struck by two statues of fauns in the Villa Borghese in Rome. In one of his notebooks he described the faun as "a natural and delightful link between human and brute life, with something of a divine character intermingled."

Such thoughts stimulated him to write again. He began another novel, *The Marble Faun,* the only Hawthorne novel that did not have an American background, although it was about American artists living abroad. The theme, though, was the same as in most of his work: the impact of sin on men and women. The novel came out to mixed reviews, first in England and then in the United States in 1860.

In that year the Hawthornes returned to their home in Concord. Soon he was planning and supervising an addition to The Wayside: a three-story tower study, in which he hoped to find the peace and quiet he needed to write. Aside from putting together his journal notes about trips around England and creating a book of essays called *Our Old Home,* he still found it difficult to concentrate on his work.

Hawthorne went into Boston at times to attend meetings of the Saturday Club with Emerson and other literary figures, including Henry Wadsworth Longfellow, James Russell Lowell, and Oliver Wendell Holmes. As time passed, though, he returned to his youthful habits of seclusion.

The beginning of the Civil War in 1861 had depressed Hawthorne, and he became increasingly pessimistic because of the large numbers of men killed and injured in the fighting. His own health deteriorated, too, to the extent that he was unable to write anymore. In May of 1863 his friend Franklin Pierce came to visit the ailing Hawthorne at The Wayside and suggested a restful trip to a

New Hampshire town they both were fond of.

After they arrived in Plymouth, Hawthorne retired to his room with tea and toast. The next morning Pierce looked into his friend's room and found him dead. Hawthorne had died in his sleep on May 19, 1864, at the age of sixty.

Washington Irving

1783–1859   Creator of Rip Van Winkle

As the Revolutionary War was ending in 1783, the American army commanded by General George Washington entered New York City, which had been occupied by British forces. In the same year, on April 3, a son, their eleventh child, was born to William and Sarah Irving.

"Washington's work is ended and the child shall be named after him," Sarah Irving said.

Washington's work, in fact, was not over. Six years later he took the oath of office as the first president of the United States in New York City, the country's first capital. And the young Washington Irving met him.

Long afterward he recalled: "My nurse, a good old Scotchwoman, was very anxious for me to see him, and held me up in her arms as he rode past. This,

however, did not satisfy her. So the next day, when walking with me in Broadway, she spied him in a shop; she seized my hand, and darting in, exclaimed in her Scotch accent, 'Please, Your Excellency, here's a bairn named after ye!' "

Irving always remembered what happened next. "He laid his hand upon my head, and gave me his blessing."

Aptly named, Washington Irving began his life with a connection to the first president and ended it many years later as the author of a five-volume biography of Washington. In between, as the author of many books, he became the first writer of the new United States to be accepted as an equal in the flourishing literary world of Europe.

Even though he wrote frequently on historical themes, he is remembered

An engraving of Washington Irving, from a drawing by Wilkie at Seville, 1828. *The Bettmann Archive.*

today mostly for two of his short fictional works, "Rip Van Winkle" and "The Legend of Sleepy Hollow." Almost everyone knows the stories of the Catskill Mountain farmer who awoke after a twenty-year sleep and of the schoolmaster Ichabod Crane's encounter with the headless horseman of Sleepy Hollow.

Few remember, however, that Irving was also a diplomat who ably served his country abroad in London and Madrid. He was, too, an astute observer of the American political scene. Surprisingly for a literary man, his advice was sought by two presidents, Andrew Jackson and Martin Van Buren. Van Buren even offered him the post of secretary of the navy, but Irving declined.

He grew up in a bustling New York just after the Revolutionary War. His strictly religious father was a prosperous merchant selling hardware, wine, and sugar. His mother, a kindly woman, kept busy with her family of eight surviving children.

Protected by his older brothers and sisters, Irving had a happy childhood, perhaps a legacy of George Washington's blessing. He learned Latin in school, but he was not a scholar. Instead of studying, he much preferred reading travel books, especially those about England.

Most of all, though, he liked to wander in the wilderness north of New York, then a small city with only around twenty-five thousand residents. He frequently visited the outlying village of Tarrytown, the home of family friends. There he enjoyed hearing spooky old local tales that he would later retell memorably—tales of a wooden bridge that a headless horseman galloped across, and of a powerful wizard who had put Indian warriors to sleep for years.

As Irving grew older he began to study law, but he was far more interested in writing and the theater. At the age of nineteen, he began to write sketches about New York society and theatrical events for his brother Peter's newspaper, the *Chronicle*. Starting in 1802, these short pieces, called "The Letters of Jonathan Oldstyle, Gent.," attracted wide attention and established him, at least in his own mind, as a writer.

But Irving's older brothers were worried about his health. They decided that a leisurely tour of Europe would be good for him. And so, in 1804, he made his first trip abroad. He wandered through France and Italy with friends, jotting down little sketches of people and places in his private journal that he hoped he could transfer into writing for publication.

Two years later Irving came back to New York in excellent health, a young man about five feet seven in height with chestnut hair and blue-gray eyes and a pleasant smile. He returned to study law, but spent most of his time with friends who put out a magazine called *Salmagundi,* a word meaning a hash consisting of pickled herring, oil, vinegar, pepper, and onions. For this rather oddly named publication he wrote satirical essays about politics, city personalities, and the theater.

Irving was admitted to the bar as a lawyer in 1806 after having completed an apprenticeship in the law office of Josiah Hoffman, a well-known New York attorney. The young man often dined with the Hoffman family, and he fell in love with a lively daughter named Matilda. But, after a sudden and short illness, she died in 1809, at the age of seventeen.

Long afterward, Irving wrote: "She died in the flower of her youth & of mine but she has lived for me ever since in all woman kind." He remained a bachelor for the rest of his life, even though he enjoyed the company of women and they admired him.

Irving found relief from his inner sadness in his writing. His first book was a comic enterprise despite its serious title, *A History of New York.* Calling himself Diedrich Knickerbocker, he declared on the work's title page that it contained "the unutterable ponderings of Walter the doubter, the disastrous projects of William the testy and the chivalric achievements of Peter the headstrong, the three Dutch governors of New Amsterdam, being the only authentic history of the times that hath been, or ever will be published."

Appearing in 1809, it was an instantaneous hit. New Yorkers roared with laughter. From Britain the famous Scottish novelist Walter Scott wrote, "our sides have been absolutely sore with laughing." Knickerbocker became a household word and Irving a celebrity.

In the next few years Irving dabbled in the family business with his brothers and traveled to Washington, where he met Dolley Madison, wife of President James Madison. Then he became the editor of a new publication in Philadelphia, *The Analectic Magazine* (the name meaning a selection from, or parts of, literary works). During the War of 1812 he wrote biographies of naval heroes for this periodical, which led later to his being offered the post of secretary of the navy. In 1814 he became an aide to the governor of New York and commander of its militia, with the rank of colonel.

That interlude in Irving's literary career ended after the war. In 1815 he sailed for England to join his brother Peter in the family business in Liverpool. On his arrival, though, his first goal was to travel through the English countryside with a friend. As was his custom, he noted everything he observed in his journal.

For the rest of his life he would remember a visit in 1817 to Walter Scott at his home in Abbotsford. They talked about legends, the folklore of various countries, and writing. Most importantly, however, Scott, the older and already famous author, encouraged the younger man.

That encouragement buoyed Irving when the family business in England went bankrupt. Without financial security, he decided that he would make his living as a writer, something that was most unusual and difficult in those times.

In his portfolio he already had some brief pieces. He therefore made his first project a book of essays, mostly about English life, but also about America. It was published on both sides of the Atlantic in 1820 under the title of *The Sketch Book of Geoffrey Crayon, Gent.*

An immediate critical and financial success, *The Sketch Book* was Irving's introduction to the literary and aristocratic social life of England and of Europe, which he greatly enjoyed. Most of the essays in this collection are forgotten today, but the stories about Rip Van Winkle and Ichabod Crane, based in part on German legends, have become a permanent part of American literature. Some critics have called Irving's *Sketch Book* the first American classic.

An amiable, friendly man, he liked the English gentry, and they liked him. He dined with the fashionable, visited them in their country homes, and made friends with other writers. Yet he considered himself a writer first and set to work on another book, this time about English country houses.

Bracebridge Hall, containing fifty-one essays, sketches, and stories, appeared in 1822, once again to critical acclaim and popularity. Irving's clear prose and his relaxed style were admired then, as they are today, but one writer of the day commented that "there is too much care bestowed on petty objects." Modern critics agree that *Bracebridge Hall* is an eminently forgettable work.

After a thirteen-month tour of Germany and a trip to Paris, Irving put together another series of sketches, *Tales of a Traveller.* He thought it included some of his best writing, but the critics thought otherwise. Despondent, Irving sought something new: He decided to learn to read and speak Spanish.

In January of 1826 a letter arrived from Madrid that changed the course of his life. An American diplomat there invited Irving to come to Spain to translate a monumental work about Christopher Columbus, just published in Spain

This drawing of Irving by Felix O. C. Darley in 1848 became one of the best known representations of the writer during his lifetime. *Sleepy Hollow Restorations.*

by Don Martín Fernandez de Navarrete. Irving would become a member of the American legation and be paid handsomely.

He arrived in Madrid in February of 1826—and thus began one of the most fruitful periods of his life. Irving began to read Navarrete. He soon came to the conclusion that a mere translation of the voluminous documents in the Spanish book would not be of general interest. He decided that he would use them as a basis for writing a new biography of Columbus.

For months his diary read, "Columb all day." Sometimes working until dawn, Irving managed to complete the manu-

script of his *The Life and Voyages of Christopher Columbus* by July of 1827. Published in four volumes the following year, it was received warmly by the public in England and America. It also won him a literary reputation in Spain, where he was elected to its Academy of History.

Entranced by the colorful history of Spain, Irving traveled by horseback through the country, drinking in the scenery and visiting libraries. He plunged into two other works about historical Spain, *The Conquest of Granada* and *The Alhambra.* A group of richly adorned buildings on a hill overlooking the city of Granada, the Alhambra (an Arabic word meaning *red*) was considered to be the finest example of Moorish architecture in Europe.

The Conquest of Granada was published in 1829, but before Irving could finish the companion work he received a diplomatic appointment—to be secretary of the American legation in London. Carrying the manuscript of *The Alhambra,* he returned to London that year.

Starting as an amateur diplomat, Irving soon gained experience and became an effective ambassador of American policy. Because of his literary fame, he was welcomed everywhere in London society. Not only did he receive the gold medal of the Royal Society of Literature, but when he went up to Oxford to receive an honorary degree, the undergraduates welcomed him with shouts of "Diedrich Knickerbocker," "Rip Van Winkle," and "Ichabod Crane."

Busy as he was with diplomatic and social affairs, Irving nevertheless completed two books. *The Voyages and Discoveries of the Companions of Columbus* came out in 1831, and *The Alhambra* in 1832.

That year, after seventeen years abroad, Irving returned to his native New York as a figure of national importance, called "the pride of American literature." He was the guest of honor at a testimonial dinner—the equivalent of a ticker-tape parade up Broadway today—and Harvard University awarded him an honorary degree.

Approaching his fiftieth birthday, Irving turned to American themes for his work. With two friends he traveled down the Ohio River to the Mississippi and then to St. Louis. With Governor William Clark, who had crossed the country much earlier with Meriwether Lewis, he rode by horseback through Missouri and Arkansas. Irving relished the outdoor life, particularly enjoying buffalo hunts and evening meals of venison or wild turkey. Above all, he admired the Indians of the Plains.

When he returned to New York he wrote *A Tour of the Prairies*, his first book about the West. Published in 1835, it was received warmly by a public fascinated by stories from the outposts of civilization in America. It led to a second western literary venture.

The famous fur merchant John Jacob Astor, who had founded the trading post of Astoria at the Pacific outlet of the Columbia River back in 1811, approached Irving. Could he write a history of Astoria? Irving consented. Using documents Astor had saved, Irving wrote *Astoria* as a rousing story of the mountain men and the western Indians who had been the backbone of the fur trade.

While living at the Astor mansion in New York, Irving met Captain Benjamin Bonneville, a native Frenchman who had attended West Point. As an American army officer, he had led an expedition to explore the then-little-known Rocky Mountains. Irving wrote the story of that intrepid soldier in a book whose title explained its contents: *Adventures of Captain Bonneville: Or, Scenes Beyond the Rocky Mountains of the Far West*.

Irving's trio of western books appealed to Americans dreaming of vast lands out west and to Europeans with a great curiosity about the West and its Indians. At the time, one reviewer called them "the very best of light reading," but scarcely anyone reads them today except as historical source material.

An engraving of Sunnyside. *Culver Pictures, Inc.*

Irving wrote *Captain Bonneville* at his own new home called Sunnyside, on the Hudson River near Tarrytown, where he had wandered in the wilderness as a boy. After moving there in 1837, he lived comfortably in what he called his "snuggery," with frequent visits from his many nieces and from other writers seeking his advice and help.

Irving's writing powers seemed to diminish in his Sunnyside years, however, and he produced only a few unimportant books or magazine articles. But he was rescued from his semiretirement by a pleasant surprise. On February 10, 1842, President Tyler appointed him Envoy Extraordinary and Minister Plenipotentiary to the court of Spain.

At the age of sixty, Irving took up his new post in Madrid, welcomed by the Spanish as an old friend. They remembered his previous visit and his books about Spanish history—and he spoke Spanish fluently. He proved to be an effective ambassador, handling the details of the embassy as ably as possible in the days when it took weeks, even months, for instructions from Washington to reach Europe by ship.

Irving returned to Sunnyside in 1846,

at the age of sixty-three, with some new projects in mind. He edited a fifteen-volume edition of his work, became the first president of the board of trustees of the Astor Library (which later became the New York Public Library), entertained numerous literary visitors, and wrote several lesser works.

In the last decade of his life, he devoted himself to a serious and detailed biography of George Washington. Even though Irving suffered from asthma, he doggedly produced five volumes between 1855 and 1859, emphasizing Washington the man as well as the hero. They were, as one critic said, "the first human study of the soldier-president."

A few months after finishing his last volume about Washington, Irving died at Sunnyside on November 28, 1859, when he was seventy-six years old.

One of his friends, the British author William Makepeace Thackeray, called Irving "the first ambassador whom the New World of Letters sent to the Old." Historically, that is true. But an even more enduring monument to Irving today is his home Sunnyside, maintained as a historical site, where the legend of Sleepy Hollow and the story of Rip Van Winkle are retold almost daily to rapt audiences of children and adults.

Henry Wadsworth Longfellow

1807–1882　The most admired American poet of his era

Only one American, Henry Wadsworth Longfellow, is represented by a bust in the Poets' Corner of Westminster Abbey in London. It sits in the company of such great British writers as Geoffrey Chaucer, William Shakespeare, Ben Jonson, John Milton, William Blake, and Robert Burns.

No one today considers Longfellow's poetry to be in the same high category as theirs. But in his own day he was the preeminent figure in American literature, read not only in the United States and England but in translation all over the world.

A versatile man, he taught foreign languages to college students, translated the works of French and Spanish writers into English, and, above all, wrote his own poetry. In his time his verses were widely read and much admired. He probably made more money from his writings than any other American poet.

From his earliest youth Longfellow knew that he wanted to be a poet. He was born on September 27, 1807, in Portland, Maine, a thriving seaport town. His father, Stephen Longfellow, a lawyer, collected books. His mother, Zilpah Wadsworth Longfellow, who had a cultivated taste for poetry, music, and the theater, frequently read to young Henry and his four brothers and four sisters.

As a boy, Henry began to write verse in his notebooks at school. He was encouraged in his ambition to become a poet by his mother, but his father looked on this goal less favorably. He believed his son needed another profession to make money, and that writing should be a sort of hobby. Why didn't Henry become a lawyer just like his father? When the fifteen-year-old Henry went off to Bowdoin College in Brunswick, Maine, in 1832, the matter seemed settled, at least in his father's mind.

But Henry had other ideas. Although he studied diligently, his main interests were in reading and writing. He kept sending verses to newspapers and magazines in hope of seeing them published. By his senior year, Henry had reached a firm conclusion about his life's work. "The fact is," he wrote to his father, "I most eagerly aspire after future eminence in literature, my whole soul burns most ardently after it, and every earthly thought centers on it."

Still, he recognized the economic realities of a literary life, as his father had painted them. Reluctantly, he agreed to study law. But he also requested and received permission to spend a year at Harvard first, studying literature and languages.

Longfellow graduated from Bowdoin in 1825. Before he could enter Harvard, though, a most surprising thing happened. The trustees of Bowdoin decided to appoint a professor of modern languages, a most unusual post in a college of those days—and they offered the position to Longfellow, then only eighteen years old.

It was a surprising choice because, even though Longfellow had been a good student, he was not the best at Bowdoin, finishing fourth in his class of thirty-nine. Also, he had only a limited knowledge of one modern foreign language, French. But he had deeply impressed his professors by a translation he made of a Latin ode. If he was so good at Latin, they decided, he could learn other languages as well. They made an appealing suggestion: that he go abroad for two or three years to become proficient in French, Italian, Spanish, and German.

Longfellow left for Europe in April of 1826, and immersed himself in European life and culture. Instead of going to universities to study languages, as might be expected, he stayed with local families wherever he went and attended many public lectures. He started in France, then went to Spain, Italy, and Germany.

Near the end of three years in Europe, Longfellow wrote to his father: "With the French and Spanish languages I am familiarly conversant, so as to speak them correctly, and write them with as much ease and fluency as I do the English. The Portuguese I read without difficulty. And with regard to my proficiency in the Italian, I have only to say that all at the hotel where I lodge took me for an Italian until I told them I was an American."

Returning to Bowdoin in 1829, the twenty-two–year-old Longfellow still looked so young that his landlady mistook him for a student. He was five feet eight inches tall, with chestnut hair and eyebrows, blue eyes, a long nose, and a clear complexion.

Despite his youth he quickly gained the respect of his students by welcoming them when they came to him with questions or problems. Lacking textbooks, he wrote his own for French and Spanish students.

At first he liked teaching, but he gradually lost his enthusiasm. He wrote to a sister, "I have aimed higher than this; and I cannot believe that all my aspirations are to terminate in the drudgery of a situation, which gives me no opportunity to distinguish myself."

His discontent at Bowdoin was eased in 1831 when he married Mary Storer Potter, the daughter of a Portland judge; Longfellow was twenty-four then, his bride nineteen.

Despite his heavy teaching load, Longfellow soon began to write—poetry and articles on languages for learned journals as well as a book about his travels in Europe. The book, called *Outre-Mer* (French for "the land beyond the sea") was published in 1835, an important year for him. After six years of teaching at Bowdoin, he accepted an appointment as professor of modern languages at Harvard. Just as at Bowdoin, the Harvard authorities suggested that he go abroad before taking up his new post, this time to perfect his German.

Despite some reluctance from his young wife, whose health had been declining, the Longfellows sailed for Europe in the summer of 1835 accompanied by two of Mary's women friends. After spending a month in London, they traveled to Germany, Scandinavia, and the Netherlands. There, Mary died in November of 1835.

Shattered, Longfellow wrote in his journal, "All day I am weary and sad—and at night I cry myself to sleep like a child." But he carried on, burying himself in work in Germany, studying both the language and the German poets. The following year he sailed back across the Atlantic to take up his duties as professor of modern languages at Harvard in the Massachusetts town of Cambridge, right across the Charles River from Boston.

Longfellow spent eighteen years teaching there, with mixed feelings. At the beginning, he felt that "no college work could be pleasanter." But he later wrote, "Poetic dreams shaded by French irregular verbs. Hang it! I wish I were a free man!"

Busy as he was in the classroom, Longfellow nevertheless found enough time to do what he wanted most to do—

An engraving of Henry W. Longfellow. *New York Public Library.*

write poetry. In 1838, still mourning for his wife, he wrote what is probably the best known of his short poems, "A Psalm of Life":

Tell me not, in mournful numbers,
   Life is but an empty dream!
For the soul is dead that slumbers,
   And things are not what they seem.
Life is real—life is earnest—
   And the grave is not its goal;
Dust thou art, to dust returnest,
   Was not spoken of the soul.
Not enjoyment, and not sorrow,
   Is our destin'd end or way;
But to act, that each tomorrow
   Finds us farther than today.

Most of today's critics ridicule the poem as trite, but it made a deep impression in its own day. Longfellow's brother Samuel defended it years later: "It has perhaps grown too familiar for us to read it as it was first read. But if the ideas have become commonplace, it has well been said that it is this poem that has made them so."

Longfellow's next literary venture was a novel, *Hyperion,* based on his own sorrow at the death of his wife and his travels in Germany. As a novel, it is a failure—overly sentimental and filled with long philosophical musings about life and death. But as therapy for the unhappy author, it served its purpose.

Longfellow completed a volume of poetry, *Voices of the Night,* that was published in 1839. Besides "A Psalm of Life," it contained many lines that aroused the admiration of a gifted young critic named Edgar Allan Poe, most particularly:

I heard the trailing garments of the Night
   Sweep through her marble halls!
I saw her sable skirts all fringed with light
   From the celestial walls!

The public liked the book, and it went into a third edition within the year. Encouraged, Longfellow produced another volume of poetry two years later, containing some of his most memorable lines. One of his most popular poems, "The Village Blacksmith," started:

Under the spreading chestnut tree
   The village smithy stands;
The smith a mighty man is he,
   With large and sinewy hands;
And the muscles of his brawny arms
   Are strong as iron bands.

At the time Longfellow wrote this, he was a widower only thirty-three years old. He lived in a room once occupied by George Washington in an old mansion called Craigie House on Cambridge's Brattle Street. A maid brought his breakfast, he walked to his classes, he visited with friends—and he wrote poetry welcomed by the public.

Yet he was unhappy. His health bothered him, he found his classes monotonous, and he argued politely with

Harvard officials about the teaching demands they made on him. Most of all, though, he felt rejected by a young Bostonian, Fanny Appleton, with whom he had fallen in love. They had met several years earlier in Germany, when she was nineteen and traveling with her family. At that time, she considered him "a venerable professor."

After another trip to Germany, during which Longfellow visited spas to regain his health, he returned home in 1842 to find that Fanny had changed her mind. They were married on July 13, 1843. As a wedding present Fanny's father, one of the richest men in Boston, gave them Craigie House for their home.

Longfellow continued to teach but, by then, even the authorities at Harvard agreed that his poetry was more important than his classroom work. In 1845 he produced *The Poets and Poetry of Europe,* including many of his translations of foreign works. The following year brought a new volume of his own poems. It contained "The Building of the Ship," which stirred the young lawyer Abraham Lincoln with these lines:

Thou, too, sail on, O Ship of State!
 Sail on, O Union, strong and great!
Humanity with all its fears,
 With all hopes of future years,
Is hanging breathless on thy fate!

Longfellow's most famous ballad, "Evangeline," came out in 1847. One critic would later describe it as "perhaps the most widely read, certainly the most wept-over, poem of the century." In Longfellow's own words, it tells of "the fortunes and misfortunes of an Acadian damsel driven by the British to this country from Canada in olden time." It starts with the often-repeated phrase: "This is the forest primeval . . ."

The public loved "Evangeline," and bought copies of it by the thousands. Longfellow, of course, was pleased. At the age of forty, he was happy in his profession and at home. In the years that followed, he and his wife had two sons and three daughters, and lived comfortably.

In 1854 Longfellow felt secure enough financially to resign from his Harvard teaching and devote full time to his poetry. He had already started another long poem, "Hiawatha." This story of a young Indian hero proved to be immensely popular. It sold ten thousand copies during the first four weeks after its publication, and thirty thousand in the first six months, remarkable figures for any sort of poetry.

Longfellow followed that with several short poems and then another long epic ballad, "The Courtship of Miles Standish," published in 1858. Like "Hiawatha," it was an immediate popular success, not only in the United States but also in England.

Longfellow's daughters: Edith (*left*), Allegra (*center*), and Alice (*right*). *Culver Pictures, Inc.*

To some readers "The Courtship" was Longfellow's masterpiece. It told the story of a triangular romantic situation in the early days of the Pilgrims in Massachusetts, and it contained the famous comment Priscilla Green makes to John Alden after he relays to her an offer of marriage from Miles Standish:

Archly, the maiden smiled, and, with eyes
    overrunning with laughter,
Said, in a tremulous voice, "Why don't you
    speak for yourself, John?"

All went well with Longfellow in those years. He received an honorary degree from Harvard, he dined with the well-known literary figures of Boston as a member of the Saturday Club, publishers sought his poetry, and the public bought his books in large numbers. He and his wife entertained frequently, and his fellow authors thought him a cheerful man with a soft voice and a delightful sense of humor.

But a personal tragedy changed him. One July evening in 1861, his wife was sitting in their library using heated wax to seal up small packages of the hair of their daughters. Suddenly, a lighted match fell to the floor and her long summer dress caught fire. As the flames enveloped her, Longfellow ran in from an adjoining room and tried to douse them by wrapping her in a rug. His own face and arms were badly burned before he could put out the fire.

But it was too late to save his wife; she died the next morning. Longfellow was too severely burned to attend the funeral service, held on the anniversary of their wedding day. When he recovered, the scars on his face made shaving impossible. So he grew the long white beard that is often shown in his pictures.

Widowed for the second time at the age of fifty-four, Longfellow felt that his life had "crumpled away like sand." Gradually, though, he realized the healing powers of work and returned to an uncompleted task, a translation of Dante's *Divine Comedy*. He also began a series of poems called *Tales of a Wayside*

Longfellow in his study at Craigie House. *The Bettmann Archive.*

Inn, published in 1863. Most of them are now forgotten, but one remains alive:

Listen, my children, and you shall hear
  Of the midnight ride of Paul Revere . . .

In 1868, Longfellow took his family abroad on a pleasure trip. It turned out to be a triumphant procession. He received honorary degrees from England's great universities of Oxford and Cambridge, Queen Victoria welcomed him at Buckingham Palace, and he dined with many eminent writers. A London reporter described his appearance: "Long, white, silken hair and a beard of patriarchal whiteness enclosed a fresh-colored countenance, with fine-cut features and deep-sunken eyes, overshadowed by massive eyebrows."

An outwardly gentle and cheerful man despite the tragedies in his life, Longfellow dressed fashionably, relished good food and wine, and had many friends. Not only did critics praise his poetry, but those who met him liked him personally. "There is a kind of halo of goodness about him," one wrote.

A friend of his, invited to comment on and criticize Longfellow's work-in-progress, later said that he spoke "with a freedom that was made perfect by Mr. Longfellow's absolute sweetness, simplicity, and modesty." After the evening's work was done, they sat down with other friends to supper, where Longfellow presided with charm, grace, and humor.

During the last fourteen years of his life, Longfellow lived quietly at Craigie House, continuing to write. He always found time to receive distinguished foreign visitors and young aspiring poets. One of the happiest days of his life came in 1879, when he was seventy-two years old. The schoolchildren of Cambridge presented him with an armchair of wood made from the "spreading chestnut tree" depicted in "The Village Blacksmith."

Longfellow died on March 24, 1882, at the age of seventy-five. Two years later, a bust of him, set on a pedestal, was dedicated in the Poets' Corner of Westminster Abbey. It was a visible symbol of the fact that he was undoubtedly one of the most famous men in the world. One contemporary said, "Surely, no poet was ever so fully recognized in his own time."

But Longfellow's reputation has diminished with the passage of the decades. His simple, melodic, rhymed poetry has come to seem out of place in a more complicated world, according to some literary critics. Nevertheless, many of his words, phrases, and images live on as part of everyday American culture. Probably not a day goes by, one biographer has written, when even lesser Longfellow verses are not quoted by his fellow Americans—verses such as:

I shot an arrow into the air,
    It fell to earth, I knew not where . . .

Or:

There was a little girl
Who had a little curl
Right in the middle of her forehead;
When she was good
She was very, very good
But when she was bad she was horrid.

Or:

Lives of great men all remind us
    We can make our lives sublime.
    And, departing, leave behind us
    Footprints on the sands of time.

And certainly almost everyone knows many of the phrases that Longfellow added to the English language, for example:

Listen, my children, and you shall hear . . .

One if by land and two if by sea . . .

Into each life some rain must fall . . .

Why don't you speak for yourself, John?

Herman Melville

1819–1891 Author of *Moby-Dick* and *Billy Budd*

Nothing in Herman Melville's early years indicated that he would become a writer. The turning point came when he went to sea at the age of twenty-one and spent three years on a whaling ship and on the romantic islands of the South Pacific. These experiences changed his life—by providing the basis for a series of remarkable books.

Melville had distinguished ancestors on both sides of his family. One of his grandfathers, Major Thomas Melville, took part in the Boston Tea Party, dumping imported tea into Boston harbor as a protest against British taxes. His other grandfather, General Peter Gansevoort, was a Revolutionary War hero who won fame by a determined defense of Fort Stanwix against English attacks.

Herman, born on August 1, 1819, grew up in comfortable surroundings in New York City with seven brothers and sisters. He idolized his father, Allan Melville, a successful merchant who imported and sold French dry goods— silks, ribbons, and gloves. His mother, who had been born Maria Gansevoort, the only daughter of wealthy parents, capably managed the large Melville household, with a staff including a governess as well as a French manservant.

In the shadow of his older brother Gansevoort during his school days, Herman was never considered bright or promising. But he surprised his family when he was nine years old by his good grades in mathematics and by winning first prize in public speaking.

The pleasant and secure world of Herman's boyhood fell apart, however, in 1830 when his father's business failed. Forced to seek financial help from wealthy relatives, the Melvilles moved north to the smaller city of Albany. Herman, eleven years old then, went to school there and once again surprised everyone by leading his class in mathematics.

But the Albany years proved to be unhappy ones. Herman's father died in 1832, leaving the family in debt and insecure. For the thirteen-year-old Herman, the death of his beloved father was a particularly serious blow. It colored his life so much that in his personal relations from then onward he always seemed to be seeking a father figure—a search reflected in almost all of his novels.

Obliged to leave school, Melville tried various means of earning money during the next several years. Gone were his dreams of going to college and becoming a great orator like Patrick Henry. Instead he held a part-time job at an uncle's bank, then worked awhile on a relative's farm near Pittsfield, Massachusetts, and taught briefly in a nearby country school. In 1838, at the age of nineteen, he studied surveying in Lansingburgh, a village north of Albany. But he failed to get a job he sought on the Erie Canal.

In those gloomy years Melville did his first writing that can be traced. He contributed a couple of mildly humorous essays called "Fragments from a Writing Desk" to the *Lansingburgh Advertiser.* Disheartened in the Albany area, he traveled down to New York City in 1839 to join his older brother Gansevoort, who was studying to become a lawyer.

Like many an unemployed young man of his era, Melville thought he could solve his problems by going to sea. Gansevoort obtained a job for him as a "boy"—an inexperienced sailor—on the *Saint Lawrence,* a sailing ship bound for Liverpool, England. It was June of 1839 when the nearly twenty-one-year-old Melville went to sea for the first time, completely ignorant of seamanship. But he soon learned to perform his duties with ropes and sails and won the respect of the other sailors.

On his return to New York that autumn, Melville traveled back up the Hudson River to Lansingburgh. He found his mother in such a difficult financial situation that she had had to sell her furniture. To make money for the family Melville taught school briefly, but soon he was unemployed again. He went all the way to Illinois to visit an uncle and look for a job there, but failed in that attempt, too.

So once more he made up his mind to go to sea, this time on a whaling ship. He signed up as a deckhand in New Bedford, Massachusetts, then one of the nation's leading seaports. His name appeared on the crew list this way: "Herman Melville; birthplace New York; age 21; height 5 feet 9 and 1/2 inches; complexion dark; hair brown."

Aboard the *Acushnet,* a brand-new sailing ship, Melville began the three-year adventure that changed his life. Like hundreds of other vessels of that era, the *Acushnet's* goal was whale oil, which was used for lighting in the days before electricity and natural gas.

Whaling was cruel, brutal, dangerous—and boring too. In between sightings of whales, there were long periods of idleness, far from any land for months at a time. Life on the *Acushnet* was so hard, as it was on other whaling ships, that seven members of her crew of twenty-three escaped as soon as they could.

After eighteen months at sea, Melville deserted, too. On July 9, 1842, he and a companion, Toby Greene, stole away from the ship when she put in at the Marquesas Islands, below the equator, not far from Tahiti.

We know how Melville felt because he described his reaction to the Marquesas later in *Typee,* his first book: "What strange visions of outlandish things does the very name spirit up!" he wrote. "Naked houris—cannibal banquets—groves of coconuts—tattooed chiefs—and bamboo temples; sunny valleys planted with bread-fruit trees—carved canoes dancing on the flashing blue waters—savage woodlands guarded by horrible idols, heathenish rites and human sacrifices."

Living on an island paradise, where no one worked because food was plentiful from the trees and the sea, turned out to be the greatest experience of Melville's life. He marveled that the Typee men and women had time to enjoy eating, singing, hunting, being sociable, making love, and occasionally fighting.

The natives welcomed Melville and Greene. Melville, who had injured his leg in reaching their community, lived with a native woman named Fayaway, as well as a man named Kory-Kory who acted as his older brother. Kory-Kory even carried Melville on his back when he had difficulty walking.

As Melville wrote later, "I often sat for hours, covered with a gauze-like veil of tappa, while Fayaway, seated beside me, and holding in her hand a fan woven with the leaflets of a young coconut bough, brushed aside the insects that occasionally lighted on my face."

Soon, however, more than insects troubled Melville. After Greene left to seek medical help, Melville noticed signs that the Typees were cannibals. He knew, of course, that the Marquesans had a reputation for being eaters of human flesh—that "long pig" was one of their favorite delicacies. It did not bother him until one day, after a short battle with a neighboring tribe, the Typee warriors returned with the bodies of three slain foes.

For two days Melville was forbidden to enter the sacred grove. The sound of drums fell continually on his ears, leading him to the conclusion that a human feast was taking place. Several days later, he passed the grove and opened a carved vessel of wood.

"Taboo, taboo," the chiefs shouted.

But Melville had had a glimpse of what was within: "My eyes fell upon the disordered members of a human skeleton, the bones still fresh with moisture, and particles of flesh clinging to them here and there."

That night Melville determined to leave the island paradise. With some difficulty he made his way to the coast, where a whaling ship from Australia, the *Lucy Ann,* was anchored. He signed on as a member of her crew. Unsuccessful in hunting whales, the *Lucy Ann* put in at Tahiti in September of 1842. There, fifteen members of the crew, including Melville, were jailed briefly after refusing to continue to work on the ship. On his release Melville and the ship's doctor wandered through the islands as beachcombers. Soon, though, Melville tired of this idle life and signed on as a seaman aboard still another whaler.

After several months at sea, the ship arrived in Hawaii, where Melville quit. To return home, he joined the United States Navy as a sailor on a warship docked there. After some delays, the vessel returned to Boston in October of 1844, and Melville was discharged from the navy.

Upon being reunited with his relatives in Lansingburgh, he amazed them with the tales he told of cannibals and beautiful maidens in the South Pacific. According to family legend, one day somebody asked him why he didn't put down his adventures in book form. Melville agreed that this was a good idea.

He had no training as a writer, however, nor had he kept a diary or journal of his travels. Relying on his memory and his imagination, he composed an account of his experiences in the Marquesas Islands. His handwriting was so bad that his sister had to copy his manuscript before it could be sent to a publisher. But his style was loose and unrestrained—and effective, as displayed in the opening sentences of *Typee,* his first book: "Six months at sea! Yes, reader, as I live, six months out of sight of land; cruising after the sperm whale beneath the scorching sun . . . and tossed on the billows of the rolling Pacific—the sky above, the sea around and nothing else!"

Part fact and part fiction, *Typee* came

An oil portrait by Asa W. Twitchell of Herman Melville in his late twenties. *The Berkshire Athenaeum, Pittsfield, Massachusetts.*

out in 1846 to high praise in New York and London, too. "A strange, graceful, most readable book, this," one reviewer wrote. And the reading public was charmed by Melville's romantic account of life among the cannibals of the South Seas.

Pleased to be recognized as an author, Melville noted the change in himself: "I am like one of those seeds taken out of the Egyptian Pyramids, which, after being three thousand years a seed and nothing but a seed, it developed itself, grew to greenness and then fell to mould. Until I was twenty-five, I had no development at all. From my twenty-fifth year, I date my life."

Delighted by his literary and financial success, Melville continued his tales of the South Pacific in another book, *Omoo*. It described and criticized the impact of white people, especially religious missionaries, on the carefree existence of the Polynesian people of Tahiti. Appearing in 1847, it was praised by critics but attacked by supporters of the missionary movement.

In that year Melville, a successful author at the age of twenty-eight, married Elizabeth Knapp Shaw, a special friend of one of his sisters and the daughter of a wealthy judge who had long been a family friend.

The newlyweds made their home in New York City in a house they shared with Melville's brother Allan and his wife. His mother and four sisters came to live with them as well. But they did not distract him from work on a new book called *Mardi*. It started as another South Sea adventure tale, but soon became a satire about contemporary life in America.

Like many authors before and since, Melville thought he had written a great book. But when *Mardi* was published in 1849, reviewers and readers were negative if not outright hostile to it. The book was a financial failure as well. So Melville made up his mind to write stories that would be popular and earn money.

An industrious worker, he returned to the subject he knew best, his experiences at sea. *Redburn*, published in 1849, is the story of an innocent young man making his first voyage as a sailor— just as Melville had on his trip to Liverpool. A year later, in *White-Jacket*, he wrote about the life of a sailor on a warship, calling upon his own experiences during his brief period in the United States Navy.

For the first time comfortably off financially, Melville became a member of the literary circle in New York City. His wife gave birth to their first son, Malcolm. Soon he moved his family to a rural home near Pittsfield, Massachusetts, that he called Arrowhead because of the Indian arrow flints he found in the fields. There he met Nathaniel Hawthorne, an older, well-known author, who became a close friend.

Melville also began to think about a book on whaling. He wrote to his publisher that it would be "a romance of adventure, founded upon certain wild legends in the Southern Sperm Whale Fisheries, and illustrated by the author's own experience of two years or more as a harpooner." Among those legends was one about an old bull whale "of prodigious size and strength," white as wool, named Mocha Dick or the White Whale of the Pacific.

A diligent worker, Melville arose at eight, went to the barn to feed his horse, ate breakfast, retired to his workroom, and wrote steadily until two-thirty. Not able to write at night because of weak eyes, he spent evenings with his family or going over his work with his wife.

Melville finished his book about the white whale in the middle of 1851. It was his sixth book in the seven years since his return from the South Pacific. Dedicated to his friend Hawthorne, it was published in England as *The Whale* and in the United States as *Moby-Dick; or, The Whale.*

It begins with the simple words, "Call me Ishmael." A whaler, Ishmael, tells the dramatic story of an expedition on a ship, the *Pequod,* with two memorable

Elizabeth Knapp Shaw Melville in a daguerreotype taken around 1847. *The Berkshire Athenaeum, Pittsfield, Massachusetts.*

characters, Captain Ahab and the great white whale Moby-Dick. But it is much more than that. Melville combined details of the practical aspects of whaling with an imaginative allegorical story of Captain Ahab's emotional fixation on Moby-Dick.

Regarded today as one of the unquestioned masterpieces of American literature, *Moby-Dick* came out to largely negative reviews and disappointing sales. It was misunderstood by the critics and ignored by the public of the time—an economic failure for Melville.

Even before the publication of *Moby-Dick,* Melville started to write his next book, *Pierre; or, The Ambiguities.* Published in 1853, it was criticized even more harshly than *Moby-Dick.* Critics found it both melodramatic and confusing, with a trite theme: the tragedy of an innocent young man facing the hypocrisy of society. The public ignored it.

Another blow hit the battered Melville that year. A fire destroyed his publisher's warehouse, taking with it all the printed copies of his books, thus effectively stopping his income from sales. Depressed, Melville nevertheless doggedly wrote short stories for magazines and a biography of a New Englander captured by the British at the Battle of Bunker Hill, *Israel Potter.*

A year later, in 1857, his most pessimistic book, a satire called *The Confidence-Man,* was published. The setting is a Mississippi River steamboat, a feature of the American scene that Melville had observed on his trip west many years earlier, with the leading man and everything around him described as a swindle. It, too, was a failure with the critics and the public.

At a low point in his career and health, Melville accepted funds from his father-in-law and went on a trip to London, the Mediterranean, and Jerusalem. "Bitter it is to be poor and bitter to be reviled," he wrote in a travel journal. At the age of thirty-seven, his life as a successful writer seemed to be over.

In a period long before radio and television, lectures by famous men and women were a popular form of entertainment. Melville tried to earn a living giving lectures, but he talked about "The Statuary of Rome," instead of topics such as the cannibals of the South Pacific, which might have interested the public more. So his lectures were not successful.

Then Melville tried to get a government job by going down to Washington to see President Lincoln. Although he shook Lincoln's hand, he did not get a job.

Following the outbreak of the Civil War, Melville sold his home in western Massachusetts and moved back to New York City. During the war he wrote poetry, which was later collected and published as *Battle-Pieces and Aspects of War* in 1866. It sold fewer than five hundred copies.

But in that same year of 1866, the financial burdens of the Melville family were finally eased. Melville received an appointment as a customs inspector in New York—at a salary of four dollars a day, considered reasonable pay in those days.

For nineteen long years Melville worked faithfully at his duties, day by day examining the cargos of ships arriving in the port of New York. His wife and family believed that regular work and hours would improve his depressed feelings and general health. But they were hard years for Melville and his wife.

Their elder son, Malcolm, committed suicide. Stanwix, their restless second son, went off to California, where he came down with tuberculosis and died. One of their daughters, Elizabeth, suffered severely from arthritis. The only bright family occasions were visits from their younger daughter, Frances, and her children.

In those troubled years, Melville did little writing. A long poem about an innocent young man seeking a mentor and faith was published in 1876 to mixed reviews. Melville himself said it was "eminently suited for unpopularity," and he was right.

A bequest from an old family friend at last enabled Melville to retire from the customs house in 1885, when he was sixty-six. Although in ill health then, he returned to writing. For five years he struggled with his last work, *Billy Budd,* the tale of a naive young sailor on a United States warship. It ended with a court-martial and Billy Budd's death by hanging. When Melville finished the

Rockwell Kent's 1930 illustration of "Moby-Dick." *Culver Pictures, Inc.*

work in 1891, the manuscript was in such bad shape that it was not published until 1924.

A largely forgotten man, Melville died on September 28, 1891, at the age of seventy-two. His obituary notices were short. One newspaper recalled him only as the author of *Typee,* his first and most popular book.

It was not until a hundred years after his birth, in 1919, that a Melville revival began. Since then, his reputation has grown to the extent that he is now regarded as one of the foremost American authors. *Moby-Dick,* largely ignored when it was published, now appears on practically every critic's list of great American novels, and since its belated publication, *Billy Budd* has been similarly acclaimed.

Edgar Allan Poe

1809–1849   America's lyric poet—and inventor of the detective story

The poetry of Edgar Allan Poe is familiar to every student of American literature. Who can forget the opening lines of "The Raven"?

Once upon a midnight dreary, while I
   pondered, weak and weary
Over many a quaint and curious volume
   of forgotten lore—
While I nodded, nearly napping, suddenly
   there came a tapping,
As of someone gently rapping, rapping at
   my chamber door.

Or of his "Annabel Lee":

It was many and many a year ago,
   In a kingdom by the sea
That a maiden there lived whom you may
   know
   By the name of Annabel Lee;
And this maiden she lived with no other
   thought
   Than to love and be loved by me.

A tormented genius, Poe wrote an amazing number of melodic poems and imaginative tales, he invented the modern detective story, and he also became America's first important literary critic. His literary life stands out as one of the greatest in this country's history, but his personal life can only be called a disaster.

Poe was born on January 19, 1809—in Boston, because his parents were there as members of a traveling theater troupe. His mother, Elizabeth Arnold Poe, was a successful actress who had married a not-so-gifted fellow performer, David Poe. He deserted his wife and three children before Edgar's first birthday.

For the next two years, Elizabeth Poe tried to support her children by continuing her stage career. She traveled

Edgar Allan Poe a year before his death. *The Bettmann Archive.*

around Southern cities despite increasingly poor health until she died in Richmond of tuberculosis when Edgar was not yet three years old. The intertwined images of mother love and death, burned into his childish mind, never left him.

While other arrangements were made for his orphaned brother and sister, Edgar was taken in by a childless couple—a prosperous Virginia merchant named John Allan and his wife, Fanny. When the Allans went off on a six-year business venture in England, Edgar accompanied them. In England he received a classical education, studying Latin, French, history, and literature.

Returning to the United States in 1820 at the age of eleven, Edgar went to school with the sons of the first families of Richmond. An all-around boy, not only was he good in his schoolwork, especially in Latin poetry, but he was a leader in other activities as well. A lieutenant in a volunteer company of Richmond boys—the Junior Morgan Riflemen—he helped welcome the Marquis de Lafayette to the city in 1824.

At the age of fifteen, Edgar became famous in Richmond for swimming six miles in the James River against a strong tide in the hot summer sun. One of his younger friends, Rob Stannard, who failed to complete the swim, took Edgar home to meet his mother. Jane Stannard

was a woman of great beauty, a splendid hostess, and she warmly encouraged the poetic aspirations of young Edgar, who had begun to write verses.

Once again, though, death separated Edgar from a loved one. Mrs. Stannard died in 1824 at the age of thirty-one. Her death inspired him later to write an ode he called "To Helen," which has endured as one of the great short poems in the English language:

Helen, thy beauty is to me
Like those Nicean barks of yore
That gently, o'er a perfumed sea,
The weary, wayward wanderer bore,
    To his own native shore.

On desperate seas long wont to roam
Thy hyacinth hair, thy classic face,
Thy Naiad airs have brought me home
    To the glory of Greece,
    To the grandeur that was Rome.

Lo! in yon brilliant window niche
How statue-like I see thee stand,
The agate lamp within thy hand!
Ah, Psyche, from the regions which
    Are Holy-Land!

That year of 1824 also marked a turning point in Edgar's relations with his foster father. Mr. Allan had come into a fortune and moved the family to a grand home. But Edgar, growing up, frequently quarreled with him, mostly about money.

In addition the fifteen-year-old Edgar

met and fell in love with a girl nearly his own age, Elmira Royster. She liked him well enough to become informally engaged, but her father strongly opposed any talk of marriage. He intercepted and destroyed Edgar's letters to his daughter. As a result the romance collapsed.

Edgar went off to the University of Virginia in 1826 at the age of seventeen. He did well in his studies in French, Latin, Greek, Italian, and even military drill. But his foster father had placed a heavy burden on him by not giving him enough money to keep up with his richer classmates.

Soon Poe began to drink and to gamble in an attempt to raise money. Instead, he sank deeper and deeper into debt. By mail, he pleaded with his foster father for help. But Mr. Allan refused to pay his debts, which led to passionate arguments and a break between them. Feeling rejected, Poe ran away to Boston.

There he met a young printer, who agreed to publish Poe's first book. *Tamerlane and Other Poems* appeared with its author identified only as "A Bostonian," and in a preface Poe said the poems included had been written when he was not yet fourteen years old. Although these early verses displayed a sense of melody and melancholy, they were really quite ordinary.

His funds exhausted, the young Poe remembered his days in the Richmond junior volunteers and enlisted in the army. Military records described him as having gray eyes, brown hair, a fair complexion, and a height of five feet eight inches.

Surprisingly, Poe made a good soldier. He did so well that on New Year's Day of 1829, shortly before he turned twenty, he was promoted to sergeant major of artillery, then the highest possible rank for an enlisted man. After two years of service, however, Poe felt he had had enough of army life. Since he had signed up for five years, he could get out only by being accepted at the United States Military Academy at West Point.

To achieve that aim, he needed the support of the foster father who had disowned him. After a series of pleading letters, Poe succeeded in getting John Allan's consent. But Allan did not soften until after the death of his wife—the third mother figure Poe had lost.

While waiting for his appointment to West Point he traveled to Baltimore, where he met some of his Poe relatives for the first time. Among them were his father's sister, Maria Clemm, and her daughter, Virginia, a pretty, laughing child of seven with violet eyes. He also had literary business in Baltimore, selling a second volume of verse to a publisher.

Al Aaraaf, Tamerlane and Minor Poems was published in 1829, before his twenty-first birthday. Unlike his first volume, this bore his name, Edgar A. Poe. It came out to mixed reviews. One Baltimore paper called some of the poems feeble, but said others might almost have been written by the great English lyric poet Percy Shelley.

Poe entered West Point on July 1, 1830, and immediately felt at home with the academy's discipline. He excelled in his studies, was well-liked by his fellow cadets, and continued to write poetry. Once again, though, just as at the University of Virginia, money problems overwhelmed him. His foster father, who had just remarried, again refused to help him.

With no money and in ill health, Poe decided to leave West Point. He ignored his duties, willingly accepting a court-martial and expulsion. Before departing, he persuaded his fellow cadets to put up about a dollar and a quarter each to cover the cost of printing another volume of his poems.

When the book, his third volume of poems, appeared in 1831, it was dedicated to the "U.S. Corps of Cadets." It contained an introduction in which Poe gave his own definition of poetry.

"A poem, in my opinion, is opposed to a work of science by having, for its *immediate* object, pleasure, not truth," he wrote. He elaborated a bit: "Music, when combined with a pleasure idea, is poetry; music without the idea is simply music; the idea without the music is prose from its very definitiveness."

Poe returned to Baltimore to live with his Aunt Maria and cousin Virginia. It was a poor household, always in need of money. Convinced that he could not earn money from poetry, Poe turned to prose and entered a newspaper contest for short stories. Although he did not win, the paper published his first tale, "Metzengerstein," the story of a fifteen-year-old orphaned baron in Germany, clearly based on his own early travel experiences.

Encouraged, Poe continued writing tales. He entered another contest and won a fifty-dollar prize from the *Baltimore Sunday Visitor* for his "Ms. Found in a Bottle." Still, telling tales did not prove to be financially rewarding.

At that time, it was almost impossible for anyone in the United States to make a living from writing. So Poe, like many other writers, turned to editing magazines, which were widely read in those days before radio and television. Poe took a job as an editor of the *Southern Literary Messenger* in Richmond in 1835.

He proved himself to be a brilliant critic and editor. He selected stories,

Virginia Poe. *Humanities Research Center, University of Texas, Austin.*

edited them, solicited manuscripts, and wrote his own reviews, editorial comments, and poems. Within months, the circulation of the *Messenger* rose by several thousand. But just as he had quarreled with his foster father, Poe was unable to get along with his employer for long—a pattern that was to continue from then onward.

His personal life was increasingly troubled. During long evenings of writing, while he was trying to give up drinking, he had become addicted to the drug opium. He lost his job. And his foster father died without mentioning

him in his will, ending all hopes of financial aid.

Despite his troubles, Poe made an attractive appearance. With almost-black hair brushed back over his ears, he dressed in raven black, wearing the large beaver hat of a gentleman. He had a sad, melancholy air, one young woman remembered, with an elegant manner. "When he looked at you, it seemed as if he could read your thoughts," she wrote.

On May 16, 1836, Poe, at the age of twenty-seven, married his cousin Virginia, then not yet fourteen years old. By this marriage he gained not only a wife but also a mother figure: He gave his Aunt Maria the nickname Muddy, a childish word for mother. After his death she would write, "At home he was simple and affectionate as a child, and during all the years he lived with me I do not remember a single night that he failed to kiss his 'mother,' as he called me, before going to bed."

After losing his job at the *Messenger,* Poe made his way north to Philadelphia and New York City, where he tried to make a living at odd literary jobs—and failed. In his Philadelphia years he wrote thirty-one tales. Among them are some of his most famous works, "The Fall of the House of Usher," "William Wilson," "The Tell-Tale Heart," and "The Pit and the Pendulum."

Poe also invented a new kind of fiction, the mystery story. His "The Murders in the Rue Morgue"—the first modern detective story—appeared in April of 1841 in *Gresham's Magazine,* of which he was the editor. In it he introduced a detective of pure intellect, C. Auguste Dupin, who solved the case by using his reasoning powers.

It was a popular success as were additional mystery stories including "The Mystery of Marie Roget" and "The Gold Bug," and later "The Purloined Letter." Poe's amateur detective, a gentleman of leisure who relies on logic and intellectual abilities, was the forerunner of other famous fictional detectives such as Sherlock Holmes and Hercule Poirot.

Despite the success of the mystery stories, though, Poe was unable to support his family on his meager earnings. He tried to get a government job, but failed. He tried to start a magazine of his own, but soon found that the idea presented too many financial difficulties. And his young wife Virginia began spitting up blood, a sure symptom of the dreaded tuberculosis.

After six years in Philadelphia, Poe moved with Virginia and her mother to New York City in 1844. Still struggling to make a living, he nevertheless created one of the most hypnotic poems ever written, "The Raven." It appeared in a newspaper, the *Mirror,* on January 29, 1845, to immediate critical and popular

Antonio Frasconi's woodcut of Edgar Allan Poe with a raven. *New York Public Library.*

acclaim. With its magic refrain, "Quoth the Raven, 'Nevermore,'" the poem was widely reprinted, quoted, and praised.

It made Poe famous, but it did not end his financial troubles. A combination of ill health, debt, his wife's illness, and his own drinking left the Poe family devastated. The only bright light in that period was the publication of his *Tales* in 1845. This book won high praise, but four months after its appearance only fifteen hundred copies had been sold, bringing its author only the small sum of one hundred twenty dollars.

In those years, the Poe family lived in poverty, nearly starving to death one cold winter. Another blow came on January 30, 1847, when Virginia died. Ill, depressed, and erratic, Poe survived that mourning period only through the help of his wife's mother and another friend, Maria Shaw.

A curious collaboration between Mrs. Shaw and Poe produced one of his most popular poems, "The Bells." Sitting in her garden one day in the spring of 1848, he mentioned that he felt no inspiration to write a poem. As the sound of church bells filled the air, she fetched paper, pen, and ink. She wrote at the top of the paper, "The bells, the little silver bells." Poe picked up the pen and wrote a stanza.

Mrs. Shaw then wrote, "The heavy iron bells." Once again, Poe wrote another stanza. When the poem was finally finished months later, it began:

> Hear the sledges with the bells—
>   Silver bells!
> What a world of merriment their melody
>   foretells
>
> How they tinkle, tinkle, tinkle,
>   In the icy air of night!
>
> While the stars that oversprinkle

> All the heavens seem to twinkle
>   With a crystalline delight;
>
> Keeping time, time, time,
>
> In a sort of Runic rhyme.
> To the tintinnabulation that so musically
>   wells
>
> From the bells, bells, bells, bells,
>   Bells, bells, bells—
> From the jingling and the tinkling of the
>   bells.

As he recovered from the shock of Virginia's death, Poe kept busy writing. Her mother described his habit of writing all night long: "He would stop every few minutes and explain his ideas to me, and ask if I understood him. I always sat with him when he was writing, and gave him a cup of hot coffee every hour or two."

In the last two years of his life, Poe was extraordinarily active. He tried to found a new magazine to be called the *Stylus;* he traveled widely, lecturing on poets and poetry in America; he wrote; and he proposed marriage to four women he had met through his and their writing. Clearly, he needed and sought out feminine sympathy.

Poe returned to Richmond in June of 1849 to lecture on American literature. He also paid a call on his childhood sweetheart, Elmira Royster Shelton, now a rich widow. For him, marriage to Elmira would mean a home in the city where he was regarded as a celebrity, work on local newspapers, perhaps money to start a magazine—and possibly even happiness at last.

The wedding was set for October 17. But first, Poe told his intended bride, he had to return to New York to wind up some business matters. He boarded a steamer in Richmond for the forty-eight-hour voyage to Baltimore, where he would take a train to New York. He began to drink on the boat to Baltimore and while waiting for the train there. Several days later, he was found semiconscious on the streets of Baltimore.

He never recovered. Poe died on October 7, 1849, at the age of forty, but he left a legacy of lyric poetry and short stories that are still read today. According to at least one modern critic, he is "America's greatest writer and the American writer of greatest significance in world literature."

Harriet Beecher Stowe

1811–1896   Her *Uncle Tom's Cabin* was one of the most influential books ever written

During the Civil War, Harriet Beecher Stowe arranged to visit President Abraham Lincoln at the White House and she brought along her twelve-year-old son. Charlie Stowe never forgot the way Mr. Lincoln wryly greeted his mother as they entered his office: "Is this the little lady who made this big war?"

Today it is hard to realize the impact that Mrs. Stowe's book *Uncle Tom's Cabin* had back in its own day. But her story of plantation life stirred so much antislavery feeling in the North—and so much anger in the South—that, after its appearance, outright conflict between these two areas of the country became increasingly unavoidable.

She also wrote dozens of other books, and at least some of them strike modern experts as important contributions to

American literature, even though they, along with *Uncle Tom,* attract few modern readers.

The main reason why this once best-selling writer now seems so out of date is that her works reflect the fondness of her own era for tales with a strongly religious flavor. Indeed her stories are really quite similar to sermons. Yet this could not be the least bit surprising to anybody aware of her extraordinary background.

If Harriet Elizabeth Beecher had been born a boy, undoubtedly she would have become a clergyman. As one of her brothers put it: "Oh, I shall be a minister. That's my fate. Father will pray me into it!" For his and Hattie's father was the Reverend Lyman Beecher, an eminent defender of old-time Puritanism as well as an overpowering parent who "prayed" his seven sons into following his own churchly example.

But the mere idea that a girl might aim for any goal beyond being a dutiful wife and mother horrified him. Even so, two of Hattie's three sisters were sooner or later led by their fervent upbringing to depart from the female pattern of their time and undertake public crusades: Catharine Beecher, her oldest sister, became prominent as a promoter of better education for girls; and Isabella Beecher Hooker, her youngest sister, took up the cause of women's suffrage.

Five Beecher babies had preceded Hattie's birth on June 14, 1811, in the pleasant New England town of Litchfield, Connecticut. As five more babies arrived after her, putting her right in the middle of this large, excitable family, it was easy for her to feel overshadowed. Also, her own mother, Roxana Foote Beecher, died when she was only four, and within a year she had a not-very-warmhearted stepmother who gave most of her attention to the infants she herself soon began producing.

Thus Hattie grew into an inward sort of child, with a tendency to slip often into daydreams. Undersized, too—she never would be more than barely five feet tall—she made her relatives say that she was all eyes. Using her "owl

eyes," they remembered, she stored up amazingly accurate pictures of whatever went on around her, even when her mind appeared to be a million miles away.

During Hattie's Litchfield girlhood, her oldest sister was her main caregiver. Catharine, called Kate within the family, took after their father remarkably; a more perfect example of a bossy big sister would be difficult to find.

For companionship Hattie depended on her brother Henry, just two years her junior. The tie they formed in their youth remained very close even after the Reverend Henry Ward Beecher began preaching spellbinding sermons at a church in Brooklyn, New York, and became the country's most famous minister. Until Hattie's book about slavery suddenly elevated her to a fame surpassing his, she by no means stood out in this exceptional family.

As early as her school days, though, Hattie showed signs of having unusual literary ability. At the age of twelve, she won a prize for her composition on one of the complicated religious questions her father often debated with his children: "Can the Immortality of the Soul Be Proved by the Light of Nature?"

Still, as she entered her teens, her father's fierce warnings about sin and hellfire upset her deeply. By then her sister Kate was operating a school for girls in

Harriet Beecher Stowe in 1853 during her first visit to England. *New York Public Library.*

the Connecticut capital of Hartford, and she insisted on taking Hattie under her own wing there. Poor Hattie!

While Kate meant well, and the sisters sometimes enjoyed playful interludes of writing nonsense verse together or taking healthful horseback rides, for Hattie the next ten years were mostly tiresome drudgery. First as a student, then as a very overworked teacher, she bore Kate's bossing uncomplainingly—many people thought of her as just the brilliant Miss Beecher's mousy assistant.

Underneath, though, Hattie seethed with suppressed emotions. Long afterward, one authority would claim that the intensity of feeling with which the plight of the slaves in *Uncle Tom's Cabin* was portrayed harked back to its author's "sense of her own suffering and oppression" in this period. Far-fetched as this may seem, she certainly put a lot of energy into spinning daydreams about someday writing something that would make her rich enough to build herself the grandest castle Hartford had ever seen.

We can be sure about her daydreams because Hattie made one close friend during these years—a fellow teacher to whom she wrote many letters. Then she made another at the age of twenty-one, soon after the whole Beecher family moved westward to the young city of Cincinnati in Ohio, where the Reverend Lyman Beecher had been summoned to head a new religious seminary.

Hattie's friend there was Eliza Stowe, the unassuming young wife of one of the seminary's professors. Eliza's gentle sympathy did much to ease the stress Hattie experienced as she helped Kate to start another school for girls in Cincinnati. Even more important, this friendship led, at least indirectly, to Hattie's escape from her older sister's domination.

A year after the Beecher arrival in Cincinnati, early in the summer of 1833, around Hattie's twenty-second birthday, she bravely traveled back east by herself to represent the family at the college graduation of her favorite brother, Henry. During her absence, an epidemic of cholera struck Cincinnati— and her dear Eliza became one of its victims.

On Hattie's return, her grief over Eliza's death melted away her shyness when she encountered her friend's bereaved husband. Month after month, as these two shared their deep sorrow over their loss, a warmer emotion began to stir in both their hearts. Yet Professor Calvin Stowe could hardly have been further from the average person's picture of a romantic hero.

Plump and nearly bald, with whiskers that were already turning gray, he looked much older than Hattie, although he was only nine years her senior. Still, his kindness as well as his keen New England sense of humor made her feel completely at ease with him. Before long they found themselves planning to marry when a proper interval after Eliza's death had elapsed.

Professor Stowe's emergence as a suitable husband could not have come at a better time in Hattie's life, for painful new difficulties between her and Kate had been developing since their move to Cincinnati. One particular source of stress involved an innovative textbook Hattie had written at Kate's request. Although it was the younger sister who ingeniously thought of teaching lessons about the lengths of rivers by means of little stories, rather than boring lists, it was the elder sister who was named on its title page as the volume's author. Also, Kate kept practically every penny that this unexpectedly successful venture earned.

Indeed Kate's total unreliability when it came to money lay behind much of the sisterly friction. However, Kate did try to make amends to Hattie by pushing her to enter a contest sponsored by a Cincinnati literary club. The story "Uncle Lot" that Hattie wrote about one of their father's relatives not only won the first prize of fifty dollars; it was even printed in the *Western Literary Magazine*—marking the literary debut of Miss Harriet E. Beecher.

But Kate's habit of losing her temper caused the parents of several of her pupils to remove them from her school. Then when an economic downturn further cut the student body, Kate suddenly closed the school. Owing Hattie months of back pay, she rushed off eastward to seek financial support for new educational ventures elsewhere.

A few weeks later, on January 6, 1836, Hattie married Professor Calvin Stowe; she was twenty-four and he was thirty-three. While becoming the wife of a brilliant expert on biblical history wonderfully raised her spirits, and the task of providing a comfortable home for such a man struck her as worthy of her best efforts, she soon discovered that her husband was as helpless as a baby when it came to practical matters like picking out a pair of matching socks from his wardrobe.

What's more, she soon found herself with two actual babies requiring constant care. That September, she gave birth to twin daughters who were named Eliza and Harriet, after both of their father's wives. From then on the Stowe family continued to be regularly enlarged—by the arrival of Henry, Frederick, Georgiana, Samuel, and Charles. Hattie surprised even herself by the capable way she rose to meet the challenges of motherhood, but the extremity of her grief when her infant Sammy died in another cholera epidemic nearly unhinged her.

Well before then, though, she had found that running her household with only the small income the professor earned was practically impossible. To pay for the assistance of a nursemaid, she began dashing off little stories during her few hours of freedom. In those days, most newspapers printed flowery fictional tales without much literary merit once or twice a week; it was mostly this type of sentimental opus that Hattie sold while her children were small.

Yet she gradually started using snippets of reminiscence she had heard from her father or her husband to compose dryly humorous pieces about colorful New England characters. Then her sister Kate, swooping down on the Stowe household for one of her periodic visits, collected the best of these efforts and took them back to New York, where she browbeat her own publisher into issuing a book of them called *The Mayflower, or Sketches of the Descendants of the Puritans.*

Its publication in 1843 so elated Hattie that she forgot about recently writing to her old friend in Hartford that she had turned into "a mere drudge with few ideas beyond babies and house-keeping." She dashed off a long letter to her husband, away attending a meeting, saying that now she needed a room of her own where she could compose more stories without being constantly interrupted by domestic crises. Calvin replied with similar enthusiasm, "My dear, you must be a literary woman. . . . Make all your calculations accordingly."

However, one family emergency after another soon undermined Hattie's health to the extent that she became more discouraged than ever. During a steamy Cincinnati summer, "sick of the smell of sour milk and sour meat and sour everything," she felt as if she never wanted to eat again. Professor Stowe was so alarmed by his wife's decline that, for once, he took decisive action and sought help from relatives, making it possible for Hattie to spend nearly a year recuperating at a "water cure" sanitorium in Vermont.

Soon after Hattie's return to Cincinnati, where she had never felt really at home, an opportunity to move back to New England presented itself: Bowdoin College, in the Maine town of Brunswick, from which her husband had graduated years earlier, asked him to join its faculty. Since the seminary he had been teaching at was by now so embroiled in controversy over the issue of slavery that nobody expected it to survive much longer, this offer struck both Stowes as God's answer to their prayers.

During the spring of 1850, approaching her thirty-ninth birthday and expecting the arrival of her seventh infant in just a few months, Hattie started east with her three youngest offspring; her husband and the other children would follow when she had found a suitable house near the college and made it ready for them. Embarking on such a long and difficult trip aboard a series of railroad trains, this small, shabby woman surrounded by babies and bundles hardly seemed about to affect the course of American history.

Despite the increasing bitterness of the national dispute over slavery, Harriet Beecher Stowe had been almost entirely taken up with her own domestic concerns during her years in Cincinnati. Once, while she was still teaching at her sister's school, she had crossed the Ohio River with a pupil who lived in slave-owning Kentucky, and the afternoon she spent visiting the plantation owned by this student's family had impressed her indelibly. So had hearing a clergyman friend of her father's describe putting lanterns in the windows of his riverside house to guide escaping slaves to freedom.

But not till she stopped off at the Boston home of one of her brothers who had become active in the antislav-

ery cause, toward the end of her journey to Maine, did she give evidence of having developed much stronger feelings about this issue than she had ever shown. At the dinner table, when the talk turned to a strict new law forbidding Northerners to assist runaway slaves, her brother's wife spoke up. "Now, Hattie," she said, "if I could use a pen as you can, I would write something that would make this whole nation feel what an accursed thing slavery is."

Those who were present always remembered that Hattie rose from her chair with an exalted look on her face. "I will write something," she promised.

After arriving in Maine, though, Hattie was so busy getting settled, then caring for her new baby, Charlie, that she seemed to have completely forgotten this pledge. But one Sunday morning the next winter, while seated in church, she suddenly saw a scene within her head that was unbelievably vivid. This picture showed a black man she instantly christened Uncle Tom, prayerfully forgiving his tormentors before he died. It moved her so deeply that she could hardly keep from weeping. As soon as she got home, she grasped a pen and put down on paper what she had visualized.

Still, week after week, the pressures of her daily existence prevented any further writing. Not until her husband happened to pick up the sheets she had scrawled that Sunday did she realize what she had to do next. As he finished reading the fragment, with tears streaming down his face, he told her she *must* compose the beginning of the story for which this was the ending.

Yes, she said, she felt that, too. She had even seen a good many more pictures in her mind that she longed to start describing. Yet there was only one way she could possibly find the time to write not merely a brief sketch but a whole book. She sent off a letter asking her sister Kate to come and take charge of their household for the next several months.

Kate had long ago assured Hattie she would drop whatever else she was doing if she ever received such a summons—and she kept her word. From out in Milwaukee, where she had been organizing a new academy for teacher training, she hurried eastward to Brunswick. By the time she arrived there, Hattie had already begun writing *Uncle Tom's Cabin.*

Also, she had arranged with the editor of a not-very-widely-circulated antislavery newspaper called the *National Era* to print weekly installments of her story. There would be about twelve installments, Hattie told him; as was customary then, he published the first the very week she mailed it, counting on receiving the next one in time for the next week's paper. Before Kate showed up, Hattie failed to finish a chapter one week, and the paper went to press without it. The flurry of letters from readers demanding that *Uncle Tom* be continued astonished both Hattie and the editor.

So did the way the story kept expanding well past the promised twelve installments. Altogether, there would be forty of them, and an effective system for producing them was adopted as soon as Kate arrived in Brunswick. After breakfast every morning, Hattie and her husband both went off to his office at the college. Away from family cares, she wrote uninterruptedly month after month.

When Hattie found herself finally approaching the end of her story, Professor Stowe traveled down to Boston to arrange for it to be printed in book form. Because of its controversial subject it seemed unlikely to attract many readers from the general public, and Hattie told her husband that she would be satisfied if her profits were sufficient to buy her the good black silk dress she had always craved. Instead, virtually overnight she became rich as well as famous.

As soon as *Uncle Tom's Cabin* appeared in bookstores in the spring of 1852, it began setting publishing

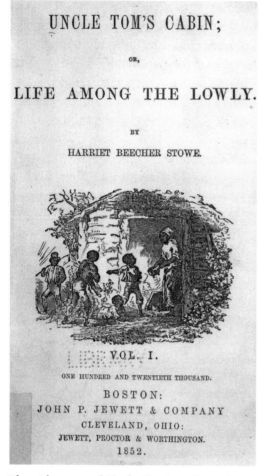

UNCLE TOM'S CABIN;

OR,

LIFE AMONG THE LOWLY.

BY

HARRIET BEECHER STOWE.

VOL. I.

ONE HUNDRED AND TWENTIETH THOUSAND.

BOSTON:
JOHN P. JEWETT & COMPANY
CLEVELAND, OHIO:
JEWETT, PROCTOR & WORTHINGTON.
1852.

The title page of *Uncle Tom's Cabin. Photosearch, Inc.*

records. The first printing of five thousand copies sold out within two days. Soon huge steam-powered presses were running day and night as the small Boston company Professor Stowe had dealt with tried to meet the unprecedented demand. Within a year three hundred thousand copies had been sold

in the United States, and more than a million in England and other countries.

In effect Harriet Beecher Stowe's creation of unforgettable characters like Topsy, little Eva, and the evil slave master Simon Legree turned the antislavery cause into a mass movement. At the same time, it infuriated people in slave-owning areas, who claimed that *Uncle Tom* presented a very unfair picture of their system. However, to examine the book's impact would require many pages; here we must concentrate on its author.

She was forty-one the year *Uncle Tom* came out, and she lived to be a very old woman. She wrote numerous other books; *Oldtown Folks, The Pearl of Orr's Island,* and *Poganuc People,* all with authentic New England settings, are generally considered the best of them. But her experience of composing her masterpiece, feeling divinely inspired, was by far the high point of her long life.

Except for taking several foreign trips, during which she dined with duchesses and was peered at by crowds of ordinary people, Stowe tried to stay out of the public eye as much as she could. After the Civil War, when her husband retired from teaching to devote himself to scholarly research, she did build the grand castle in Hartford that she had dreamed of. Alas, it cost so

Harriet Beecher Stowe with her brother, Henry Ward Beecher. *UPI/Bettmann.*

much to live in this magnificent residence that she had to work her fingers to the bone turning out magazine articles to pay its expenses.

In addition Stowe endured much sorrow from tragedies involving her children. One son, severely wounded while fighting in the Union army, became an alcoholic who disappeared on a trip to San Francisco and was never heard of again. Another drowned a few weeks before he would have graduated from Dartmouth College.

Still, her twins, who never married, were great comforts to her, eventually taking over all housekeeping and secretarial chores so that she could concentrate on her writing. After life in the castle became too expensive, the Stowes moved to a less elaborate home on the outskirts of Hartford, where another famous writer, who was one of their new neighbors, seemed much impressed by the differences in the twins' personalities. "Hellfire" and "Soft Soap," Mark Twain called them in his private journal.

As Stowe and her husband grew older, they began spending their winters amid blossoming orange trees in Florida. Even at their cottage there, she kept on writing while he dozed in the sunshine. But soon after Professor Stowe died in 1886, his wife's mind began failing. For another ten years, watched over by her twins, she gathered little bunches of flowers in her Hartford garden or sat peacefully singing to herself, with no connection whatever to the changing scene beyond her own home.

She died there at the age of eighty-five, on July 1, 1896.

Henry David Thoreau

1817–1862   A most original thinker

It often happens that writers who win fame during their lifetimes fade into obscurity after their deaths—but the case of Henry David Thoreau is just the opposite. Nowadays many of his opinions about the evils of civilized society that were mostly ignored or dismissed as quirky back in the 1800s are familiar to millions of readers. For instance:

"The mass of men lead lives of quiet desperation."

"Our life is frittered away by detail. . . . Simplify, simplify."

"I say beware of all enterprises that require new clothes."

Even though Thoreau's world was far simpler than ours, he thought that ordinary daily life in rural Massachusetts over a century ago had already become too complicated. Today he seems re- markably ahead of his own era. Still, his particular surroundings as well as his own family background did much to turn him toward becoming a rebel.

He was born, on July 12, 1817, in the historic village of Concord, where one of the first battles of the American Revolution had been fought just forty-two years earlier. During Henry's youth, two outstanding literary figures—Ralph Waldo Emerson and Nathaniel Hawthorne—settled in this outwardly placid community twenty miles northwest of Boston, so the air there was "simmering with ideas."

In addition Henry had an abundant supply of independent-minded relatives to inspire him. On his father's side, he was descended from Protestants who had left France because of religious persecution by that country's Catholic majority. When they arrived in Boston, some of them became prosperous merchants or shipowners. But Henry's father, John Thoreau, a man who most enjoyed quietly reading his newspaper or playing his flute, earned barely enough as a Concord storekeeper to support his wife and children.

That wife—Henry's mother—had grown up in New Hampshire as Cynthia Dunbar. Besides having a grandfather stubbornly in favor of the British during the Revolutionary War, she also had several other kinfolk known for holding unpopular opinions or behaving rather strangely. In Concord, however, she herself struck many of her neighbors as more of a character than any of her relatives.

A large woman, towering a full head taller than her husband, she never hesitated to express her views on any subject—so she earned the reputation of being the village's most talkative woman. At a time when speaking out against the black slavery system of the American South still seemed extremely radical to most New Englanders, she organized a women's antislavery society and held its meetings in her front parlor.

Nevertheless, nobody could say that she neglected her family. Most of the time, she had several needy relatives living under her roof—along with a few strangers, whose weekly rent supple-

mented the small income her husband brought home. Since they had four children, their modest gray frame house was certainly crowded.

Henry, the third of these children, had an older sister and brother as well as a younger sister. One of the girls became a teacher, the other an artist, not especially gifted, and neither of them ever married. Remaining closely tied to their childhood home, they were always a source of affectionate support for Henry.

Yet it was his brother John to whom Henry felt the strongest connection. Just two years apart in age, the Thoreau boys explored the woods near Concord together, fished in nearby rivers together, and attended school together. Much as they enjoyed each other's company, though, their personalities could hardly have been more different.

John was outgoing, carefree, a leader in school yard games, while the shy and silent Henry seemed "an odd stick" to most other boys. Also, his appearance was against him. Despite being thin as a rail, he had a surprisingly big nose, and his deep blue-gray eyes had a way of appearing to stare right through whatever he was looking at. Because Henry spent a lot of time reading, he was considered the more scholarly of the brothers, even though his marks on exams were not outstanding.

Only when it came to writing compositions did he really excel. And by the time he was eleven, he had already found that he liked writing about nature. In a small sheaf of papers saved from the Concord Academy of his day, one headed "The Seasons" has his name on it. The young Thoreau had started with a short poem:

Why do the seasons change? and why
Does Winter's stormy brow appear?
Is it the word of him on high
Who rules the changing varied year?

Although his essay only hinted at the unusual mind he was developing, along with other early efforts it convinced his mother to focus her own ambition on him. A few of the men on her side of the family had attended Harvard College, and she decided that this literarily inclined son of hers must follow in their footsteps.

The full cost for attending Harvard in those days was one hundred seventy-nine dollars a year. By the time Henry finished his final year at the Concord Academy, Mrs. Thoreau had scraped together enough money to promise him a higher education if he passed Harvard's entrance exams. In the summer of 1833, when he was sixteen, he took this series of tests—and even though he came very close to failing Latin, Greek, and mathematics, he was accepted with about forty other young men as a member of the Class of 1837.

Only fifteen miles lay between Concord and Cambridge, where Harvard occupied a small cluster of old brick buildings. Across the Charles River not far away was Boston, but Henry found to his happy surprise that a short walk from his dormitory in practically any direction brought him to open fields. Almost daily during his college years, he went off by himself to study the habits of birds and other wildlife in the Cambridge area.

But Henry's main refuge throughout his Harvard career was the institution's fine library. Unwilling to join in any lighthearted extracurricular activities, he spent long hours poring over poetry and natural science books, copying passages he admired. As far as his classes were concerned, he did just enough work to rank a bit above average.

At that time a Harvard rule decreed that every student had to attend religious services regularly, and Henry did not defy it. He still showed his spark of rebellion, though, by going to chapel in a green coat "because the rules required black."

There is a widely believed myth that Thoreau's first major protest against established practices was his refusal to accept his Harvard diploma when he graduated. However, the actual certificate was saved by his family, proving that he was awarded a bachelor of arts degree, at the age of twenty, in the summer of

Henry David Thoreau. *Culver Pictures, Inc.*

1837. Still, his studies had not led him toward any of the three professions—the ministry or law or medicine—that most of his classmates entered. As he would have to earn his keep somehow, he decided that he might as well try teaching.

Immediately, Thoreau found an opening right in Concord at the grammar school where he had once been a pupil himself. Since the country was suffering then from an economic depression, it seemed that he was very lucky. But only two weeks after the term started, a member of the school committee paid a visit to see the new teacher at work. When this upstanding pillar of the community found the classroom less than totally silent, he called Thoreau into the hall and told him it was his duty to whip students who made the slightest noise, or "the school would spoil." Thoreau stiffly nodded.

As soon as the committee member left, Thoreau picked out several pupils at random. Although he hated the idea of hurting them, he felt that he had to show the absurdity of such punishment. So he grasped the cane traditionally used for keeping discipline and did some whacking—then wrote a letter resigning his post.

Thoreau told his family that he just could not teach in any school where he was not allowed to teach in his own way.

Yet many neighbors shook their heads over his foolishness in quitting a job that paid five hundred dollars a year, especially during a period when jobs were hard to find. But another step he took soon afterward may have done even more to convince his neighbors of his oddity.

Around twenty years earlier he had been christened David Henry Thoreau, but now he announced that he wished to be known as Henry David Thoreau. Since he had always been called Henry anyway, what possible difference could it make? Perhaps, though, he was influenced in this minor matter by the same man who had such a major influence on his whole outlook.

Ralph Waldo Emerson—the mere sound of his name could hardly be more impressive. Among those who analyze such matters, it is clear that the ringing Rs at the beginning and near the end create much of the grand resonance. As a similar effect could be achieved by reversing the order of Thoreau's two given names, possibly a strong inner desire for a similar grandeur made Thoreau become Henry David.

At any rate there can be no doubt that right at this same period Thoreau came under Emerson's spell. Emerson had just published a masterly essay entitled "Nature," which had a profound impact on Thoreau's thinking. In addition, Emerson soon became a close neighbor of Thoreau's, as well as the most devoted friend he ever had.

Fourteen years Thoreau's senior, Emerson had first attracted attention as a Boston clergyman, but he found being a minister too restricting. Instead he began giving lectures open to the public at large, in which he stressed his belief that every person should rely more on the promptings of his or her own inner voice than on any established pattern of rules. Of course, this Emersonian doctrine of self-reliance deeply appealed to an individualist like Thoreau.

At least for the next several years, though, Thoreau's brother remained more important to him than anyone else. When John came home between terms from the school in a nearby town where he was teaching, they roamed the countryside together. They also rowed their small boat up the Concord River, then down the Merrimack, for a marvelous trip into New Hampshire. They even both fell in love with the same young woman.

Ellen Sewall was the sister of a pupil at the private school they were by then running together. When Henry realized how John felt about her, he stepped aside to let his older brother court her. Only after Ellen told John that she could not marry him did Henry try to win her himself. But she turned him

down, too—it seems that her strictly religious father did not consider the Thoreau family sufficiently orthodox to suit his daughter.

Following this one disappointment, Henry never again gave any sign of wanting to get married. For the next few years, he and John were very involved in operating their school. More at ease among children than adults, Henry liked teaching without having a committee looking over his shoulder. He especially enjoyed leading nature walks, a new idea of his that helped to make the school gain an increasing number of pupils.

But suddenly, in 1841, his brother developed tuberculosis, the lung disease that was a leading cause of death at that time. When John could no longer continue teaching, Henry had no heart for continuing to operate the school alone and closed it just as it was beginning to really thrive.

Emerson, seeing Henry at loose ends, invited him to come live in his own household, where a handyman was urgently needed. In return for keeping the garden free of weeds and coping with other maintenance jobs that defeated Emerson, Thoreau received room and board plus unlimited access to a large collection of books. Besides, he had plenty of time for carrying out his aim of doing some serious writing himself.

So Thoreau was living as practically a member of Emerson's family when an awful blow struck him. John, who seemed to be recovering from his lung condition, cut himself one morning while he was shaving—and this minor injury brought on the dreaded symptoms of lockjaw. With his face paralyzed, and suffering terrible pain, he died within just a few days.

Henry spent those days tirelessly taking care of John. After John died, Henry sank into a strange silence, and then he horrified his family by showing all the symptoms of lockjaw himself. Even if no cause could be discovered, it seemed that he, too, was doomed. But gradually Henry began to recover, although he was not strong enough to leave his room for almost a month.

It took several more months until he could walk outdoors or even think of working. He was twenty-five when his brother died in 1842, and his drastic reaction to this tragedy might have been at least partly caused by his own deep disappointment over having thus far failed to write anything he was satisfied with himself.

Emerson, from all the hours he had spent listening to Thoreau talk brilliantly on many subjects, still felt convinced that his young friend had a touch of genius. Hoping to bring him out of his depressed mood, he arranged an easy job for him teaching the young sons of a relative of his on Staten Island, just a short ferry ride from New York City. Also, Emerson gave Thoreau letters of introduction to several prominent literary figures there.

Thoreau realized that he was being given a good opportunity to get some poems or magazine articles published and he tried to take advantage of it. At least one of the men Emerson sent him to—Horace Greeley, the editor of the *New York Herald*—was much impressed by the originality of Thoreau's ideas. From then on he became something like Thoreau's literary agent.

Still, Thoreau could not stand the hectic atmosphere of New York. In a letter to his family giving his impressions of the country's largest city, he wrote: "It is a thousand times meaner than I could have imagined. It will give me something to hate. . . ." So his relatives were hardly surprised when he returned home after just a few months there.

Back in Concord, Thoreau buckled down to work at a little factory adjoining his family's house. An uncle from New Hampshire had acquired the rights to mine a substance called plumbago, from which the graphite, or "lead," in lead pencils could be extracted. Then Henry's father had begun making pencils in what had once been a woodshed.

Yet it was Henry, with his gift for fixing almost anything, who figured out how to make pencils more efficiently than any competitors. He worked hard at improving the procedure so that the business would yield a profit. But was this a reasonable goal for someone who much preferred reading and writing and communing with nature?

Henry thought not. It struck him with increasing force, while working at the factory, that work like this left him hardly any energy for the activities he really cared about. Instead of spending six days a week striving to earn money and only one day doing as he liked, why couldn't he turn this ridiculous arrangement around?

Toward that end, early in the spring of 1845, Thoreau embarked on a great experiment. A few months before his twenty-eighth birthday, he started cutting down pine trees in a patch of woods about two miles outside Concord. This land on the edge of Walden Pond was owned by Emerson, who had gladly offered to let his friend clear a space there and put up a small cabin. Fittingly, Thoreau moved into his hut on July 4, the anniversary of another famous declaration of independence.

During the two years Thoreau spent in the woods, he finished a book he called *A Week on the Concord and Merrimack Rivers*. Filled with disconnected musings, it satisfied its author's yearning to write something that might serve as his memorial to his brother even though it never attracted many readers. But two other much more important literary works also had their beginnings while he was living in the woods.

One stemmed from a brief but extraordinary adventure during Thoreau's second summer at Walden. For the past several years he had refused to pay a small tax that Massachusetts levied on every male citizen. Because the state did nothing to oppose black slavery, he reasoned, in effect the tax was supporting this hateful system. So he felt a duty to make his own antislavery protest in the only way available to him.

As a result, one day when Thoreau walked into Concord to visit his family he was arrested by the local constable, then put in jail. He spent just one night behind bars—an aunt of his could not bear this disgrace, and she paid his tax the next morning. Even so, Thoreau wrote an essay entitled "Civil Disobedience," which would prove to be one of the most influential documents in the world's history.

It was "Civil Disobedience" that Mahatma Gandhi, in India, and Martin Luther King, Jr., in Alabama, both read while they were leading protests against injustice. Later, they both testified that Thoreau's lofty words had given them renewed courage to defy governmental policies their own consciences told them were wrong. Wherever rebellious individuals have been persecuted for their beliefs, very likely they, too, have quoted from the same source in their defense.

The second of Thoreau's works that stemmed from his solitary experiment was his masterpiece *Walden.* Ever since his college years, at his friend Emerson's suggestion, he had kept a journal where he carefully wrote down his daily thoughts. In this, throughout the time he spent alone, he jotted notes that during the next eight years he kept polishing and repolishing.

In 1854 he was at last ready to publish *Walden; or Life in the Woods.* By then Thoreau had made several trips to Maine and to Cape Cod, and he had written magazine articles about these experiences. He had also delivered a few dozen lectures, none of them drawing much attention. With the appearance of *Walden,* he hoped that at last he would achieve recognition as a major writer.

But hardly anybody read the book; of the one thousand copies printed, only about two hundred were sold. Although one reviewer commented favorably on Thoreau's "habit of original thinking," the majority either ignored him or agreed with a reader who commented,

The opening page of Thoreau's manuscript, *Walden. The Henry E. Huntington Library and Art Gallery.*

"He is a good-for-nothing, selfish, crablike sort of chap."

Nevertheless, Thoreau seemed to be content with his life. Becoming a skilled land surveyor, he also managed to spend many hours just roaming the countryside, collecting specimens of rare plants or rocks to add to the bins of his treasures that made his attic room at his family's house practically a museum of local natural history.

Indeed Thoreau was aiming to write a book about nature's amazing variety right in the Concord vicinity, but he could not complete this ambitious

Walden pond as seen from Thoreau's hut. *The Bettmann Archive.*

project. In 1856, when he was only thirty-nine, he showed alarming symptoms of having tuberculosis. He still continued to write daily entries in his journal and, during periods when he felt a little better, went by railroad to visit supposedly more healthful areas. Even after a difficult trip to the dry climate of Minnesota failed to accomplish the healing miracle that had been predicted, he remained in cheerful spirits.

On May 6, 1862, about two months short of his forty-fifth birthday, Thoreau died peacefully in Concord, surrounded by his family. At his funeral, his friend Emerson said, "The country knows not yet, or in the least part, how great a son it has lost."

Gradually, though, his greatness was recognized. Today, the leading textbook for college classes studying the long sweep of this country's literature calls Thoreau "the most challenging major writer America has produced."

PART II
The Middle Period

Louisa May Alcott

1832–1888   Her stories, based on her own family life, still attract millions of young readers

One cold morning in March of 1840, when Louisa was only seven, she discovered a half-starved bird near her family's front door. After crying out for her sisters to help her warm and feed it, she suddenly found herself inspired to compose a poem. As soon as the small creature had been cared for, she wrote down:

> To the First Robin
>
> Welcome, welcome, little stranger,
> Fear no harm, and fear no danger;
> We are glad to see you here,
> For you sing, "Sweet Spring is near."
>
> Now the white snow melts away;
> Now the flowers blossom gay:
> Come dear bird and build your nest,
> For we love our robin best.

Louisa's mother was so delighted by her daughter's first literary effort that she fondly exclaimed, "You will grow up a Shakespeare!"

Spurred on by both of her parents, Louisa May Alcott did become an outstanding writer—of children's books. Her most popular work, *Little Women,* about four sisters living in a New England household very similar to her own, would be laughed over and cried over by many generations of girls. Despite its old-fashioned tone, it still sells thousands of copies every year.

But even though Louisa's best-loved book was closely based on her own memories, *Little Women* differed from her real life in some important ways: What she wrote was not nearly as harsh as what she actually experienced. Today, when people are far more open about their problems than they were in her day, the parts of her story that she did not confide make her seem like a surprisingly modern heroine.

Louy, as her family always called her, was born on November 29, 1832, in Germantown, Pennsylvania, not far from Philadelphia. Both of her parents had firm New England ties, and she herself would live most of her life in Massachusetts. Yet her birthplace happened to be elsewhere because her father briefly tried running a school away from his familiar surroundings.

Louy's father, Bronson Alcott, was unusual in many ways. "He is the best-natured man I ever met," his neighbor Henry David Thoreau once noted. Also, though, according to another writer, "No sane man, it seems probable, has ever shown a more complete indifference to money than he did."

So in spite of Bronson's intense love for his children, which made him keep detailed records about their growth and development, he could not take the responsibility of being his family's breadwinner seriously. Only rarely did his head-in-the-clouds approach to teaching and lecturing earn enough to pay his bills. Still, his serene quest for the answers to deep questions about human nature won him the affectionate admiration of some of his century's leading intellectual figures, and they often dug into their own pockets to help him financially.

Mostly, however, it was his wife's relatives who came to his rescue. Louisa's mother, born Abigail May—Abba, her many friends called her—had been accustomed to every comfort during her own girlhood, for she belonged to a solidly established old Boston family. Several rungs higher on the social ladder than the young man who came courting her, Abba nevertheless felt sure that worldly prosperity could not guarantee happiness. So her suitor's high ideals impressed her much more than his lack of concern about money.

Bronson never ceased following his own path, not even seeming to notice other people's head shaking. Nor did his wife ever seem to doubt his greatness or regret having married him, despite some periods of severe hardship throughout the years their children were growing up. Indeed, the Alcott pattern of periodically hovering on the brink of hunger might have marked their whole lives—if not for the second of their four daughters.

Louy had stood out even as a little girl. Because of her having been born on her father's birthday, he seemed to feel a particular bond with her. But it was her own lively personality that set her apart even more, and tales of her youthful mischief won a special place in her family's stock of memories.

The earliest of these harked back to when she was only about eighteen months old. After her father's Pennsylvania school had failed, one morning Louy and her elder sister, Anna, were nicely dressed up in clean frocks, then taken to board a northbound steamship with their parents. Soon after the ship sailed, the children's mother suddenly realized that her baby was missing.

After a long search, Louy was discovered all the way down in the ship's engine room—having a wonderful time because her eager curiosity had led her to "plenty of dirt" with which to amuse herself. Unlike Anna, or later her younger sisters, Beth and May, Louy constantly defied many of the rules about proper behavior set for girls of her day.

So she grew up accustomed to being called a tomboy, a title she relished. In an era when rolling a large hoop was the most active exercise allowed to girls, Louy started to practice running sturdily after a hoop much bigger than she was soon after settling with her family in Boston. During the next several years, she kept increasing the distance she rolled her hoop uninterruptedly, eventually managing to go completely around the parklike Boston Common without stopping.

During these years the Alcott girls never attended any regular school. They received all their teaching from their parents—and a very thorough teaching it was, turning them into great readers.

However, the family kept moving, every year or two, into smaller, cheaper quarters. Between the moves, there were often interludes during which they had to stay with relatives. Louy and her sisters wore shabby clothes handed down by cousins, and their meals were very frugal.

Because their father disapproved of eating meat, the entire family followed a strictly vegetarian diet. Also, a combination of poverty and high principles made them give up sugar and molasses. Sometimes their dinners for days in a row were just plain boiled rice, with raw apples for dessert. Still, Louy thrived to the extent that one day she rolled her hoop for five solid hours, covering almost twenty miles.

Despite all of the hardships of her youth, she was taught to feel lucky because so much love bound her family together. While she and her sisters sometimes felt sharp stabs of envy when they saw other girls wearing new dresses, mostly they did manage to rise above such unworthy emotions. Looking back, Louy would gloss over the harsh moments and decide she really had had a wonderfully happy childhood.

But there was a summer—in 1843, when she was ten years old—over which no amount of wishful thinking could cast a rosy glow. That year her father brought his family to a run-down farm called Fruitlands, where he and some

Louisa May Alcott. *The Bettmann Archive.*

like-minded idealists aimed to create a model community. They hoped to prove that if all of the residents spent a few hours doing chores every morning, they could devote the rest of the day to carefree study and enjoyment.

This starry-eyed experiment proved, within less than a year, to be totally impractical. But the sad story of how dismally Fruitlands failed to fulfill the aims of its sponsors cannot be told here; we can only note that the pressures of communal life almost made the Alcott family fall apart. In her diary, soon after her eleventh birthday, Louy wrote, "In the eve father and mother and Anna and I had a long talk, and we all cried. Anna and I cried in bed, and I prayed God to keep us together."

As if in answer to Louy's prayers, her mother inherited a little money soon afterward, and her father's friend Ralph Waldo Emerson added some from his own pocket that made it possible for the family to buy a small house near his own in the historic village of Concord, where one of the first battles in the American Revolution had been fought.

Concord had a pleasantly rural setting, despite being only about fifteen miles from Boston. Settling there was one of the best things that ever happened to the Alcott family. Although their new house, called Hillside, had long been neglected, Bronson Alcott possessed sufficient carpentry skill to repair its worst faults. Meanwhile, the girls and their mother planted flower and vegetable gardens, besides coping with countless indoor duties.

During the next several years, the Alcotts were still poor because Bronson's teaching and lecturing brought in hardly any income. Nevertheless they found much to enjoy. The spacious old barn in back of their house gave Louy the idea of using it as a theater, where she started by producing her own versions of tales like "Jack and the Beanstalk," then went on to compose all sorts of wildly romantic dramas, in which she herself always played the hero.

By the time Louisa Alcott was fifteen, she had begun writing stories that she dreamed of seeing in print. But that year acute money problems drove the family to start spending winters in Boston. There Louy's mother earned a modest salary, contributed by some well-off ladies, for serving as a "missionary" to the poor in a slum area. The two older daughters did their share, too. Anna was both teacher and nursemaid for the spoiled children of a rich family, while Louisa spent long hours reading religious books aloud to a cranky old lady.

She also worked at sewing and "schoolmarming," becoming more and more discouraged as she discovered how poorly females were paid for the kind of jobs available to them. Yet she longed to be able to become her family's financial mainstay. At the age of eighteen, Alcott wrote about her mother in her diary: "I often think what a hard life she has had since she married—so full of wandering and all sorts of worry! so different from her early easy days. . . . My dream is to have a lovely, quiet home for her, with no debts or troubles to burden her. But I'm afraid she will be in heaven before I can do it."

Along with her various moneymaking efforts, Alcott kept sending poems as well as stories to the editors of magazines. In 1852, at the age of twenty, she scored her first literary success when a fanciful tale of hers entitled "The Rival Painters" was printed by a religious weekly. Although she was paid only five dollars for it, she felt sufficiently encouraged to begin calling herself a writer.

Over the next decade, Alcott doggedly kept writing while she also earned what she could from sewing and teaching. Mostly, she dashed off lively stories without much literary merit, like the blood-and-thunder plays she had put on in their Concord barn. For instance, the hero of her "Pauline's Passion and Punishment," upon discovering the treachery of a supposed friend, turned to Pauline and asked, "Shall I kill him?"

Pauline replied grandly, "There are fates more terrible than death, weapons more keen than poniards, more noiseless than pistols. . . . Leave Gilbert to remorse—and me."

Although Alcott sometimes earned as much as fifty dollars for such stories, her income still did no more than slightly ease her family's financial worries. Also, she longed to prove herself capable of a higher level of literary composition. Within the next few years she did manage to sell a few short pieces to respectable magazines, but it was the Civil War that put her on the road toward fame.

Alcott turned thirty in November of 1862, over a year after the war had started. By then her older sister, Anna, was married and living with her husband at Hillside in Concord, while the rest of the family had moved into a more convenient residence nearby, called Orchard House. Alcott had set her mind so firmly on supporting her aging parents that she felt sure that she herself would never marry.

Still, she knew that, if she had been born a boy, she would certainly have answered President Lincoln's call for volunteers to save the Union. Thus, even though she could not join the fighting, during a crucial period of the war Alcott signed up to serve as a nurse at an army hospital in the nation's capital.

Hardly more than a month after she began the harrowing task of caring for wounded soldiers, she fell dreadfully ill with typhoid fever. She had such alarming symptoms that her father was summoned to Washington, and somehow he managed to bring her home to Concord. She would never be able to recall more than a few confused impressions of their difficult railroad journey; nor did the next several weeks ever cease to seem like a series of terrible nightmares.

But gradually Alcott grew stronger. While she was still recuperating, her worries over the expenses of her illness made her undertake to write a series of magazine pieces about the wartime experiences of "Nurse Periwinkle." And these touched the hearts of readers to the extent that a leading publisher agreed to reprint them in book form.

Alcott's first book, *Hospital Sketches*, not only sold well, it also proved to her father's friends that his daughter really did have some literary talent. Soon she was receiving writing and editing assignments that brought her a modest income as well as a modest amount of acclaim. However, she boldly put her work aside when she was invited to accompany an elderly woman planning just the sort of extensive tour of Europe that she had long dreamed of being able to take.

Soon after returning to Boston, Alcott was asked to call on a friend of her fa-

The frontispiece illustration for the original edition of *Little Women. Culver Pictures, Inc.*

ther's. Thomas Niles of the Roberts Brothers publishing firm had noted the healthy profits that one of his competitors was reaping from the sale of "Oliver Optic" books for boys. He urged Alcott to consider composing a full-length story about domestic life that might be as popular among girls.

So in 1868, at the age of thirty-six, Louisa May Alcott wrote *Little Women*—or, as she would often put it, the book all but wrote itself. Years later, after producing many other highly regarded children's books as well as a steady stream of magazine stories, she explained in a letter to a friend:

My methods of work are very simple. . . . My head is my study & there I keep the various plans of stories for years sometimes, letting them grow as they will until I am ready to put them on paper.

Then it is quick work, as chapters go down word for word & need no alteration. I never copy, since I find by experience that the work I spend the least time upon is best liked by critics & readers.

Little Men, An Old-Fashioned Girl, and *Jo's Boys* were some of her other much-admired books. But few of her works have stood the test of time the way *Little Women* has—for Alcott had somehow given a universal appeal to this heartwarming story of the family she called the Marches. Although its four daughters were very much like herself and her sisters, the fictional Meg, Jo, Beth,* and Amy seemed to possess a magical sort of reality, perhaps because Alcott poured the whole power of her personality into picturing the uncomplicated childhood she wished that she had had.

---

* Beth was the only one of the fictional March girls to receive the same name as the real-life Alcott she had been closely modeled on; the actual Beth had also died young of tuberculosis.

At any rate, from the 1868 appearance of *Little Women* onward, Alcott was able to provide ample financial support for her parents: By 1870, she had ten thousand dollars—a substantial sum in those days—safely invested. Although the needs of those depending on her kept increasing, so did her income. Furthermore, she felt the satisfaction of having earned a respected place among Boston's literary celebrities.

But much as Alcott enjoyed some aspects of her new status, such as being able to attend all sorts of concerts and theatrical performances without closely calculating whether she could spare the price of a ticket, her success did not bring her much personal happiness. Unfortunately, health problems of her own, together with a series of family tragedies, put her under constant strain.

Ever since her terrible bout of typhoid, Alcott had kept falling prey to one set of symptoms or another. Most seriously, she found it less and less possible to sleep at night unless she took ever stronger doses of a medicine she had first been given during the worst of her fever. At a time when the dangers of becoming addicted to drugs were not generally recognized, this thoroughly upright woman had come to depend on a sleeping potion containing opium.

While Alcott did often try to do without her medicine, this upset her to the extent that she could not work—and so she would start relying on it again because she felt so much pressure to keep making money. The death of her older sister's husband had required her to support a second household, that of Anna and her children. What's more, Alcott could not help lavishing affection and money on her youngest sister, May.

Alas, though, while May was in Europe to study art, she had married a penniless fellow student—then died shortly after giving birth to a little girl named after her Aunt Louy. Of course, Alcott adopted her namesake. By then Alcott's adored mother had died, too, but she still had to worry about her increasingly frail father. To fulfill all of her responsibilities, it seemed to her that with every passing year she had to work harder than ever.

Yet the pressures of her fame made it difficult for her to do any work in Concord. Tormented by the "impertinent curiosity" of sightseers, she adopted a sort of disguise to thwart them and newspaper reporters. Coming to the front door carrying a dustmop, she would pretend to be a servant and say that Miss Alcott had gone out of town.

In Concord, however, Alcott demonstrated her full support of the growing national movement demanding that women be allowed to vote in all elections. When local authorities decided to let females cast ballots for school-board members, she was the first woman in line at the polling place.

But Alcott spent an increasing amount of time in Boston, working with frantic urgency as her health continued to deteriorate further. Although she was only entering her fifties, by early in the 1880s she had become so fragile that she entered a private nursing home. She remained there, ever weaker, until her death, at the age of fifty-five, on March 6, 1888.

More than a century later, several of the stories Louisa May Alcott wrote about childhood in a less complicated era are still considered classics. Even some of her earlier sensational tales, originally printed anonymously, have been reissued under her own name and judged as possessing more literary merit than critics of her day had perceived. Her Orchard House in Concord remains one of New England's most popular tourist attractions.

Emily Dickinson

1830–1886   Regarded by many as one of the greatest poets in the
English language

"I'm Nobody!" Emily Dickinson ex-
ulted in one of the most playful of her
poems, which goes on to provide a wonderfully lighthearted example of her
unique way of expressing herself:

How dreary—to be—Somebody!
How public—like a Frog—
To tell one's name—the livelong June—
To an admiring Bog!

But even though she did remain a nobody during her lifetime, since then she
has come to be recognized as a truly
great poet. Also, because her own story
is so mystifying, she has inspired the
weaving of many romantic tales with her
as the heroine. Only by much sifting
through boxes of old letters have her biographers managed to make sure of
some basic facts about her.

Emily Elizabeth Dickinson was born,
on December 10, 1830, in the Massachusetts village of Amherst, about a
hundred miles west of Boston. Ancestors of hers had settled in that area back
in the 1600s, producing generation after
generation of solid citizens who were
well respected among their neighbors.
One of her grandfathers had won wider
notice by taking a leading part in the
founding of Amherst College a generation earlier.

Emily's father stood out still more. An
imposing-looking lawyer, Edward Dickinson continued his father's efforts on
behalf of the local competitor to Harvard and Yale by serving as its treasurer.
In addition, he promoted so many community projects, ranging from a hospital
to an agricultural fair, that he acquired

an honorary title: Squire Dickinson, he was called, in the style of old England.

Yet the squire's cold and austere manner, reminiscent of the original New England Puritans, would give rise to questions after his older daughter became famous. Within the Dickinsons' large brick house, had he played the part of a terrible domestic tyrant? Was some conflict with him the root cause of Emily's strange retreat from the outer world?

For even among people who are not fond of reading poetry, the name Emily Dickinson is associated with oddity: It conjures up the image of a ghostlike woman, always clad in white, flitting silently out of sight whenever visitors came to her family's house. However, all efforts to explain why Dickinson withdrew this way while she was in her twenties have been thwarted by the burning of drawers full of her private papers right after her death. As a result, a variety of dramatic explanations have been proposed over the years.

Although Dickinson's father has often been cast as the villain, there are good reasons for doubting that he deserves this role. Nevertheless, it seems clear that he did cherish old-fashioned ideas about male superiority. He certainly intimidated his wife with his definite opinions on every subject.

She had grown up as Emily Norcross, the daughter of a well-off farmer in the vicinity. Although she had taken singing lessons and attended lectures on chemistry, after marrying Edward Dickinson she found it easier to give up any interests of her own than to risk displeasing him. At least partly because she became so self-effacing, concentrating on cookery and other household chores, the belief that her husband must have been a fierce ruler of his own domain would spread widely.

But several dozen letters dating back to the poet's youth, which turned up only a few decades ago, do not bear this out. They show that the three Dickinson children—Emily; her older brother, Austin; and her younger sister, Lavinia, nicknamed Vinnie—joked a lot about their father's explosive temper. When they wrote to one another during periods when they were separated, the ones at home frequently used phrases like "a storm blew up," but their references to these episodes displayed more amusement than fear.

While the squire obviously awed his son and daughters, the main emotion he appears to have aroused in them was love, not terror. Indeed, all of the available evidence indicates that Emily actually had quite a normal childhood, even though she constantly astonished the rest of her family. For the oddest,

A daguerreotype of Emily Dickinson at about sixteen. *The Robert Frost Library, Amherst College, Amherst, Massachusetts.*

shrewdest, funniest notions kept emerging in a breathless rush from her prodigiously busy brain.

At the age of five, she entered the local primary school. Then, when she was ten, she moved on to the Amherst Academy for more advanced lessons and spent seven very happy years there. "You know I am always in love with my teachers," she once confided to a friend.

Among her friends—and Emily made the warmest of friendships with those she trusted—she joked even about her own appearance. The only existing picture of her, an early type of photo that was taken when she was around sixteen, shows a wispy thin young woman wearing a plain dark dress. Her pale oval face looks solemn, a book rests on the table beside her, and the mood conveyed is certainly studious. But "I am growing handsome very fast indeed!" she wrote to a girl she liked immensely. "I expect I shall be the belle of Amherst when I reach my 17th year."

Upon arriving at that milestone, however, Emily accepted her father's decision to send her to the recently founded Mount Holyoke Female Seminary. Only about ten miles from Amherst, it gave girls more exposure to higher education than they generally received during that period; soon it would evolve into one of the country's first colleges for women. Yet Dickinson found moving even such a small distance from her own familiar environment a painful experience.

To say that her concern over her lack of beauty lay behind her distress would be overly simplifying the reaction of someone with her complexity. Still, in Amherst, where, regardless of her plain exterior, she had long since demonstrated how exceptionally clever she was, she had thoroughly relished companionship. At Mount Holyoke, though, she felt much less secure.

Writing to her brother, Dickinson tried, not very successfully, to disguise her sense of apartness. For instance, after telling him about the flurries of valentines descending on the other girls, she could not help adding that "your *highly accomplished & gifted elder sister* is entirely overlooked." On another occasion, when some sort of entertainment had been made available: "Almost all of the girls went & I enjoyed the solitude finely."

Yet the pressure for religious conformity exerted by Miss Mary Lyon, Mount Holyoke's high-minded founder, disturbed Dickinson far more deeply. All of the students there were expected not only to attend regular prayer meetings, but also to stand up and publicly proclaim their faith. Dickinson could not do this, and her insistence on thinking her own thoughts made her feel still more isolated.

So even though she probably bene-
fited intellectually from some of the
courses she took at Mount Holyoke,
Emily was not sorry when she developed a bad cough during her second semester, causing her father to send
Austin to escort her home. On her return to the school a month later, she
knew the worst was over—her father
had promised that she need not endure
a second year there.

Back in Amherst, Dickinson's daily
life was restricted in many ways that
would seem oppressive a century later
to any young woman with even a much-
less-intensely independent mind. She
wore cumbersome long skirts as a matter of course, accepted the prevailing
limits on womanly behavior, and did her
share of household tasks, mainly baking
bread. Yet she felt safe in her own
home—safe and free to think her own
thoughts.

Though she and her sister shared the
same bedroom, Vinnie's kind heart un-
failingly told her when Emily needed
solitude. For Dickinson had already perceived a need to put down some of her
thoughts on paper, mostly in letters to
cousins or close friends. Often Vinnie
shut her eyes and went to sleep while
Emily sat up by candlelight, writing on
and on in her tiny script.

These letters showed Dickinson's dis-
dain for many rules of proper English
composition, particularly her preference
for dashes instead of periods or com-
mas. In addition she did a lot of under-
lining to stress certain words, besides
compressing her ideas into phrases that
could be very puzzling. She also made
much use of comparison—metaphor, as
teachers of grammar called it—to etch a
deeper impression than any simple description could accomplish. The same
very individual style marked the verses
that she frequently included when she
wrote to her closest friends.

We do not know when Dickinson decided that she could be a poet, or how
she came to arrive at her decision. Most
likely her first efforts were spontaneous
outpourings, like the one she sent the
editor of an Amherst College student
paper when she was eighteen. There
had apparently been an informal contest, but hers was the sole entry printed.
Mostly in prose, it started with a comic
burst of words that were recognized by
a few readers as brilliant nonsense
verse: "Magnum bonum, 'harum
scarum,' zounds et zounds and war
alarum, man reformam, life perfectum,
mundum changum, all things flarum?"

A law student working as a clerk in
her father's office, a young man named
Benjamin F. Newton, was one of the
few who saw Dickinson's rare potential.
As she later recorded, this "gentle, yet
grave Preceptor, teaching me what to

read, what authors to admire, what was most grand or beautiful in nature" exerted a tremendous influence over her following her return from Mount Holyoke. If he had not died a few years later, perhaps the course of her life might have been quite different.

As it was, Newton was just the first of several more or less shadowy figures who would later be brought forward and given the role of the tragic hero in Dickinson's life story. But the main candidate for this distinction is a man she encountered early in 1855, not long after she turned twenty-four. Practically nothing is really known about her meeting with the Reverend Charles Wadsworth except that it happened on her way home from the longest journey she ever took.

The previous year the voters of the Amherst area had elected her father to the United States Congress. As he hated being separated from his family, he insisted on having his wife and daughters accompany him to Washington. The only evidence we have regarding Dickinson's stay there is a letter in which she told a friend how she and Vinnie "on one soft spring day glided down the Potomac in a painted boat," then jumped ashore, hand in hand, to explore General George Washington's "sweet Mount Vernon."

Traveling back to Massachusetts, the Dickinsons stopped off and visited relatives in Philadelphia, where they were introduced to the Reverend Wadsworth, noted for his thoughtful as well as inspiring preaching. Dickinson, according to the most prevalent myth about her, fell instantly and irrevocably in love with him. And though he, too, lost his heart, they forever renounced each other because he already had a wife.

But researchers who have probed as deeply as possible into this tale do not believe it. They think that Dickinson's relationship with Wadsworth amounted to no more than the exchange of occasional letters in which she sought spiritual guidance and received what amounted to private sermons—the same type of student-teacher connection that her diffidence about asserting herself would draw her into repeatedly.

Still it is easy to understand why various mythical romances involving Dickinson would be invented and believed. Depicting her as the heroine of an unhappy love affair served two purposes: These fanciful tales not only provided a motive for her becoming a recluse toward the end of the 1850s, but they also explained an otherwise perplexing aspect of her poetry.

For readers can hardly doubt that Dickinson knew the supreme joy of loving, besides the anguish of blighted love, because she wrote so convincingly about these emotions. Nevertheless, only one actual attachment of hers can be proven, and that did not start until she was in her late forties. But since many of the people who knew her would recall having been overwhelmed by the intensity of feeling that she lavished on them, some biographers ask:

Is it possible that Dickinson *imagined* a number of love affairs? That she intensely exaggerated friendships that were much less important to the objects of her affection? And is it possible that she withdrew from the world because she herself could not stand the continual draining of her emotional power from her poetry?

Certainly, by her thirtieth birthday in 1860, Dickinson had an unshakeable confidence in her own genius. She had also realized that any ordinary pattern of life would not allow her the concentration on her work it required. Given the playful side of her nature, were the white dresses she always wore from then onward just her playful way of saying she was married to her poetry?

Yet Dickinson's deep commitment to writing remained hidden even from most of those closest to her. While the letters she sent to relatives and friends often contained stanzas of verse, only a few of the recipients suspected how seriously involved she was in composing poetry on grand themes like love and death. At least for a brief period, however, Sue Gilbert, the dear friend of hers who married her brother Austin, served as her poetic mentor, providing much helpful advice.

But even though Sue and Austin lived in a house that had been built right next to the Dickinson homestead, behind the same high hedge, Sue soon showed a craving to become the social leader of Amherst. The spiteful way she went about achieving this ambition created so much family tension that, a few years after her marriage, practically all contact between Sue and Emily ceased.

Still, Dickinson's father had many influential associates, among them the publisher of the area's leading newspaper. Samuel Bowles, whose *Springfield Republican* was one of the entire country's most noted journals, has been suggested as another candidate for the great love of Dickinson's life—and he surely received some unusually cryptic letters from her. Perhaps, though, her main aim in cultivating his acquaintance was to see if he would introduce the world to her poetry.

In 1861 his newspaper did print her poem starting, "I taste a liquor never brewed," which eventually would be among her most often quoted works because of its magical second stanza:

Inebriate of Air—am I—
And Debauchee of Dew—
Reeling—thro endless summer days—
From inns of Molten Blue—

But Sam Bowles, despite his lively journalistic outlook, had very conventional literary tastes. Over the years five of Dickinson's poems appeared in his paper, anonymously filling a few inches of space between news items; and yet in each case he changed some of her words to simplify her meaning. He also eliminated her dashes—Dickinson's device for indicating pauses that were necessary to preserve the rhythmic pattern she intended. As a result she ceased expecting him to appreciate her work.

In this period, though, Dickinson still must have wished that her poetry might win some notice during her own lifetime. For she was moved to boldness when she read an essay by Thomas Wentworth Higginson, one of the most highly regarded literary figures of the day, in the April 1862 issue of the *Atlantic Monthly*. Because he urged "new or obscure" writers not to give up hope, she mailed him four of her poems and a brief letter:

Mr. Higginson,
   Are you too deeply occupied to say if my verse is alive?
   Should you think it breathed—and you had the leisure to tell me, I should feel quick gratitude—

While Higginson replied within just a few days, this prominent writer and critic was a sort of mirror reflecting the accepted literary tastes of his era so he did not immediately perceive Emily Dickinson's genius. But he felt sufficient curiosity to ask her numerous questions, which started a regular exchange of letters. As she kept refusing to come see him in Boston, at last, in the summer of 1870, he paid her a visit in Amherst—and his report provides the only reliable firsthand description we have of Emily Dickinson at the peak of her poetic power, approaching the age of forty.

Higginson wrote to his wife right after this encounter, telling her of waiting in a "dark & cool & stiffish" parlor until: "A step like a pattering child's & in glided a little plain woman with two smooth bands of reddish hair [wearing] very plain & exquisitely clean white pique & a blue net worsted shawl. She came to me with two day lilies which she put in a sort of childlike way into my hand & said "these are my introduction" in a soft frightened breathless childlike voice—& added under her breath Forgive me if I am frightened; I never see strangers & hardly know what to say. . . ."

While Higginson could not help sharing the general opinion in Amherst that Dickinson was eccentric to the point of being mentally unbalanced, he kept writing her encouraging letters throughout the rest of her life. Although her output of poetry gradually diminished, during her forties she produced some of

Emily Dickinson's home on Main Street in Amherst. *The Jones Library, Inc., Amherst, Massachusetts.*

her most complex work—despite a terrible series of family tragedies.

The sudden death of her father in 1874 was the first of these blows. A year later, Dickinson's mother suffered a severe stroke that left her bedridden. Together with the sturdy Vinnie, Dickinson cared devotedly for their invalid parent, carrying endless trays of delicacies up to the sickroom. Nevertheless, during this period she had the only ro-

mantic adventure of her life that we can be sure really happened.

Following her father's death, Dickinson had found a special comfort in talking about him with one of his old friends, Judge Otis Lord. When the judge's wife died a few years later, Dickinson sympathized with him so warmly that, even though she was forty-seven by then, and he had reached the age of sixty-five, these two fell deeply in love.

Yet the judge's home was miles away in the seaport of Salem. While a cache of old letters indicates that he and Dickinson seriously thought of marrying, her reluctance to uproot herself delayed any decision. Then he had a serious heart attack. Her mother's death further shocked her. Finally, her brother's young son Gib, a child Dickinson adored, developed a mysterious fever and, to her horror, died.

Gib's death in the autumn of 1883 seemed more than Dickinson could bear. A few months afterward, when Judge Lord died, too, she collapsed, and the family doctor found that she had developed an incurable kidney ailment. For more than two years, Dickinson—waited on day and night by the faithful Vinnie—grew ever weaker. She died on May 15, 1886, at the age of fifty-five.

Right after a very simple funeral at which Dickinson's friend Higginson spoke briefly, Vinnie went home alone to carry out her sister's last wish. She emptied out drawers filled with every letter Dickinson had ever received and burned them all.

Then Vinnie opened a large box whose contents she had not been asked to destroy. It contained about sixty hand-sewn little booklets stacked in tidy piles, each page filled with Dickinson's handwritten poetry. All together, there were nearly eighteen hundred poems.

Just seeing them gave Vinnie "a Joan of Arc feeling," she later confessed, and she vowed that somehow she would bring Emily's genius to the world's attention.

It was no easy task. Owing to Emily's nearly indecipherable script, as well as the emnity of her brother's wife Sue, more than four years elapsed before a slender silver-and-white volume containing just about two hundred of Dickinson's least-confusing poems was published in the autumn of 1890. Thomas Wentworth Higginson—at last he had come to realize Dickinson's great gift—was listed as the book's editor, along with a young woman named Mabel Loomis Todd, an Amherst neighbor particularly hated by Sue Dickinson.

While some critics objected to Emily Dickinson's defiance of accepted rules of poetic expression, this first book received far more praise than disapproval. So did two similar volumes issued during the next few years. Then the extraordinary tangle of emotions in which the surviving members of the Dickinson family were embroiled prevented further publication for several decades.

Not until the 1950s did authoritative versions of all of Dickinson's poems finally appear in print. Meanwhile, myths about her personal life proliferated. But discoveries of hoards of old letters in various New England attics have gradually enabled biographers to dispel at least some of the mysteries in her story.

Numerous researchers keep delving further, still hoping to find answers to the many remaining questions. No longer a nobody, Emily Dickinson now securely ranks among this country's most outstanding literary figures. Indeed, her nontraditional verse patterns particularly appeal to modern readers—today, she is often called America's greatest poet.

Theodore Dreiser

1871–1945   A one-man literary factory

As a boy in Terre Haute, Indiana, Theodore Dreiser walked along the railroad tracks picking up lumps of coal that fell from passing trains. He brought them home so that his mother could heat their house in the winter. His pieces of coal were needed because the Dreisers were a poor family with ten children, who frequently went to bed both cold and hungry.

His father, John Dreiser, an immigrant from Germany, worked at the weaver's trade, but went into debt when he tried to become a wool manufacturer on his own and failed. A stern, religious man, he did his best to force his beliefs on his children, but met only rebellion. He had married Sarah Maria Schanab, who grew up on a farm, when she was only seventeen. A kindly woman, she tried to shield the children from her husband's constant anger. One by one, though, the older daughters and sons ran away from home.

The ninth of ten children, Theo was born on August 7, 1871. Growing up in poverty, he often wore ragged clothing and shoes with holes. His mother became a washerwoman and took in boarders to earn money, but that was not enough to keep a stable home. The Dreisers had to move repeatedly, usually because they could not pay their rent.

At first Theo and his brothers and sisters went to parochial schools at the insistence of their religious father. But when the family settled in the Indiana town of Warsaw, in 1884, his mother enrolled the thirteen-year-old Theo in the

111

public school. There, for the first time, the shy, gangling boy found some encouragement. He always remembered a young teacher, May Calvert, who told him, "You read beautifully."

But Theo did poorly in grammar and, nearing the end of the school year, he thought that he would be left back. Miss Calvert surprised him, however. "I'm going to pass you just the same," she said. "Grammar isn't everything." Years later, even after Dreiser became a world-famous writer, he still had not mastered the elements of English grammar.

Another teacher, Mildred Fielding, encouraged Theo in high school. "You must study and go on, for your mind will find its way," she told him. "I know it."

Still, Theo considered himself a failure at the age of sixteen. He dreamed of money, fine clothes, beautiful girls—a glamorous life far beyond Warsaw's limited possibilities. In the summer of 1887 he decided to try to better himself in Chicago, where two of his sisters lived.

He failed in Chicago, too. He was fired from a job as a car washer in a railroad yard, he quit as a dishwasher, he was fired as a stove polisher in a hardware store, and he gave up a job as a freight-car tracer in a railroad yard because it was too hard, before finding work as a stock boy in another hardware store. He was rescued from that monotonous job by an unexpected visitor: Miss Fielding, his high school teacher from Warsaw, who had become a school principal in Chicago.

"Theodore," she said, "work of this kind isn't meant for you, really." She arranged for him to be accepted as a freshman at the University of Indiana, and she even paid his tuition. In 1889 Theo went to college. He passed his courses with fair grades, but failed at what interested him most: girls. He adored them from a distance, but they ignored him.

Returning to Chicago after just one year at the university, he again began bouncing from job to job, but now they were somewhat better jobs. He worked as a real estate salesman, a driver for a laundry, and as a bill collector for a company that sold furniture to poor people on the installment plan. As he made his rounds on foot, he saw the underside of the busy city of Chicago and began to write short pieces about life in the slums.

"I seethed to express myself," Dreiser would recall years later in his memoirs. "I had a singing feeling that someday I should really write and be very famous into the bargain."

He decided that working for a newspaper could be the path toward realizing his dream. He haunted the offices of the *Daily Globe* until an editor gave him a

Theodore Dreiser in his early twenties. *Van Pelt-Dietrich Library, University of Pennsylvania.*

chance to try out as a reporter, even though he had absolutely no experience. The year was 1892, and the Democratic party was holding its national convention in Chicago. "Cover the hotels for political news," the editor told him.

Thrown into a world about which he knew nothing at all, the twenty-one-year-old Dreiser floundered. Yet he found that the politicians he met were friendly. One day a member of the United States Senate told him that Grover Cleveland would be nominated for president—news that none of the experienced reporters had yet gathered. When Dreiser returned to the newspaper office with his scoop, another reporter got to write the story—but he himself got a job, at fifteen dollars a week.

Eager to write, Dreiser worked hard to improve at his chosen craft. His factual reporting, the heart of any newspaper article, could not always be relied on. However, his observations were keen and his descriptive feature stories were excellent. On the recommendation of one of his colleagues, he found a job at a bigger newspaper, the *St. Louis Globe-Democrat,* at a salary of twenty dollars a week.

In the next few years, Dreiser worked as a reporter for a variety of newspapers in St. Louis, Toledo, and Pittsburgh. During this period, he branched out to become a theater critic as well, gaining information that would be useful afterward when he started writing a novel. While on an assignment for a St. Louis paper, he met Sara Osborne White, a schoolteacher just a few years older than he was, whom he later married. In Toledo he became friendly with a young editor, Arthur Henry, who encouraged him to write fiction.

On the invitation of his older brother Paul, an actor and songwriter who had changed his name to Paul Dresser, Dreiser moved to New York City in 1895. Unable to find a newspaper job, he convinced his brother and some of Paul's associates to let him edit a magazine to help them sell their songs. Dreiser called the magazine *Ev'ry Month* and filled it with fiction, poetry, pictures, and songs.

One day in 1897, Paul put a question to his younger brother: "Why don't you give me an idea for a song once in awhile, sport?"

Dreiser replied, "Why don't you write something about a state or a river? Take Indiana—what's wrong with it—the Wabash River?"

Paul said he would write the music if Theo would write the words. Dreiser sat down and wrote the chorus of what became one of Paul Dresser's most famous songs, "On the Banks of the Wabash":

Oh, the moonlight's fair tonight along the
    Wabash,
    From the fields there comes the breath
      of new mown hay,
Through the sycamores the candle lights
    are gleaming,
    On the banks of the Wabash far away.

Soon Dreiser quit his job on *Ev'ry Month* and worked as a freelance magazine writer, interviewing men of wealth and achievement. A fast writer, he had no time for revising or editing his own manuscripts because 'he was always working on three or four articles at a time. "I have an easy pen," he said.

At last, having achieved some financial success, Dreiser felt the time had come to marry the patient Sara Osborne White, who had been waiting for him for years. They were married in 1898; she was just short of thirty then, and he was twenty-seven.

The newly married couple went to visit Dreiser's friend Arthur Henry in Ohio. Henry had started to write a novel, and he urged Dreiser to do so, too.

"Finally," Dreiser would recall, "I took out a piece of yellow paper and to please him wrote down a title at random—*Sister Carrie.*"

He said he had no plot in mind. As he began to work, though, he recalled an older sister who had run away to Chicago with a man. He remembered his own poverty, the life of the bustling city, his theatrical experiences, and a streetcar strike he had covered as a reporter. Writing quickly, he described his heroine Carrie, an innocent girl of eighteen who went to Chicago to find a job, then he told about her discouraging work as a shop girl and her love affairs—all with compassion and understanding.

Dreiser finished *Sister Carrie* in seven months, writing magazine articles at the same time to earn some money. He submitted the manuscript to a publisher, where the reader was Frank Norris, an author himself. Norris accepted the book enthusiastically, calling it one of the best he had ever read.

Unfortunately, however, when the publisher, Frank Doubleday, read the manuscript, he rejected it as immoral. He felt that the theme of the novel violated the conventions of the times: Carrie was not punished for her sins, and was even rewarded with fame and fortune.

Dreiser insisted that the Doubleday company live up to its contract to publish the book. When it appeared in print, a majority of the critics condemned the book's immorality, but some recognized the power of the writing. Only four hundred and fifty-six copies were sold, and Dreiser received royalties totaling just sixty-eight dollars and forty cents. It was a crushing blow to him—at a time when light romantic books sold hundreds of thousands of copies.

The next few years were hard for Dreiser. He separated from his wife, he found himself unable to write, and he descended once more into poverty, even picking up discarded fruit and vegetables at markets for food. After a short stay in a sanitorium, paid for by his brother Paul, he recovered from his bout of depression. He found a job as an editor for a publisher of cheap novels.

A competent editor, Dreiser moved soon to *Broadway* magazine, at a salary of forty dollars a week. In an era of much lower prices, he could live comfortably again and he could even afford to buy the plates of *Sister Carrie* from its original publisher, then reissue it in cooperation with a new publishing firm. The book came out again in 1907 to better reviews and brisk sales.

In that same year, Dreiser got a new, high-paying job as editor of three women's magazines at another publishing company. Ironically, Dreiser, the realistic writer, put out magazines devoted to frothy fiction and fashion. But his salary of five thousand dollars a year, a very substantial amount in those days, soothed him.

As an editor Dreiser dealt with most of the famous authors of the early 1900s and also with many young writers. He became a friend of one of them, Henry L. Mencken of Baltimore. Together, they shared a contempt for what they considered the dull nature of American society.

Dreiser was fired in 1910, not because of any failings as an editor but because he paid too much attention to the seventeen-year-old daughter of one of the other editors. In those years, and for the rest of his life, Dreiser was unable to resist young women. Although far from handsome, he was nevertheless a magnetic man who attracted women of all ages by his ability to talk compellingly—and he was also a good listener. Separated from his wife, he carried on numerous love affairs, often two or three at the same time.

Freed from the daily chores of an editor's desk, Dreiser returned to serious writing after a ten-year lapse. A one-man literary factory, he worked from nine in the morning to four in the afternoon every day at a big rectangular desk made from the old rosewood piano that his brother Paul had owned. He wrote fast—too fast, the critics said—pouring out thousands of words a day, never editing his own work. He depended on his women friends for that.

Dreiser finished his second novel, *Jennie Gerhardt,* in early 1911. It was the story of a poverty-stricken woman who had an illegitimate child by a man who died. As originally written it had a happy ending, with Jenny marrying a rich man. But Dreiser always showed his manuscripts to friends, asking their opinion, and in this case the verdict was unanimous: The happy ending was wrong, and the book was too long. Dreiser changed the ending and let others shorten it.

In a burst of creative energy, Dreiser busied himself with three other novels: *The Financier* (1912), *The Titan* (1914), and *Genius* (1915). He also wrote the first volume of an autobiography, *A Traveler at Forty,* and several one-act plays.

During this period before and during the First World War, Dreiser found himself at home in the free and easy atmosphere of the New York neighborhood called Greenwich Village. Political radicals and rebels against conventional social rules congregated there. His own thinking had crystallized into what one critic called Dreiser's Laws: "Beliefs held by the multitude and their leaders are likely to be wrong. . . . Beliefs held by the unconventionalists which fly in the face of orthodoxy are probably right."

After the war, in 1919, Dreiser met Helen Patges Richardson, a beautiful young actress who was his second cousin. Despite a wide difference in age—he was forty-eight, she twenty-

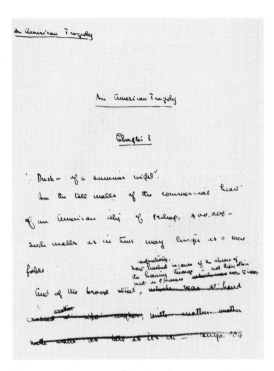

The opening page of Dreiser's manuscript, *An American Tragedy. Van Pelt-Dietrich Library, University of Pennsylvania.*

five—they fell in love and began to live together.

And Dreiser began to work on what became one of his most successful novels, *An American Tragedy.* He based it on a true story, that of a young man in an upstate New York town who killed his pregnant girlfriend when she stood in the way of his getting ahead socially and economically. For Dreiser, though, the tragedy was more in the false values of American society than in the individual case.

The book came out in December of 1925 to glowing reviews and large sales. Many critics, including his friend Mencken, pointed out that the novel was too long, that the writing was crude, and that the author's grammar was faulty. But, as Mencken said, "as a human document, it is searching and full of a solemn dignity and at times rises to the level of genuine tragedy."

For the first time in his life, Dreiser had riches to match his dreams. *An American Tragedy* was a best-seller, and a play based on the book ran for more than two hundred performances on Broadway. Magazines and newspapers begged him to write articles, for which they paid handsomely.

Dreiser and Helen Richardson moved into a splendid apartment in New York. She bought herself gowns, a Russian wolfhound, and a grand piano. He indulged himself with colorful clothes, notably expensive shirts, bright bow ties, and a new walking stick.

Together they opened their new apartment every Thursday evening for an informal gathering of men and women in the arts. They toured Europe, including the Soviet Union, in 1927. Two years later Dreiser built a large country home that he called Iroki, a Japanese word meaning "beauty," in Mount Kisco, north of New York City.

Despite his riches, he faced a major disappointment in 1930. Dreiser had hoped to win the Nobel Prize in literature that year. Instead it went to Sinclair Lewis.

In the depression years of the 1930s, Dreiser became active as a social reformer. He became chairman of the National Committee for Political Prisoners and publicly supported causes sponsored by the Communist Party. During this period, his emergence as a public figure paralleled his decline as a writer.

In 1931 he published *Dawn*, an autobiographic book about his early years. It sold only a few thousand copies. The following year he wrote *Tragic America*, a violent attack on big business, banks, the Supreme Court, and other American institutions. Badly written and riddled with errors, it attracted few readers.

Although his works sold briskly in Europe, Dreiser became a forgotten man in America. Many people thought he had died. In 1940 he and Helen left the bustling literary world of New York and moved to California—once again poor. They lived in a cramped apartment, filled with cheap furniture, and had few close friends.

Dreiser was rescued from poverty by the sale of his first novel, *Sister Carrie*, to a movie producer. He bought a six-room Spanish-style house in Santa Monica, with a study big enough to hold the

Theodore Dreiser in 1931 when he was becoming active as a social reformer. *Culver Pictures, Inc.*

large desk that had once been his brother Paul's piano. At the age of seventy, Dreiser went back to work.

In 1944 he received the Award of Merit from the American Academy of Arts and Letters. In that same year, following the death of his first wife, he and Helen were finally married. A year later, physically and mentally weary, Dreiser struggled to finish his last two novels.

On December 27, 1945, with Helen's help, he completed his work. They walked on the beach and watched the sun set. On their return home, Dreiser collapsed. He died the next day, at the age of seventy-four.

Dreiser is remembered today mostly for two books, *Sister Carrie* and *An American Tragedy.* But he played an important role in the development of American literature as well. Sinclair Lewis, in his 1930 acceptance speech for the Nobel Prize, the award that Dreiser wanted and did not get, put it this way: "Usually unappreciated, often hounded, he had cleared the trail from Victorian . . . timidity and gentility in American fiction to honesty, boldness and passion of life. Without his pioneering I doubt if any of us could, unless we liked to be sent to jail, express life, beauty and terror."

O. Henry

1862–1910   Master of the short story

Although his real name was William Sydney Porter, the world came to know him as O. Henry.

When he first began to write he used various pseudonyms, such as Howard Clark and T. B. Dowd, which are now forgotten. But the last one he chose, O. Henry, became one of the most famous pen names in American literature.

How did he choose it? There are several stories, among them that he knew a rancher in Texas called Old Henry, or simply O. Henry. Also, at a bank where he once worked a porter was often summoned with the call, "Oh, Henry, come here." And in Texas he no doubt became familiar with a cowboy song containing these words:

Along came my true love about twelve
    o'clock

Saying Henry, O Henry, what sentence
    have you got?

He himself once told an interviewer that he picked the name Henry from the society columns of a New Orleans newspaper and the initial O because it was "the easiest letter written." To an editor he explained that he used O. Henry because "it looked good in print and is easy for the lips."

Whatever the reason, he felt comfortable with his pen name and so did his readers. O. Henry's stories became popular around the world, in English and in translation. By 1920 nearly five million copies of books containing his short stories had been sold in the United States alone. "No other American writer of stories had ever been so widely read, enjoyed, discussed, approved of, and imitated," one literary historian has noted.

The future storyteller was born in the small, elm-shaded village of Greensboro, North Carolina, on September 11, 1862. His parents named him William Sydney Porter, but everybody called him Will. He had a brother two years old at the time of his birth.

Will's mother, Mary Virginia Jane Swaim Porter, was an educated woman, a graduate of the Greensboro Female College. She had married one of the most eligible bachelors in town, Algernon Sidney Porter, the local doctor. An amiable man, considered to be the leading physician in the entire county, he had a major problem: collecting his fees.

As a wedding present, Mary Virginia Porter's family gave the newlyweds a house. But they lived there only a short time before they were forced to give it up because of Dr. Porter's unwillingness to ask for payment for his medical services. The young family went to live in an unpainted old house with the doctor's mother and sister, Evalina.

Will's mother died when he was three years old, shortly after giving birth to another son who did not survive infancy. After his wife's death, Will's father lost interest in medicine. He spent his time in the barn trying to build a perpetual-motion machine and drinking.

As a result, Will was raised in his grandmother's house, largely by his aunt—known to the town as Miss Lina—who also ran a small school, which he attended. Will grew to be a shy boy, just like his father. He did not get along with his rough and tough older brother. But he was a good student at his aunt's school, ranking at the top of his class.

In school Will displayed one remarkable talent. When he was up at the blackboard doing an arithmetic problem with chalk in his right hand, at the same time he would draw a sketch of his aunt with his left hand. He would do this quickly while Miss Lina, who always carried a switch to discipline unruly students, was marching to the back of the classroom. Somehow he always managed to get the sketch erased before she turned around, and escaped punishment.

A born teacher without formal training, Miss Lina strongly influenced Will, as well as her other pupils. One of her teaching devices was to begin a story in class and then call on one student after another to continue the story. She took her classes on wildflower hunts, staged exhibitions in which all the children participated, and read good books to them.

Will became an avid reader. He later said that he did "more reading between my thirteenth and nineteenth years than I have done in the years since, and my taste was much better than it is now, for I used to read nothing but the classics." His favorite books were *The Arabian Nights* and Burton's *Anatomy of Melancholy.*

Will's formal schooling ended in 1877 when he was fifteen years old. He went to work in an uncle's drugstore, which was a gathering place for the town's leading men. Not only did he learn how to mix and dispense drugs, but he stored up impressions of the people who came in and their mannerisms, gestures, and speech—all of which were reflected later in his stories. His ability to sketch came in handy, too. When an unknown customer came in, he drew a likeness so that his uncle could identify and charge him.

In this period, Will was a red-cheeked, black-haired boy, about five feet six inches tall. Despite his shyness, he took time off from the drug and soda counters to go out back to pitch horseshoes and practice pistol marksmanship with the other young men of the town. He also loved to play tricks on some of his customers. Once he displayed a snake in alcohol, telling people it had been extracted from someone's stomach.

By the age of nineteen, Porter had learned his trade so well that his name appeared on the first list of druggists in the records of the North Carolina Pharmaceutical Company in 1881. But he was unhappy, both in his work and in his grandmother's house. "The grind in the drugstore was agony to me," he told an interviewer years later.

Rescue came from one of his customers. Dr. James K. Hall and his wife invited Porter to accompany them on a visit to their sons in Texas. He accepted eagerly. In 1882 he went to live with Richard Hall and his wife, Betty, on a small sheep ranch, forty miles from the tiny town of Cotulla. He showed no signs of regret at leaving his family in North Carolina and seldom wrote to them.

Porter lived as a guest with the Halls, almost as if he were one of their children. He made friends with the cowboys, went to town for the mail, occasionally baby-sat for the Hall children, learned to speak Spanish, and sometimes even served as the substitute cook. It was a lonely life for a young man of twenty out there in the wide open spaces. He filled his long hours of leisure time by reading all the books available, as well as mail-order catalogs and the dictionary.

The Halls liked Porter. But they were realistic in their appraisal of him. Betty Hall said later that he had showed "no sense of responsibility or obligation or gratitude" to them, just as he had failed to express thanks to his aunt and grandmother for his upbringing. To another friend, Porter appeared to be "a child-like individual" who accepted help and favors but not responsibility, characteristics that he was to show for the rest of his life.

After Porter had spent two years on the ranch, the Halls introduced him to another family that came from Greensboro. Joe Harrell, a cigar store owner, and his wife took Porter into their home in Austin, the Texas state capital, as a member of their family. "He was like a brother to me," one of the Harrell sons would recall.

Porter, now twenty-two years old, lived with the Harrells for three years. He thrived in Austin, sketching, writing, and becoming friendly with many other young men and women. He fell in love with a high school girl, Athol Estes. Shortly after she graduated in 1887, they got married. They had one child, a daughter named Margaret, who was born in 1889.

Porter's nineteen-year-old bride encouraged him to write. Only three months after his marriage, his first letter of acceptance arrived—from the *Detroit Free Press,* to which he had sent a short, humorous sketch. Still, he had to have a job to support his family.

Porter worked briefly as a pharmacist, bookkeeper, draftsman, and finally as a teller in a bank. But writing remained his major interest. He established his own humor newspaper by buying a cheap printing press and the rights to a magazine, which he renamed *The Rolling Stone* (not in any way connected with today's magazine of the same name).

For a year, starting in 1894, Porter put out a weekly while he also worked at the bank. He filled his magazine's eight pages mainly with his own writing. But the *Rolling Stone* was a financial failure. Porter borrowed money from family and friends to keep it afloat. In addition he took some money from the bank, with the intention of returning it later.

When a bank examiner found that about a thousand dollars was missing, Porter resigned. After his friends repaid what he had taken, a grand jury refused to indict him on criminal charges, probably because such borrowing from banks was common in those days of lax regulation.

Porter got a job in Houston, writing a humor column for its leading newspaper. His column in the *Houston Post* contained characters like a sensitive tramp, ill-starred lovers, struggling artists, and likable grafters, a foretaste of the short stories that he was to write later. But his past caught up with him in 1896. A second grand jury in Austin indicted him for embezzlement from the bank, and he was ordered to stand trial.

At this point Porter made the major

mistake of his life. If he had returned to Austin, he probably would have been acquitted because of the loose management of the bank. Instead he acted like a guilty man. He ran away, first to New Orleans and then to the Central American country of Honduras. He remained there until 1897, when he heard that his wife was fatally ill. He returned to Austin.

It was a terrible time for Porter. Not only did his wife die, but he stood trial, was convicted of embezzlement, and was sentenced to five years in jail. He entered a federal prison near Columbus, Ohio, in April of 1898 at the age of thirty-five. Prison records described him as five foot seven in height, with a dark complexion and chestnut hair sprinkled with gray.

Porter had a relatively easy time in jail. As a registered pharmacist, he was assigned to the prison pharmacy. He made friends with other inmates easily, listened to them, and wrote stories when his duties were over.

O. Henry was born as a professional short story writer in jail. Under that name, three of his stories were published almost immediately: "Whistling Dick's Christmas Stocking," "Georgia's Ruling," and "Money Maze." One critic has pointed out that most of his early stories had a theme with obvious autobiographical overtones: "The plot in-

evitably turns on the regeneration of an admitted delinquent, not on the vindication of a character who is blameless."

After serving a sentence of three years, reduced from five because of good conduct, Porter came out of prison in 1901. He stopped first in Pittsburgh, where his daughter was being cared for by friends. He kept on writing. In less than a year, nine of his stories were published in magazines, and others were accepted for later publication.

His career blossomed when he went to New York City in 1902 at the invitation of his editors. "If ever in American literature the place and the man met, they met when O. Henry strolled for the first time along the streets of New York," one biographer would declare. For O. Henry prowled the city streets, absorbing the color and texture of city life and turning what he observed into memorable short stories.

His work appeared in many national magazines. In 1903, though, the *New York World* became his major outlet. Then the newspaper with the largest circulation in America, the *World* had begun to attract some of the country's outstanding writers. Porter wrote a story a week about life in New York for a hundred dollars apiece, a large amount of money for those times. He also kept on writing stories for magazines.

With ample funds for the first time,

O. Henry in a photograph taken in 1904. *The Bettmann Archive.*

Porter enjoyed his life in New York. He lived near Gramercy Park, a pleasant neighborhood but close to the seamy side of the city—its saloons, shooting galleries, and vaudeville halls. He spent lavishly, giving big tips to working people. In the three years from 1904 to 1907, Porter indulged in what he called "the business of caliphing"—behaving like a caliph, or rich Arabian prince, in the exotic tales from the Near East he had loved as a child.

It was during this period that Porter, as one writer put it, "became the O. Henry of fact and legend, the O. Henry whose stories suggested to his friends the role in which he is familiarly pictured—that of the Caliph of Bagdad-on-the-Subway." For he acted as if he had unlimited money to spend and give away to needy people on the streets of New York.

Porter paid for his generous, and irresponsible, habits with an amazing productivity. In two years, he wrote one hundred and thirteen stories for the *World* and at least twenty-five longer stories for magazines. Almost all of them follow the O. Henry pattern: a chatty opening, a confidential narrator, the chance meeting of old pals, an ironic tone, love triumphant, and, above all, a surprise ending.

A fast writer, Porter sometimes worked best under deadline pressure.

Probably his most famous story, "The Gift of the Magi," was written while an illustrator for the *World* waited for the copy so that he could do the drawings. Porter told him to draw a poorly furnished room, with a man and woman sitting on a bed, talking about Christmas. The man was to have an old-fashioned watch in his hand, the woman to have beautiful long black hair.

In three hours, using a pencil on yellow copy paper, Porter completed the story. It ended when the man sold his watch to buy his wife some elegant combs for her hair and the woman sold her hair to buy him a chain for his watch. It was a typical O. Henry story, sentimental and ironic, glorifying love and sacrifice, complete with a surprise ending.

Perhaps his funniest story is "The Ransom of Red Chief." It begins with the simple words of a kidnapper: "It looked like a good thing; but wait till I tell you." What he told was how two crooks succeeded in taking a boy for ransom, but found him so obnoxious that they paid their own money to have him taken back.

The first collection of O. Henry stories in book form, *Cabbages and Kings,* came out in 1904. It drew favorable reviews and sold reasonably well. His second collection, *The Four Million,* (a reference to the population of New York

City at the time) made him world famous after it appeared in 1906. It not only sold well in this country, but it also was translated into many foreign languages, and it is still one of his best-read books.

Volumes of his short stories appeared at a fast pace from then on. *The Trimmed Lamp* and *Heart of the West* came out in 1907; *The Voice of the City* and *The Gentle Grafter* in 1908; *Roads of Destiny* and *Options* in 1909; *Strictly Business* and *Whirligigs* in 1910; and others later.

But success as an author masked a failure in his personal life in those years. His generous gifts of money often led to problems in paying his own lavish living expenses. To earn more, he drove himself to writing so unceasingly that he grew weary of the pace. He began to drink heavily.

When a friend inquired about how to go about writing, Porter replied in his usual ironic manner: "The first step is to get a kitchen table, a wooden chair, a wad of yellow writing paper, one lead pencil and a drinking glass. Those are the props. Then you secure a flask of Scotch whiskey and a few oranges, which I will describe as the sustenance. We now come to the plot, frequently styled the inspiration. Combining a little orange juice with a little Scotch, the author drinks the health of all magazine editors, sharpens his pencil and begins to write. When the oranges are empty and the flask is dry, a saleable piece of fiction is ready for mailing."

One of the stories he produced in 1909, "A Municipal Report," was among his best. In a 1914 symposium conducted by the *New York Times*, it was voted "the greatest American short story." In it, Porter has three characters: a black carriage driver, an aging woman author, and an utterly despicable Southern gentleman. After a dramatic and mysterious murder, the story ends with the O. Henry trademark, a surprise last paragraph.

In a way that seemed to duplicate one of his own sentimental stories, in 1907 Porter, at the age of forty-five, made a completely unexpected second marriage. It happened because the mother of the thirty-seven–year-old Sara Lindsay Coleman discovered that the famous New York writer O. Henry was the same Will Porter who had played with her daughter back in Greensboro many years before. This discovery led to an exchange of letters, then a wedding.

But it was not a happy marriage. Not only did two middle-aged people have difficulties adjusting to one another; in addition, Porter's teenage daughter Margaret came to live with her father and his new wife. The need for additional money drove Porter to write ever more furiously, and his health cracked. By 1909, only two years after his marriage, Mrs. Porter had returned to North Carolina, Margaret had gone back to school, and Porter himself had reverted to his old bachelor habits.

Increasingly ill, Porter lived alone in a hotel room during the last year of his life, relying on whiskey to keep himself alive. He died on June 5, 1910, at the age of forty-eight.

Henry James

1843–1916   Brilliant novelist and literary critic

At the age of only six months, Henry James took his first trip to Europe and he lived there with his parents for the next year and a half. So the earliest picture stored away by his amazing memory was of a grand Paris monument he saw before his second birthday.

Then when he was twelve, he and his family spent another few years in England, France, and Switzerland. These youthful travel experiences strongly influenced his whole outlook—and his work. Throughout his career as a writer, the plight of Americans facing the complexities of Old World society gave him his main theme.

From the subtle nuances in human relationships on both sides of the Atlantic, James spun out dozens of novels that have never been widely popular.

But his acute psychological probing is far more admired today than it was in his own era, and a select company of devoted readers considers him the most brilliant literary figure the United States has ever produced.

Like many of the characters he created, Henry James himself had some puzzling elements in his own story. Yet at least two of his basic problems are easy to understand: He grew up feeling a compelling need to avoid being doubly overshadowed—by his father and also by his older brother.

Right from his birth in a fashionable neighborhood of New York City, on April 15, 1843, he bore a burden bound to weigh heavily on a very sensitive child. Even his name did not seem to belong to him because it was the same as his father's: he was just Henry James, Junior. What's more, he lacked the special status of being his parents' firstborn son—for he had a remarkably bright brother, William, sixteen months his senior.

But before taking a further look at the complicated mixture of love and rivalry that marked the relationship between this pair of exceptional brothers, it is necessary to make the acquaintance of their father. He was a rich and amiable man, whose eminence during the 1800s is hard to explain today because the numerous books that he wrote about religious and moral issues baffle practically everybody who tries to read them. Even in his own era, one critic, reviewing an opus of his entitled *The Secret of Swedenborg* (Emanuel Swedenborg was a noted Swedish philosopher), good-humoredly wrote that Mr. James "kept the secret very well."

Nevertheless, the elder Henry James had such a wonderfully sunny disposition—and such disarmingly eccentric habits—that the intellectual leaders of his era were delighted by him. Ralph Waldo Emerson was a close friend of his, and so was Britain's Thomas Carlyle. As a result, all of his children were awed by his famous associates as well as by his many differences from ordinary fathers.

These could be traced to his rebellious feelings during his own strict up-bringing in a wealthy household in Albany, New York, and also to the terrible experience he had endured at the age of thirteen: He had almost died from being severely burned while helping to fight a fire. After an operation amputating one of his legs, he spent two years flat on his back in bed before he could begin learning to walk with a leg made of cork, and this long period of invalidism turned him into a reader and thinker always seeking solutions to the mysteries of human existence.

His father—the future novelist's grandfather—was a merchant who had amassed a large fortune by investing in real estate. When he died several years after the fire, he left property valued at the then-enormous sum of three million dollars, to be divided among eleven children and their mother. So the injured Henry—the future novelist's father—in his early twenties inherited a sufficient income to find himself "leisured for life," as he contentedly put it.

Marrying Mary Walsh, the self-effacing sister of one of his classmates at the Princeton Theological Seminary, he soon began testing his unusual ideas about raising a family. Having felt extremely oppressed by the narrow world of his own youth, he aimed to expose his children to the widest possible range of possibilities: Instead of living only in one place—always attending the same

Mathew Brady's daguerreotype of Henry James at the age of eleven, photographed in New York with his father. *The Bettmann Archive.*

school and being obliged to accept the religious beliefs of one church—he set out to give his offspring endless opportunities to broaden their minds.

That was why he kept uprooting his family every few years, enthusiastically making available new sights and new lessons. But as he himself was more interested in European civilization than in the discovery of gold in California, his educational efforts were focused eastward, not westward. Also, he shared the prevailing ideas about the proper role of females to the extent that his daughter Alice, born after William and Henry and two other boys, was expected to concentrate on encouraging the men in her family, rather than to develop any talent of her own.

The two brothers closest to her in age would have unhappy lives. Despite their youthful glimmers of ability, neither of them could achieve the high intellectual level expected of them. Yet their father's system for spurring genius certainly worked in the cases of his two eldest sons. Possibly, though, their own talents were just as much stimulated by the competition between William and Henry junior that started practically with Henry's birth.

In his old age James ruefully admitted feeling from his first stirring of consciousness as if William "had gained such an advance of me in his sixteen months' experience of the world before mine began that I never . . . in the least caught up with him or overtook him. He was always round the corner and out of sight." Even when Henry briefly found himself in the same schoolroom or the same game, "it was only for a moment— he was clean out before I had got well in."

So the young Henry behaved quite a bit like a typical little brother, forever trying to copy whatever William did in the hope of showing that he was equally worthy of their father's approval—even though William kept defeating him in one way or another.

For instance, because William was good at drawing pictures, Henry took up drawing, too. Around the age of ten, he ambitiously made a sketch showing a stormy ocean scene and, to be sure anybody who saw it knew what he had in mind, he wrote underneath it, "The thunder roared and the lightning followed." William, far more interested in science than Henry was, teased him so unmercifully for not remembering that the lightning came first that Henry had to run to their mother demanding protection.

As Henry kept losing brotherly battles, he depended more and more on maternal help. To win it he cultivated such good manners that he became their mother's special favorite, and this status surely did not help him when he begged to accompany his big brother on some after-school outing. "*I* play with boys who curse and swear!" William informed him.

Even though brothers everywhere were likely to have similar difficulties, the intensity of the rivalry between Henry and William—as well as the depth of their brotherly affection—went much beyond the ordinary. For, owing to their father's policy of moving his family so often, they were unusually de-

pendent on each other for companionship.

During Henry's first dozen years, he no sooner got used to one neighborhood or school in New York City or Albany than his surroundings changed. Besides reducing his opportunities to form boyhood friendships, however, all of this upheaval had a more positive effect. It stirred him to become a very careful observer of people and places, always quietly storing up detailed impressions of everything he saw.

Then his father decided that the time had come to take his whole family on a prolonged tour of Europe. The Jameses boarded the steamship *Atlantic* in New York on June 26, 1855, two months after Henry's twelfth birthday—and they did not return to America until early in the summer of 1858, when Henry had already turned fifteen.

Those three years abroad had an enormous impact on him. While depriving him of an American setting as he entered his teens, they gave him a familiarity with the Old World that would make him feel more at home there than anywhere else. They also gave him such a variety of fascinating scenes to observe that his tendency toward regarding himself as a watcher rather than a participant in whatever was going on around him was much reinforced.

Being shy and bookish, Henry began

doing some writing during this period. Europe's artistic treasures, its castles, and its ruins excited his imagination much more than anything his own land had offered.

His first literary efforts were all about glorious heroes of the past. Imitations of the sort of historic tales that many people admired in those days, they showed that Henry knew how to use words effectively, but his father could not believe this type of fanciful composition was worth attempting. In a letter he sent to relatives back in the United States, he described this son at the age of thirteen: "Henry is . . . a devourer of libraries, and an immense writer of novels. . . . He has considerable talent as a writer, but I am at a loss to know whether he will ever accomplish much."

When the James family finally returned to the United States, their destination was the pleasant old seaside town of Newport in Rhode Island, where some close friends had settled. Soon to emerge as this country's leading summer resort for the rich, in 1858 it already could boast of numerous cultural advantages, including one of the country's best public libraries—so the Jameses could not have chosen a more congenial atmosphere.

Here William began taking serious painting lessons, but when he himself decided that he lacked enough talent to become a great artist he abruptly changed his course and aimed instead for a career as a scientist. He departed to study in Europe, then at Harvard—on his way to winning international renown. During his twenty-five years as a Harvard professor, William James would write many books about philosophy and psychology that are still regarded as his century's most important contribution to these fields.

As for Henry, in Newport he briefly studied painting, too, but not as seriously as his brother. Then, when William embarked on a new path where he could not follow him, Henry spent a few seemingly aimless years during which he must have been striving to find his own course. The outbreak of the American Civil War further complicated his inner struggle.

Henry turned eighteen the day the fighting started. Any young man with his bookish preferences would have felt unfit for the life of a soldier, and even after a system for drafting recruits took effect, it undemocratically excused those who were called to serve if they could pay a substitute. Yet Henry created a small mystery about why he never donned a uniform to defend the Union cause.

When he long afterward came to write his memoirs, he noted cryptically that he had suffered "a horrid even if an obscure hurt" the spring the war began. Providing a fine example of his method of letting readers draw their own conclusions, he implied that this mysterious injury had kept him out of uniform. However, a professor who a century later would devote nearly twenty years to composing an authoritative biography of James found a much more complicated puzzle.

The horrible "hurt" probably was a comparatively minor, although painful, back problem. But because it first troubled James while he was helping in a frantic effort to rescue horses from a stable fire, the experience reminded him inevitably of his father's severe injury during quite similar circumstances. And he could not help exaggerating the importance of his own lesser impairment.

From then onward, James himself seems to have blamed his back for preventing him from many different activities. With his passion for personal privacy, though, he disguised his ailment so successfully that all sorts of other reasons would be proposed to explain the rather restricted way he eventually chose to live. Still, he only rarely gave any outward signs of being hampered by backaches once he started writing in earnest—when he was just twenty.

James took this momentous step during his final effort to copy his older brother by enrolling at Harvard. But it was the university's law school that he entered in 1862, even though he had not the least interest in becoming a lawyer. From the various schools and tutors he had been exposed to during his growing-up years he already had a good basic education, so he decided that he might as well see what a few law courses might teach him.

However, Harvard's location right near Boston proved to be just the spur he needed to begin his literary career. Owing to his family's many connections, and his own acute mind, he quickly formed friendships with editors and other literary figures in this center of American intellectual life. Soon "the young James" was contributing thoughtful book reviews to some of the country's major magazines, and within a year he gave up law school.

Between 1865 and 1869, James also wrote his first short stories—rather solemn but promising efforts, mostly printed by the popular *Atlantic Monthly*. To give himself a more mature look, he grew a dark beard, which he kept neatly trimmed. By the time he was twenty-six, in 1869, he felt sufficient confidence in being able to earn his keep literarily that he sailed for Europe on his own and sent back short pieces about his travel experiences to leading magazines and newspapers.

Henry James as a law student at Harvard University. *The Bettmann Archive.*

James crossed the Atlantic repeatedly during the next several years, alternating between a hotel existence and the domesticity of living with his parents, who were now settled in Cambridge, near the Harvard campus. Wherever he was, he kept quietly and purposefully writing increasingly polished stories. Despite the closeness of his ties to his family, though, among his relatives he was still just Henry junior, and even if they warmly congratulated him on his literary progress they were also his severest critics.

Too much togetherness could be particularly painful in the case of his brother William, already lecturing at Harvard and starting a family of his own. The superior tone that William took when he read anything Henry wrote almost approached ridicule; spending time with him somehow seemed to bring on attacks of Henry's back trouble. However, the letters they exchanged when separated by the width of the Atlantic Ocean were always long and affectionate.

Thus there were personal as well as professional reasons why Henry James decided in 1875, at the age of thirty-two, to become a permanent resident of Europe. That year saw the publication of his first novel, along with a book of short stories, plus another one containing his travel pieces—but he felt certain that he could achieve more as a writer if he made his home where his imagination was especially active.

Throughout the rest of his life, James would write an amazing number of novels, shorter tales, and essays—enough to fill thirty-five large volumes. But because his prose was so densely crammed with hints about hidden motives that it required extremely careful reading, few of his works attracted much notice from the general public. Indeed, a brief novel of his that appeared in 1878 was his only best-seller.

Named *Daisy Miller*, after its enchanting heroine, it showed how a high-spirited young woman from the upstate New York city of Schenectady naively defied Old World rules of proper behavior, with tragic results. Her innocent insistence on spending an evening alone with a handsome Italian man, just to absorb the moonlit splendor of Rome's ancient ruins, made her a social outcast—and also cost her her life, for her outing brought on a fatal attack of malaria.

Since the moral climate on both sides of the Atlantic has changed so much since Daisy's day, modern readers may wonder why her story made its author famous. But Daisy herself was something new in literature: a flirty American girl embodying her young country's breezy lack of concern over the Old World's rigid standards. It was as if

The James brothers: Henry (*left*) and William (*right*). *The Bettmann Archive.*

James had written the perfect parable to explain the differences between people in the United States and Europe.

However, when he continued to explore the same subject in increasingly complex novels, he lost much of his audience. And James's own status as a transplanted American offended many of his fellow citizens. England's cosmopolitan capital of London had become his headquarters; residing in a comfortable flat there, he regularly dined out with the top level of British society, also traveling often to Paris and other major European cities. His absorption with upper-class life wherever he went further alienated him from the American mainstream.

When James did visit his family in the United States, the many changes caused by the country's increasing industrialization made him feel more and more a stranger there. Yet he remained closely tied to his relatives, writing countless letters to them as well as to numerous friends and editors. In Europe he also did much patient shepherding of American tourists.

Although James enjoyed the company of women and created a large gallery of feminine literary portraits, he never married. Devoting so much of his energy to his writing and to the social activities that provided him with a constant stream of plot ideas to be jotted in his private journals, it was as if he had no time for a personal life of his own. Nor did he have enough money.

During his middle years James found that his share of the family fortune had dwindled to the extent that he needed every penny he earned from his writing to pay his bachelor expenses. Despite already being regarded by sophisticated readers as a literary master, his literary income was much less than some authors of trash received. In 1890 he felt so distressed over his financial inferiority that he embarked on a calculated effort to "cash in" on his talent—by writing plays.

But his talky dramas bored London audiences. On the opening night of his fifth play, such a chorus of booing broke out that the humiliated James forever gave up any hope of becoming rich. Retreating to a charming but inexpensive old house in the English village of Rye, a few hours south of London, he resumed writing novels and highly perceptive essays about other literary figures.

In Rye, James capped his career with a trio of masterpieces: *The Wings of the Dove, The Ambassadors,* and *The Golden Bowl.* These long and subtle novels about Americans victimized by wily Europeans convinced his admirers that beyond any doubt he ranked with his century's greatest literary masters, France's Honoré de Balzac and Russia's Fyodor Dostoyevsky. Yet some of James's short novels, like *Washington Square* and *The Turn of the Screw,* would always be more popular.

During his old age James only occasionally left Rye. But a circle of other writers, who only half-jokingly referred to him as The Master, formed around him. Plump and bald by now, he had long since shaved off his beard because he looked abundantly impressive without it. He had become noted, too, as a brilliant, if rather pompous, conversationalist.

Soon after the outbreak of the First World War in 1914, James felt so disturbed by his own country's delay in supporting the Allied cause that he formally became a British citizen. Not long afterward, he suffered a severe stroke and, on February 28, 1916, he died at his Rye home a few months before he would have turned seventy-three.

In the wartime atmosphere of crisis, not much attention was paid to his passing from the literary scene. Then during the 1920s, a new generation of American readers, with much broader international interests than their forbears, owing to United States' participation in the recent European war, "discovered" Henry James. Since then his fame has kept increasing—and nowadays, the literature collections of major college libraries are likely to contain more shelves filled with books by him, or about him, than by or about practically any other American author.

Jack London

1876–1916   Novelist of adventure

At the age of fifteen Jack London became known as the Prince of the Oyster Pirates in San Francisco Bay. At night, when the tide was low, he and his crew sailed out to scoop up oysters for sale in the city's saloons. It was dangerous work, stealing from privately owned oyster beds in shallow waters. If captured by the California Fish Patrol, London could have gone to jail.

With borrowed money he had bought his tall-masted sailing sloop, the *Razzle Dazzle*, from another oyster pirate, French Frank. Along with the sloop came a crew of two, Spider Healy and a sixteen-year-old girl named Mamie, who was called the Queen of the Oyster Pirates. Because of their youth, good looks, and success in gathering oysters, she and Jack were the royalty of their illegal trade.

In that year of 1891, oyster pirating was a cutthroat business, with armed competitors vying with one another to plunder the rich oyster beds. Sturdy, strong, and an able sailor, Jack held his own with the other tough pirates despite his youth.

After his oysters were sold, Jack would swagger into the Last Chance Saloon and order drinks for his rowdy companions with colorful names such as Joe Goose, The Clam, Big George, and Whiskey Bob. Drinking with them seemed to the adventurous fifteen-year-old like a badge of manhood.

Jack enjoyed the wild and free life of a pirate prince. But he differed from the other pirates in one major way: He loved to read. As a boy he had discovered the Oakland Public Library and its books. He did not lose his craving for them when he became a pirate. "Always a book," he remembered years later, "and always reading when the rest were asleep; when they were awake I was one with them, for I was always a good comrade."

Those twin impulses in Jack—reading and being a good comrade—remained with him for the rest of his life. Both of them played an important part in his becoming a famous writer of adventure stories. Many years after his death Jack London is still one of the most popular American writers around the world.

On the surface his stories seem to be uncomplicated tales about the sea, the gold rush in Alaska, or life among the natives of the islands of the South Pacific. But they are more than that. They are also stories about men facing adversity and death, and not always conquering them. Almost everything he wrote was based on his experiences, leading one critic to say that London's best adventure story was his own life.

He had been born in Oakland, California, on January 12, 1876. His mother, Flora Wellman, had gone West from Ohio, supporting herself by giving piano lessons. Her major interest, though, was in spiritualism—listening to voices from beyond the grave, relayed through mediums.

Jack's father was William Henry Chaney, a Maine man who had become a wandering astrologer, spreading the message that every person's destiny was governed by the position of the stars and planets on his or her date of birth. Chaney never married Flora Wellman and left her before Jack was born. Later, Chaney denied any connection with Jack London.

Shortly after Jack's birth, his mother married John London, a former farmer from Iowa who had come West seeking an easier life. As a widower with two young daughters, Eliza and Ida, he had been looking for a wife to take care of them. Following this marriage of convenience, Flora's son was given an impressive new name, John Griffith London.

Jack grew up in poverty, though, for his stepfather failed in a number of business ventures, including farming— no doubt at least partly because Jack's mother insisted on handling the family's money, with advice from spirits that came to her at seances. She showed little interest in Jack, so his stepsister Eliza took care of him during his early years as she would throughout his life.

This is how Jack remembered his youth:

I was eight years old when I put on my first undershirt made or bought at a store. Duty—at ten years I was out on the streets selling newspapers. Every cent was turned over to my people, and I went to school in constant shame of the hats, shoes, clothes I wore. Duty—from then on I had no childhood. Up at three in the morning to carry papers. When that was finished I did not go home but continued on to school. School out, my evening papers. Sunday I went to a bowling alley and set up pins for drunken Dutchmen. Duty—I turned over every cent and went dressed like a scarecrow.

At thirteen, Jack graduated from grade school. Instead of going on to high school, he had to work full-time to help support his family. He swept out saloons, sold newspapers, and did odd jobs. For enjoyment, he saved his pennies until he had enough to buy an old rowboat. He became an expert sailor in the rough waters of San Francisco Bay, enjoying the challenge of the sea.

That pleasure ended when his stepfather became ill and unable to work. Jack, then fifteen, got a job in a fish cannery—ten cents an hour for ten hours a day, and sometimes twelve or sixteen hours at a stretch. He could see no future in the backbreaking toil at the cannery. It was then that he turned to the romantic crime of oyster pirating.

His carefree life as a pirate ended when he almost died at sea after a night of drinking. He fell overboard from his boat and was swept by the current farther and farther from land. He was a good swimmer, though, so he was not worried about surviving. But as he rested, floating, in the choppy water, he began to reflect on his life. He decided that he wanted more than crime, fighting, and drinking with his comrades.

After being rescued by a passing fishing boat, Jack gave up the merry life of an oyster pirate. In a dramatic switch of roles, he became a deputy patrolman for the California Fish Patrol. He chased illegal salmon fishermen, shrimp raiders, and even, at times, oyster pirates. "I felt fearless and a man when I climbed over the side of a boat to arrest some marauder," he later recalled.

A restless young man, a few days after his seventeenth birthday in 1892 he signed on as a seaman aboard the *Sophia Sutherland,* a schooner bound for the seal-hunting grounds off Japan. He proved to be an able sailor and got along well with his shipmates.

Jack's seven-month voyage to the seal-killing grounds furnished him with material he would later use in writing his greatest novel, *The Sea-Wolf.* The voyage also started him on his literary career. On his return to San Francisco, he entered a newspaper contest for young writers. His entry, called "Story of a Typhoon off the Coast of Japan," describing an experience aboard the *Sophia Sutherland,* won the first prize of twenty-five dollars.

For Jack it was an economic lesson. He earned more by this writing than he did in a month of hard physical labor at his current job in a jute mill, where the pay was ten cents an hour. But he was not yet a writer. He had to work, at physical labor, for a living. He got a job shoveling coal at an electric power plant, which was so hard that he soon gave it up.

He became a hobo, riding eastbound freight trains to join an army of unemployed marching on Washington in 1894. But he never got there. Arrested as a tramp in Niagara Falls, New York, he spent thirty days in jail. He returned home determined to get an education and thereby climb out of the underclass of society.

In 1895 Jack entered the freshman class at the Oakland High School. At nineteen, he towered over his younger classmates. They looked upon him with a mixture of awe because of his experiences and of contempt because of his age. But he persisted. In school he wrote articles for the student magazine, and outside school he joined a group of radical reformers. The *San Francisco Chronicle* wrote about him: "Jack London, who is known as the boy socialist of Oakland, is holding forth nightly to the crowds that throng City Hall Park. . . . London is young . . . scarcely 20, but he has seen many sides of the world and has traveled extensively. He is a high school boy and supports

himself as a janitor in the institution."

In 1896 Jack decided that he could not waste two more years in high school before entering college. So he began to study chemistry, mathematics, history, and English by himself, cramming nineteen hours a day to prepare for the entrance examinations at the University of California. He passed, and became a freshman there in the fall.

He also fell in love—with Mabel Applegarth, a girl whose respectable middle-class family had many things he craved, books, music, and stimulating conversation. Jack described her in a later novel as "a pale ethereal creature, with wide spiritual blue eyes and a wealth of golden hair . . . a pale, gold flower upon a slender stem . . . a spirit, a divinity, a goddess."

Jack himself was a handsome young man of middling height, with tousled brown hair and glittering blue eyes. He came into a room with gusto, one of his friends said. His high spirits and easy way of conversing made him interesting to new acquaintances, especially to women. He loved to argue, defending his belief in socialism, and spent many happy hours at meetings of the university's debating club.

Impatient to make good, Jack gave up college after just one semester. He began to write, sometimes working fifteen hours a day. He sent his work to maga-

Jack London (*left*) as a war correspondent in Japan. *The Bettmann Archive.*

zine after magazine, and got back nothing but rejection slips. Seemingly at a dead end, he was rescued by the exciting news of the Klondike gold rush in Alaska. With his sister Eliza's husband, he joined the army of men who traveled north in 1897.

London did not find gold in Alaska but came back richer than those who did. After making the rugged trek over the mountains to the goldfields, he returned a year later via a two-thousand-mile raft trip down the Yukon River. He had spent many evenings debating politics with passing strangers or listening to the tales of veteran miners in the cold and primitive Alaska wilderness. So he returned filled with the raw materials that he would soon start processing into dramatic fiction.

"It was in the Klondike I found myself," he later wrote. "There you get your perspective. I got mine."

Determined to be a writer, London was actually penniless when he returned to San Francisco. First he had to find a job to pay basic living expenses for himself and his mother. By day, he looked for work; by night, he wrote stories about Alaska. He wrote, he always said, solely to make money. He told his friends that his objective was not to create literature but to produce a thousand words a day and sell them at a penny a word.

He was unsuccessful in both endeavors, his job quest and his writing. Of necessity, he took odd jobs and pawned his belongings. He spent almost all his nights at his desk, scribbling down stories, then typing them and sending them to magazines and newspapers. None of them were accepted. His biggest expense was postage, and he often went hungry.

A critical point in London's life came in 1899. After taking a civil service examination, he was offered a post office job at sixty-five dollars a month, very good pay then. If he went to work for the post office, he would be set for life, able to support his mother as well as a family of his own with no trouble.

He and his mother talked about the choice he had to make. She might have been expected to urge him to grasp this chance for a secure future, but instead she made up for years of neglect by warmly encouraging a braver course. Do not settle for a humdrum, safe job, she told him—continue to write.

London returned to his desk—and little by little things began to change. *The Overland Monthly* offered him five dollars for a story, "To the Man on the Trail." Another magazine sent him a check for forty dollars for a science fiction story, "A Thousand Deaths." Later in 1899 the *Atlantic Monthly,* then the country's leading magazine, accepted "An Odyssey of the North," and paid him one hundred and twenty dollars.

That story's opening words give a good indication of London's style: "The sleds were singing their eternal lament to the creaking of the harnesses and the tingling bells of the leaders; but the men and dogs were tired and made no sound. The trail was heavy with new-fallen snow, and they had come far, and the runners, burdened with flintlike quarters of frozen moose, clung tenaciously to the unpacked surface with a stubbornness almost human."

In the spring of 1900, a Boston firm published London's first book of collected short stories, *The Son of the Wolf.* It was an immediate hit. One reviewer said, "The Klondike has waited three years for its storyteller and interpreter to set it in an imperishable literary mold."

On the same day his book came out, London got married—but not to Mabel Applegarth, whom he had loved so long. Their romance had broken up when her mother insisted that she would have to live with the couple if they got married. London discovered other women.

He was particularly impressed by a friend of Mabel's, Bess Maddern. Serene and unassuming, Bess was interested in mathematics but not in art or politics. They decided to marry on the basis of "affectionate companionship,"

not love. Their wedding took place on April 7, 1900, and within the next two years they had two daughters, Joan and Becky.

After his marriage, London's literary position kept improving, and so did his finances. Magazines competed for his stories by offering him more money than he had ever expected to make. In addition, he began writing longer works. *The Call of the Wild,* which would turn out to be his most famous novel, was published in 1903.

Based on his observations in the Klondike, it was the story of a dog called Buck, who had been raised on a ranch in California. Taken to Alaska, Buck became part of a dog team pulling a sled. After learning how to survive "the law of the club and fang" in that brutal atmosphere, Buck escaped and returned to the wild ways of his ancestors.

One critic said that the last sentence of *The Call of the Wild* was the most vibrant Jack London ever wrote: "When the long winter nights come on and the wolves follow their meat into the lower valleys, he [Buck] may be seen running at the head of the pack through the pale moonlight or glimmering borealis, leaping gigantic above his fellows, his great throat a-bellow as he sings a song of the younger world, which is the song of the pack."

An instant best-seller, *The Call of the*

Wild made the twenty-seven-year-old London famous. He rented a cottage in Glen Ellen, a picturesque hamlet about fifty miles north of Oakland. Immediately he began work on another novel, *The Sea-Wolf,* which turned out to be just as popular as *The Call of the Wild.*

"My idea," he wrote to a friend, "is to take a cultured, refined, super-civilized man and woman . . . and throw them into a primitive sea environment where all is stress & struggle and life expresses itself, simply, in terms of food and shelter; and make this man and woman rise to the situation and come out with flying colors." He did that, but the most memorable character in the book is Wolf Larsen, the tough captain of the *Ghost,* a schooner bound for the seal-hunting grounds off the coast of Japan.

By the time *The Sea-Wolf* came out, London had left on another adventure—as a war correspondent covering the Asian war between Russia and Japan. When he returned, he began a busy period of writing more short stories, working on a new novel, and plunging into politics by running as the socialist candidate for mayor of Oakland. He lost, receiving only nine hundred and eighty-one votes.

In addition, during that same year of 1905, London bought a ranch near Glen Ellen, lectured at Harvard and Yale, and decided to divorce his wife, for he had fallen in love with Charmian Kittredge, whom he married as soon as the divorce had been granted.

Two years later they set out to sail around the world on their new forty-five–foot boat, the *Snark,* but they ended their trip after a series of illnesses in the South Seas. Instead of island paradises, London had found disease, headhunters, cannibals—and material for short stories that later thrilled a worldwide audience.

At the age of thirty, London also discovered that there was no place like home, his beautiful ranch in California. Spending money lavishly, he expanded it to fifteen hundred acres and used the most modern techniques to grow crops like prunes and grapes. Becoming involved with soil conservation and raising animals, he even built a "pig palace" that was a model of sanitation and efficiency.

And he continued to write, keeping to his schedule of a thousand words a day. London earned enough money—by one estimate, seventy-five thousand dollars a year—to live like a lord. Not only did he farm, but he took great pleasure in entertaining guests, horseback riding, driving a coach with four horses, and sailing his new boat, the *Roamer,* on inland bays and rivers. He also spent many nights making the rounds of the Glen Ellen saloons, drinking heavily.

Jack London (in white shirt) photographed by Laurence M. Kane at the start of his cruise on the *Snark*. *Acme/UPI/Bettmann*.

But London had little sense of money. Although by 1913 he was the highest-paid, best-known, and most popular writer in the world, he was always behind in his financial affairs. A generous man, he supported fourteen relatives, lent large amounts to friends, and never considered the cost of anything he wanted to do. His ranch house was open to anyone who came by—not merely friends, but hoboes, convicts, former comrades, and even strangers.

To make the money he constantly needed, London kept coming out with book after book. Most of them were adventure stories, but he also wrote novels about his own early struggles and his drinking problem. Altogether, forty-three of his books were published before his death, and seven more appeared later.

London developed a number of ailments, and he died on November 22, 1916, when he was only forty. Since then, some academic critics have tried to downplay the importance of his work. But his books, translated into almost every known language, still are widely read all over the world.

Mark Twain

1835–1910   Creator of Huck Finn and Tom Sawyer

His real name was Samuel Langhorne Clemens, as if his parents had expected him to become a serious sort of lawyer. When he began writing comic items for newspapers, he signed them with two words he liked the sound of. "Mark twain!" was a Mississippi riverboat cry signifying water deep enough for a vessel to proceed safely. Under this name he gave himself, he won more fame and fortune than even he could have imagined.

Not only did Twain's work prove to be enormously popular all over the world, but it also led many literary experts to include him among the very best writers the United States had yet produced. "The Lincoln of our literature," a leading critic of his own day called him.

Besides creating a long list of fictional characters, in particular Tom Sawyer and Huckleberry Finn, Twain did a lot of traveling around giving lectures. His talks displayed such a special blend of humor and sharp comment that his own personality struck some people as his greatest creation. Here are just a few examples of typical Twain remarks:

"It is difference of opinion that makes horse races."

"Cauliflower is nothing but cabbage with a college education."

"Be good and you will be lonesome."

But this extremely successful writer had a not-very-promising start in life. Born in an isolated Missouri village named Florida, on November 30, 1835, he was the sixth of the seven children of a couple with grand dreams and hardly any worldly possessions. Both of Sam's

151

parents came from lesser branches of "ancestor-proud" Virginia families.

His father, John Marshall Clemens, bragged that one of his forbears back in England had been the judge who ordered its King Charles beheaded for bad behavior. And Sam's mother, Jane Lampton Clemens, believed that she was closely related to an English duke. A cousin of hers with the same idea even tried in vain for many years to have himself proclaimed the rightful holder of the title—giving Mark Twain the idea for one of his novels, *The American Claimant.*

Long before "Little Sam" Clemens thought of doing any writing, though, his parents took the step that would inspire his greatest efforts. Around his fourth birthday, they moved their family to the Missouri town of Hannibal right on the Mississippi River. It was only forty miles from Florida, but what a difference those forty miles made!

For the mighty river was then the main route up and down the middle of the young United States. Boats of all sorts stopped at Hannibal's dock, bringing constant excitement as well as thriving commerce. In the ten years prior to the Clemenses' arrival, the town had grown from a raw settlement amid dense woods to a rural sort of metropolis with three sawmills, two hotels, and a population of some three thousand people.

Being such a thriving community, it attracted a variety of traveling shows featuring animals like giraffes or performers in gaudy costumes. No matter how scarce money was at Sam's house, his mother still had the heart of a young girl and she saw to it that he got the price of admission. As he had been sickly as an infant, and also because three of her older children had died of sudden fevers, she could not help favoring this high-spirited son whose red hair and readiness to laugh made people say he took after her.

But Sam's mischief tried her sorely. "He drives me crazy with his didoes," she fretted. Whenever he went out, "I am expecting every minute that someone will bring him home half dead." The sort of adventures he enjoyed—exploring local caves or camping out on uninhabited islands—would eventually enchant millions of readers when they read *Tom Sawyer.*

However, Sam's own boyhood ended abruptly during the year he turned twelve. His father, trained as a lawyer, had always found it easier to daydream about various schemes for making money than actually to earn any. A dignified-looking man, he had a few times served briefly as a judge, and he relished being called Judge Clemens. He kept failing as a storekeeper, though, while his health declined, too; in 1847, he died.

So Sam had to help his older brother,

Orion, support their mother and younger sister and baby brother. As Orion had already learned the printing trade well enough to get a job in St. Louis, Sam followed his example by working after school at a Hannibal printer's shop. His task of putting tiny metal letters into trays bored him—but the idea that famous men like Benjamin Franklin had got their start this way appealed to him.

Within two years Sam had enough skill to start on the rolling-stone sort of life common among printers of those days. When he swore on the Bible to his mother that he would not touch liquor or cards, she tearfully let him go. Young as he was, it suited his restless nature to wander from place to place, all the way from St. Louis to New York City and Philadelphia, always sure of finding work even if it might not pay very well.

What's more, being around print shops—which were usually associated with newspapers—could not help but turn an active mind toward reading. In that period, newspapers frequently ran installments of books by well-known writers. One way or another, Sam got his hands on other books, so the seven years he spent as a wandering printer gave him an informal yet wide-ranging higher education.

Also, by the age of sixteen Sam began doing some writing himself. His first efforts were short pieces, signed with his own initials, that were mildly amusing but nothing out of the ordinary. Instead of thinking about becoming a writer, though, in typical Clemens style he dreamed up a much more dramatic scheme. At twenty-one, he brashly announced that he was starting out for South America, where he aimed to get rich quickly collecting cocoa along the Amazon River.

Sam had saved enough from his printer's pay to board a Mississippi River steamboat bound for New Orleans. After just a day or two afloat, however, his boyhood ambition to be a riverboat pilot revived with such force that he completely forgot about the Amazon—and paid all his savings to the pilot of the *Paul Jones*, who promised to teach him this glorious trade.

The two and a half years Sam spent on the Mississippi as an apprentice and then as a licensed pilot were perhaps the most important of his life. They gave him not merely an awesome familiarity with every bend and landmark along the country's greatest river, but also a deep feeling of identity with the assortment of people comprising the American traveling public. In effect he turned into Mark Twain during these years right before the outbreak of the Civil War.

Still he was not yet ready to begin his real career. When the war started in 1861, cutting off normal Mississippi River traffic, Clemens joined a company of volunteers loyal to the Southern cause. But even though his family's Virginia background made him tend in this direction, his own upbringing in Missouri, where there had also been a lot of Northern sympathizers, kept him from being a very eager fighter.

Because of the informal way the volunteers had organized, it was easy for him to quit soldiering as soon as a wonderful new opportunity arose. His older brother, Orion, had somehow managed to get appointed to a government post in the Nevada Territory, and he invited Sam to accompany him out West as his secretary. By stagecoach, they journeyed beyond the last traces of civilized society and into the spectacular scenery of the Rocky Mountains.

It turned out that Clemens had no secretarial duties, after all, which suited him fine. At a booming miners' camp grandiosely christened Virginia City, he failed to find any silver himself, but he did find very congenial work as a reporter for the area's leading newspaper, the *Territorial Enterprise.*

Tall tales became his specialty, and if he embroidered the outrageous boasting he heard from various miners, nobody minded a bit. Soon his pieces—signed Mark Twain—were being reprinted all over the West. After a few years, he moved on to San Francisco, the unofficial capital of the West, and the lively

group of writers making their headquarters there welcomed him enthusiastically.

Clemens joined them, writing more pieces and enjoying his first taste of celebrity. Never noted for false modesty, in 1866, when he was thirty-one, he wrote to his mother, "I am generally placed at the head of my breed of scribblers in this part of the country." By then, however, he could have made a somewhat broader claim because a tall tale of his about a jumping frog had recently delighted newspaper readers all the way from California to New York City.

So, in 1867, Clemens journeyed eastward to see about publishing his first book, *The Celebrated Jumping Frog of Calaveras County and Other Sketches.* While in New York, he happened to hear of a church group's plans for a five-month tour of Europe and the Middle East. His notion of joining this group to report on its travels at last brought him the fame and fortune he craved—and personal happiness, too.

The publication of his book *The Innocents Abroad,* coming just as the United States was emerging from the great trauma of the Civil War, could not have been more perfectly timed. In this period of surging economic growth, it suddenly struck a lot of Americans that they were a different breed from the people of the Old World. So they relished reading page after page on which Clemens humorously, and yet with an underlying pride in American quirks, let Mark Twain display his fellow tourists' reactions to European culture.

For instance, while describing a museum visit to inspect the famous portrait of Mona Lisa by the Italian artist Leonardo da Vinci, he observed, "They spell it Vinci and pronounce it Vinchy; foreigners always spell better than they pronounce."

As the book sold so well, it finally freed Clemens from money worries—and, again, from his personal standpoint, this new freedom could not have been better timed. During his travels with the high-minded churchgoers, he had gotten friendly with a young man who showed him a miniature painting of his sister. While Clemens may have exaggerated when he said later that he had fallen in love with the picture of Olivia Langdon, when he got around to visiting his shipboard companion's home in Elmira, New York, he unquestionably fell in love with Livy herself.

Livy's father was a wealthy as well as an extremely religious businessman, who especially cherished this beautiful daughter because a fall on ice when she was sixteen had left her in delicate health. The idea that a coarse sort of fellow from out West, eleven years older than she was and without any steady job, wanted to marry her at first horrified him.

However, Clemens made Livy herself laugh. When he swore to give up cusswords and cigars—and when some book critics highly praised his *Innocents Abroad*—her father finally gave up his objections. Clemens and Livy got married in Elmira on February 2, 1870; he was thirty-four then, and she was twenty-three.

Despite the many differences in their backgrounds, the marriage proved very happy. Following a difficult first year, during which Clemens vainly tried to enjoy editing a Buffalo newspaper that Livy's father had helped him buy and Livy suffered the pain of losing a baby son, the couple made a fresh start in a city he had much admired when visiting a publisher there. Moving to Hartford in Connecticut, Mark Twain—as most people now thought of him—embarked on a remarkable period of both literary and personal fulfillment.

Almost as if he had actually been reborn, as Mark Twain he lived in an elaborate nineteen-room brick mansion that was part of a select community called Nook Farm on Hartford's outskirts. Among his neighbors were a prominent clergyman, the area's leading newspaper editor, and several other notables, including the old lady looked up to as the

Mark Twain at his home in Hartford, photographed with his wife Livy and their daughters Clara, Jean, and Susy. *The Mark Twain Project, University of California, Berkeley.*

country's most famous living writer, Harriet Beecher Stowe, author of *Uncle Tom's Cabin.*

In this thoroughly respectable setting, so different from his accustomed surroundings, Twain flourished remarkably. As Livy's devoted husband and the adoring papa of three daughters, he presided over a home furnished in lavish style and staffed with a horde of servants. While all of the Tiffany stained glass and carved cherubs on the ceilings must have reflected Livy's taste, he did not seem a bit ill at ease.

Up on the third floor Twain had his own private domain, complete with a billiards table around which he and his friends could smoke cigars to their hearts' content. He also had a desk at which he composed some of the world's best-loved books.

Twain had already completed *Roughing It*, about his Rocky Mountains adventures, by the time he and Livy moved into their Nook Farm mansion. The first book he wrote there, and also his first full-length fictional effort, was *The Gilded Age*, which he collaborated on with his neighbor Charles Dudley Warner, then a popular novelist. Although its title was seized on as the perfect way to describe the post–Civil War era, this long-winded satire about life in the 1870s would not otherwise be remembered.

The most memorable of Twain's own works harked back to his boyhood. Starting in *The Adventures of Tom Sawyer*, then in his masterpieces *The Adventures of Huckleberry Finn* and *Life on the Mississippi*, which both were finished during a great surge of creativity in 1885, he achieved a magical sort of transformation. He was somehow able to give the America of his youth a universal appeal, so that readers as far away as Russia shared his own nostalgic feelings.

In addition, though, Twain wrote numerous other books. Some, like *The Prince and the Pauper* and *A Connecticut Yankee at King Arthur's Court* testified to his early fascination with his family's stories about their British ancestry. Others, like *The Tragedy of Pudd'nhead Wilson* had solidly American themes. Practically all of them won wide popularity, even if the verdict of future generations would sometimes be less favorable.

Today it might seem strange that in Twain's own day *Huckleberry Finn* was much less appreciated than several of his lesser works. In fact it was banned in a Boston suburb on the grounds that its scoffing at the rules of genteel society set a very poor example for "our pure-minded lads and lasses." Although this book's underlying defense of individual freedom would later be seen as the essence of Americanism, at that time its slang words aroused so much controversy that Twain felt tempted to give up writing.

Instead, though, from then on he just put away whatever he wrote that seemed likely to offend his critics and published mainly lightweight fluff, for his expenses at Nook Farm required a high income. Also, he had become involved in two costly business ventures— a book-publishing company and an effort to turn an inventor's contraption for automatically doing the job he had done as a young printer into a marketable typesetting machine.

Yet all seemed well with him during the 1880s: In 1888, at the age of fifty-three, his stature as more than just an entertaining humorist was certified when Yale University awarded him an honorary master of arts degree.

Then came a succession of severe blows. An economic downturn caused the failure of the publishing company in which Twain had invested heavily. He lost even more when his typesetting venture had to be abandoned after a

Mark Twain in 1905 wearing his customary white suit. *The Bettmann Archive.*

Mark Twain was honored in 1905 on his seventieth birthday at a dinner at Delmonico's restaurant in New York. Left to right: Kate Douglas Wiggin (author of *Rebecca of Sunnybrook Farm*), Twain, his friend Rev. Joseph H. Twichell, the poet Bliss Carman, writers Ruth McEnery Stuart and Mary Freeman, Henry Mills Alden, and Henry H. Rogers, Twain's financial advisor. *The Bettmann Archive.*

better machine was produced by another company. On top of everything else, one of his daughters developed epilepsy, and his wife's health seemed increasingly fragile.

Under mounting financial pressures, Twain closed up his mansion in 1891 to live more cheaply in Europe. Although he expected to return to Hartford within a few years, he never did. His favorite daughter's sudden death from

meningitis, combined with crushing money troubles that resulted in his personal bankruptcy, made him unable to bear going back there.

In this terribly dark period, a millionaire admirer of Twain's took charge of his tangled finances while he himself traveled all around the world earning as much as he could by giving lectures. Thanks to expert guidance from his friend Henry Rogers of the Standard Oil

Company, Twain was able by the end of the 1890s to pay every penny he owed—not only regaining his self-respect but also erasing every trace of tarnish from his public reputation.

When he disembarked from a steamship in New York in November of 1900, after having been away from the United States for nearly a decade, the sixty-five-year-old Twain received a hero's welcome. The rest of his life was filled with similar tributes. By that time his hair as well as his bushy mustache had turned white, and he had also taken to wearing only white suits in the winter as well as in the summer. Recognized immediately wherever he went, he had become, as he cheerfully put it himself, "the most conspicuous person on the planet."

Twain survived even the death of his adored wife in 1906. The following year, he gave one of the most moving speeches of his long career when England's Oxford University honored him with its degree of doctor of literature. After that his health began failing and,

on April 21, 1910, at the age of seventy-four, Mark Twain died at his home in Redding, Connecticut.

Since then Twain's literary reputation has grown rather than diminished. After various of his unpublished works appeared in print—and proved that he had done a lot of private brooding about serious moral issues—a few critics held that he had been prevented from developing into a truly great writer by his marriage, which had forced him to concentrate on making money rather than on questioning prevailing values. But this view won few adherents.

Instead Twain's *Huckleberry Finn* has come to be widely regarded as a work of genius, and several of his other books are ranked almost as high. Twain himself remains one of the most beloved figures of the American past. "Like Lincoln, he spoke to and for the common man of the American heartland that had nourished them both," an influential college textbook informs students of the 1990s.

Walt Whitman

1819–1892   From printer's devil to poet

At the age of twelve Walt Whitman went to work as a printer's devil for the *Long Island Patriot,* a newspaper in Brooklyn, New York. The year was 1831, when many printing operations were done by hand. As an apprentice Walt learned how to take metal letters one by one from a box and make words and sentences out of them.

For young Walt it was an exciting time. Besides learning a trade, every day he listened to fascinating behind-the-scenes stories of politics in New York. He particularly enjoyed the tales of William Hartshorne, an old-timer who had known George Washington, Thomas Jefferson, and Benjamin Franklin. After the papers were printed, Walt drove out with the editor in a horse-drawn buggy to deliver them to subscribers in rural Brooklyn.

During his apprenticeship Walt dealt with type and printing, not writing. The first time he wanted to write anything came one day when he saw a ship under full sail—and "had the desire to describe it exactly as it seemed to me," as he later recalled. But his first actual writing was what he afterward called some "sentimental bits" for the *New-York Mirror,* a weekly of literature and the fine arts.

"I used to watch for the big, fat, red-faced, slow-moving, very old English carrier who distributed the *Mirror* in Brooklyn," he would remember. "How it made my heart double-beat to see my *piece* on the pretty white paper, in nice type."

In his growing-up years Walt was enthusiastic about everything he saw and did. Whenever he had any spare time, he wandered around Brooklyn's waterfront. Most of all, he loved to take the Fulton Street ferry across the East River to Manhattan and walk to the theaters on Park Row, Chatham Square, and the Bowery.

He always remembered his first visit to a theater. "The play was 'The School for Scandal,'" he recalled. "I had a dim idea of the walls of some adjoining houses suddenly and silently sinking away to let folks see what was going on. Then the band, O never before did such heavenly melodies make me drunk with such pleasure so utterly sweet and spiritual!"

Walt devoured novels, attended every opera he could, loved to ride the horse-drawn buses on Broadway listening to the stories of the drivers, and talked to everyone he met. He showed the same enthusiasm about swimming during visits to the sandy beaches farther east on Long Island: "I loved after bathing to race up and down the hard sand, and declaim Homer and Shakespeare to the surf and sea gulls by the hour."

It was out on the island, near the north-shore village of Huntington, that Walt had been born on May 31, 1819. His father, Walter Whitman, came from a long line of farmers who had left England around the middle of the 1600s to settle in the colony of New York. His mother, Louisa Van Velsor, was the daughter of a Dutch family transplanted to the same area. Walt was the second in a family of eight children.

He was particularly close to his mother, who had been a daring horseback rider as a girl growing up on a horse farm. She told him stories, comforted him, and backed him in everything he did. She would even support his wish to become a poet, despite not understanding much of what he wrote.

Walt's relationship with his father, who was a carpenter and a builder, was sometimes stormy. His father could not approve of a son who preferred to write stories and poems rather than farm. Yet this strict parent somehow could not succeed financially; he moved his family frequently, from Huntington to Brooklyn and then back again, seeking to make a living.

Walt attended a Quaker school in Brooklyn, but at the age of eleven his formal schooling came to an end. He went to work, which was not unusual then for the son of a poor family. His first job was as an office boy in an attorney's firm. He worked there only briefly, though, before becoming a printer's devil. By the time he was sixteen, he was an experienced printer.

Big for his age, he was already six feet tall, heavy in appearance, with black hair, a broad strong nose, full lips, and pale gray-blue eyes. With a friendly manner, Walt had the knack of striking up conversations with everybody he met. And he had no trouble finding new jobs when the papers he worked for went out of business.

In 1836 his family moved back to Huntington because his mother was ailing, and the seventeen-year-old Walt returned, too. He found a job as a schoolteacher. An easygoing instructor, he went from school to school, boarding with the parents of his pupils.

After two years of such wandering, Walt bought a used press and a case of type and moved them to rented space above a stable in Huntington. At the age of nineteen he became the editor, publisher, and printer of his own newspaper, the *Long Islander.* He even delivered copies of his weekly paper himself, riding his newly purchased white mare, Nina.

Walt enjoyed himself in Huntington and at the nearby beaches with the other young men of the community, but showed no interest in young women. "I was a first-rate aquatic loafer," he recalled later. "I possessed almost unlimited capacity for floating on my back." The wife of one of his associates called him "a dreamy, impracticable youth."

Little wonder, then, that the *Long Islander* lasted only one year. After a brief period of teaching again and working on a local newspaper, Whitman moved in 1841 to New York City, where jobs for experienced printers were available on many publications. At the age of twenty-one, he began a new life—becoming involved in politics, speaking in public to support the Democratic party, writing, and editing newspapers.

During the next few years Whitman worked for at least ten different newspapers, writing editorials about the state of the nation. In addition he wrote short stories, articles about the theater and music, and also a novel, *Franklin Evans, or The Inebriate, A Tale of the Times.* Whitman himself described the novel later as "rot of the worst sort."

But his reputation as a capable newspaperman led to his being appointed editor of the *Brooklyn Daily Eagle,* one of the city's leading papers, in 1845. He bought a house, took a major role in supporting his younger brothers and sisters, became an official of the Democratic party, and even marched in patriotic parades.

"I had one of the pleasant sits [situations] of my life," Whitman said later about his job on the *Eagle.* He got along well with the paper's owner, he received good pay, and he enjoyed the work. But it lasted only two years. Whitman wrote strong editorials opposing the extension of slavery into new states, one of the most controversial issues facing the country. That led to a dispute with the *Eagle*'s publisher, and Whitman was fired.

Then a chance encounter in the lobby of a New York City theater set Whitman on a new course. He met a newspaper proprietor from New Orleans who offered him a job on a new paper there, the *Crescent*. Whitman accepted. Two days later, accompanied by his fifteen-year-old brother, Jeff, he started south. It was his first trip outside New York, his first sight of the vastness of America.

He went by railroad to Baltimore, by stagecoach to the Ohio River, and then by a side-paddling steamer down the Ohio and Mississippi rivers. At the age of twenty-nine, Whitman was enchanted by the beauty of New Orleans and the pleasantness of life there.

Yet he returned to Brooklyn after only four months to become the editor of the *Freeman,* a newspaper opposed to slavery in the expanding United States. After a year, though, he left the paper because of a dispute with its owners, who were ready to compromise their antislavery principles to keep their political party in power.

Jobless once again, Whitman lived with his family in Brooklyn while working as a carpenter and house builder. He occasionally wrote freelance pieces for newspapers, went frequently to the opera, and kept his notebook filled with random observations, thoughts, and ex-

periments in verse. At the age of thirty, his transition from printer, newspaper editor, and carpenter to poet had begun.

Whitman probably began to accumulate ideas for a book of poetry in the late 1840s. Starting in 1847, he carried a notebook small enough to fit in his pocket so that he could jot down ideas as they came to him. The first entry in the first notebook said, "Be simple and clear—Be not occult."

By 1855, at last he was ready. On May 15 he received a copyright for a work to be called *Leaves of Grass*. Then Whitman found two printer friends in Brooklyn who let him set the type for his book and help operate their presses. On July 6 the following announcement appeared in the *New York Tribune:*

WALT WHITMAN'S POEMS
LEAVES OF GRASS

1 vol. small quarto, $2, for sale by SWAYNE, No. 210 Fulton St., Brooklyn, and by FOWLER & WELLS, No. 308 Broadway, N.Y.

Only seven hundred ninety-five copies were printed. A thin book, it contained ten pages of introduction, followed by twelve poems on eighty-three more pages. Whitman's name did not appear as the author, but an engraving near the front of the book pictured him.

At the time, Whitman described himself this way: "Of pure American breed,

This engraving of Walt Whitman, made from a daguerreotype by Gabriel Harrison in 1854, was used as the frontispiece for *Leaves of Grass*. *The Library of Congress.*

large and lusty—age thirty-six years—
never once using medicine—never
dressed in black, always dressed freely
and clean in strong clothes—neck open,
shirt collar flat and broad, countenance
tawny transparent red, beard well-mot-
tled with white, hair like hay after it has
been mowed in the field and lies tossed
and streaked."

In his introduction to his book, Whitman defined himself as a poet of America, of the common people. In his own
words, "*Leaves of Grass* . . . is the song
of a great composite democratic individual, male or female . . . an attempt
from first to last to put a Person, a human being (namely myself in the later
half of the nineteenth century in America) freely, fully and truly on record."
The great American poet, he said,
would create new forms and new subject matter for poetry.

Whitman tried to do this in the first
poem in the book, a long one, untitled
then but later called "Song of Myself,"
which started:

I celebrate myself, and sing myself,
And what I assume you shall assume,
For every atom belonging to me as good
    belongs to you.

It also contains these famous lines:

Do I contradict myself?
Very well then I contradict myself.
(I am large, I contain multitudes.)

Many modern critics call "Song of Myself" one of the great long poems in the
English language.

It and the other poems in *Leaves of
Grass* represented a radical departure
from the traditional poetry of rhythm
and rhyme. Whitman rejected the example of his contemporaries—the melodi-
ous lines of Poe, what he called "the
pleasing ripples" of Longfellow, and the
refined verse of England's Tennyson. He
was the first poet to exploit to the full
the possibilities of free verse—free-
flowing lines with a rhythm of their own.

No wonder, then, that *Leaves of
Grass* met a cool reception. It did not
sell, and some critics were puzzled and
offended by its frank language.

But the foremost man of letters in
America at the time, Ralph Waldo
Emerson, recognized the revolutionary
merits of the poems and their author.
He wrote to Whitman about his book, "I
find it the most extraordinary piece of
wit & wisdom that America has yet contributed. . . . I greet you at the beginning of a great career."

Emerson's endorsement established
Whitman as a major American poet, but
did not help sell his book. Still, the small
sale of the first edition did not discourage Whitman from publishing a new
edition of *Leaves of Grass* two years
later, containing twenty new poems.
Among these was one of his finest,

"Crossing Brooklyn Ferry." Another was "Song of the Open Road," with these often-quoted lines:

Afoot and light-hearted I take to the open road,
Healthy, free, the world before me.
The long brown path before me leading wherever I choose.

Like the first edition, this one did not sell well either.

In the next few years, Whitman earned money once more as a newspaperman, serving as editor of the *Brooklyn Times*. Other writers, including Henry David Thoreau and even Emerson himself, came to visit him at his home in Brooklyn. Many evenings, Whitman rode the ferry across the river to Manhattan, where he frequented Pfaff's beer cellar, a meeting place for young writers, musicians, artists, and newspapermen.

By 1860 Whitman had written one hundred twenty-four new poems for a third edition of *Leaves of Grass*. Visiting a publisher in Boston, he stopped off to see Emerson. As the two writers strolled on Boston Common, Emerson tried to persuade Whitman to refrain from printing some of the more sexually explicit of his poems. Whitman refused.

Perhaps the most memorable poem in the third edition of *Leaves of Grass* is the one named after its first line:

A manuscript page in Whitman's handwriting shows the revisions he made in one of the poems in *Leaves of Grass*. *The Henry E. Huntington Library and Art Gallery.*

Out of the cradle endless rocking,
Out of the mocking-bird's throat, the musical shuttle,
Out of the Nine-month midnight,
Over the sterile sands and the fields beyond, where the child leaving his bed wander'd alone, bareheaded, barefoot . . .

The Civil War reduced Whitman's publishing firm to bankruptcy, halting the sale of his book. When his young brother George was wounded in battle, Whitman hastened down to Washington to see him in an army hospital. The sight of thousands of suffering men changed the poet's life. At the age of forty-three he decided to devote himself to visiting and comforting the wounded.

Day after day, with a basket on his arm filled with oranges, jelly, tobacco, and candy, he made the rounds of wards filled with wounded soldiers. He wrote letters for them, read the Bible to the dying, and even helped to bandage wounds. At first he made money to support himself by sending articles to New York newspapers, but later he found a job as a clerk in the Department of the Interior that left time for his hospital visits.

For the bedridden soldiers Whitman was a grandfatherly figure, an older man with a white beard, broad hat, blue flannel coat, and flowing tie. They welcomed him because he always had time to talk to them. He once wrote, "To many of the wounded and sick, especially the youngsters, there is something in personal love, caresses, and the magnetic flood of sympathy and friendship that does, in its way, more good than all the medicines in the world."

Somehow, Whitman also continued to write poetry, a volume based on his wartime experiences called *Drum Taps.* It was published in 1865, the year the war ended and President Lincoln was assassinated. He wrote two poems about Lincoln's death. The shorter was a routine sort of elegy, which became vastly popular:

O Captain! my Captain! our fearful trip is
    done.
The ship has weather'd every rack, the
    prize we sought is won . . .

But the other longer poem, "When Lilacs Last in the Door-yard Bloom'd" has come to be included among the greatest American poems ever written. One of its stanzas starts:

O powerful western fallen star!
O shades of night—O moody tearful
    night!
O great star disappear'd—O the black
    murk that hides the star!

The year 1865 was a busy one for Whitman. He met Peter Doyle, an eighteen-year-old horsecar conductor in Washington. Despite a thirty-year age difference, Doyle appealed to Whitman's affectionate nature, and they became close friends. But Whitman lost his job as a government clerk because a new boss objected to the sexual passages in some of his poems. Within days friends found him another job in another federal department, where he continued to work until 1873.

That year the fifty-four-year-old Whitman met a series of reverses. Early in the year he suffered a slight stroke. Then his mother, who had always comforted and encouraged him, died. And after being away from Washington on a leave of absence, he lost his job along with the financial security it had provided him.

Whitman went to live with the family of one of his brothers in Camden, New Jersey, where he spent the remaining years of his life. Even though his health and spirits gradually improved, his creative energy was much diminished. He supervised several new editions of *Leaves of Grass* without making many changes, and his only other writing was a volume of recollections he called *Specimen Days*.

Except for a trip to the Rocky Mountains during this period, Whitman stayed in Camden, often receiving friends and admirers. One of those admirers was an English woman, Anne Gilchrist, who had written warm love letters to him after reading *Leaves of Grass*. A widow, she traveled to America and settled in Philadelphia to be near him. She even proposed marriage, but he was not interested. They remained friends, though, for the rest of his life.

In those years he concentrated on putting *Leaves of Grass* into the form he wanted. Nine editions of the book were published in Whitman's lifetime, the last one in 1891. Each one was slightly different, with old poems revised and new ones added. It might be said that Whitman spent a lifetime writing one book—but that one book established him as one of America's great poets.

He died in Camden on March 26, 1892, at the age of seventy-two.

PART III

Modern American Writers

Pearl S. Buck

1892–1973   The first American woman to be awarded a Nobel Prize in literature

Around 1880, two adventurous and deeply religious young people astonished their relatives in the small town of Hillsboro, West Virginia. Nobody could be very surprised that Caroline Stulting and Absolom Sydenstricker wanted to get married; it was the career they planned to embark on together that stirred a lot of talk, along with some strong protests.

But the couple would not give up their goal of spending their lives thousands of miles from any familiar surroundings—working as Presbyterian missionaries in China. Right after their wedding they set forth for that vast Asian land, and they remained there decade after decade despite all sorts of difficulties.

Still, they went back to Hillsboro for two years early in the 1890s, following a harrowing series of personal tragedies. One after another, three of the four children born to them in China had sickened then died, and a doctor had prescribed a long rest back in America for the heartbroken mother. It was during the last few months of this period, on June 6, 1892, in the large white house where Caroline herself had been born, that she gave birth to a new little girl.

The child, named Pearl Comfort Sydenstricker, forty years later would win international fame; by then, her own marriage had changed her name to Pearl S. Buck. The first step toward her future renown as the first writer to "humanize" the people of the Far East for Western readers was taken when she was just three months old. At that tender age, she was carried aboard a steamship bound for China.

Even though her parents taught her to regard the United States as her own country, this extremely bright and sensitive little girl grew up absorbed by the Chinese world in which she found herself. Many years later, she would tell an interviewer about her early childhood in a hilltop bungalow overlooking a crowded city on the Yangtze River called Chinkiang, whose tiled roofs, from her vantage point, "overlaid each other as closely as the scales upon a fish."

Then she added, "On the other side of our house there were low mountains and lovely gardened valleys and bamboo groves. At the foot of the hill where we lived was a big, dark temple where lived a dour old priest who used to chase me with a bamboo pole if in my wanderings I came too near the gates. I was deliciously afraid of him."

Pearl learned from her nursemaid to speak Chinese fluently at the same time her parents were teaching her English. Because they preferred having Chinese neighbors, rather than residing within a separate walled-off area as most other foreigners did, practically the only people she knew then were Chinese. Although she had blue eyes and a braid of long yellow hair, instead of the black eyes and black hair she saw all around

her, she did not realize there was any major difference between her and her Chinese neighbors until she was nearly eight years old, in 1900.

That was a very troubled year in China's history—the year of the Boxer Rebellion, a brief but violent uprising by a militant group aiming to kill all foreigners on Chinese soil. This bitter protest grew out of widespread resentment against Western business interests, backed up by Western governments, which for the past fifty years had been seizing more and more control over the very profitable East-West trade.

But an even broader sort of struggle was also symbolized by the Boxer violence. During many centuries of isolation China had developed its own distinctive civilization with a very high level of culture, at least for the privileged few. However, its ancient ways were proving incapable of resisting Western pressures effectively—and this conflict between two sets of values played an important part in shaping Pearl's whole outlook.

To start with, when reports of the bloody attacks on some Western settlements reached Chinkiang, her father decided to take his wife and daughter a few hundred miles down the Yangtze to the great coastal city of Shanghai. Feeling they would be safer there, he set them up in an apartment with loyal Chinese servants to watch over them, and sailed back upstream to resume his own religious teaching.

Happily, no outbreak of anti-Western fury occurred in Chinkiang. In Shanghai, however, antiforeign feeling reached such a pitch that Pearl became accustomed to a horrible experience. Almost every time she was taken out for a walk, her yellow hair and blue eyes stirred angry muttering. "Little foreign devil," she was called repeatedly.

For all the rest of her life, Pearl would remain very aware of the evil of racial prejudice. "I have had that strange and terrible experience of facing death because of my color," she would tell audiences many years later, after she had returned to her own country and become noted as a fervent supporter of better treatment for African Americans.

But even during the remainder of her Chinkiang childhood, her warm connection with Chinese neighbors and Chinese schoolmates in the Presbyterian school she attended led her to ask herself some hard questions about her own parents. Although she adored her mother, and gradually came to feel equally fond of her strict father, she could not help wondering, Why were they trying to impose their own religion on people who preferred other time-honored religions like Buddhism?

Pearl knew that her parents felt sure

they were helping those they preached to, and they could not see that their missionary work might actually stimulate more antiforeign feeling. She never argued with them, nor did she tell them any of the feelings her Chinese friends freely confided to her. She would later explain, "I grew up in a double world, the small white clean Presbyterian world of my parents and the big loving merry not-too-clean Chinese world, and there was no communication between them. When I was in the Chinese world I was Chinese . . . I shared their thoughts. . . . When I was in the American world, I shut the door between them."

Although Pearl did have an older brother, who would later become one of her closest confidants, she hardly knew him until she grew up because he went off to school in the United States when she was just three years old. And the beloved baby sister she acquired at the age of nine could not provide much in the way of companionship, either, during this period.

So Pearl, despite her outgoing nature, suffered a great deal of loneliness—until she discovered a wonderful way to cure it. She accomplished this by writing stories for an English-language newspaper, the *Shanghai Mercury,* which had a children's page featuring literary efforts by young readers. The paper even sent

Edwin, Pearl, and Grace Sydenstricker with their mother. *Photograph by Elliott Erwitt. © Magnum Photos, Inc.*

small sums of money to contributors whose offerings were printed.

Pearl was so thrilled by her first sight of her own words in the newspaper that from then on she wrote little stories regularly. They not only earned her enough to keep her well supplied with pocket money, but they also gave her a definite goal for her future: Someday, she decided, she was going to be a real writer.

First, though, she needed a broader education than she could receive in China. In 1910, at the age of eighteen, she traveled all the way back to the land of her birth, and enrolled at Randolph-Macon Woman's College in Lynchburg, Virginia. By then, Pearl's brother was married and living in that small city, so she did not feel entirely removed from family ties during her four years there.

Otherwise, however, those years were not too happy. Pearl had brought along a trunkful of fine Chinese silk or linen dresses made by a Chinese tailor trying to copy pictures of American styles from an American magazine—and she soon realized that all of her clothes looked ridiculous to American eyes. But even after buying herself a new American-made wardrobe, she still did not feel at ease with her classmates because she had not shared any of their ordinary American growing-up experiences.

Nevertheless, by her junior year Pearl had conquered her unaccustomed shy-

ness to the extent that she was elected president of her class. In addition she proved to be such an outstanding student that she graduated with high honors and was offered a job teaching freshman students while also earning a master's degree. Just as she was starting to enjoy her new status as a teacher, however, she received a cabled message summoning her back to China: Her mother was seriously ill with a tropical disease that often proved fatal.

Pearl spent the next two years taking care of her mother, whose health gradually improved to the extent that her daughter could devote an increasing number of hours to teaching at a Chinese boys' school. Right around the time her mother no longer needed any nursing, Pearl met a handsome young American agricultural scientist named John Lessing Buck, who had come to China to teach up-to-date farming methods.

After four brief meetings, they became engaged and they were married in May of 1919, a month before Pearl turned twenty-five. Very soon, alas, she realized that she and her husband had such entirely different interests that they could never be happy together.

Yet their marriage would endure for eighteen years because Pearl's parents had strong feelings against divorce—and one of the basic rules of behavior she had absorbed from her Chinese friends was obedience to parental guidelines. So she tried hard to make the best of her new status.

Indeed, the next five years would be the source of some of her richest memories, both personal and professional. For during this period she gave birth to a cherished little girl she named Carol, whose infancy was suffused with an especially rosy glow after Pearl developed a health problem that made any future pregnancy impossible.

Professionally, the same period was of great importance to Pearl Buck because right after her marriage she accompanied her husband to a North China town where he had been hired to teach agricultural subjects. Her new home was surrounded by a rural area whose customs had hardly changed for many centuries. Here, she soon learned to understand an unfamiliar dialect, and she formed warm friendships with peasant women who had never before even seen any foreigner; in effect, she was doing research that would prepare her to write *The Good Earth.*

Yet Buck started her writing career much more modestly, in 1922 when she was thirty years old, by sending an essay to the *Atlantic Monthly.* Somehow she had happened to see a copy of this highly regarded American magazine containing an article about "the new woman" who wore much shorter skirts than her older sisters and disregarded many long-held ideas regarding proper female behavior. Pearl mailed off a vivid description of the way revolutionary political currents were bringing similar changes even in Far Eastern cities like Shanghai—and her piece appeared under the title, "In China, Too."

After this first success, Buck began writing regularly for a magazine called *Asia.* But throughout the rest of the 1920s she had to cope with two overwhelming emotional traumas—the discovery that her daughter was mentally retarded to a very serious degree, and the eruption of outright revolutionary fighting in her beloved China. Her days were crammed with so much anguish and excitement that she had to keep putting off various ambitious literary projects.

In 1924 a trip to the United States brought the medical verdict that Carol's condition would only worsen. Back in the Chinese city of Nanking, where Carol's father was then teaching, the family only narrowly escaped being murdered in an outbreak of fierce rioting. Then came another journey to America for the purpose of placing Carol in a New Jersey training school said to be the best existing institution for children with her very limited ability to learn.

When she returned alone to Nanking, Pearl Buck missed her daughter terribly.

Also, she felt such a pressing need to earn money to pay for Carol's care that she quickly turned a short story she had written on shipboard into a novel, *East Wind: West Wind.* It was published in 1930 by a new firm in New York whose founder, Richard J. Walsh, had the then-unusual idea that the American reading public could be drawn to buy books about China—if the Chinese people depicted were treated as real human beings, not just exotic, doll-like creatures.

Whether Walsh and Buck had already met while she was in the United States neither of them ever confided; possibly they became acquainted during the months she had spent at Cornell University completing her studies for a master's degree. At any rate, their aims surely were similar and, right after her first book appeared, at the age of thirty-eight she began writing another one that would earn both of them a fortune. It took her only three months at her typewriter to tap out the entire manuscript for *The Good Earth* because, as she later explained, "My story had long been clear in my mind. Indeed, it had shaped itself firmly and swiftly from the events of my life, and its energy was the anger I felt for the sake of the peasants and the common folk of China, whom I loved and admired."

The Good Earth, nearly four hundred absorbing pages starting with the marriage of a poor farmer named Wang Lung to a former slave called O-lan, became an unprecedented international best-seller. Critics everywhere acclaimed the simplicity and clarity of Buck's writing, which somehow gave her scenes a timeless sort of universal appeal; she herself attributed this to her ability to think in the Chinese language and then mentally translate her thoughts into English.

Yet her book also stirred unfavorable comment because of its frankness about topics that had until then been out of bounds for novelists—in particular, its descriptions of O-lan all by herself giving birth to her children caused some reviewers to label the book immoral.

Nevertheless, *The Good Earth* won the 1932 Pulitzer Prize as that year's best novel by an American writer. It was also turned into a Broadway play as well as an award-winning movie. Meanwhile, during the next few years, Buck wrote two related novels, *Sons* and *A House Divided,* and all three were eventually grouped together in one large volume entitled *House of Earth.*

Although Buck still considered China her home, the smashing success of *The Good Earth* stimulated another trip to the United States. Finding herself famous dismayed her at first, but she was immensely relieved to have enough money now to set up a trust fund guaranteeing that Carol would be well cared for as long as she lived. In addition, her

Pearl Buck photographed in Sweden in 1938 when she received the Nobel Prize. *The Pearl S. Buck Foundation.*

new fame required her to have frequent lunch meetings with her publisher—and, as she later explained, "we slowly fell in love."

Walsh, too, was unhappily married. After Buck returned to her Nanking home, he arrived there the following year to try to persuade her to accompany him back across the Pacific. By then Buck's marriage was all but formally over, and she thought her father had mellowed sufficiently not to oppose

her seeking a divorce. However, despite China's increasing political troubles, making life for foreigners increasingly difficult, she and her father could not bring themselves to leave their beloved country permanently until another year had elapsed.

At last, on June 11, 1935, in the Nevada city of Reno, Pearl Buck and Richard Walsh both were granted divorces from their former spouses—and they got married there that very day. At the age of forty-three, she might almost have been the heroine of a modern sort of fairy story who from then on lived happily ever after.

With a spacious apartment on New York's Park Avenue, as well as a farm about a two-hour drive southward in Pennsylvania, the couple certainly had ample room for a large family. After just a few months, they adopted two infant boys. They would eventually have nine adopted sons and daughters, some from mixed racial backgrounds, for Buck became an outspoken crusader against all kinds of bigotry, while continuing to devote much of her energy to her writing.

Although most book reviewers thought her later work was inferior to *The Good Earth,* Buck remained the favorite author of many thousands of ordinary readers. To them, her position as a major writer was beyond debate after she won the prestigious Nobel Prize in

Pearl Buck in 1968 with one of the Amerasian children being cared for by the Pearl S. Buck Foundation. *UPI/Bettmann Newsphotos.*

literature in 1938; she was the first American woman to be honored this way.

But some leading figures in the American literary world, largely a man's world during this era, wondered aloud whether *any* woman writer could ever deserve such an award. Others merely insisted that Buck did not deserve it. She herself good-humoredly recalled this "great outcry of dissent" years later, adding, "I agreed with them! . . . My first reaction was to say, 'Oh, what a pity they didn't give it to Theodore Dreiser.' "

As the years passed, Buck's steady output of novels and short stories and personal reminiscences continued to arrive in bookstores; all together she would be the author of the astonishing total of eighty-five books. But because her publisher-husband advised that she would wear out her welcome if she came out with more than one new book every year, she took to signing some of her work with assorted made-up names. Her clear, uncomplicated storytelling captured the attention of readers even when she pretended to be "John Sedges."

The very ease with which she turned out book after book seemed to offend some critics, as if they felt that any writer who wrote so much could not possibly be worth serious attention. Yet novels by Pearl Buck continued to appear on best-seller lists; some of her most popular were *Dragon Seed, This Proud Heart,* and *Portrait of a Marriage.* As her familiarity with China receded further and further into the past, she gradually changed over to American themes but, by and large, these works were less successful.

Still, Buck's reputation as a defender of human rights kept growing. In 1949, she founded an adoption agency with the special mission of finding homes for children of mixed Asian and American ancestry, a legacy of World War II when United States soldiers stationed in the Far East had fathered numerous unwanted youngsters. She also supported many efforts to foster Asian-American cultural exchanges.

As her health began failing in her old age, Buck still kept on writing. During her last years she published several books of stories for children as well as *Pearl Buck's Oriental Cookbook.* She spent much of her time at a Vermont farm, where she and her family had with their own hands built a comfortable cabin some years back. It was at this farm near the town of Danby that she died on March 6, 1973, a few months short of her eighty-first birthday.

From the White House, President Richard Nixon issued a tribute to the author of *The Good Earth,* praising her as "a human bridge between the civilizations of the East and West."

Willa Cather

1873–1947   Her novel *O Pioneers!* was called the best book ever written "about the actual soil of our country"

She was just nine years old when she moved with her family from their fine brick home in the beautiful Shenandoah Valley of Virginia to a seemingly endless expanse of empty Nebraska prairie.

Willa Cather never forgot the intensity of her sense of loss then. "I felt a good deal as if we had come to the end of everything," she remembered years afterward, and she added:

I would not know how much a child's life is bound up in the woods and hills and meadows around it, if I had not been jerked away from all of these and thrown out into a country as bare as a piece of sheet iron. I had heard my father say you had to show grit in a new country . . . but . . . I thought I should go under.

Instead, though, as she began riding around on horseback with her brothers, she found unexpected excitement in the extremes of the Nebraska weather. And when she met pioneer families who had traveled all the way from Europe, her imagination was greatly stirred by their stories as well as by their dauntless spirits. Maybe she might have become a writer even if she had never left Virginia, but what she wrote about would surely have been very different.

Willela—as her name appeared in the Cather family Bible—had been born, on December 7, 1873, into a particularly picturesque and long-established farming community. Until she moved to Nebraska, she had "never before looked up at the sky when there was not a familiar mountain ridge against it." Also, the blue hills surrounding her native village of Back Creek had protected it during the Civil War, when bitter fighting had blackened many other areas of the Shenandoah Valley.

Her family's spacious old house, surrounded by towering trees, was called Willow Shade. Of red brick, with a white-pillared front porch, it stood on land that had been farmed by six generations of her ancestors. But her father, Charles Fectigue Cather, was not cut out to supervise an extensive farm profitably.

A kind and trustful man, he had married Mary Virginia Boak, from a respected family of longtime settlers quite similar to his own. Both of them had relatives who had served in Virginia's state legislature. Some of their adventurous kin were already thinking, however, about going west in search of richer soil while the couple's first child was still an infant.

Willie, they affectionately called her. A sturdy little girl with a warm and eager manner, she soon had a pair of younger brothers; later, in Nebraska, there would be an additional two brothers as well as two sisters. But the three eldest of the seven Cather children would always feel a special bond because of their happy times together in Virginia.

As if she were a boy, too, Willie roamed the outdoors with Roscoe and Douglas. She especially enjoyed going fishing or searching for animal tracks. But she also spent many hours down in Willow Shade's kitchen, listening to stories about days gone by, besides taking lessons in some proper female accomplishments like cooking and baking.

In addition, Willie picked up an amazing amount of book learning from her grandmothers. Both of these women had somehow acquired a wide knowledge of literature—and even an acquaintance with the ancient languages of Latin and Greek—despite the very limited educational opportunities open to females in their area then.

So Willie already was a tomboy, and bookish, too, by the time money troubles made her father decide to join some of their relatives out in Nebraska. Since there had recently been a great burst of railroad building, the family's westward journey involved no more hardship than repeatedly changing trains at transfer points along their route. Only after the Cathers reached the prairie town of Red Cloud did they board a horse-drawn wagon for the final few hours of their trip.

"I was sitting on the hay in the bottom of the wagon," she would always recall, "holding on to the side to steady myself—the roads were mostly faint trails over the bunch grass in those days.

The land was open range and there was almost no fencing." It was April, and spring had already arrived in Virginia, but the bleak Nebraska vistas in every direction gave Willie the feeling that her heart was breaking.

The Cathers, as it happened, spent only a little more than a year out in the remote area where Willie's father had hoped to develop a prosperous farm. Living conditions there proved harsher than he had expected, and Willie's mother, expecting a new baby, hated being so far from a doctor. So in the autumn of 1884, when Willie was approaching her eleventh birthday, the family moved again—into a plain frame house in Red Cloud.

This young town, hardly older than Willie herself, had started growing rapidly just a few years earlier after railroad tracks connected it with the rest of the country. Eight trains stopped at its station every day en route to Denver or Chicago, bringing storekeepers as well as farmers; the population of Red Cloud had reached about three thousand when the Cathers took up residence there and, within the next five years, that figure doubled.

While Willie's father worked for a bank, and her mother kept busy with new babies, Willie herself started showing signs of being exceptional. Attending school regularly for the first time in her life—when she enrolled, she said she wanted to be called Willa—she did outstandingly well, and she also made a few lifelong friends. Still, she was too much of a loner to join any group.

Having exceptionally strong emotions, she never ceased to feel the loss of Virginia, yet she also came to feel a deep tie to Nebraska during the years she lived in Red Cloud. For her, the town's main attraction was the remarkable variety of recently transplanted Europeans who had settled in its vicinity. Maybe she felt so drawn to them because her own uprooting made her very sensitive to what they must be enduring so far removed from their native countries. In any case, she spent as much time as she could getting to know them.

On the Sundays of her early teens, Willa often turned up at a Norwegian or Danish or Swedish church to observe their services. With her brothers she rode to an outlying settlement of Catholics from France or to the Bohemian community, where the sermons were delivered in the French or Czech languages.

Years later it would be clear that she had unconsciously been behaving like a writer gathering material for future stories. But the notion of becoming a writer had not yet occurred to her. Willa brashly aimed instead to be some sort of scientist, even though girls in those days were not supposed to harbor any such ambition.

One summer she convinced the local doctor to let her ride all over the area with him in his horse-drawn buggy when he went to see sick people. Sometimes she even assisted him—most memorably on the day he found it necessary to amputate a boy's leg, when he put her in charge of giving the patient whiffs of the sleep-inducing drug chloroform.

More startling, as far as Red Cloud was concerned, Willa managed to acquire a set of surgical tools herself and she started operating on small animals in the Cathers' basement.

Then, at the age of fourteen, she gave the town something outright scandalous to talk about. She cut her curly, chestnut-colored hair as short as a boy's, and she displayed her scorn for accepted ideas about proper female garb by walking around wearing a pair of trousers borrowed from one of her brothers.

During the next several years, Willa often dressed like a boy. When she did appear in a skirt, she usually wore a boy's shirt and tie with it. In addition, she took to signing her name *William* Cather.

Her reason for all of this was simply that more opportunities were available to boys than to girls, as she told anybody

who asked. But even though during this period a campaign was going on all over the country to win the right to vote for America's women, and other efforts were being made to expand women's employment possibilities, Willa Cather never showed any interest in such reforms.

Instead, she just refused to consider herself bound by the usual restrictions limiting other females. This outlook made her the topic of a lot of gossip, besides causing much friction with her mother. Nevertheless, Willa remained closely tied to her whole family—and if someone else made fun of her, her family members always defended her.

In an album saved by a friend of hers, Willa at the age of fifteen answered a list of personal questions flippantly. "To be an M.D." was her chief ambition, and her idea of perfect happiness was "amputating limbs." Having to do any fancy sewing was her idea of real misery. More seriously, Shakespeare and Ralph Waldo Emerson were her favorite writers.

Bent on attending the University of Nebraska, a few months before her seventeenth birthday Willa boarded a train to the state capital of Lincoln, one hundred fifty miles from Red Cloud. It was in September of 1890 that Willa enrolled at the university, and she did not try to avoid attracting attention.

One of her fellow students never forgot the first time he saw her: "The door opened and a head appeared, with short hair and a straw hat; a deep masculine voice inquired whether this was the class in elementary Greek. A boy nodded yes, and as the newcomer entered and was a girl, the entire class burst out laughing."

Willa's fearless way of defying the prevailing views about female behavior won her friends as well as enemies; it seemed that, because her own personality was so decisive, most people she met either liked her very much or hated her. Like her or not, though, her new acquaintances could hardly doubt her intellectual ability. While she still planned to concentrate on science and become a doctor, soon after arriving in Lincoln she wrote a paper for a literature course that had a great impact.

Her professor was so impressed by the brilliant essay she handed in on one of Britain's most eminent literary figures, Thomas Carlyle, that he told the editor of the *Nebraska State Journal* about it. The next Sunday, the area's leading newspaper printed the entire essay, calling it "a remarkable product," by a student who was still only sixteen. Such public praise was, of course, widely noticed on the campus.

Willa herself had no advance hint that her composition was going to be published. At her first sight of her own words in print, she felt as if she had been hypnotized; she suddenly forgot all about studying medicine—and set her future course on becoming a writer.

It would be over twenty years before Willa Cather began to be hailed by book reviewers as a major American novelist. Another ten years would elapse until her name became widely known to the general public. Still, she never wavered in her belief that she was on the right path.

By the time she graduated from the university, Willa knew that, most of all, she wanted to write fiction. Already she had seen several of her short stories appear in a student literary magazine—and one had actually been accepted by a weekly journal in distant Boston. As satisfying as these fictional beginnings were, however, she realized that for the time being, in order to support herself, she would have to concentrate on journalism.

During her sophomore year Willa had started contributing regularly to the *Nebraska State Journal*. Despite her youth and inexperience she had total confidence in her own opinions, and she did so well at writing about the local performances of traveling companies of actors that upon her graduation she was hired as the paper's drama critic.

By now Cather had gradually ceased

Willa Cather photographed while she was managing editor of *McClure's. The Bettmann Archive.*

cutting her hair very short and dressing in a notably mannish style. But a theatrical streak in her own nature made her immensely enjoy associating with the acting troupes that often came to a state capital like Lincoln in those days. Sometimes even the most famous stars of the era appeared on the stage there, and Willa wrote very perceptively about them, as well as about the arts in general.

Yet as Cather approached her twenty-second birthday, she felt a mounting frustration because she had hardly any time for the creative writing she kept hoping to do. Furthermore, she had no intention of spending her entire life so far away from the nation's artistic mecca of New York City. So she eagerly grasped an opportunity to move eastward—to the Pennsylvania steel-manufacturing metropolis of Pittsburgh.

In 1896 Cather became the editor of a homemaking magazine there. After she realized that the job did not suit her at all, she quickly found other work on a local newspaper and then as a high school English teacher. Pittsburgh offered a wide range of cultural attractions, which strongly appealed to her. At its grand marble concert hall, built with money contributed by the millionaire steelmaker Andrew Carnegie, she turned into a fervent lover of classical music.

At a backstage party in a Pittsburgh theater, Cather met a charming young woman who would play a major role in her life. Isabelle McClung, the daughter of a wealthy and respected judge, enthusiastically did all she could to support the arts. Soon Isabelle prevailed on Willa to leave the shabby boardinghouse where she had been living and move into her family's mansion.

Part of its attic was fitted up as Cather's own private workroom—a luxury she had only dreamed of previously. Up there, on weekends and after school hours, during the next several years she wrote short stories that showed more evidence of a real talent than anything she had done before. In 1905, when she was nearly thirty-two, seven of them were published in a small book.

Although this literary debut brought Cather neither fame nor fortune, it led to her being offered a job assisting the editor of a nationally known magazine published in New York. Despite the fact that *McClure's* was famous for its muckraking articles on political and economic matters, which hardly interested her, she did not hesitate an instant. In 1906, she departed from Pittsburgh after having spent ten increasingly satisfying years there.

Willa Cather's move to New York City caused her much personal unhappiness because it meant separating from Isa-

A photograph of Willa Cather during the *McClure's* magazine period, 1906 to 1912. *The Bettmann Archive.*

belle McClung. Her friend's father held that his unmarried daughter must continue to live in her parents' home, and she did not dare to defy him. Even though the two women remained deeply fond of each other all the rest of their lives, their emotional tie inevitably grew less binding as they both formed other friendships.

Professionally, however, Cather's arrival in New York opened an exciting new period. Her quick grasp of literary details soon led to her being appointed *McClure's* managing editor. As her duties consisted mainly of dealing with other writers, during the four years she held this post she grew into a self-confident resident of the city's artistic community. At the same time, her intense remembrances of Nebraska finally began taking a novelistic form in her mind.

Still, her first full-length work of fiction was *Alexander's Bridge,* about a brilliant engineer whose powerful drive to succeed leads only to a feeling of emotional emptiness—and the collapse of his largest bridge. But even though its author would never rate this book very highly, it attracted enough favorable attention for her to resign from her magazine job so that she could concentrate thenceforth on her own writing. By the following year, in 1913, she had produced her first masterpiece.

Cather's *O Pioneers!* had very little plot or fictional embellishment. The tone of this simple and yet lyrical story about an immigrant family bravely farming their new land was set by its opening sentences:

One January day, thirty years ago, the little town of Hanover, anchored on a windy Nebraska tableland, was trying not to be blown away. A mist of fine snowflakes was curling and eddying about the cluster of low drab buildings huddled on the gray prairie. . . . On the sidewalk in front of one of the stores sat a little Swede boy, crying bitterly.

Book reviewers wrote many kind words about *O Pioneers!* One critic called it "far above the ordinary product of contemporary novelists," while another marveled that no man in the whole history of American literature had written "as good a book as this about the actual soil of our country." And leading critics in England said it would be hard to praise this book too highly.

Pleased as she was to win the admiration of her peers, Cather earned only a modest income from *O Pioneers!* and her next several books because none of them became best-sellers. Nor did her name become widely known among the general public. Even so, she was able to live very comfortably in a large apartment in one of the city's most pleasant neighborhoods because, by then, she and a fellow Nebraskan named Edith Lewis had settled into a lifelong companionship.

Lewis, a self-effacing woman who had no doubt that her friend was a genius, worked as an editor at various publications. Besides the money she contributed to pay their joint expenses—in those days of lower wages, the pair could easily afford a French cook who doubled as their housekeeper—Lewis also shielded Cather from unwanted interruptions. In effect she became something like her private secretary as fame started to descend on Cather following the publication in 1918 of her other great prairie novel, *My Antonia.*

Although Cather continued to pay extended visits to her family in Red Cloud every summer, after *My Antonia* her writing began to veer off onto other themes, as if she had said all she wished to about the pioneer experience. Increasingly fond of traveling, she became enchanted by the American Southwest. During several trips there, she and Edith Lewis boldly rode out on horseback with Indian guides to explore New Mexico canyons where ancient cliff dwellers had lived. From these expeditions came her serenely poetic book about old Santa Fe, *Death Comes for the Archbishop.*

By its publication in 1927, Cather had received many awards, including hon-orary degrees from more than a dozen of the nation's leading universities. One of her lesser works, *One of Ours,* a novel about Midwestern soldiers fighting in the First World War, won a Pulitzer Prize, and she was continually invited to all sorts of literary gatherings.

But as she advanced in years, her craving for personal privacy grew to such an extent that she made almost no public appearances. Major changes in manners and morals during the 1920s, and then the Great Depression of the 1930s, left her feeling as if the world she knew had disappeared. Still, she wrote another few books; the last of them— *Sapphira and the Slave Girl,* harking back to her childhood memories of Virginia—was published in 1940.

Willa Cather died at her New York apartment on April 24, 1947, when she was seventy-three. In her will, she forever forbade any publishing of her private letters, and she also tried to forbid dramatizing any of her stories because she hated the way Hollywood had treated some of her favorite books by other authors.

Despite these restrictions, however, during recent years Cather herself has been the subject of several admiring biographies. And her reputation as an outstanding American writer has grown rather than diminished in the decades since her death.

William Faulkner

1897–1962   The creator of Yoknapatawpha County

Billy Falkner grew up surrounded by the legend of William Clark Falkner, the founder of his family in northern Mississippi. As a boy, Billy loved to sit on the porch of his grandfather's house and listen to stories about his famous great-grandfather.

When the Civil War broke out in 1861, Colonel Falkner had organized a regiment of cavalry in the Confederate army. At the Battle of Bull Run in Virginia, he helped turn back a Union advance despite having two horses shot from under him.

As he mounted his third horse and charged forward again, his commander cried out, "Go ahead, you hero with the black plume, history shall never forget you!" But Colonel Falkner is remembered today because his great-grandson used his life as raw material for his novels, not because of his heroism in battle.

After the Civil War, Falkner—always called the Old Colonel to distinguish him from his son, the Young Colonel—had a notable career. He practiced law, built a railroad, operated a saw- and gristmill, managed a twelve-hundred-acre plantation, raised cotton, and lived in an ornate mansion. Somehow he found time to write books, too, among them a popular novel called *The White Rose of Memphis.*

Years later, as Billy Falkner handled mementos of his famous ancestor—his cane, his silver watch, his pipe, and his books—he strongly identified himself with the Old Colonel, whose first name he shared. In school, when asked what he wanted to be when he grew up, he replied, "I want to be a writer like my great-granddaddy."

Billy Falkner did grow up to be a writer, known to the world as William Faulkner. He won many awards, including the Nobel Prize in literature. More important than the prizes, though, are his novels, which are studied in college classrooms and widely read today.

The story of Billy Falkner begins in the tiny town of New Albany, where he was born on September 25, 1897. His parents named him after his great-grandfather, who had died eight years before, but gave him a new middle name, Cuthbert, instead of Clark.

His father, Murry Falkner, served as the general passenger agent of the railroad line that the Old Colonel had built. A year after Billy's birth the family moved to a larger town, Ripley, where his father acted as treasurer of the railroad. His mother was the former Maud Butler, a graduate of the Women's College in Columbus, Mississippi, who had worked as a secretary before she married.

The pleasant life of the Falkners was turned upside down in 1902 when the Young Colonel, Billy's grandfather, decided to sell the railroad line. This decision devastated Billy's father, who loved the railroad that was affectionately called The Doodlebug Line because its small engines ran on narrow tracks.

Feeling miserable, Murry Falkner moved his family to Oxford, home of the University of Mississippi.

Despite the obvious unhappiness of his father, who took to operating a livery stable hiring out horses, Billy lived in a closely knit family. He was the oldest of four boys in a household that included his mother's mother, called Damuddy by the boys, and a tiny old servant, Caroline Barr, called Mammy Callie.

Mammy, who had been born a slave, rocked Billy on her knees and told him stories about slavery, the Civil War, and Ku Klux Klan members wearing white sheets terrorizing black communities. But the major influence in his early years was his mother, who taught him how to read and draw pictures. Billy was a reader before he entered grammar school in 1905.

At first, he was quiet and studious. He made the honor roll in the first grade, doing so well that he skipped the second grade entirely and went on to the third. Billy cared only for his writing and drawing, though. "I never did like school," he once said, "and I stopped going to school as soon as I got big enough to play hooky and not get caught at it."

In those growing-up years, Billy and his brothers lived a normal rural childhood. They played baseball, hunted, built a playhouse, ran to the town square to see the first automobile in the area, and went to parties. Once they built a flying machine of wood and paper. Billy became the pilot as his brothers pushed it over the side of a deep ditch, hoping it would fly. Instead, it slid down the slope of the ditch, breaking into pieces, but left Billy unhurt.

As he moved into high school, he showed little interest in his formal studies. He read at home, drew pen-and-ink sketches for the yearbook, and played baseball and football. Even though he was small in size, only five feet five inches tall in his senior year, he became a quarterback for the high school football team.

"I hung around school just to play baseball and football and then I quit," he later said. Just a few months short of graduation in 1915, Billy gave up attending any classes at all.

In the troubled years that followed, there were two major influences on his life. One was Phil Stone, a neighbor who had graduated from the University of Mississippi. He asked to see Billy's poems and encouraged him to write. Stone, four years older than Billy, became his guide into the works of the great poets. They often read together, especially the lyrical verses of Keats, Shelley, and Swinburne.

The second influence was Estelle Oldham, the girl who lived down the street—a pretty, laughing belle with blue eyes, reddish brown hair, and an alluring smile. Popular with many boys, Estelle always had time for Billy and his first attempts at poetry. When Estelle enrolled at the University of Mississippi, Billy gave her a gold ring with an *F* carved on it, a symbol of his love.

To the outside world, Billy Falkner was a failure—a high school dropout who had a job only because his grandfather owned a bank. Billy hated his job as a bookkeeper, working in a back room, entering numbers in ledgers. Money was a contemptible thing to work for, he confided to Estelle.

Trapped in a situation he detested, Billy began to drink heavily, dipping into his grandfather's closet of fine whiskey. He began to spend less time at the bank and more at the nearby university campus, contributing drawings to student publications. In 1918 two of his drawings appeared in *Ole Miss*, and they were his first published work.

That year, under increasing family pressure, Estelle became engaged to another man, a lawyer. In tears she came to Billy and told him, "I'm ready to elope with you." But he refused. In the old-fashioned tradition of a Southern gentleman, he said, "No, we'll have to get your father's consent."

Her father was furious. How could his daughter marry a man who could not support himself, much less a wife? Billy's parents were angry, too. Estelle and Billy were unable to stand up to the combined opposition of both sets of parents.

When Estelle married the other man later in 1918, Billy's "world went to pieces," one of his brothers would recall. So Billy decided to join the glamorous air corps of the army and take part in the great war then raging in Europe. He tried to enlist for pilot training but was turned down because he was underweight and undersized.

In despair Billy went to visit his friend Phil Stone, then studying law at Yale University. There, all of the students were talking about which branch of the armed services they would enter. Their talk gave Billy the idea of joining Canada's branch of the British Royal Air Force, where his size and weight were no problem.

When Billy enlisted, he changed the spelling of his name as a way of symbolically casting aside his past unhappiness. He signed himself as William Faulkner, adding a *u* to his last name, which most critics would later decide was a means of turning his back on his alcoholic father in Oxford and his own troubled youth. At the age of twenty-one, William Faulkner thought he could start life all over again with an almost new identity.

He traveled to Canada for training, and learned to fly. However, when World War I ended before he could go overseas, he was discharged as a cadet. Faulkner went back to Oxford proudly wearing the blue uniform of the Royal Air Force, as if he were seeking recognition from those at home who had previously looked down on him.

But things had not changed for the better; the next few years were unhappy ones for him. He spent most of his time alone in his room, writing poems. All of them were rejected by various publications until he wrote his own version of a well-known verse by the French poet Stéphane Mallarmé. It was printed in *The New Republic* magazine on April 6, 1919—the first published writing by William Faulkner.

That did not open the doors of literary success for him, though. For the next ten years, Faulkner struggled to make a living. He attended classes briefly at the University of Mississippi, served as an assistant scoutmaster, and, on a brief trip to New York City, worked in a bookstore. On his return to Oxford, he got a job as postmaster at the university, but was fired for inefficiency. In those years he turned once again to alcohol, at times drinking heavily to escape from his troubles.

In 1924 his first book was published: *The Marble Faun*, a collection of pastoral poems. It came out only because Phil Stone had paid a publisher to issue it. The book impressed Faulkner's family and friends because it proved that he really was an author, but made little impact outside his immediate circle. In Oxford, in those years, Faulkner was regarded as a most peculiar young man, a scribbler without talent.

At one point he escaped to New Orleans, where he found a number of young writers like himself and a well-known writer, Sherwood Anderson, who became his mentor. Faulkner wrote a series of sketches about New Orleans for the local newspaper. He also began to write a novel about his war experiences—even though he had never seen any action—and those of his brother Jack, who had been wounded in France.

That first novel, *Soldier's Pay*, was published in 1926. It received good reviews but did not sell very well. By the time it came out, Faulkner was already at work on another novel about a writer and his disappointments. Called *Mosquitoes*, it was greeted with mixed reviews when it appeared in print in 1927. Both of these books are remembered today only as early works of Faulkner.

At the age of thirty, he certainly seemed to be a failure. In New Orleans he had fallen in love with a young woman named Helen Baird, but she had rejected him and married another man just as Estelle had. Faulkner followed the advice of his fictional writer in *Mosquitoes*: "You don't commit suicide when you are disappointed in love, you write a book."

Back in Oxford, unable to earn a living, he stayed with his parents. In his room, he remembered a suggestion of Sherwood Anderson—to write about his own Mississippi. Long after he became famous, Faulkner recalled those days: "I discovered that my own little patch of native soil was worth writing about and that I would never live long enough to exhaust it."

In 1927 Faulkner created the fictional Yoknapatawpha County, naming it from a Chickasaw Indian word meaning "water flowing slowly through the flatland." In one of his later books, he described it and its capital as follows: "JEFFERSON, YOKNAPATAWPHA CO., Mississippi. Area: 2,400 square miles. Population, Whites 62,988; Negroes, 9,313. WILLIAM FAULKNER, Sole Owner and Proprietor."

Writing a novel called *Sartoris*, Faulkner peopled his fictional county with the aristocratic Sartoris clan. He transformed his great grandfather, the legendary Old Colonel, into Colonel John Sartoris, and his grandfather, the Young Colonel, into Bayard Sartoris.

Sartoris was published in 1929, an important year to Faulkner emotionally

William Faulkner and his wife outside their home in 1955. *UPI/Bettmann Newsphotos.*

as well as professionally. His childhood sweetheart Estelle had returned to Oxford a divorced woman with two children. They were married on June 20. By then he had already completed another novel, *The Sound and the Fury,* a complicated story of a beautiful young woman told through the eyes of her brothers. Published in 1929 it received warm critical attention but did not attract many readers.

In need of money Faulkner worked nights in the university powerhouse, shoveling coal into the furnaces. During the early-morning hours there, he used an overturned wheelbarrow as a writing table. *The Saturday Evening Post* bought one of his short stories for seven hundred fifty dollars, more than he had earned from any of his early novels, encouraging him to write more stories.

Faulkner's financial situation brightened in the early 1930s with the publication of *Sanctuary,* a lurid story of a young woman raped by a gangster. Not only did it sell well, but it led to a contract to write movie scripts in Hollywood. Although he was well paid there, he hated the atmosphere of Hollywood and resumed drinking heavily.

His home life deteriorated, too, as his wife also began to drink. As a diversion from his problems at home and from his distaste for Hollywood, Faulkner took up flying again. With the money from the movie sale of *Sanctuary,* he bought a small airplane of his own. Despite the growing estrangement between him and his wife, their only child, Jill, was born in 1933.

For the next several years, Faulkner continued to write for the movies so that he could afford to write more novels. On one of his trips to Hollywood, he fell in love with a young woman, Meta Carpenter, and began a long-lasting love affair, one of many in his life.

His major novel *Absalom, Absalom* came out in 1936. It was a complicated story about "a man who wanted a son through pride, and got too many of them and they destroyed him." One typical reviewer called Faulkner's way of writing "one of the most complex, unreadable and uncommunicative prose styles ever to find its way into print."

But he made it a little easier for some readers by including a map of Yoknapatawpha County. He marked the homes of all the characters in *Absalom, Absalom* and his other novels. Despite that detail, his aim was to capture the universal human spirit, not limiting himself to colorful Southern characters. Nevertheless, he did create colorful characters. Among them was Flem Snopes, a backwoodsman with no redeeming qualities. Faulkner chronicled the rise of the Snopes clan to money and power, as the aristocratic Sartorises

William Faulkner in his library. He wrote in longhand, he said, because "I've got to feel the pencil and see the words at the end of the pencil." *UPI/Bettmann Newphotos.*

declined, in three novels: *The Hamlet* (1940), *The Town* (1957), and *The Mansion* (1959).

In those years, Faulkner's reputation grew in literary circles, but his books did not reach a large audience until he published *Intruder in the Dust* in 1948. In it he tackled race prejudice squarely, telling the story of a black man accused of murder who is helped by two white boys and a white woman. When it was sold to the movies, he achieved financial independence for the first time—at the age of fifty-one.

Yet these were unhappy years for him. He and his wife were emotionally separated although there was no divorce. Periodically he went off on alcoholic binges, at times being hospitalized before he recovered. However, his drinking did not affect his literary production.

Faulkner wrote in longhand with a pencil in a cramped, almost illegible script. At the end of a day's work, he would type what he had written because he was afraid he would not be able to decipher it later. He revised his work constantly, rewriting and rearranging his words, sentences, paragraphs, and even chapters.

Recognized as one of America's outstanding writers, Faulkner received many awards and other honors—including the Nobel Prize in literature in 1950. At the presentation ceremony in Stockholm, he was described as the "unrivaled master of all living British and American novelists as a deep psychologist."

Nervous because it was the first time he ever made a speech in public, Faulkner rose to reply. The audience saw a short man with gray hair and a full and bristly mustache. He spoke so softly and quickly that his words were scarcely heard.

What he said was memorable, though. He addressed his remarks to young writers in a world facing the danger of nuclear conflict. For writers, he said, there was no subject but "the old universal truths lacking which any story is ephemeral and doomed—love and honor and pity and pride." Then he went on: "I believe that man will not merely endure; he will prevail. He is immortal, not because alone among creatures he has an inexhaustible voice, but because he has a soul, a spirit of compassion and sacrifice and endurance. The poet's, the writer's duty is to write about these things."

Faulkner returned to Oxford to be greeted by the high school band and seven drum majorettes. An admirer proposed that the legend on the city's water tower be changed to read OXFORD HOME OF OLE MISS AND WILLIAM FAULKNER. When there were some objections,

Faulkner was pleased that the chamber of commerce honored him in another way, with a fish fry.

Despite his new fame, Faulkner was still an unhappy man. Depressed about his work, he continued to drink to excess. He led what he called a dull, busy, purely physical life on his farm in Mississippi, training and riding his horses. But he also traveled, meeting friends, publishers, and young women with whom he had brief love affairs.

In those later years of his life, more honors came his way. In 1951, he received the National Book Award for his collected stories. In 1955 he won another National Book Award and the Pulitzer Prize for a new novel, *The Fable*. It was a retelling of the Christ story, set in the French army during troop mutinies in World War I.

Faulkner made many trips abroad for the United States State Department, speaking on writing in Japan, the Philippines, Italy, France, England, and Iceland. At home, in his native South, he spoke out against racial segregation. "To live anywhere in the world of A.D. 1955 and be against equality because of race or color is like living in Alaska and being against snow," he said.

Faulkner became the writer-in-residence at the University of Virginia in 1958, answering student questions about his work.

"Mr. Faulkner," one student asked, "in *As I Lay Dying* did Jewel purchase the horse as a substitute for his mother?"

"Well, now, that's something for the psychologist," he replied. "He bought the horse because he wanted that horse." His intention, he said, was to write about people, not sociology or symbolism.

His last book, *The Reivers*—an old Scottish word meaning robbers—came out in 1962. It was a mellow story about a grandfather, someone like Faulkner himself, recalling his boyhood. When he went down to the post office to mail off the manuscript, he told a friend, "I been aimin' to quit this foolishness."

He had completed his life's work: nineteen novels, five collections of stories, a collection of three short novels, two editions of his New Orleans sketches, and two volumes of poetry. In May of 1962, he won his last honor, the gold medal for fiction from the National Institute of Arts and Letters.

In June, injured in a fall from one of his horses, Faulkner entered a hospital. He died on July 6, 1962, at the age of sixty-five.

F. Scott Fitzgerald

1896–1940   Novelist of the Jazz Age

He was named for a distant relative, Francis Scott Key, the author of the words to "The Star Spangled Banner." Even though he was proud of that connection, naming his only child Frances Scott Key Fitzgerald, he wrote under the name of F. Scott Fitzgerald. His friends called him Scott.

Scott was born in St. Paul, Minnesota on September 24, 1896. Two older sisters had died before his birth. As an only son, Scott grew up rather spoiled despite having a younger sister, Annabel.

His mother, Mary McQuillan Fitzgerald, was the daughter of a poor Irish immigrant who had arrived in St. Paul while it was still a frontier town with Indians walking on the unpaved streets. Nevertheless, he made a fortune in the wholesale grocery business. But the quiet, mannerly man Mary married—Edward Fitzgerald, from Maryland—proved to lack any similar talent for moneymaking. When the furniture factory he was managing failed during Scott's infancy, the family moved to upstate New York.

As a boy growing up in Syracuse and Buffalo, Scott was a bit of a dandy. His mother bought him clothes from a fashionable New York City store, and he wore bow ties to go with his high stiff collars. Even though his parents were hard-pressed financially, they sent him to dancing school, where he associated with the sons and daughters of wealthy families.

In 1908, when his father lost his job the Fitzgeralds moved back to St. Paul.

His mother had inherited enough money to be able to send Scott, then twelve years old, to the St. Paul Academy, an elite private school. Once again he became part of a circle of rich families despite his own family's lesser affluence.

A slender blond boy, with attention-attracting green eyes, Scott was not popular with his classmates. He talked too much. Perhaps that was because, among the wealthy boys who came to dancing school in black limousines with monograms on their doors, he felt ashamed of his father's failure in business and his mother's lack of style.

At school Scott went out for sports, starred in dramatic performances, wrote his first short stories for the literary magazine, and learned a little Latin and Greek. As he paid scant attention to his studies, his grades were poor. His parents, deciding that he needed the discipline of a boarding school, sent him to the Newman School in New Jersey, which drew its pupils from wealthy Roman Catholic families all over America.

At the age of fifteen, Scott went east determined to make good. He wrote a self-appraisal: "I considered that I was a fortunate youth capable of expansion to any extent for good or evil. I thought there was nothing I could not do, except, perhaps, become a mechanical genius." Then he listed his advantages:

"Physically—I marked myself handsome: of great athletic possibilities, and an extremely good dancer. . . . Socially—magnetism, poise, and the ability to dominate others. Also, I was sure that I possessed a subtle fascination over women. . . . Mentally—I was vain of having so much, of being so talented, ingenuous [ingenious] and quick to learn."

It was partly true. Scott was handsome, a good dancer, and an excellent conversationalist. But he was also spoiled, vain, moody, and unpopular with the other boys—mainly because he talked too much, just as he had in St. Paul. Even though he was slight in build, he went out for sports, playing intramural football and becoming a substitute on the baseball and basketball teams. Paying little attention to his formal studies, he read widely. He also wrote for the school newspaper, and went into New York City often to go to the theater.

Perhaps the major influence on him in his boarding-school years was his friendship with Father Sigourney Webster Fay, the school's headmaster. A sympathetic priest, he treated Scott as if he were his own son. Scott would show his appreciation by later dedicating his first book to Father Fay.

As he neared graduation, Scott determined that he would attend Princeton

University. But getting admitted there was not easy. At first, he was turned down because of poor grades. Then he failed the entrance examinations. As a last resort, he appeared in person before the admissions committee to appeal his case. Among the arguments he cited was the fact that that very day was his seventeenth birthday, so it would not be charitable to exclude him. As he often said later, he talked his way into Princeton.

In September of 1913, Scott became a freshman. He sent a telegram to his mother: "ADMITTED SEND FOOTBALL PADS AND SHOES IMMEDIATELY PLEASE WAIT TRUNK." But there was no place on the football team for a young man only five feet seven inches tall, weighing just a hundred thirty-eight pounds. He lasted one day on the freshman football squad.

Looking around for another way to make his mark on the campus, Scott settled on the Triangle Club, a group that produced musical comedies, and the *Tiger,* a humorous literary magazine. He bombarded both with comic sketches. Writing mainly for the Triangle Club, he followed the pattern he had set earlier at boarding school: He paid so little attention to his studies that he failed three subjects in the first part of his freshman year.

Despite his scholastic problems, Scott loved the atmosphere at Princeton—its buildings with their Gothic spires and gargoyles, the colorful crowds at the football games, the songs of marching men on the campus, the camaraderie of his fellow students. He was pleased to be invited to join the Cottage Club, one of the elite eating clubs at Princeton.

Among his friends at college and after were Edmund Wilson, editor of the literary magazine, and John Peale Bishop, a poet. Under their influence, he began to write more serious pieces than his lyrics for the Triangle Club. He made up his mind to become a writer.

"I want to be one of the greatest writers in the world, don't you?" he said to Wilson. As usual, he talked so much about himself and his ambitions that even his friends found him irritating.

He also found time for less serious pursuits. He frequently went into New York City for dances and he began to drink, sometimes heavily. His attention to play and writing affected his grades: He failed exams in chemistry and Latin. As a result, under the college rules he became ineligible for an important office that he had sought—president of the Triangle Club.

He never forgot that. "To me, college would never be the same," he wrote many years later. "There were to be no badges of pride, no medals, after all."

Disappointed, he was rescued from

despair when the United States entered World War I in 1917. Along with many other Princeton men, Fitzgerald joined the army. Sent to Fort Leavenworth, Kansas, for officer's training, he served under a hard-driving regular-army officer, Captain Dwight D. Eisenhower.

Not interested very much in the military life, Fitzgerald spent his free hours in the officers' club, ignoring the drinking, the chatter, and the noise, to work on a novel. It was a thinly disguised story of himself and Princeton, which he called *The Romantic Egoist.* He paid so little attention to his duties that one of his colleagues later called him "the world's worst second lieutenant."

In 1918, Fitzgerald was assigned to an infantry regiment stationed at Camp Sheridan, near the Alabama city of Montgomery. At a country-club dance one Saturday night, he met Zelda Sayre, a beautiful Southern belle not yet eighteen years old but already the most popular young woman in Montgomery. The youngest of five children, Zelda had grown up with few restraints; talented and tomboyish, she was also utterly enchanting.

Fitzgerald saw Zelda across a crowded room and went up to introduce himself. Thus began a romance that made literary history because this pair came to personify the devil-may-care outlook of the Jazz Age of the 1920s.

"For the first time, Fitzgerald had found a girl whose uninhibited love of life rivaled his own and whose daring, originality, and repartee would never bore him," one of his biographers would write.

When the war ended, Fitzgerald went to New York. On his arrival, he sent an exuberant telegram to Zelda: "DARLING HEART . . . I DECLARE EVERYTHING GLORIOUS THIS WORLD IS A GAME AND WHILE I FEEL SURE OF YOUR LOVE EVERYTHING IS POSSIBLE I AM IN THE LAND OF AMBITION AND SUCCESS." His success was not long in coming.

His novel, much-revised and with its name changed from *The Romantic Egoist* to *This Side of Paradise,* was published in 1920. A week after its appearance in print, Scott and Zelda were married in St. Patrick's Cathedral in New York City; he was twenty-four years old, and she was twenty.

In *This Side of Paradise,* Fitzgerald displayed an attitude typical of all his work: a preoccupation with the rich, seen by a skeptical eye. "That was always my experience," he wrote much later, describing himself as "a poor boy in a rich town; a poor boy in a rich boy's school; a poor boy in a rich man's club at Princeton." He added bitterly, "I have never been able to forgive the rich for being rich, and it has colored my entire life and works."

This Side of Paradise made Fitzgerald himself rich for a brief time, and also famous. The critics praised the book, and it sold well. At the age of twenty-four, he found himself being hailed as a spokesman for the new postwar generation of young people who were determined to be amused.

Fitzgerald was rather amused by his new position as "the laureate of the Jazz Age." He once described himself as a boy from Minnesota who knew less of New York than any young reporter and less about the city's high society than any young man dancing at the Ritz Hotel.

However, Scott and Zelda plunged enthusiastically into having a good time. With good looks, wit, and charm—and money—they became involved in a continuous round of theatergoing, parties, and drinking. Zelda danced on tabletops to the cheers of Scott's Princeton friends. They went to gala gatherings with Scott riding on the hood of a taxi while Zelda perched on the roof. Once they were thrown out of the hotel where they were living because of their noisy carryings-on.

Somehow, in between the parties and their heavy drinking, Scott found time to write short stories that he sold to popular magazines. Despite Scott's being well paid for the stories, the Fitzgeralds' wild life-style left them short of cash often—a problem that was to persist throughout his life. In 1920, for instance, he published sixteen short stories, for which he earned about twenty thousand dollars, a large amount of money for those days; but by December he was overdrawn at his bank. His and Zelda's expensive habits forced him to borrow money from his literary agent as advances against stories he had not yet written.

The couple's only child, Frances Scott Key Fitzgerald, was born in 1921 in St. Paul. The Fitzgeralds had gone there to visit his parents and to revise his second novel, *The Beautiful and the Damned.* It was published in 1922. The story of a young and glamorous pair who end up desperate and degraded, to some it seemed like a self-portrait of Scott and Zelda, but he insisted it was not.

Short of money as usual, Fitzgerald thought he could make a lot with a hit play. He wrote a comedy called *The Vegetable, or from President to Postman.* It opened in Atlantic City in 1923 and closed there, a complete failure. Disappointed, the Fitzgeralds decided they could live "on practically nothing a year" in France.

They became part of the American scene in Paris. Among their friends were Ernest Hemingway, then a

F. Scott Fitzgerald at the height of his fame. *Culver Pictures, Inc.*

beginning writer; Gertrude Stein in her salon; Sylvia Beach in her famous bookstore Shakespeare & Company; and Gerald and Sara Murphy, who were well known socially. On the surface, the Fitzgeralds were living very stylishly. But their friends could see that they were erratic—drinking too much, fighting, and often acting peculiarly.

In between parties and pranks, Fitzgerald settled down to serious work and completed *The Great Gatsby*. It was published in 1925 to excellent reviews but disappointing sales. Some critics now call it the best of Fitzgerald's novels. As he himself described it, "the whole idea of Gatsby is the unfairness of a young man not being able to marry a girl with money."

After a brief trip to Hollywood to make money writing for the movies, Fitzgerald and his wife returned to Paris in 1928. Zelda began to write and sell stories that appeared sometimes under her name, sometimes under Scott's name or both of their names. Restless and obviously unhappy, she started taking intense instruction in ballet dancing.

But Scott and Zelda and their marriage were beginning to disintegrate. He was drunk frequently and she behaved so oddly that some of her friends thought she must be mentally ill.

The golden couple who had thrived in a giddy era came into hard times. The world had changed from the optimistic prosperity of the 1920s to the Great Depression of the 1930s, when many people in the United States were jobless, hungry, homeless. It seemed to many that the charming, party-loving Fitzgeralds were out of place.

In 1930, Zelda entered a private sanitorium to be treated for a nervous breakdown. For the rest of her life she remained under medical care, in and out of institutions in both Europe and the United States. In 1931, the Fitzgeralds returned to America. He lived near Baltimore so that he could be close to a hospital where she spent most of her time.

Despite being confined there, Zelda was able to continue her efforts at writing and painting. Her novel, *Save Me a Waltz*, was published in 1932. In it, a thinly disguised Zelda, named Alabama Beggs, marries a young artist who is an army lieutenant stationed in the South during the First World War, a character obviously based on Scott. Later, an exhibit of Zelda's paintings opened in New York City.

Scott's drinking problem had become acute, his debts were increasing, and he was deeply worried about Zelda, but in 1934 he managed to finish another novel, *Tender Is the Night*. It is the story of the decline of a young American psychiatrist whose life and career are ru-

The Fitzgeralds with their daughter Scottie, photographed in the 1930s as they arrived in the United States from Europe. *The Bettmann Archive.*

ined by his marriage to a young, beautiful, wealthy patient. It was his favorite novel, with obvious overtones from his own life and those of other Americans he had known in France.

No matter that *Tender Is the Night* received generally favorable reviews; it did not sell very well. Appearing during the depth of the Great Depression, its focus on the problems of the rich put off many people. Today, though, it is required reading in many college literature courses.

Discouraged and in debt as usual, Fitzgerald returned to writing routine short stories merely to earn money. "The history of my life is the history of an overwhelming urge to write and a combination of circumstances bent on keeping me from it," he once noted. But many of those circumstances, particularly his heavy drinking and his inability to handle money, were at least partly under his own control.

In 1937, at the age of forty, Fitzgerald decided to give up serious writing and concentrate on making money by writing movie scripts in Hollywood. Even though the pay was good—more than a thousand dollars a week—the work was discouraging. Frequently his scripts were rewritten, a normal procedure in the movie business, but galling to Fitzgerald.

His personal life changed somewhat when he met Sheilah Graham, a Hollywood columnist. They fell in love, and for a while Fitzgerald was happy. But he was unable to break his habit of heavy drinking, especially when his script writing did not go well or when he visited Zelda, still in a hospital back east.

In the autumn of 1939, Fitzgerald began to put together notes for another novel—his last. Sitting in his bathrobe in bed, he scribbled furiously with a pencil on yellow sheets, telling the story of the head of a movie studio, Monroe Stahr, who meets an English woman, Kathleen Moore, and falls in love. This relationship was obviously derived in part from his own connection with Sheilah Graham. His secretary typed the pages he wrote, and he went over them carefully, revising, rewriting, and editing the book he called *The Last Tycoon*.

But he did not finish *The Last Tycoon*. On December 21, 1940, he died after a heart attack, at the age of only forty-four. Zelda lived on, still in and out of sanitoriums, for another eight years. In time to come, after a great rebirth of interest in Fitzgerald's writing, not only would all of his work be reprinted, but many books about Scott and Zelda would restore their fame as leading figures of the 1920s Jazz Age.

Robert Frost

1874–1963   The most admired American poet of the twentieth
century

There had been a blizzard the day before, but the sun shone brightly over the
nation's Capitol on January 20, 1961.
Robert Frost, nearing his eighty-seventh
birthday, sat waiting to read the poem
he had composed especially for President John F. Kennedy's inauguration.
Until then, no poet had ever been asked
to take part in any similar ceremony.

Millions of people watching via television saw Frost step forward at the right
moment, and they never forgot what
happened next: A sudden gust of wind
ruffled the old poet's white hair, also dis-
arranging the pages of verse he had just
placed on the stand in front of him. He
tried to start reading, but could not.
Blinded by the glare of bright sunlight
on the snowy scene he faced, he seemed
to dissolve in confusion. The new vice

president hastily moved to his side to try
to help him.

All at once, Frost squared his shoul-
ders. In a wonderfully strong, clear
voice, he began to recite an earlier patriotic poem of his, "The Gift Outright."
As newspapers from coast to coast
would put it, he had heroically turned a
personal disaster into a triumph.

As for Frost himself, he grumbled
that if he had not kept revising his inau-
gural verses up to the very last minute
he probably could have said them without needing his manuscript. For he still
prided himself on his memory. Also, he
did such an amount of what he called
"barding around," speaking his verses to
all sorts of audiences, that sometimes he
wondered whether he hadn't ended up
more of an actor than a poet.

Indeed a few critics in the literary establishment went even further, claiming that throughout his career he had merely been playing the part of a lovably humorous New England farmer-poet. Nevertheless, most authorities agreed that a good many of his shorter poems—including such popular favorites as "Birches," "Mending Wall," and "The Road Not Taken"—were works of genius. According to these experts, Frost's seemingly simple verse actually displayed, beneath its surface simplicity, a great mastery in the use of language unsuspected by readers unaware of such subtle nuances.

In one respect, though, Frost's severest critics were on unquestionably sound ground. Despite the poet's rock-ribbed New England image, he really was a native Californian. Born in San Francisco, on March 26, 1874, he spent the first eleven years of his life there. No doubt because he did not have a very happy childhood, he rarely referred to this period after he became famous.

It appears that his father's inability to conquer a streak of wildness caused many family problems. William Prescott Frost, Jr., named after his own solidly respectable Massachusetts father, had tried to run away during the Civil War—to join the *Confederate* army. Then, after his graduation from Harvard, he had started west in search of adventure.

On his way, he stopped off to earn some money by teaching at a small college in Pennsylvania. There he was enchanted by Isabelle Moodie, one of his fellow teachers. Born in Scotland, she had been orphaned during her girlhood and sent to live with American relatives. Gentle and high-minded, she could not have imagined what her life would be like after marrying her handsome suitor.

Soon after the couple arrived in San Francisco, William Frost began working as a reporter for a local newspaper. But during the next decade he developed an increasingly serious drinking problem that undermined his health. Despite showing unmistakable symptoms of the dreaded disease tuberculosis, one day in the spring of 1885 he rashly went swimming in icy water for more than an hour—and he died only a few weeks later, at the age of thirty-four.

His son Rob was a few months past his eleventh birthday then. Rob had been so protectively guarded by his mother that he did not even attend school: When he had complained of a stomach-ache the morning after his first day at kindergarten, she had decided that serving as his teacher herself would be the safest course. As a result, he had grown very accustomed to having his own way.

But everything changed for Rob and his similarly protected younger sister,

Jeanie, following their father's death. Their mother, left practically penniless, bundled them aboard an eastbound train. A long, tiring journey brought them at last to the large gray frame home of their elderly grandparents in the Massachusetts town of Lawrence. They were welcomed without much warmth, though, and were expected to obey a long list of strict rules.

After just a few weeks, Rob's mother felt that staying in such a gloomy place was impossible. Not far north of Lawrence, right across the border between Massachusetts and New Hampshire, she found a job teaching at a one-room school in the village of Salem. She also found a farmwife willing to provide room and board for her and her children quite inexpensively. Even so, her pay could hardly support them.

Fortunately, it turned out that the grandparents meant well despite their strictness, and they regularly contributed helpful sums of money. Rob did his part, too, earning whatever he could at part-time jobs like berry picking or as an errand boy for a cloth-making factory. Yet he also spent many hours in his mother's classroom and, at the age of fourteen, he entered Lawrence High School.

Rob blossomed forth there as an exceptional student who got high marks in every subject, from Latin to science.

Also, in his sophomore English class he discovered a book called *The Golden Treasury*, by Francis T. Palgrave—and this collection of the best poetry in the English language inspired him to start writing poetry himself.

Walking home from school one March afternoon, as he later told an interviewer, he "began to make" his very first poem. "It burned right up, just burned right up," he said, and the hours he spent going over and over what had "burned up" inside his head were more exciting than anything else he had ever experienced.

Clearly, that first poem, "La Noche Triste," or "The Sad Night," had been influenced by his recent reading about Spain's conquest of Mexico: Its subject was the death of the native ruler Montezuma. In telling this story, Rob used some trite phrases like "brightest fame" and "faithful steed," but he also displayed an impressive sense of poetic rhythm. "La Noche Triste" was printed in the Lawrence High School *Bulletin* in April of 1890, shortly after Rob turned sixteen.

By the beginning of his senior year, Rob had become the *Bulletin*'s editor. As he was the top student in his class, it seemed all but certain that he would be the valedictorian when graduation day arrived. That autumn, though, a newcomer named Elinor Miriam White began challenging his right to the title—and he did not mind the competition a bit because he and Elinor liked each other immediately.

Within a few months, they had fallen deeply in love. While school authorities were deciding to proclaim these two outstanding students co-valedictorians, Rob and Elinor came to a decision of their own. Soon after they both delivered their graduation speeches, they held a private ceremony at which they exchanged plain gold rings. But three more years would elapse before they actually got married, and for Rob these were extremely troubled years.

As his good marks at high school had won him some money for college expenses, and his grandfather was willing to provide further financial help, Rob enrolled at Dartmouth in upper New Hampshire. However, he dropped out after just one semester. By then, he would wryly explain long afterward, he was "getting past the point where I could show any interest in any task that was not self-imposed."

Returning to the Salem area, Rob flitted from one boring job to another, hoping that Elinor would soon give up her quest for a college education at St. Lawrence University in upstate New York. The one positive aspect of this period was that he completed several poems much better than anything he had

yet composed—and he boldly sent one of them to a New York magazine called the *Independent*, known for encouraging new poets.

When the *Independent* accepted "My Butterfly," Rob felt so elated at this first recognition of his talent, even though he received only fifteen dollars for it, that he impulsively paid a local printer practically every penny he possessed. A few days later he picked up two copies, one for Elinor and the other for himself, of a small book containing "My Butterfly" as well as three other poems. Then, without giving Elinor any advance warning, he boarded a train and appeared late the following evening at her dormitory. Holding out her copy of the book, he demanded, almost fiercely, that she quit school and marry him right away.

Her refusal triggered a reckless several months. After tearing up his own copy of the book, Rob took a series of trains to the most horrible area he could think of—the part of Virginia known as the Dismal Swamp. As if he hoped to drown there, thereby making Elinor terribly sorry for her unkindness, he began to wander alone on foot. But soon he met some drunken duck hunters, who made him laugh so much that he at least temporarily forgot his anguish.

Not long afterward, Elinor did relent. On December 10, 1895, when he was twenty-one, she finally became his wife.

In those days, most women devoted themselves entirely to family duties after they got married; Frost knew that he was expected, from then on, to support Elinor and any children they might have. Although he had never earned more than very minor sums of money, the prospect ahead still seemed golden to him.

Even so, it was only after several more years of floundering—and another brief college experience, this time at Harvard—that he thought of a way to keep on writing poetry, and at the same time provide a home for his family.

With money advanced by his grandfather, in the summer of 1900 the Frosts bought a small poultry farm near the village of Derry, New Hampshire. By then, their first son had tragically died of cholera, but they had a healthy two-year-old daughter, and four more children would be born during the nine years they lived there.

While his wife spent long hours caring for all of them, Frost devoted just a limited amount of time to farming chores and slept much of the day. Then, after the rest of the family went to bed, he did his real work, sitting up at the kitchen table and writing by the light of a kerosene lantern. Many of the poems he wrote then would, in the years ahead, be cherished by millions of readers.

One of the best-loved of these early works was "The Pasture," starting:

I'm going out to clean the pasture spring;
I'll only stop to rake the leaves away
(And wait to watch the water clear, I
    may):
I sha'n't be gone long.—You come too.

While Frost was living on the Derry chicken farm, however, he could hardly have been less famous. Indeed, he had almost no dealings with outsiders. Yet his own family gave him much joy, and also sorrow. During this period the death of his mother sent him into a deep depression, from which he only slowly recovered. Then he was intensely upset by the collapse of his sister, Jeanie, who had to be confined to a mental hospital for the rest of her life. His grandfather died, too, leaving Frost a small annual income.

By 1909 Frost felt a compelling need for a change of scene. He tried teaching school in nearby Derry, and he did so well at it that he was offered a post at New Hampshire's teacher-training academy in the town of Plymouth. There he attracted much favorable notice by giving his classes an air of cheerful informality, quite different from the usual stodgy educational atmosphere. But he yearned for a far wider eminence; in his own words, there were times when even he himself could hardly believe "the astonishing magnitude of my ambition."

In 1912 Frost was thirty-eight years old and practically nobody knew that he had written dozens of exceptionally fine poems. To expand his own horizons, while also seeking the recognition he felt he deserved, that autumn he sailed across the Atlantic Ocean with his family. His destination was England, "the land of *The Golden Treasury,*" where it seemed to him that poets were held in a much higher regard than in his own country.

By then Frost had acquired the accustomed-to-being-out-in-all-sorts-of-weather look of a sturdy Yankee farmer, with remarkably deep blue eyes. Soon after settling his family in a cottage about an hour's train ride from London, he dug a thick parcel from the bottom of his trunk and carried it to the city office of one of England's leading book publishers.

No doubt Frost's disarmingly American appearance and manner helped him past the reception desk there. Still, it was only after the manuscript he left in London had been carefully read by a series of experts that he received doubly exciting news: *Two* books of his poems would shortly appear in print.

The first volume, *A Boy's Will*, was published in 1913, and *North of Boston* came out the following year. Together, they set Frost firmly on the path to fame, for they were highly praised by several influential reviewers.

What's more, somehow Frost knew exactly how to insure that his work was widely noticed. By turning up at a party

celebrating the opening of a large new bookshop in London, he met—and charmed—many of the leading figures in England's literary establishment. By encouraging his new friends to write about him, he saw to it that word of his overseas success spread in the United States.

So when the Frosts sailed home early in 1915, shortly after the outbreak of the First World War, the way was already well paved for a triumphant future. American editions of both of his books soon appeared in print, and received immensely favorable reviews. One prominent critic called his poems "masterpieces of deep and mysterious tenderness," while another compared him with two of the English language's greatest poets, William Wordsworth and Walt Whitman.

At the same time, Frost's life as a celebrity commenced. He was showered with invitations to join all sorts of literary groups. But even highly regarded poets did not earn much money; it was unheard of for books of poetry to become best-sellers, so the question of how he could support his family again arose.

An answer immensely satisfying to Frost soon presented itself. Despite his lack of any college diploma, he was asked to read from his works at a Harvard conference and also to teach a few courses at Amherst in western Massa-

Robert Frost with his wife and children at their home in New Hampshire in 1915. *Lawson Library, Plymouth State College, Plymouth, New Hampshire.*

chusetts. Thus started his secondary career as a lecturer and professor, which made it financially possible for him to continue writing.

With an irrepressibly playful spirit, Frost once described his teaching as a process of "seeking kindred souls—to comfort them, and to comfort me." Yet he had serious topics to talk of, such as the overwhelming importance he assigned to poetry. When an interviewer suggested that writing poems was his way of escaping from life's problems, Frost sharply replied, "No, it's a way of taking life by the throat."

Still, none of his pithy sayings as a public figure were nearly as important as his continuing output as a poet. During the next several decades, he kept striving to express deep thoughts and emotions in the rhythms of ordinary speech—"to make music out of the sound of sense," as he liked to put it himself. Every few years a new book of his poetry was published, further enhancing his reputation.

Proof that he had acquired an extraordinary stature was provided by the sponsors of this country's most prestigious literary awards. To win the Pulitzer Prize was the goal of many notable authors—but Robert Frost won the Pulitzer *four* times: in 1923 for his book of poetry entitled *New Hampshire;* in 1930 for his *Collected Poems;* in 1936 for *A Further Range;* and in 1942 for *A Witness Tree.* Also, he eventually accumulated a grand total of forty-four honorary degrees, from universities on both sides of Atlantic.

Even though Frost himself thrived on public acclaim, however, his eminence was hard on his family. Frequent moves back and forth between campus towns and a succession of New England farms seemed to cause increasing stress, and then the 1930s brought one tragedy after another.

In 1934 the Frosts' beloved youngest daughter died from a complication following the birth of her first child. A few days later, the grief-stricken Elinor Frost suffered the first in a series of heart attacks, from which she never quite recovered, and she died in 1938.

Robert Frost was sixty-four years old when he lost his wife, and her death plunged him into such deep gloom that his closest friends feared he might commit suicide. How much he had depended on Elinor was something nobody else could really know, but those who knew him well thought that his intense reaction to her death was at least partly caused by his sharp pangs of guilt about putting his own career above her desire for a more private sort of life.

At any rate, still another blow fell just two years later when Frost's only remaining son did commit suicide. It was mainly because the poet now had a dependable secretary—Kathleen Morrison, the wife of a Harvard professor—that he was able to weather this new crisis without giving much outer evidence of his profound inner turmoil.

As far as the world at large was concerned, Robert Frost in his old age combined wisdom and wit in a wonderfully American way. However, some literary figures were so irritated by his staunchly conservative political opinions that they spread rumors during World War II accusing him of sympathy with the Nazi enemies of the United States. Yet the general public paid no heed at all to any such charges.

Indeed, in 1961 Frost played his symbolic role at the inauguration of the liberal President Kennedy without any regard to politics. And the tremendous outpouring of affection he stirred then marked the summit of his long career.

In 1962 his last book, *In the Clearing,*

Robert Frost reciting his poem "The Gift Outright" at the inauguration of President John F. Kennedy in 1961. *George Silk, Life Magazine,* © *Time Inc.*

was published. Late that autumn, after a faltering public appearance, he was persuaded to enter a Boston hospital. While doctors were conducting a lengthy series of tests, he died there on January 29, 1963, two months before he would have marked his eighty-ninth birthday.

The tributes to Frost that followed his death could not have been more filled with praise. However, a few years later the literary world was stunned by a biography claiming that, privately, he had really been a hateful monster, motivated mainly by selfishness and spite. Gradually, though, a more balanced picture has come to prevail: of a great poet who did, after all, possess his share of human failings.

Ernest Hemingway

1899–1961   Grace under pressure

At the age of eighteen, Ernest Hemingway began his career as a professional writer by working as a reporter on the *Kansas City Star,* one of the leading newspapers in the United States in the early 1900s. Despite his youth and inexperience, he got his job through influence—his uncle knew the editor. But Hemingway was bright and industrious, and quickly learned how to gather facts and put them together in a readable way.

His editors drummed into him a series of basic writing rules. Use short sentences. Use short paragraphs. Use vigorous English. Be positive, not negative. Avoid the use of adjectives. Hemingway followed those rules so well that later, when he became a famous author, his style was a model for young writers all over America.

"Those were the best rules I ever learned for the business of writing," he once said. "I've never forgotten them. No man with any talent, who feels and writes truly about the thing he is trying to say, can fail to write well if he abides by them."

Hemingway went to Kansas City from the Chicago suburb of Oak Park, Illinois, where he had been born on July 21, 1899. He was the second child in a family of six children, with four sisters and a younger brother. They were raised in a prosperous, middle-class community.

His mother, Grace Hall Hemingway, a former music teacher, gave Ernest a cello when he was a boy and made sure he learned how to play it. His father, Dr. Clarence Edmonds Hemingway, was a physician more devoted to hunting and

Ernest Hemingway with his four sisters, his baby brother, and his mother *(left)* in 1916. *John F. Kennedy Library, Boston, Massachusetts.*

fishing than to his medical practice. Ernest adored his father and, as he said later, hated his mother because she tried to make all the men in her family obey her rules.

He remembered growing up as an obedient child, working hard in school and getting good grades. Well-liked by the other boys, he had many nicknames, among them Hem, Hemmie, Nesto, and Hemingstein, which he liked best of all. Later, when he became a celebrated writer, he was widely known as Papa, after what his firstborn son called him.

In high school, Ernest was an all-around student. Not only did he main-

tain a ninety average in his classes, but he played the cello in the school orchestra, sang in the glee club, managed the track team, captained the water polo squad, and played second-string guard on the varsity football team. He also wrote for the literary magazine and was one of the editors of the school newspaper.

Above all, though, he waited for the summer. Every year, the Hemingway family went to their vacation cottage on a lake in northern Michigan, where Ernest could go around barefoot. He called himself Huck Hemingway, after one of his favorite characters in fiction, Mark Twain's Huckleberry Finn.

His father gave him a fishing rod when he was only three years old and a shotgun when he was ten. The doctor taught him to shoot, to make fires and cook game in the woods, to make woodland shelters out of boughs, to tie flies for fishing, and to make bullets in a mold—along with all sorts of other lessons about the proper way to handle guns and fishing tackle. For the rest of his life, Hemingway loved to hunt and fish.

As a writer he made constant use of his familiarity with these and similar activities: He wrote about game hunting in Africa, deep-sea fishing in the Caribbean, bullfighting in Spain, and war in Europe. In his own life as well as in his literary efforts, he relished violence and all sorts of pursuits that he considered manly, including hard drinking.

To Hemingway, being a writer meant observing life in the raw—men displaying courage under extreme conditions—and recording what he saw faithfully.

His first opportunity to observe the reality of bravery and death came when the United States entered World War I in 1917. Just graduated from high school, Ernest faced three alternatives: the army, college, or work. He rejected college. His father thought he was too young at eighteen to be a soldier. And so they agreed that he would get a job, which he did in Kansas City.

During the period of his work as a cub reporter on the *Star,* Hemingway again thought of enlisting in the army, but he was turned down because of defective vision in his left eye. Still seeking to serve somehow, he volunteered to become an ambulance driver for the Red Cross in Italy—and proudly wore the uniform of a second lieutenant, with red crosses on his collar and cap to distinguish him from an army officer.

On July 18, 1918, while passing out chocolate candy to frontline troops, Hemingway was severely wounded by an enemy mortar shell. After twenty-eight metal fragments were removed from his leg, he spent months in a hospital recovering. He received a high Italian award, the Silver Medal for Military Bravery, during this period. He also fell in love with a nurse who later became the model for one of his memorable characters, Catherine Barkley in *A Farewell to Arms.*

Returning home at the age of nineteen, Hemingway found another newspaper job through the influence of a friend. He wrote feature stories for the *Toronto Star,* a major daily in Canada. He also began to experiment with short stories and poems. A new friend, Sherwood Anderson, already an established author, suggested a trip back across the ocean to Paris, then the major center of literary life for young American writers.

When Hemingway expressed a desire to go to Europe, his editors had no hesitation in sending him abroad as a foreign correspondent. He and his new wife, Hadley Richardson, arrived in France in 1922. Not yet twenty-three years old, he was an established professional newspaperman at an age when many aspiring writers were just beginning their careers.

Even though Hemingway wrote vivid news stories from Italy, Germany, Afghanistan, Turkey, and Greece, he became more and more disenchanted with daily journalism. "You have to learn to forget every day what happened the day before," he once explained. "Newspaper work is valuable up to the point that it forcibly begins to destroy your memory. A writer must leave it before that time."

With a letter of introduction from Anderson, Hemingway visited Gertrude Stein, a well-known American writer then forty-eight years old, old enough to be his mother. In those early writing years, Stein was the greatest influence on him. Writing, he once said, had been easy before he met her. But she criticized his work on a technical level, suggesting better ways of arranging his words in sentences to gain the desired impact. He was a good pupil, learning quickly.

By the age of twenty-five, Hemingway had completed his apprenticeship as a writer. His first short stories appeared in *The Little Review* in Paris in 1923. In that same year, a small volume of his stories and poems came out, also in Europe. His second book, *In Our Time,* containing eighteen short stories, appeared in 1924. A year later it was published in the United States, his first book to reach an American audience.

After several trips back to the United States and Canada, Hemingway, his wife, and their new son, John, took up residence once more in Paris. They became part of the American literary set there, numbering among their friends the novelist Scott Fitzgerald and his wife, Zelda, as well as the poet Ezra Pound and many other art-minded expatriates.

A good-looking man of sturdy build, six feet tall, Hemingway made a vivid impression on the writing colony. He drank heavily, talked well, argued often, and dramatized his adventures in war and peace. Zelda Fitzgerald and some others considered him "phony as a rubber duck" because of his exaggerations, but her husband Scott called him "the one true genius" of their literary generation.

In those early years, Hemingway made several trips to Spain, falling in love with the country and the nation's favorite sport of bullfighting. He began his first novel, *The Sun Also Rises,* in 1926. On the surface it is a simple story of a wounded war veteran, Jake Barnes, who travels to Spain to see a bullfight, as Hemingway himself often did.

But in *The Sun Also Rises,* as in all his other books, his prose is deceptively uncomplicated. Hemingway felt that if a writer's work was simple and honest, readers would find the deeper meaning in it. "I always try to write on the principle of the iceberg," he once told an interviewer. "There is seven-eighths of it under water for every part that shows."

Hemingway asked the more experienced Scott Fitzgerald to read the manuscript of his first novel, and Fitzgerald suggested that it be shortened by eliminating some of the background in the story. Hemingway responded by cutting out the first fifteen pages. In a letter thanking Fitzgerald, he coined a memorable phrase that would later be associated with Hemingway himself: He defined courage as "grace under pressure," citing as an example the bravery of a matador in the face of a bull that might kill him.

Book reviewers praised *The Sun Also Rises* and it sold well. Magazine editors called on Hemingway for short stories, and he wrote many. Among them were some of his famous ones, "The Killers" and "Fifty Grand." These also appeared in a collection of short stories, *Men Without Women*, published in 1927.

In that year Hemingway and his wife were divorced. Shortly after, he married a magazine editor named Pauline Pfeiffer. In 1928, they returned to the United States, settling in Key West, Florida, where he could go deep-sea fishing as well as write. He began *A Farewell to Arms*, drawing on his experiences as an ambulance driver on the Italian front during the world war.

A hard-working writer, Hemingway usually began work at six in the morning, continuing until noon. Then he had his afternoons and evenings free for drinking and meeting his friends, usually at a nearby bar. He once told a student audience that it took him eight

months to complete the first draft of *A Farewell to Arms* and another five months to rewrite it—a total of thirteen months.

One of the few romantic Hemingway novels, it is the tragic story of a wounded American officer who falls in love with a nurse and flees with her to Switzerland, where she dies in childbirth. Both the critics and the public received *A Farewell to Arms* warmly when it was published in 1929. It sold very well, making large amounts of money for Hemingway, then thirty years old.

He and his wife bought a house in Key West, which became their home. They had two sons, Gregory and Patrick. Just as his father had done before him, Hemingway taught his three sons to hunt and fish.

After assembling new short stories for another collection, Hemingway worked hard at a novel about a bullfighter. Published in 1932, *Death in the Afternoon* became a popular success. Some critics have said that it demonstrated Hemingway's preoccupation with death following the suicide of his father, who had shot himself in the head in 1928 at the age of fifty-seven.

Financially secure, Hemingway was now able to indulge himself in something he had always longed to do: big-game hunting in Africa. In a nonfiction book, *Green Hills of Africa,* written as if

Ernest Hemingway fishing in Sun Valley, Idaho, in 1939. *UPI/Bettmann Newsphotos.*

it were a novel, he told how he had hunted and killed animals such as the kongoni, kudu, and oryx, as well as buffalo, lion, and rhinoceros. This book was published in 1935.

That same year, he bought a large fishing boat named the *Pilar.* He used it for relaxation from writing, fishing for marlin and other big-game fish in the Atlantic Ocean and the Caribbean Sea.

Hemingway used Key West as the background for *To Have and Have Not,* his only full-length novel set in America. Published in 1937, it is the story of a Florida boatman who takes to smuggling during the Depression in an effort to survive.

Next, Hemingway returned to an African setting for two memorable short stories, which are still widely read, "The Snows of Kilamanjaro" and "The Short Happy Life of Francis Macomber."

The outbreak of the Spanish Civil War in 1936 was a call to action for Hemingway. As a strong anti-Fascist, he went to Madrid to support the Loyalist government of the country he loved. He wrote about the war as a newspaper correspondent, helped to prepare a propaganda film, *The Spanish Earth,* and returned home to raise money for ambulances for the Loyalists.

His Spanish Civil War period produced two literary results. One was *The Fifth Column,* a melodrama about spies in Madrid, then under attack by the Fascist forces. The other was perhaps his most popular novel, *For Whom the Bell Tolls,* published in 1940. Its title came from a haunting meditation by the English poet John Donne, who had written back in the 1600s, "any man's death diminishes me, because I am involved in mankind; and therefore never send to know for whom the bell tolls; it tolls for thee."

Made into a very successful movie, *For Whom the Bell Tolls* is both a love story and a political tract. Its hero, a Montana teacher fighting for the Loyalists in Spain, follows orders even though he realizes that his military mission is bound to fail, and he dies while protecting the escape of the Spanish girl he loves.

For Hemingway himself, love and war were intertwined as they were in his novels. He fell in love with Martha Gellhorn, a journalist also covering the war in Spain. After a divorce from his second wife, he and Gellhorn were married in 1940.

With the outbreak of World War II, Hemingway went to London, then under air attack by the Germans, to report on the activities of the British Royal Air Force. Under the pressures of bombing, fires, and death, the American correspondents formed a tightly knit group, covering stories and going to parties together. Hemingway met Mary Welsh, a correspondent for *Time-Life* magazines, in London and, even though both of them were already married, told her, "I want to marry you."

After the D-Day invasion of France, Hemingway accompanied the first French forces to enter Paris. "I liberated the Ritz Hotel," he liked to say later, using it as a center for his drinking, parties, and receiving visits from soldiers and a variety of celebrities. Later, he attached himself to an American infantry regiment as it pursued enemy forces across France, Belgium, and Germany.

When the war ended, another divorce led to the marriage of Hemingway and Mary Welsh in 1946. It was his fourth and last marriage. The couple established their home in Cuba, just outside the city of Havana. With ample money from his books and their sales to Hollywood, the Hemingways regularly entertained other writers, movie stars, and well-known figures from other walks of life.

By this time, Hemingway had established himself in the public eye as "a man's man"—a hunter, fisherman, heavy drinker, amateur boxer, and war correspondent. He looked the part, burly with a grizzled gray beard, and talked it as well. Noted for being moody, he was frequently rude, even to his friends, but treated working people considerately. He had many admirers, but others thought his macho manner masked a man who really doubted his own strength.

In his first postwar novel, *Across the River and into the Trees,* Hemingway returned to his favorite themes of love and war. In this book, an infantry colonel, obviously modeled after an officer he had known in Europe, recalls his activities in two world wars. In Venice, he falls in love with a young girl, who listens with sympathy to the colonel's bitter reminiscences before he dies of a heart attack.

It was, the critics agreed, probably the worst of Hemingway's novels. A parody of it entitled "Across the Street and into the Grill" amused many readers of the *New Yorker* magazine, and the same influential weekly printed a series of articles about Hemingway himself, making fun of him and his life-style. When these pieces were printed as a book, good-humoredly he said that it was one of the three best books he had read that year.

But Hemingway surprised his critics in 1952 by producing a new small masterpiece, *The Old Man and the Sea.* On the surface it is the simple tale of a fisherman who catches the greatest marlin of his life, only to have it eaten to a skeleton by sharks before he can bring it into port. Yet it is also about a man who carries on against great odds with courage and endurance, the two qualities that Hemingway most admired.

The reaction to *The Old Man and the Sea* was all that its author could have wished. "Superbly told," one reviewer proclaimed, and several called it the best story Hemingway had ever written. It was not only a best-seller for many weeks, but in 1953 it also won the Pulitzer Prize for the best novel of the year.

The following year Hemingway received the Nobel Prize in literature. This prestigious award was based on "his powerful, style-forming mastery of the art of modern narration, as most recently evidenced in *The Old Man and the Sea.*" In addition, at the ceremony presenting the honor, he was praised not only for his "manly love of danger and adventure," but also for his "admiration for every individual who fights the good fight in a world of reality overshadowed by violence and death."

Hemingway was proud of the prize, but it came at a time when his health was deteriorating. Too ill to attend the ceremony in Stockholm, he wrote a short speech that was delivered on his behalf by the American ambassador there.

In that year of 1954, Hemingway, at fifty-five, was falling apart both mentally and physically. Early in the year, he had been severely injured in two airplane crashes during a hunting trip to Africa. Besides the concussion and the severe bruising resulting from these accidents, he also suffered from liver and kidney problems, high blood pressure, and partial deafness—and he began to complain that he was being followed by FBI agents. He talked frequently of suicide as a means of solving his problems.

Hemingway tried to write, but the creative spark was gone. He did summon enough energy to put together a series of sketches on his life in Paris back in the early 1920s, called *A Moveable Feast;* it would be published in 1964, after his death. Upon completing this project he traveled to Spain once more to attend bullfights, but could not really enjoy them because of persistent health problems.

Hemingway and his wife returned to Ketchum, Idaho, where they had bought a hideaway surrounded by the wild game that he loved. However, his health deteriorated so badly that his wife convinced him to enter the Mayo Clinic in Minnesota for treatment. He was given electric-shock therapy to relieve his mental depression, and for a short time he seemed better.

But he had lost the capacity to concentrate and write—and with that, the will to live. Back in Ketchum, on the

morning of Sunday, July 2, 1961, a few
days before his sixty-second birthday,
Hemingway awoke very early. He
walked downstairs and found the keys to
his gun cabinet where his wife had hidden them on a window ledge above the
kitchen sink. Opening the gun cabinet,
he took out a double-barreled shotgun
and loaded it. Then he shot himself in
the head, committing suicide just as his
father had done many years before.

Langston Hughes

1902–1967   The poet laureate of black America

When he was thirteen years old, Langston Hughes was elected poet of his graduating class in elementary school although he had never written any poems. It was an unusual selection because at that time, in 1915, he was one of only two black children in his class in Lincoln, Illinois.

It happened like this, he later wrote in his autobiography, "there was no one in the class who looked like a poet, or had ever written a poem. In America, most people think, of course, that all Negroes can sing and dance, and have a sense of rhythm. So my classmates, knowing that a poem had to have rhythm, elected me unanimously— thinking, no doubt, that I had some, being a Negro."

Langston went home and wrote a poem about his teachers and his school. When he read it at graduation, everybody applauded loudly. Even though he had never before thought of being a writer, that experience set him on the path toward becoming one. During the rest of his life he wrote an impressive number of poems, plays, short stories, children's books, newspaper columns, song lyrics, and histories—so many and so well that he was often referred to as "the poet laureate of the Negro people."

Unlike most other blacks of his era, who came from the South or the big cities of the East Coast, Hughes was a son of the Middle West. Like other blacks, he faced prejudice and discrimination, but there was less of it in the small cities where he grew up than in some other areas. He had been born in Joplin, Missouri—on February 1, 1902—and lived in Kansas, Illinois, and Ohio before he moved East.

Langston came from a broken home. His father, James Nathaniel Hughes, was bitter about the discrimination he had faced in the United States. Even though he had worked in a law office, he had been refused admission to law school because of his color. He was so angry that he moved to Mexico and became a rancher there.

That left Langston alone with his mother, Carrie Mercer Langston Hughes, a proud woman who refused to do menial work. A rare woman for her times, Carrie Hughes had studied at the University of Kansas and longed for a career on the stage. She traveled widely, just as her son did later, trying to find jobs that suited her.

As a result, Langston was raised largely by his grandmother, Mary Langston, in Lawrence, Kansas. She told him stories about her first husband, who had been one of the men who took part in John Brown's raid on Harper's Ferry just before the Civil War. Her second husband, Langston's grandfather, had been active in the Underground Railroad traveled by blacks in the South to escape slavery.

Langston's mother came on an occasional visit and took him to Kansas City,

where they both delighted in going to the theater. He found another escape in the public library. He loved the librarians, the big chairs, the long tables, and, above all, the books. Langston became a reader, devouring books of poetry, stories, books by black authors, and translations of French novels.

In 1914, Langston went to live in the Illinois town of Lincoln with his mother, who had remarried after divorcing his father. In his new home, he found a younger brother, Gwyn, the son of his new stepfather. He liked his new brother, ten years younger than he was, and called him Kit.

Langston's stepfather, Homer Clark, was a restaurant chef who wandered from job to job. In 1916, he began to work in a new restaurant in Cleveland. After Langston joined him and his mother there, he went to Central High School as one of the few blacks in an overwhelmingly white school.

Despite that, he met no hostility from either his fellow students or his teachers. He did well in his schoolwork and began to write for the school publications. He ran on the relay team that won a citywide championship. He became a lieutenant in the military training corps. He also edited the school yearbook, made the honor roll, was elected class poet, and became president of the Americanism Club in a sort of reverse discrimination—just because he was black.

This was how he explained it: At school, there was a frequent division between his Jewish and Christian classmates when it came to electing officers. "They would compromise on a Negro, feeling, I suppose, that a Negro was neither Jew nor Gentile!"

In 1919 the seventeen-year-old Langston received a surprise invitation from his father, whom he had not seen in ten years. He enjoyed visiting him in Mexico, and returned there the following year after graduating from high school. As his train crossed the Mississippi River, Langston began to think about blacks who had been sold down the river into slavery many years earlier. He thought about rivers in Africa, too—the Congo, the Nile, and the Niger.

Langston pulled an envelope out of his pocket and began to write in pencil. What resulted is "The Negro Speaks of Rivers," still one of his best-known poems:

I've known rivers:
I've known rivers ancient as the world and
    older than the flow of human blood
    in human veins.
My soul has grown deep like the rivers . . .

That summer in Mexico was the beginning of Hughes's career as a poet. He wrote many poems there because, as he said, "I was unhappy." His unhappiness stemmed from fights with his father, who wanted him to study mining engineering. But Langston was determined to be a writer.

He succeeded in that first year. He sent "The Negro Speaks of Rivers" to *The Crisis,* the official magazine of the National Association for the Advancement of Colored People, known as the NAACP. It was printed in June of 1921. He followed it with seven other poems, five prose sketches about life in Mexico, and a one-act play.

Hughes also found time to learn Spanish, ride a horse, attend bullfights, and teach English to Mexicans to earn money. After many arguments, he convinced his father to pay for a year of study at Columbia University in New York City.

In September of 1921, Hughes made his first trip to New York—and discovered Harlem, the capital of black America. Bored with his classes at Columbia, Hughes fell in love with Harlem in the 1920s, and later made it his home. Many of the era's best-known blacks lived there, and the possibility of encountering them thrilled him. He later wrote: "I was nineteen years old when I first came up out of the Lenox Avenue subway one bright September afternoon and looked around in the happy sunlight to see if I saw Duke Ellington on the corner of 135th Street, or Bessie Smith passing by, or Bojangles Bill Robinson in front of the Lincoln Theater, or maybe Paul Robeson or Bert Williams walking down the avenue."

Harlem was the inspiration for Hughes's new poems. In the year 1922, thirteen of his poems appeared in *The Crisis*. Probably the most famous is the one that begins:

I am a Negro
    Black as the night is black
    Black like the depths of my Africa.

After finishing his first year at Columbia, Hughes decided that he had had enough of college. But he had difficulty finding a job in New York. Remembering the smell of the sea on his trip from Mexico to New York, he decided to see the world by finding a job on a ship.

His first job was on a ship that never went to sea, though. Hughes became a mess boy—a waiter—on a rusty old freighter anchored in the Hudson River along with many other ships stored there. It was not a demanding job, so Hughes spent his time reading, talking and listening to the other sailors, traveling in the area, and writing more poems.

After almost a year at that job, Hughes decided it was time to get onto a moving ship. So in the spring of 1923 he signed on as a mess boy on a freighter bound for Africa. His first

sight of Africa touched him deeply: "My Africa," he wrote. "Motherland of the Negro peoples! And me a Negro! Africa. The real thing to be touched and seen, not merely read about."

One thing surprised him. The Africans he encountered looked at him—dressed like a westerner, speaking English, brown in color rather than black like them—and would not believe that he was a Negro. To them, he was an American. For Hughes it was ironic because in America he was treated as a Negro—and discriminated against because of his color.

Hughes made several trips across the Atlantic. On one of these voyages, when the ship arrived in the Dutch seaport of Rotterdam a piece of chicken ended his oceangoing life. As a mess boy, he served chicken to the ship's officers and, as usual, expected to eat some himself. But the cook refused to let the crew eat the leftovers. "So I quit and went to Paris," Hughes recalled later.

With seven dollars in his pocket, he arrived in Paris in February of 1924. Hughes found a low-paying job as a doorman at a nightclub, then another as a cook's helper in a club that featured black performers. He also made many friends, including a young woman named Anne Cousey.

But her parents objected to the penniless young man of twenty-two, who seemed to have a far-from-promising future. And he was not ready for a permanent relationship with a loving young woman. Her father insisted on her returning home, ending the romance. Hughes met many other attractive young women after that, and even said he loved some, but he never married.

Late in 1924, Hughes returned to the United States. He stopped first in Harlem, where he met a well-known black poet, Countee Cullen, and then went on to Washington D.C., where his mother now lived. Penniless, he got a job as a busboy in a hotel restaurant. But his real work was writing poems. He entered some of them in a literary competition in New York, which received over seven hundred entries.

On May 1, 1925, Hughes traveled up to New York to attend the ceremony at which the contest awards would be announced. He heard his name called as the third-prize winner, sharing it with Countee Cullen. Cullen won the second prize, too. But then Hughes once more heard his own name. He received the first prize (of forty dollars) for his poem "The Weary Blues."

Now well-known, at least in the literary circles of New York, Hughes became front-page news shortly after because a famous poet named Vachel Lindsay had dinner at the hotel where he worked. Hughes placed three of his poems next to Lindsay's plate. Lindsay was so impressed that he read the poems aloud at a public meeting later that evening, announcing that he had discovered "a busboy poet." The story and a picture of Hughes carrying a tray of dirty dishes was printed in newspapers all over America.

The year 1926 was a good one for Hughes. His first book, *The Weary Blues*, was published, his poems appeared in various magazines, and he achieved another ambition—getting a second chance at going to college. With a scholarship from a New York woman, he attended Lincoln University near Philadelphia. Even though he was twenty-four, much older than his fellow students, his classmates considered him "a regular guy." They called him Lank despite his shortness; he was only five feet four inches in height.

During his four years at Lincoln, Hughes did a lot more than just schoolwork. He wrote many poems, he frequently went to Harlem to visit other black writers, and he traveled around the country reading his poetry. Hughes recited his poems in a sort of singsong voice. Even so, he made a hit with his audiences, who received him and his work warmly.

His second collection of poems, *Fine Clothes to the Jew*, was published in 1926. Afterward, he apologized for the

Langston Hughes as the "busboy poet" at a Washington, D.C., hotel in 1925. *UPI/Bettmann Newsphotos.*

title, which some people found offensive; but few criticized the poems. He also wrote a novel, *Not Without Laughter,* about a boy growing up in the Midwest, and collaborated with Zora Neale Hurston on a Negro folk comedy, *Mule Bone.*

After graduation, Hughes—now twenty-eight years old—traveled widely. He visited Cuba and Haiti, made a nine-month poetry-reading tour across the United States, and joined a group of blacks making a movie in the Soviet Union. There, he wrote articles for Russian newspapers, as well as poems and short stories.

Back home, his short stories were collected in a book, *The Ways of the White Folks,* with settings ranging from Harlem to Paris, from Alabama to the Middle West of his boyhood. He also wrote a play, *Mulatto,* about conflict between a college-educated black son and his white father, which opened on Broadway in 1935. Even though it received unfavorable reviews, it ran for a year.

When Hughes's own father died, he returned to Mexico for a short time. While there he read *Don Quixote* in the original Spanish, then translated several Mexican stories into English. He also went to bullfights as often as he could.

From Mexico, Hughes went to Cleveland where his mother was then living.

Even though his income from his writing was small, he supported his ailing mother and paid college tuition fees for his stepbrother.

Hughes escaped by traveling again, as a war correspondent for the *Baltimore Afro-American,* covering the activities of black volunteers in the Spanish Civil War. As usual, he wrote poetry while performing other duties. Three of his best-known poems from Spain were "Air Raid: Barcelona," "Moonlight in Valencia," and "Madrid—1937."

Back in Harlem in 1938, Hughes turned to the stage again. He founded the Harlem Suitcase Theater, which presented his play *Don't You Want to Be Free?* In the following year, he moved to Los Angeles, where he founded another group, The New Negro Theater, which presented several of his short plays. Always a hard-working writer, he also put together another collection of poetry and worked on a scenario for a Hollywood movie.

In addition, when he was only thirty-eight years old he wrote an autobiography he called *The Big Sea.* It told, in episodic fashion, about his experiences with race prejudice, his loss of faith in religion, his hatred for his father, and his contacts with other black writers in Harlem. It ended with these words: "Literature is a big sea full of many fish. I let down my net and pulled."

The Big Sea came out in 1940, a year of transition for Hughes. He was sick with a variety of ailments and he was broke. Despite the volume of his work, his income for the year totaled only twelve hundred dollars. He also lost his faith in left-wing movements, describing himself as a radical at twenty who had become a conservative at forty.

When the United States entered World War II in 1941, Hughes threw himself into war work as a writer. He wrote war songs, radio scripts, and verse to help boost morale and end race discrimination at home. He also began to write a column for *The Chicago Defender,* the largest black newspaper in America.

In his column Hughes introduced a folk character, Jesse B. Semple, called Simple for short. Simple asked basic questions, and an unnamed character—Hughes himself, of course—answered them. The comic contrast between the uncomplicated questions and the complicated answers made Simple the most popular character that Hughes had ever created. He wrote the Simple columns for twenty-three years, to the delight of black audiences across America.

Hughes remained a busy man in those years. He lectured at colleges, traveled around the country reading his poems, wrote the lyrics for Kurt Weill's songs in a memorable Broadway musi-

cal, *Street Scene,* and also kept producing poetry. In the 1940s he wrote more poems than in any decade of his life. Among his books were *Shakespeare in Harlem, Jim Crow's Last Stand,* and *One-Way Ticket.*

During this period he received many honors. In 1943 he was awarded an honorary degree from his alma mater, Lincoln University, and he later received similar degrees from Howard University and Western Reserve University. In 1961, he was elected a member of the National Institute of Arts and Letters.

His friends marveled at Hughes's productivity in the 1950s and early 1960s—lecturing, traveling, and writing at the same time. He collected his Simple columns into five books, he wrote books for black children, he translated numerous works from Spanish into English, he produced anthologies of black writing, and he completed the second volume of his autobiography, *I Wonder As I Wander.*

One of his biographers summarized his almost half-century as a writer this way: playwright, novelist, song lyricist, journalist, essayist, editor, translator, lecturer, humorist, social activist, freedom fighter, dream keeper, integrationist, Pan-Africanist, world traveler, international voice for the oppressed, and, above all, poet. But near the end of his life, Hughes himself was uncertain of

Langston Hughes surrounded by young admirers in 1943. *United Press International.*

his accomplishments. One of his last poems indicated how discouraged he felt:

On the shoals of Nowhere
Wasted my song—
Yet taken by the sea wind
And blown along.

Hughes died in a hospital in New York on May 22, 1967, at the age of sixty-five.

Sinclair Lewis

1885–1951   The first American to win a Nobel Prize for literature

His parents named him Harry Sinclair Lewis, but he had many nicknames: Hal, Doodle, Mink, Minnie, Sink, Ginger, Bonfire, and Red. His family called him Harry, his wife Hal, and his friends Red. When he became an author, he dropped the Harry and became simply Sinclair Lewis.

A son of the Midwest, he grew up in Sauk Centre, Minnesota, where he had been born on February 7, 1885. He remembered his boyhood as lonely and unhappy. His father, Edwin John Lewis, was a hard-working doctor with a cold, methodical personality. His mother, Erma Kermott Lewis, a schoolteacher before her marriage, died when he was six years old.

His two brothers, Fred and Claude, were much older and quite different. Fred, who worked in a flour mill, moved away and played no role in his younger brother's life. Claude, on the other hand, became Harry's idol. A happy, good-looking, ambitious young man, Claude was everything that Harry was not. The young boy tagged along with Claude and his friends and became the butt of their jokes.

At home Harry's unhappy life was eased somewhat by his stepmother, Isabel Warner, who married his father a year after his mother's death. A kindly woman, active in many Sauk Centre clubs, she read to him and took him on trips. But he did not get along well with his father, who imposed his own sense of what was fit and not fit on his family.

In school Harry started out as a poor

student. As a sixth grader, he failed in music, drawing, and penmanship. When he entered high school, he ranked seventeenth in a class of eighteen. By his junior year, though, determined to go to a good college, he scored in the nineties in all his subjects except Latin and deportment. Outside the classroom, he read every book in sight—one summer he listed fifty books he had read.

Successful in his studies, he was a clown at school, always trying to win friends. He joined the literary society, played the lead in a class play, and took part in debates, but he did not enjoy the class meetings, which were usually held at night, as if they were social events. Although he admired several of the girls in school from a distance, he never had a real girlfriend.

Like the other boys in the community, Harry worked after school—sawing wood, mowing lawns, shoveling snow, setting up pins in a bowling alley, and as a night clerk in the local hotel. He also worked for the local newspaper, setting type and writing articles on local news—his first published writing.

Harry even wrote some poetry, sending it to *Harper's* magazine, which rejected it. He wrote another poem for a magazine called *The Youth's Companion,* and that, too was turned down. In 1902, when he traveled to Minneapolis to take the entrance examination for Yale, he began keeping a journal, a practice that he continued afterward.

"I am 17," he wrote as he prepared for college. "Tall, ugly, thin, red-haired but not, methinks, especially stupid."

A gangling young man, with flaming red hair and blue eyes, he called himself ugly because of a severe case of acne. He took X-ray treatments to cure it, but they left his face pitted and gave him a permanent scar on his right cheek. For the rest of his life, he posed for photographs with his hand on his chin or his face averted to hide the scar.

Harry entered Yale as a freshman in the fall of 1903. A midwesterner from a public high school, not from a fashionable eastern prep school, he found himself considered an outsider. He tried to be accepted by the "big men on campus," but was, as one of them later said, "kicked in the face over and over again." He was a nuisance, naive, ugly—and talked too much. His cruel classmates called him God-Forbid because of a speech he made as a freshman at a mock trial, at which he shouted, "God forbid that this villain should go free!"

With no friends, Harry took long walks alone, and began to submit poems to the *Yale Literary Review.* During his first summer vacation, he worked on a boat carrying cattle to Europe and then traveled through England before returning to Yale for his sophomore year.

He submitted so many pieces—anecdotes, poems, and stories—to the *Lit* that he became editor of the magazine.

He also began to send manuscripts to off-campus publications. His first effort, an essay on plagiarism in a new novel, appeared in a national magazine called *The Critic* in 1905 under the name of Sinclair Lewis. From then on, he never used his first name, Harry, in his writing.

At the age of twenty, while still a student, Lewis was a busy writer. He contributed to the *Lit,* he worked summers for the *New Haven Journal and Courier,* and he bombarded national publications with his efforts. His first commercially published fiction was an improbable tale called "Matsu-No-Kata, a Romance of Old Japan." It was published in the *Pacific Monthly,* a small magazine that paid him the very small sum of seven and a half dollars.

In the autumn of 1906 Lewis left Yale with a new friend, Allan Updegraff, to join a utopian community in New Jersey. By his own account, Lewis worked as janitor, furnace man, carpenter, ditchdigger, and cleaner—and did none of his chores well. After a month, both young men had had enough. They left for New York in an effort to make a living by freelance writing.

Lewis wrote light verse, short stories, and essays for various magazines for very little money. But the end of 1907, he had earned a total of two hundred forty-two dollars and sixty-nine cents for fifty-five pieces. Restless, he decided to look for a job helping to construct the Panama Canal in Central America. Once there, though, he found no work, and so returned to New York and Yale. In June of 1908, he graduated from Yale.

At the age of twenty-three, faced with the prospect of earning his own living, Lewis got his first job—on the *Daily Courier* in Waterloo, Iowa. He read proofs, wrote editorials, and acted as telegraph editor, all for eighteen dollars a week. After just a brief time there, he began a period of flitting from job to job, all the way from New York to California to Washington, D.C. In those days, as one biographer would put it, Lewis lived in "a miscellany of false starts, lost jobs, lost hopes, loose ends, and erratic wandering."

Although he did not sell many stories, Lewis had a fertile imagination and he kept devising new plots. By chance, in California he met the well-known author Jack London, who had no difficulty in writing but a major problem in thinking up ideas for his stories. They made a deal: London would buy plots from Lewis at five dollars each.

In Lewis's diary during 1910, there were several notations such as "14 sh. st.

pl. sold to Jack London—$70." Some of the plots he sold actually became London stories. But as much as Lewis needed the money London paid him, he was determined to become a writer himself.

So Lewis got a job in New York as an editor with the Frederick A. Stokes publishing firm. Along with his editing duties, he wrote his first book for Stokes— an adventure story for boys called *Hike and the Airplane.* His pay for the book was two months' salary, which gave him the time to write his first novel, *Our Mr. Wrenn.*

In those days Lewis lived in Greenwich Village, sharing an apartment with some other aspiring writers. The novelist Edna Ferber would describe him as "a gangling, red-headed popeyed fellow, shambling, untidy, uproariously funny." He had a vast knowledge of English poetry and recited verse after verse at all sorts of gatherings. Also a gifted mimic, Lewis often amused his friends by repeating funny conversations he had overheard.

Now twenty-seven years old, he pursued a dozen young women, fancying himself in love with each. He proposed marriage to some of them, half in jest, but none took him seriously. Lewis himself became serious about marriage when he met Grace Livingston Hegger, who wrote for *Vogue* magazine. She was

everything he was not—chic, poised, careful about appearances, and respectful of social conventions.

They were married in 1914, the same year that *Our Mr. Wrenn* was published. *Our Mr. Wrenn* introduced a theme that Lewis would use in many of his later novels: the conflict between the exotic—in Mr. Wrenn's case, travel—and the real satisfactions of ordinary Americans. The book received good reviews, but sold poorly.

To earn money Lewis took a job as an editorial assistant in the George H. Doran publishing company. But he was a tireless writer as well. He wrote many short stories that were printed by one of the country's most popular magazines, *The Saturday Evening Post.* In addition, from 1914 to 1918 he wrote four more novels, all of them competent but forgettable.

In that period he also wrote a play, *Hobohemia,* about life in Greenwich Village, which achieved a modest success. And, in 1917, he and his wife had a son they named Wells.

All the while, though, he had been thinking of another novel, based on his recollections of life in Sauk Centre. Published in October of 1920, his *Main Street* became, as one of Lewis's biographers would put it, "the most sensational event in twentieth-century publishing history." Within days, bookstores were sold out and printers could not keep up with the orders for additional copies.

A controversial novel, *Main Street* provoked strong reactions from its readers. It depicted a small, complacent American town, with a strong tendency to suppress individuality in manners, taste, dress, and thought. To some, it was a revelation of the narrowness of life in small-town America; to others, it was an unfair libel about cherished American traditions.

Lewis had started the novel:

This is America—a town of a few thousand, in a region of wheat and corn and dairies and little groves.

The town is, in our tale, called "Gopher Prairie, Minnesota." But its Main Street is the continuation of Main Streets everywhere. The story would be the same in Ohio or Montana, in Kansas or Kentucky or Illinois, and not very differently would it be told up York State or in the Carolina hills.

Gopher Prairie is, of course, Sauk Centre, where Lewis grew up. Its heroine, a librarian named Carol Kennicott who attempts in vain to bring culture to the smug town, is a thinly-disguised Lewis himself. Asked once if that were so, Lewis replied, "Yes, Carol is 'Red' Lewis; always groping for something she isn't capable of attaining, always dissatisfied, always restlessly straining to see what lies just over the horizon, intoler-

ant of her surroundings, yet lacking any clear vision of what she really wants to do or be."

With the success of *Main Street*, Lewis entered a remarkable period of literary productivity. During the next ten years, he wrote four more novels that became American classics: *Babbitt, Arrowsmith, Elmer Gantry*, and *Dodsworth.*

In those years, Lewis's life changed dramatically. His money problems were over. He and his family traveled to Europe—first class, in contrast to his earlier trip by cattle boat. They lived in the best hotels and mingled with American writers abroad as well as with the literary leaders of England, France, and Italy.

Although Lewis could be charming and gracious when he chose to be, he could also be rude and arrogant. His talk was lively and his impersonations of other people entertaining. But he talked too much. And he began to drink, sometimes heavily. "In many ways, he was a spoiled boy," one friend would write. "He always had to be at the center of the stage."

Despite his personal excesses, though, Lewis was a hard-working author. Before he began writing his second major novel, *Babbitt*, he planned it all carefully in advance. He put together biographies of his main characters, made detailed maps of the setting, drew floor plans of the houses, and outlined the plot, step by step. It was a method he used in all his later novels.

Babbitt, published in 1922, is about a prosperous real estate man in the fictional city of Zenith, living an empty life chasing material possessions. It not only sold well, but it also gave the English language a new word. According to the *American Heritage Dictionary* (third edition), a Babbitt is "a member of the middle class whose attachment to its business and social ideals is such as to make that person a model of narrow-mindedness and self-satisfaction."

Even before finishing *Babbitt,* Lewis was thinking of his next novel. It was to be the story of a young doctor dedicated to pure research. The idea came to him after he met Paul de Kruif, who had a doctorate in bacteriology and had been a medical researcher prior to becoming a scientific journalist. With de Kruif, Lewis took a two-month cruise to the Caribbean, studying bacteriology and the methods of medical research.

Lewis was enthusiastic, remembering his youth as the son of a country doctor and his brother Claude, who was a doctor, too. In a letter to a friend about his new project, he wrote, "It's going to be my best book—although it isn't just *mine* by a long shot," referring to de Kruif's contributions.

When *Arrowsmith* came out in 1925 it was an instant success. Unlike the characters in his previous books, in this one Lewis created a heroic figure. Although there had been books about doctors before, Martin Arrowsmith was a new kind of doctor—a research scientist fighting to maintain his integrity. The critics hailed *Arrowsmith* and Lewis.

As his biographer Mark Shorer would put it, "Sinclair Lewis had recognized at last the best as well as the worst in the American experience."

The acclaim *Arrowsmith* received led to a major literary controversy. In 1926, Lewis was awarded the Pulitzer Prize for writing the year's best novel. But he felt strongly that he should have received the prize for *Main Street* back in 1920, and he rejected the belated award with an attention-getting letter:

Between the Pulitzer Prizes, the American Academy of Arts and Letters, amateur boards of censorship, and the inquisition of earnest literary ladies, every compulsion is put upon writers to become safe, polite, obedient, and sterile. In protest, I declined election to the National Institute of Arts and Letters some years ago, and now I must decline the Pulitzer prize.

I invite other writers to consider the fact that by accepting the prizes and approval of these vague institutions, we are admitting their authority, and publicly confirming them as the final judges of literary excellence, and I inquire whether any prize is worth that subservience.

Lewis's next novel, *Elmer Gantry,* caused a different kind of furor. His pic-

Sinclair Lewis and Dorothy Thompson in 1928. *Culver Pictures, Inc.*

ture of a hypocritical minister whose personal behavior completely ignored his own preachings was bitterly attacked. On the grounds that it ridiculed a religious leader, the book was banned in Boston. Elsewhere, many bookshops refused to stock it, and it was denounced from many pulpits. Even so, it became a best-seller.

But Lewis's personal life was not as successful as his novels. He sailed for Europe in 1927 without his wife, and stayed there for more than a year. In the following year, he and his wife were divorced. Almost immediately, he married Dorothy Thompson, well-known as a foreign correspondent, whom he had met in Berlin.

When they returned to the United States in 1928, they bought a farm in Vermont. It was the first house that the forty-three–year-old Lewis had ever owned, and the only permanent home he would ever have as an adult. In 1930, the couple's only child, Michael, was born.

In those years of the late 1920s, Lewis wrote several minor novels and one major one, *Dodsworth*. His earlier books had satirized stuffy midwestern customs. But Sam Dodsworth, a successful automobile manufacturer, was an admirable character, even though his wife Fran was not; one reviewer called Fran "a well-groomed female American mon-

ster." Her husband, instead of being an unthinking conformist as Babbitt had been, was an example of the best of America. Despite finding himself trapped in an unhappy marriage, he showed himself capable of growth and understanding.

With the beginning of the new decade in 1930, Lewis at last achieved the international recognition he had craved. He became the first American to win the Nobel Prize in literature. But how could he accept it after rejecting the Pulitzer Prize? Lewis's only answer was that the Nobel Prize was for a body of work, whereas the Pulitzer was for a single novel.

In his acceptance speech, Lewis called attention to the fact that American literature had come of age. Also, he himself, at the age of forty-five, had reached the peak of his fame and literary production. The direction of the rest of his career, unhappily, was mostly downhill.

For the next twenty years, Lewis kept writing steadily, but none of his work reached the quality—or the audiences—of *Main Street* or *Arrowsmith*. He wrote nine novels and many short stories, he worked on plays, and he even became active as a producer, director, and actor in the theater. But he obviously was unhappy and had an increasingly severe drinking problem.

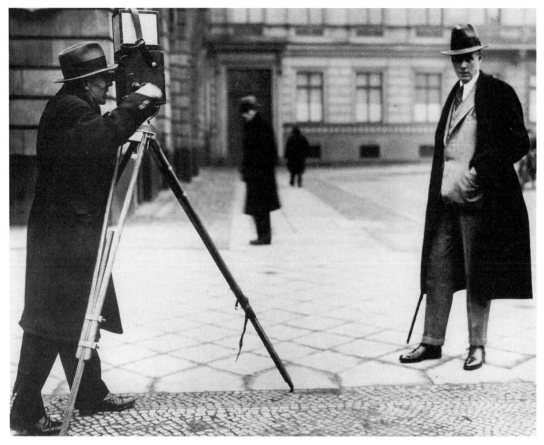

Sinclair Lewis being photographed in Berlin around 1930. *Culver Pictures, Inc.*

Only one of his novels in that period, *It Can't Happen Here,* struck the public fancy. Published in 1935, it was a fictional account of how dictatorship could come to the United States, obviously based on the rise of Adolf Hitler in Nazi Germany. Lewis helped dramatize the book, and it opened as a play in New York, then in about twenty other cities around the country. As a political document it was a success, but the critics called it a poor play.

During the next several years, Lewis devoted much of his time to theatrical efforts. He played the leading role in a touring company putting on one of his own plays, and wrote a novel about this experience, but none of these projects was successful.

After a long separation from his second wife, he was divorced again in 1942. Two years later, his older son, Wells, a lieutenant in the United States Army serving in Europe during World War II, was killed by a sniper's bullet. Lewis, frequently drunk and often rude to other people, moved around the country, still somehow producing stories and books.

Once again he sailed to Europe in 1949, and took up residence in Italy. He died in Rome on January 10, 1951, at the age of sixty-six. Lewis left behind five major novels—*Main Street, Babbitt, Arrowsmith, Elmer Gantry,* and *Dodsworth*—that are still regarded as very important contributions to American literature because they changed the way Americans look at themselves.

Eugene O'Neill

1888–1953   America's first great playwright

"Born in a hotel room," Eugene O'Neill said bitterly as he lay dying, "and—God damn it—died in a hotel room."

His complaint was accurate. Eugene O'Neill was born in the Barrett House, a hotel on Times Square in New York City, in 1888. He died in the Shelton Hotel in Boston, overlooking the Charles River, in 1953. Between his birth and his death, he lived in many houses, from coast to coast in the United States, but none of them became his permanent home.

Yet the lack of a place that he could call home did not prevent him from working at his trade—writing plays. He became America's greatest dramatist, the winner of four Pulitzer Prizes and the Nobel Prize in literature. Today, his plays are still highly regarded in his own country and throughout the world.

From the day of his birth, O'Neill's life was connected to the theater. His father, James O'Neill, was a famous actor who regularly toured the country with a traveling troupe of players. His mother, Ella Quinlan O'Neill, left the tour only briefly when this son was about to be born.

Both of his parents came from Irish Catholic families that had immigrated to the United States. Despite their similar background, their marriage was not a happy one. Ella, the pampered daughter of a middle-class family, was shy, unable to make friends, and a little spoiled. By contrast, James, a dashing and handsome man, was friendly as well as charming—and he was often drunk. The emotional gap between the pair was apparent to their children and would become the theme of many of Eugene's plays.

James O'Neill did interrupt his travels

to be present at his third son's birth on October 16, 1888; James, Jr., ten years older than Eugene, was already away at school, and another boy had died in infancy. Ella O'Neill had a hard time giving birth to Eugene and began to take medicine with morphine in it to ease her pain. During much of his life, this son would live with the belief that his birth had made his mother a drug addict.

A month or so after Eugene's birth, he and his mother joined his father as he traveled around the country playing the leading role in *The Count of Monte Cristo.* Eugene would often say in later years that his mother had nursed him in the wings and in dressing rooms. He even said he remembered being put to sleep in small hotel rooms in a sort of cradle made by tucking a pillow into a bureau drawer.

For seven years, Eugene traveled with his parents to theaters all over the United States. Their only home was a summer cottage on the water in New London, Connecticut. He escaped the theatrical atmosphere surrounding him most of the year by burying himself in books. Summers, he learned to swim so well that in later years he astounded his friends by swimming so far out to sea that he could not be seen from the shore.

At the age of seven, Eugene began to attend a Catholic boarding school in New York City. A quiet boy, he was unhappy there, preferring to spend his time reading rather than playing with the other boys. At home, his adolescent years were very troubled. When he was fifteen, one day he entered his mother's hotel room and found her giving herself a morphine injection.

Eugene prayed to God to cure his mother and worked hard at school to show that he was serious. He received an 88 in history, 87 in English, and 84 in religion, but he could not master geometry or algebra, receiving a failing grade of 57 in mathematics. And his mother remained addicted.

Eugene lost his religious faith and made up his mind never to go to church again. That caused a furious fight with his father, one of many over the years between James O'Neill and his two irreligious sons.

By this time Eugene was attending another school, the Betts Academy in Stamford, Connecticut. His teachers would remember him as a dreamer who often liked to go off walking alone. But he did take part in the normal student rebellions, playing tricks on the faculty and sneaking off to town to smoke cigarettes or try a sip of beer. He liked Betts and became a good student, except in mathematics. He got excellent grades in English, good marks in natural history, fair ones in Latin and French, and did well in Greek and Roman history.

During his summers in the seaport city of New London, Eugene loved to wander around the harbor. He spent hours watching ships with beautiful white sails, which still cruised the seas in the early 1900s. For him, they were the reality of the romantic tales he read in the novels of Jack London and Joseph Conrad.

In 1906, at the urging of his father, Eugene went to college, at Princeton. He quickly came to the conclusion that it offered little in the way of intellectual stimulation. As a result, he devoted himself to reading, girls, and drinking, paying little attention to his classes. At the end of his first year he was dropped for "poor scholastic standing."

At the age of eighteen Eugene decided to become a self-educated man. For the next six years, he held a variety of jobs. He looked for gold in El Salvador and Honduras; sailed for South America on one of the last sailing ships; shipped out on a coal-fired steamer to England; spent a lot of time drinking in shabby bars in England, Argentina, and New York City; worked briefly as a reporter for the *New London Telegraph;* and even acted as an assistant stage manager for one of his father's plays.

In between, O'Neill—a tall, slender, handsome young man with black hair and large, dark eyes—always found time for women companions. His brooding air was attractive to women of every social rank, from those who frequented the low-down bars where he drank to those he met at the homes of well-off neighbors in New London.

At the age of twenty, in New York he met Kathleen Jenkins, an attractive young woman with blue eyes and fair hair piled high on her head. She fell in love with this unusually intense young man. O'Neill, coming out of a home that was beset by drink, drugs, and discord, could not resist being loved for himself.

In 1909, he and Kathleen were secretly married. But almost immediately he felt trapped. After just a week of marriage, he went off to sea and did not see his wife again for a long time. They were divorced in 1912, two years after their son, Eugene Jr., was born.

Back in the United States, O'Neill, obviously unhappy, began to drink heavily like his father and brother. At one time he even attempted suicide. In addition, he contracted tuberculosis and was confined to a sanitorium for six months in 1912.

It was at the sanitorium in Connecticut that O'Neill found an escape from the hostile world around him—by writing. Although he had tried to write poetry before, he now began to write short plays. Later, he would call his time at the sanitorium and his discovery that he could write plays "a rebirth."

Cured of tuberculosis, O'Neill returned to New London in 1913. In eight months, he wrote six one-act plays, none of them very good. But his father paid to have them published in a thin volume called *Thirst and Other One-Act Plays.*

One critic made a comment that changed the course of O'Neill's writing. He suggested that O'Neill should write about what he knew best—the sea. The advice was heeded: His next work was a one-act play about a sailor dying in his bunk on a tramp steamer. It was called *Children of the Sea.*

After completing it, O'Neill decided that he really needed more training as a playwright. He applied for admission to the well-known playwriting class of Professor George Pierce Baker at Harvard, and was accepted as a student there. According to one of his classmates, O'Neill was no better or worse than any of his fellow students.

Upon finishing the course in 1915, O'Neill went back to New York City. He lived in the artistic neighborhood that was known as Greenwich Village, drinking at a bar called The Hell Hole, where gangsters, homeless people, political radicals, and would-be artists gathered. He listened carefully, storing up impressions of people and how they talked.

In the summer of 1916, with some other young writers and artists, he moved to Provincetown, then a quiet fishing village on the northern tip of Cape Cod in Massachusetts. Some of the actors organized the Provincetown Players, but had a problem finding short plays to present. They were delighted when O'Neill offered *Children of the Sea,* now renamed *Bound East for Cardiff.*

Years later, O'Neill was in a reminiscent mood. "It was a rather curious coincidence," he said, "that my first production should have been on a wharf in a sea town. *Bound East for Cardiff* [took place] on shipboard and while it was being acted you could hear the waves washing in and out under the wharf."

That play launched O'Neill's career. During the next four years he was a remarkably busy playwright. In 1917 alone, he wrote four plays: *Ile, The Moon of the Caribees, The Long Voyage Home,* and *In the Zone.* But he also found time for fun.

A shy, quiet man, he liked to sit in shabby saloons near the waterfront, talking to sailors. He was addicted to spectator sports, too. He loved to watch six-day bicycle races, attend prizefights, and follow the batting averages of his favorite baseball players.

In 1918, O'Neill married Agnes Boulton, a writer. They had two children: a son, Shane, and then a daughter given the unusual name of Oona, the equiva-

Eugene O'Neill photographed in Bermuda in 1926. *UPI/Bettmann.*

lent of Agnes in the old Irish language of Gaelic.

O'Neill also began to work on his first long play, *Beyond the Horizon,* in 1918. He began, as usual, by writing a scenario, or outline, of the entire play before attempting to set down the actual dialogue and stage directions.

He sat at a table with twelve sharpened pencils before him. On the table were also his papers and his notes, written in small notebooks. His handwriting was neat and precise as he worked steadily for about seven hours, starting at seven o'clock in the morning. Later, a secretary or his wife or even he himself made a typed copy of his manuscript.

Beyond the Horizon dealt with the conflict between two brothers, one an idealist and the other a materialist. It was his first play produced on Broadway, in 1920. Surprisingly for a tragedy, it was a hit. It also won for him his first Pulitzer Prize for the best play of the year.

The early 1920s were extraordinarily emotional for O'Neill. His father died in 1920, his mother in 1922, and his brother Jamie in 1923. They all lived on in his memory, though, and he turned them, only thinly disguised, into characters in several of his later plays. Churning with ideas, he wrote seven more plays during this decade.

One of his most innovative plays, *The Emperor Jones,* the story of a black railroad porter with delusions of grandeur, was a huge success on Broadway toward the end of 1920. A year later, *Anna Christie,* a tragedy about a prostitute and her Swedish-immigrant father, proved to be equally successful. It brought O'Neill his second Pulitzer Prize. But a short play about a coal stoker on an ocean liner, *The Hairy Ape,* received only lukewarm reviews.

While these plays were being produced, O'Neill started what proved to be one of his greatest works, *Desire Under the Elms.* Using themes from ancient Greek tragedies, he wrote about the tortured relationships of a twentieth-century New England family with obvious similarities to his own. It was produced in 1924.

In 1926, the thirty-eight–year-old playwright, who had spent only one year at college, received an honorary degree from Yale. The citation described him as "a creative contributor of new and moving forms to one of the oldest of the arts" and as "the first American playwright to receive both wide and serious recognition upon the stage of Europe."

As usual, O'Neill was working on several new plays at the time. In one, *The Great God Brown,* he used masks for some of his characters, enacting the tragic story of an artist in conflict with a materialistic society. In another, *Marco*

Millions, O'Neill wrote about the legendary Marco Polo and his trip to China.

In *Strange Interlude*, O'Neill again used an innovative technique: His characters spoke their thoughts aloud in asides to the audience. When it opened in 1928, it became his biggest hit and made him more money than any other of his plays. It also won for him a third Pulitzer Prize.

By that time, O'Neill had left his wife and run off with a beautiful actress, Carlotta Monterey. Married in 1929, they settled for a time in France. O'Neill began a lengthy retelling of one of the ancient Greek legends, set in New England at the end of the Civil War. Called *Mourning Becomes Electra*, it opened in New York in 1931. Despite its length— it played from five in the afternoon to after eleven at night—it received enthusiastic reviews.

Restless, the O'Neills settled down in a beach house on Sea Island, Georgia. There, and for the rest of his life, Carlotta acted as a buffer for her husband, protecting him from the outside world, preserving his seclusion, and creating a legend that he wanted to be left alone. "I was Gene's secretary, I was his nurse," she later recalled. "I loved it."

In a burst of energy, O'Neill wrote his only comedy, *Ah Wilderness!* in just six weeks. A gentle picture of his boyhood in New London, it opened in 1933 and became one of his biggest hits. It was made into a popular movie too.

After an exceptionally hot summer, the O'Neills decided to leave Georgia. They moved to Seattle, once again near the sea. While there in 1936, he received a telephone call notifying him that he had won the Nobel Prize in literature, becoming the first American dramatist to be so honored.

O'Neill was ill in a hospital when the award ceremony took place. The citation sent to him said he had been selected for his creative drama, especially for the honesty and strong emotions of his characters "as well as for depth of interpretation."

Soon the O'Neills moved to a house they built in the hills near Danville, California. There he wrote *The Iceman Cometh*, called by many his greatest play. On the surface it is a simple story of a group of derelicts in a saloon, dreaming about how they will pull themselves together someday. But it also raises broad questions about dreams, drunkenness, and death. Although written in 1939, it did not open on Broadway until 1946, after the end of World War II.

In that period, O'Neill's creative energy began to fade. His physical condition deteriorated, too. Now over fifty years old, he suffered from a brain dis-

Eugene O'Neill at the age of fifty, then acclaimed as America's leading playwright. *UPI/Bettmann*.

order that made it difficult for him to hold a pencil. But he did manage to write three more memorable plays about his tortured family, all produced on Broadway after his death.

The first, *Long Day's Journey into Night,* deals with the complicated relationships among his mother, a drug addict; his father, a frustrated man; his brother, an alcoholic; and himself, a disillusioned youth. It was not produced until 1956, three years after his death, when it received the Pulitzer Prize, the fourth he had won.

He completed *A Touch of the Poet* in 1942. The leading character is a tavern keeper, an immigrant from Ireland, but he is a thinly disguised James O'Neill, Eugene's father, with a love-hate relationship with his family. It was produced on Broadway in 1958, five years after O'Neill's death.

His last play, *A Moon for the Misbegotten,* was written in 1943 as a sequel to *Long Day's Journey into Night.* It is the story of his brother Jamie, an embittered alcoholic, and his strange romance with a farmer's daughter. It was staged out of New York, to basically negative reviews, and not presented on Broadway until 1957, again after O'Neill had died.

From 1943 until his death ten years later, O'Neill's life was far from happy. Not only did his declining health make it impossible for him to write, but his family was falling apart, too. As a parent, he was a notable failure.

For years he was out of touch with his oldest son, Eugene Jr., a professor at Yale who committed suicide in 1950. O'Neill's second son, Shane, was basically a drifter who drank too much. After Shane's son, Eugene O'Neill III, died as a two-month-old infant, O'Neill never saw him again.

The story of his daughter, Oona, was quite different. At the age of eighteen, she married the famous comedian Charlie Chaplin, then fifty-four years old. "Oona broke Gene's heart," his wife Carlotta said. But it was O'Neill himself who cut off relations with her and he never saw her again, even though she tried to repair the breach. As for her unusual marriage, it turned out very successfully.

O'Neill and his wife remained in California for six years before moving back east in 1945, first to New York and then to a cottage by the sea at Marblehead, Massachusetts. Ailing and miserable, he lived on for several years. He died in the Shelton Hotel in Boston on November 27, 1953, at the age of sixty-five.

John Steinbeck

1902–1968   Author of *The Grapes of Wrath*

He always wanted to write. After John Steinbeck became a famous author one of his sisters recalled that, as a child, "John always had to write things." He wrote verses for place cards used at parties, jingles for special events, a poem for the tombstone of his dog Jiggs who was run over by a fire truck, and poems for the birthdays of his relatives. He told ghost stories to neighborhood children in his basement and he read stories and poems to his friends.

It was when he entered high school as a freshman that he decided he wanted to be a real writer, not a doctor or a lawyer or a public official like his father. But he was not quite sure how one became a writer, except by writing. So he spent much of his time for the next few years in his bedroom, sitting at his desk, daydreaming, thinking, and writing. Many years later, he remembered:

I used to sit in that little room upstairs . . . and write little stories and little pieces and send them out to magazines under a false name and I never knew what happened to them because I never put a return address on them. But I would watch the magazines for a certain length of time to see whether they had printed them. They never did because they couldn't get in touch with me. . . . I wonder what I was thinking of? I was scared to death to get a rejection slip, but more, I suppose, to get an acceptance.

John grew up in Salinas, California, where he had been born on February 17, 1902. He had two older sisters, Elizabeth and Esther, and a younger one, Mary. Salinas, a small town then, was the center of a major agricultural valley south of San Francisco and not far from the Pacific Ocean at Monterey. All around the town were the Salinas Valley farmers and farmworkers who were to become important figures in John's novels and short stories.

His father, John Ernst Steinbeck, was of German descent. John's grandfather, John Adolph Grossteinbeck, had shortened his name to Steinbeck when he came to the United States and settled in Florida. After the Civil War, the family moved to California, where John Ernst followed his father into the miller's trade. An experienced manager and accountant, he later became treasurer of Monterey County, a position of prominence in the community.

John's mother, Olive Hamilton Steinbeck, was of Irish ancestry. Her father, Samuel Hamilton, had immigrated to the United States, and there met and married a young girl who had also come from Ireland. In 1850, at the height of the California gold rush, they joined the westbound tide, but, instead of fortune hunting, the Hamiltons prudently took up farming and operating a blacksmith shop.

Olive, the youngest of their five daughters, became a schoolteacher at the age of eighteen. On horseback, she rode fifteen miles every day to a one-room schoolhouse where she taught a wide range of subjects—math, reading, science, history, and even art and music. She gave up teaching, however, after she met and married John Ernst Steinbeck.

Their son John was raised in a house filled with books and magazines. He and his sisters were also encouraged to use the nearby public library, and they always received books as birthday gifts. On his ninth birthday, John was given a handsome volume of old-time tales about the adventures of England's legendary King Arthur and his knights of the Round Table. This present greatly influenced John then and many years later when he was a professional writer.

"I loved the old spelling of the words—and the words no longer used," he would recall. "Perhaps a passionate love of the English language opened to me from this book. I was delighted to find out paradoxes—that 'cleave' means both to stick together and to cut apart . . . for a long time, I had a secret language."

But John was not only a bookworm. With a mischievous streak, he loved to play tricks and he became the leader of the boys who lived nearby. When he was ten years old, his father gave him a pony, Jill. John groomed Jill carefully, and the relationship between the two of them later became the basis for one of his best-known books, *The Red Pony.*

In 1915, when he was thirteen, John entered high school. He did enough work to get above-average grades. Although he took part in school activities along with the twenty-four other members of his graduating class, he was shy with girls and not good at athletics. But he worked as an associate editor of the yearbook and for one semester he was even president of his class.

John's interest in writing led him to become an English major when he entered Stanford University as a freshman in 1919. He was an unusual student, going to classes for half the year and working the other half. Not interested in getting a degree, he took only the courses that he thought would help him to become a writer—history, literature, advanced composition, journalism, and the classics.

He also learned to play poker and drink. Once shy with girls, he now acquired several girlfriends who were attracted by his seriousness and his literary ambitions. Six feet tall, he was anything but handsome, with a plain face as well as large ears and nose.

As an aspiring writer John was an active member of the English Club. Once when another student asked whether it was worth joining, a professor advised, "Stay away. A fellow named Steinbeck comes every meeting and insists on reading his stuff to everyone." It was a

John Steinbeck and his sister Mary on Jill, the "red pony." Valley Guild, *John Steinbeck Library, Salinas, Steinbeck Archives.*

habit Steinbeck followed the rest of his life—he always liked to read his work aloud, but he did not welcome criticism or comment. "I don't want a critic," he once told his wife, much later. "I just need an audience."

He did listen to one teacher, however. Edith Mirrielees, who taught a class in short-story writing, became a major influence on him. A writer herself, she was an old-fashioned strict teacher who emphasized a commonsense approach, logical plot development, and revision to eliminate wordiness.

In the six years that Steinbeck intermittently attended Stanford, he held a variety of jobs—laborer, farmhand in sugar-beet fields, salesman, ranch hand, chemist, and surveyor—all of which would be reflected in stories later. He left Stanford in 1925 without a degree and, at the age of twenty-three, went to New York.

After working briefly as a laborer on the construction of Madison Square Garden, Steinbeck got a writing job. Through the influence of an uncle, he became a reporter for the *New York American*. But he showed no aptitude as a journalist, finding the rules of the craft irksome, and was soon fired. Trying fiction again, he wrote several short stories he failed to sell and then returned to California.

For the next two years Steinbeck supported himself by working as a caretaker of vacation cottages on Lake Tahoe. The job provided plenty of free time that he could devote to writing, enabling him to complete a novel he called *Cup of Gold*. A story based on the life of the famous Caribbean pirate Henry Morgan, it was not a very good novel and it was largely ignored by the critics as well as the public when it was published in 1929.

Although Steinbeck was enduring semipoverty at the time, he made three connections that changed his life. He met a lively young woman from San Francisco named Carol Henning, whom he married in 1930. He also met Edward F. Ricketts, a marine biologist who became his best friend. And another

friend put him in touch with a literary agent in New York City, who would work with him for the rest of his writing career.

In those years Steinbeck wrote by pen in a commercial ledger book, about twelve inches high by seven-and-a-half inches wide, the kind that businesses used to record their finances before the age of computers. On one side of the opened pages he wrote stories; on the other, notes about his stories. He used different-colored inks: green, purple, and blue-black. In one of the notes, he explained that the color did not reflect his mood—he had simply bought the cheapest ink available.

After Steinbeck's marriage he and his wife moved to his family's oceanside cottage at Pacific Grove. They lived there rent-free, further helped by a twenty-five-dollar-a-month loan from his father. The couple gathered food from the ocean and their garden, and Carol worked in a variety of jobs to support them. John diligently wrote daily until four o'clock in the afternoon. After that, their house was open to friends.

"For entertainment, we had the public library, endless talk, long walks, and a number of games," Steinbeck would later recall. "We played music, sang, and made love. Enormous invention went into our pleasures. Anything at all was an excuse for a party: all holidays, birthdays called for celebration. When we felt the need to celebrate and the calendar was blank, we simply proclaimed a Jacks-Are-Wild Day."

Steinbeck also wrote many letters to his friends, a habit he continued for the rest of his life. He used pencils for his letters because he liked the way they felt in his fingers. Every morning, he would sharpen all his pencils and write letters before getting down to the serious business of fiction. His handwriting was small—once he boasted that he had squeezed more than five hundred words onto a postcard.

Although he and his wife were poor, it was a happy and productive time for Steinbeck. On his thirtieth birthday, he received a welcome present: *The Pastures of Heaven* was accepted by a publisher, and it appeared in 1932. A year later, *To a God Unknown*, now largely forgotten, came out. He began writing two more books, *The Red Pony* and *Tortilla Flat*, that were really collections of short stories about the same characters. He also continued to write separate short stories. One of them, *The Murder*, was selected for the O. Henry Award as the best short story of the year in 1934.

A year later *Tortilla Flat* came out and became a best-seller, giving Steinbeck his first taste of financial success. It was a warm and sentimental series of tales about a group of idlers who pursue

their own eccentric ways while avoiding the normal routine of ordinary life. In it, he sounded a theme that would be repeated in many of his novels—that those condemned or looked down on by society are often the best people.

Steinbeck's strong sympathy for the underdog was reflected in his next book, *In Dubious Battle*, a novel about a strike in the apple orchards of California, published in 1936. Its title conveyed the author's doubts about the merits of both sides, the left-wing union organizers and the antiunion growers.

With their financial burdens now relieved, the Steinbecks built a new house in Los Gatos. He began to work on a novel about two wandering ranch hands that he called *Of Mice and Men* (a reference to the poet Robert Burns's familiar lines, "The best laid schemes o' mice and men/Gang aft a-gley.")

The book leaped to the top of best-seller lists in 1937. Then Steinbeck collaborated with George Kaufman on a play with the same title, which became a hit on Broadway. It won the New York Drama Critics Award as the best play of its year and later became a successful movie, too.

Back in California, Steinbeck busied himself on another project—one that would make him world-famous. On an assignment for the *San Francisco News*, he investigated the plight of thousands

John Steinbeck photographed in the early 1930s. *Photograph by Sonya Noskowiak. Courtesy Arthur F. Noskowiak. The John Steinbeck Collection, Stanford University Libraries.*

of farm families who had fled a terrible drought in Arkansas and Oklahoma to look for work in California's farm fields. He wrote a series of seven articles called "The Harvest Gypsies" about the miserable conditions in the migrant labor camps where they lived. The assignment gave him the idea for a new book.

Steinbeck and his wife worked as a team on the new novel, a devastating story about one family of "Okies" who made the trip from Oklahoma to California during the Great Depression of the 1930s. He turned out two thousand words a day in pen and ink, and she typed what he wrote, editing it as she did so.

It was Carol, too, who came up with a brilliant idea for the title: *The Grapes of Wrath*. It was a phrase from the opening lines of the great antislavery marching song of the Civil War, "The Battle Hymn of the Republic":

Mine eyes have seen the glory of the
    coming of the Lord;
He is trampling out the vintage where the
    grapes of wrath are stored . . .

The title was also an obvious allusion to one of California's major crops. What's more, it stirred a glimmer of hope that the oppression of the migrant workers of the 1930s could be overcome.

Published in 1939, *The Grapes of Wrath* was an instantaneous success, both with the critics and the public. Even though some attacked the book as radical propaganda, it was squarely in the American tradition of social protest. The best-selling book of its year, it won the Pulitzer Prize in fiction and it was also made into a memorable motion picture. More than half a century later, it is still required reading in many schools and colleges and is regarded as an American classic.

It established Steinbeck as a major American author—and made him an unwilling celebrity, too. Although he appreciated the fact that people were reading his books, he regretted the loss of privacy accompanying his new eminence. After he was elected a member of the National Institute of Arts and Letters, he continued to dodge interviews and declined to pose for photographs. "They ain't going to lionize me," he told a friend.

To avoid publicity, Steinbeck and his wife made several trips with his friend Ed Ricketts to collect specimens of marine life from the Gulf of California for Ricketts's biological laboratory. Out of the trips came another book, *The Sea of Cortez,* published in 1941.

Despite his literary success, these were troubled years for Steinbeck. Increasing tensions in his marriage led to a divorce in 1942. Then Steinbeck moved to New York City. He had met another

John Steinbeck receives the Nobel Prize for literature in 1962. *Courtesy Mrs. E. G. Ainsworth, John Steinbeck Library, Salinas, Steinbeck Archives.*

woman, Gwyn Conger, a young singer, and they were married in 1943. They had two children, Thom, born in 1944, and John, born in 1946.

During World War II, Steinbeck, in his early forties, was considered too old to serve in the armed forces. He did, however, write for the Office of War Information and the Army Air Corps, and he worked briefly as a war correspondent for *The New York Herald Tribune.* He also wrote *The Moon Is Down,* a novel about Nazi-occupied Europe that was turned into a successful play, as well as the script for a movie called *Lifeboat,* about the survivors of a ship sunk by a German submarine.

As the war ended, Steinbeck returned to a California theme in *Cannery Row,* a series of stories about local residents who plan and throw a party for a character modeled after his friend Ed Ricketts. Next came two short novels, *The Pearl,* about a fisherman who finds a magnificent gem, and *The Wayward Bus,* about a group of stranded bus riders.

In the postwar period, Steinbeck did a lot of traveling as well as writing—to Mexico, to Europe, to the Soviet Union. He felt the pressure to live up to the promise of *The Grapes of Wrath* by tackling another major theme, but his new work seemed to be of minor significance. His personal life was falling apart, too. His second wife sought a divorce in 1948.

Steinbeck, a strong believer in marriage despite his divorces, married Elaine Scott in 1950, and this marriage was apparently a happy one. Once more, he moved from California to New York City, where he wrote another play and a movie script as well as magazine articles, short stories, and novels.

One of his better books of this period was *East of Eden,* published in 1952, which was made into a popular movie. After several lesser efforts, in 1962 one of his best-loved books appeared. *Travels with Charley* was a whimsical account of a car trip Steinbeck had taken across the United States with his dog, Charley, a large poodle. Although it was praised for its relaxed style and thoughtful observations of life in America, many critics called it second-rate, obviously not in the same category as *The Grapes of Wrath.*

So Steinbeck himself, as well as the entire literary world, was stunned in 1962 when he was awarded the Nobel Prize in literature. The citation called attention to his "sympathetic humor and social perception." He was praised as a teacher of goodwill and charity and as a staunch defender of human values.

Reaction in the United States was mixed. Sales of his books zoomed. But literary critics were furious. One wrote, "It is difficult to find a flattering explanation for awarding this most distinguished of literary prizes to a writer whose real but limited talent is, in his best books, watered down by 20th rate philosophizing."

Steinbeck himself was deeply wounded by such criticism. In his acceptance speech, he said, "In my heart, there may be doubt that I deserve the Nobel award over other men of letters for whom I hold respect and reverence—but there is no question of my pleasure and pride in having it for myself."

He went on to define his concept of the writer: "He is charged with exposing our many grievous faults and failures, with dredging up to the light our dark and dangerous dreams for the purpose of improvement. Furthermore, the writer is delegated to declare and celebrate man's proven capacity for greatness of heart and spirit—for gallantry in defeat, for courage, compassion, and love."

After receiving the Nobel Prize, Steinbeck declined as a writer. In the last years of his life, he traveled often, spent much time at his country home at Sag Harbor, Long Island, and went abroad frequently as a cultural ambassador for the United States, but wrote little of consequence. He died in New York on December 20, 1968, at the age of sixty-six.

Edith Wharton

1862–1937   Chronicler of the privileged world of old New York
society into which she had been born

She could not remember a time when she did not like to make up stories. By the age of four, she had found a procedure that she particularly enjoyed: She would walk around her room with an open book in her arms, speaking out a rapid stream of words and turning the pages at regular intervals. Anyone peering through a crack of her door might think she was reading aloud—except that she often held her book upside down.

Her private game never involved knights in armor or ancient Greek gods, as did the tales her nurse and her father read to her. Instead, her own imagining was always about the grown-ups who came to dine with her parents, and other ladies and gentlemen she saw in the park opposite the hotel where her family had a spacious apartment.

This park adorned one of the most fashionable neighborhoods of France's capital city of Paris. There, in 1866 shortly after the American Civil War ended, a shy, lonely, rich little girl from New York named Edith Newbold Jones started on the path toward becoming a writer.

But no matter that her solitary "making-up" would always stand out in her early memories; Edith was by no means an unloved child. Even her mother, mostly absorbed with dinner parties and dressing stylishly, sometimes called her Puss or Pussy. Her father, much more warmhearted, seemed to enjoy nothing more than their occasional walks together.

Yet she might have felt deprived of any constant source of affection if not for her dear Doyley. Years later she would write, "I pity all children who have not had a Doyley—a nurse who has always been there, who is as established as the sky and as warm as the sun, who understands everything, feels everything, can arrange everything." In her world, it must be noted, all children were, as a matter of course, brought up by hired nursemaids.

Edith, born at her parents' New York City home on January 24, 1862, belonged to a small and elite group of families there. Descended from early English or Dutch settlers, they did not claim any close connections with kings or dukes because their ancestors had been merely canny businessmen. But over the years, mainly as a result of vast increases in the value of land they owned on the island of Manhattan, they had grown very rich as well as very snobbish. They comprised the city's top "society," from which outsiders were sternly barred.

Even though Edith's father, George Frederic Jones, had a commonplace last name, his family tree made him a member in good standing of this New World aristocracy. Her mother, Lucretia Rhinelander Jones, possessed an even more impressive ancestry. So Edith was required to start learning many complicated rules about acceptable behavior during her earliest years.

She had two older brothers from whom she might have received some help—except that Harry and Freddy,

twelve and sixteen years her senior, were both away at school. Thus, she grew up almost as an only child. When she was just three, though, her longing for companionship was perceived by a family friend, who gave her a little white puppy that she adored. Named Foxy, he was the first in a long series of little white dogs she would cherish throughout her life.

Despite the firmness of her family's social and financial position, however, an economic downturn right after the Civil War made Edith's father take a step that greatly influenced her future. He decided to put their winter and summer residences up for rent—and take his wife and daughter to Europe, where the cost of living elegantly was much less expensive than on their own side of the Atlantic.

So it happened that Edith, between the ages of four and ten, acquired a lifelong feeling of being more at home in Europe than America. From 1866 through 1872, settled for months at a time in one grand hotel or another, she not only painlessly learned to speak proper French, Italian, and German along with English, but she also formed definite ideas about what cities should look like from her exposure to Rome's splendor and the charm of every Paris street scene.

Not quite jokingly, many years later she would say that she really could not

Edith Wharton in her teens. *The Beinecke Rare Book and Manuscript Library, Yale University.*

help liking Europe much better than the United States. "It's the curse of having been brought up there," she explained. At any rate, she certainly did develop many of her lasting opinions on the basis of her early European experience.

During these six important years when she lived overseas, she never attended any school. Her mother thought that private lessons from a series of governesses were all the formal education needed by any daughter of hers. Still, Edith did manage to read a large range of books on her own, besides starting to scribble bits of stories or poems.

All such activities ceased when Edith fell ill at a summer resort in Germany. Her fever rose so alarmingly that her parents searched out the only doctor in the vicinity—who spoke no language except his native Russian. This physician plunged his patient into an ice-cold bath repeatedly, until her temperature at last began dropping. Only later did Edith's parents learn that his drastic treatment for a severe case of typhoid had probably saved their daughter's life.

Yet it was many months before Edith felt well enough to play with a new puppy, and when she had finally regained her strength the family embarked on a ship bound for New York. Although the noisy, dirty pier where they landed disgusted her, she found it delightful—after six years of hotel life— to have a whole house where she could wander up and down stairs as much as she wished without any outsiders' eyes observing her.

Following just a brief period of reacquaintance with New York, however, the Joneses departed for their summer home in Newport, Rhode Island. This picturesque old waterfront town had been gradually attracting so many wealthy residents that it was becoming known as America's foremost playground for millionaires. The seaside residence owned by Edith's family had its own private dock, along with many other amenities, although it was not nearly as spectacular as the huge and ornate "cottages" being built by the Vanderbilts and the Astors. Still, her parents received invitations to all of the most fashionable gatherings, while their daughter attended countless swimming, sailing, tennis, and archery parties for young people.

From the age of ten onward, the pattern of Edith's life remained unchanged: For the next seven years her summers were devoted to Newport's approved amusements, and her winters to lessons or entertainments in New York City that were considered appropriate for girls in her social position. As she developed into an outwardly self-confident young woman, not quite beautiful but with a striking halo of red-gold hair, she gave every sign of being able, in due course, to attract a suitable husband from a background similar to her own.

Yet close friends of her family wondered if Edith was not perhaps too "clever." Among New York's social leaders, the notion that men preferred wives without any intellectual interests was widely prevalent. While art and music were to be applauded, the creators of any sort of art seemed somehow dangerous because they so often defied society's firm rules governing manners and morals.

Therefore, Edith's mother did all she could to discourage her daughter's habit of scribbling. No paper was provided for her use, so most of what Edith wrote had to be set down on wrappings saved from parcels she received.

However, at the age of twelve she hopefully showed her mother a story of hers that started, " 'Oh, how do you do, Mrs. Brown?' said Mrs. Tompkins. 'If I had known you were going to call, I should have tidied up the drawing room.' " Lucretia Jones, after just one glance, handed it back with the cold comment, "Drawing rooms are always tidy."

Still, when Edith was fifteen, she secretly wrote a far more shocking long story, which she called *Fast and Loose*, about an English girl who married a rich lord she did not love. In the same period she also composed some high-minded verse, which became the first of her work to appear in print. A friend of her brother Harry's sent copies of her poems to the eminent poet Henry Wadsworth Longfellow—and he said a good word about them to the editor of *The Atlantic Monthly*.

Even Edith's mother could not feel disgraced when a few of her daughter's poems appeared anonymously in this respected magazine. Indeed, she arranged for the private printing of a booklet of all of Edith's verse. In addition, though, because she believed Edith was spending far too much time reading and writing, she convinced her husband that instead of waiting till their girl turned eighteen to introduce her formally to New York and Newport society, they should let her "come out" a year in advance, while she was just seventeen.

Edith would always remember the ball at which she made her social debut as a "long cold agony of shyness." Nevertheless, during the next several years she surely seemed to be enjoying her almost-continuous party going. And before her family could have any serious worries about her failing to find the right sort of husband—the underlying purpose of the coming-out ritual—on April 29, 1885, at the age of twenty-three, she married Edward Robbins

Wharton, an amiable and wealthy Bostonian thirteen years older than she was.

Teddy, as his friends called him, had been a schoolmate of Edith's brother Harry. Like many of the men in their circle, he had never felt a need to take up any business or profession because he had inherited enough money to live comfortably. Accustomed to spending most of his time playing games or paying visits, he was quite willing to fit in with his adored wife's Newport and New York social round.

Since she was so fond of Europe, however, the couple devoted several months every year to touring off-the-beaten-path hill towns in Italy or visiting Paris, Edith's favorite city. As far as any observer could see, she and Teddy were very happy together. Yet the young Mrs. Wharton felt so much inner conflict that in 1894, nine years after her marriage, she suffered a frightening nervous collapse.

Unable to cope with daily life, she was put under the care of the foremost American specialist in mental illness, Dr. S. Weir Mitchell of Philadelphia. Off and on for the next several years, Edith spent long periods of total rest at a hotel suite there while Dr. Mitchell tried to help her recover from her breakdown. With an outlook far ahead of his time, he strongly encouraged her

to dare society's disapproval by adopting writing as a career.

Till then, Wharton had written occasional short stories and sent them to an editor at *Scribner's* magazine, who printed several of them. But even though she felt proud of these efforts, she also could not help feeling ashamed of them; she had absorbed enough of her mother's attitude to be torn by an extremely intense interior conflict. Thanks to Dr. Mitchell, however, she began, while she was in her early thirties, to evolve her own unique solution to her problem.

In effect, she chose to devote herself to both writing *and* society. Wherever she happened to be, she would spend her mornings in bed with a little table on her lap, turning out page after page of clear and polished prose. Then around noon she would appear downstairs, elegantly dressed and ready for entertaining guests or going on an outing with Teddy in the new "motorcar" he loved to show off.

The most remarkable aspect of Wharton's program, however, was the high quality of what she wrote. Even her first book, a sort of guide for well-off homemakers called *The Decoration of Houses*, on which she collaborated with an architect friend, had such a decisive flavor that it sold far more copies than its publisher had expected. Then her

Edith Wharton in a photograph taken in 1905. *The Bettmann Archive.*

first collection of short stories, published in 1899 when she was thirty-seven, established her as a very promising new literary figure.

Wharton's strong talent for probing "the underground movement of women's minds" was especially noted by one critic. Three years later, her first novel, *The Valley of Decision,* received glowing reviews calling it a "splendid achievement" and calling her "one of the great novelists of the day." However, this long and complicated historical romance, which took place during the 1700s in Italy, is all but forgotten today—because its author soon began to focus her fictional attention on another setting, one with which she herself was intimately familiar.

In 1906, at the age of forty-four, Wharton scored her first major success with the publication of her brilliant novel about New York society entitled *The House of Mirth.* Its satiric picture of this world of wealth and privilege—and the moving struggle of her heroine, Lily Bart, to survive after she was no longer rich—made the book a best-seller that substantially increased its author's income.

But even though casual acquaintances of the Whartons still thought that Edith and Teddy got along wonderfully well together, in fact their marriage had begun to distress both of them. As she

became increasingly prominent and formed friendships with many literary figures, he felt increasingly bored by much of the talk in his own house. At the same time, she felt more and more like a prisoner, condemned to spend the rest of her life with a husband who could not share any of her intellectual interests.

By then the Whartons had built a large country home in the Berkshire Mountains of western Massachusetts, where they spent about half of every year. Wharton saw to it that she had a steady stream of friends visiting The Mount, and the snobbery she had absorbed from her upbringing kept her from getting to know any of poor families native to the area. Still, her imagination was stirred by a run-down farm she saw on one of her drives; and then, further stimulated by the intensity of her own inner misery, in 1911 she wrote her grimly fascinating short novel *Ethan Frome.*

This wintry New England tale could hardly be more different from the usual Wharton story set in the glittering world of high society, and yet its very strong emotional impact has made it more widely read than anything else she ever wrote. Included in many collections of outstanding American literature, it also has been translated into numerous foreign languages.

Within two years after the publication of *Ethan Frome,* the private unhappiness of the Whartons reached a critical point. Teddy had developed a drinking problem, which led to his stealing a large sum of his wife's money and spending it to woo another woman. Then she gave up the viewpoint she had been taught, which harshly condemned any wife who tried to end her marriage, and, in 1913, she secured a divorce. That same year Wharton began to regard the apartment she had rented in Paris as her only real home.

In 1913 she also finished writing *The Custom of the Country,* which some critics consider her most powerful novel. Undine Spragg, the book's brash heroine from the American Middle West, personified the whole category of newly rich outsiders who had, by then, successfully invaded New York society. Although Wharton treated this invasion as high comedy, her underlying contempt for Undine could easily be perceived.

The outbreak of the First World War in 1914 sharply interrupted Wharton's writing, but it did not send her back across the Atlantic to escape the dangers that threatened even noncombatants in Europe. On the contrary, she plunged into organizing a series of agencies to help families forced by the fighting to flee from their homes—and she contributed so much of her own energy and

money to this cause that the French government awarded her its Legion of Honor medal.

Unlike her great friend Henry James, who formally became a British subject during this period, Wharton never gave up her American citizenship to demonstrate her loyalty to her adopted country. But after the coming of peace, when she sailed back across the ocean for a brief visit, she could hardly wait to board a Europe-bound ship again. By then both of her parents had died and, even though she still had her brothers as well as many American friends, she much preferred keeping up with them during their European visits.

So Wharton proceeded to establish *two* elaborate residences where she could regularly entertain her guests—a house just twelve miles outside of Paris and another, for the winter months, in the south of France. Now an imposing woman in her middle fifties, she might have convinced any stranger that she must be a duchess.

Yet she mostly surrounded herself with literary figures, and she continued her longtime pattern of writing in bed every morning. Wharton's *The Age of Innocence,* about New York back in the 1870s, was welcomed on its appearance in 1921 as her finest work of art. It won the Pulitzer Prize as the best American novel published that year.

In addition Wharton became the first

woman ever awarded an honorary degree by Yale University; she even made a brief trip to the United States in 1923 to accept this honor in person. It would be her last Atlantic crossing, for American manners and attitudes had by then diverged so far from her own standards that she had come to feel entirely a stranger there.

Still, Wharton could not give up her writing. As her expenses for the upkeep of her two elegant homes kept mounting, she wrote less carefully, however, and sold many short stories to magazines with low literary standards but high rates of payment. Altogether, her published works would eventually fill over thirty volumes.

At the age of seventy-five, on August 11, 1937, Wharton died at her home near Paris. Since then, her renown as one of this country's outstanding novelists has continued to grow and, early in the 1990s, new motion-picture versions of *Ethan Frome* and *The Age of Innocence* further added to her fame.

E. B. White

1899–1985   Essayist and author of the classic children's books
Stuart Little and *Charlotte's Web*

His five older sisters and brothers all had ordinary names like Clara or Stanley. But shortly before his birth, his mother met a woman from Wales who had a little boy named Elwyn. And she fell under a sort of spell.

His father, who was the president of their church's board of trustees, thought that naming their new son after their minister would be more appropriate. Yet even though he took his role as the head of his household very seriously, he was a loving ruler. So a compromise was arrived at, and the youngest member of this family became Elwyn Brooks White.

No wonder, then, that he hid behind his initials throughout his literary career. In the many "Notes and Comment" columns he wrote for the sophisticated

New Yorker magazine, as well as in the seemingly simple animal stories he told in his immensely popular children's books, his own unassuming personality was really the most important factor. So a fancy first name like Elwyn certainly did not suit him.

Apart from his unusual name, however, he had a most fortunate start in life. He was born, on July 11, 1899, at his family's large and comfortable home in the suburb of Mount Vernon, about a half hour's train ride north of New York City. There he enjoyed many advantages that came of being the baby in a big, affectionate, and increasingly prosperous family.

For instance one of his early Christmas presents was the first small-sized bicycle to be seen in his neighborhood.

When he was just eleven, for his birthday he got the best canoe money could buy up in Maine, where the Whites regularly spent a month every summer.

His father, Samuel Tilley White, had endured poverty during his own youth and left school at the age of thirteen. But he poured so much energy into his first job as an errand boy for a company that manufactured pianos that soon he was promoted—and around the time Elwyn arrived on the scene, he became the piano company's president.

The future writer's mother, Jessie Hart White, was a warmhearted woman who seemed entirely contented with her busy household routine. Still, she liked to brag a bit about the artistic talent on her side of the family: Her father, who had started out working for a carriage maker, had developed such a skill at painting scenes on door panels that he eventually became one of the most prominent landscape painters of his era. Perhaps hearing repeatedly about this grandfather contributed toward forming the unconventional outlook of the Whites' youngest son.

While it appears that his parents and schoolteachers really did call him Elwyn, younger people often shortened this in one way or another. The brothers and sisters nearest to his own age, who were his main companions during his growing-up years, favored just plain En.

That nickname also caught on among his few good friends—boys who shared his fondness for animals, bicycles, and sailboats.

Only the friends and relatives he felt thoroughly at ease with realized what a bright sense of humor En had. Among strangers he always suffered great waves of shyness, perhaps at least partly because he was smaller than most boys of his age and felt insignificant. But he also had an unusual number of other worries.

Most of all he dreaded having to stand up on the platform at a school assembly and make a speech, a test that every pupil was supposed to pass once every semester. En lived in terror as each new term started—until the day he realized that the speech-making assignments always went in alphabetical order. And he could hardly have had a luckier last name: White came so far down in the alphabet that, all through his school days, he was actually called on only once to address his fellow students. Still, he never lost this fear and throughout his life he would never accept any invitation to speak in front of an audience.

Yet writing was a totally different matter. That method of expressing himself came easily to him, and by the age of eight En had already formed the habit of keeping a diary recording his daily activities and also raising various questions he wanted to think about. "Why does a fox bark?" he asked himself. "How does a bird know how to build a nest?"

Around the time En turned ten, he began entering the writing contests that some of the popular children's magazines of the era sponsored. When he was eleven, he won a silver medal for a poem about a mouse. Then, at fourteen, he got a gold medal for "A True Dog Story"—telling how his big, friendly Irish setter named Beppo suddenly turned ferocious to scare away a herd of menacing steers. Something like this had actually happened one day when he was out walking with some of his family across a hilltop pasture up in Maine.

These early literary successes gave En more of a feeling of self-confidence than anything else he did. He thoroughly enjoyed trying out different combinations of words and, like a natural athlete taking up a new game, he knew, without anybody having to tell him so, that he was good at it. By the time he started college, when he was eighteen, he already felt pretty sure that he would aim to be a writer.

Very soon after his arrival at Cornell University, in upstate New York, one of his basic problems was happily solved. Again because of his last name, which reminded his fellow students of the university's popular president, Dr. Andrew

D. White, he quickly acquired the nickname Andy. For the rest of his life, he would be Andy to everybody who knew him well.

Despite the shyness that still plagued him, Andy was asked to join one of the leading fraternities on the campus. Writing to his sister Lillian, he confided that he was going to turn down the invitation because he couldn't possibly live up to the favorable impression he'd somehow given. Lillian immediately sent him a letter urging him to reconsider. "For Heaven's sake *don't be scared,*" she wrote. "Have confidence in yourself."

So Andy did join the fraternity—and he gradually relaxed to the extent that, three years later, he was elected its president. During his senior year, he also served as the editor in chief of the *Cornell Daily Sun,* considered one of the best newspapers on any college campus. By the time he graduated, in the spring of 1921, he surely appeared to be on the brink of a promising journalistic future.

However, Andy himself was far from enthusiastic about the prospect ahead of him. He wanted to write whatever he felt like writing, whenever he felt like writing it, and he realized by now that the newspaper business did not work that way. Yet he could not count on having his father support him forever, nor could he hope to earn a fortune as the

author of a great American novel because he had very little interest in either reading or writing fiction.

So he got a job, which distressed him as much as he had expected, requiring him to compose routine prose for a New York City news agency. After several painfully boring months of commuting back and forth from his parents' home in Mount Vernon, he suddenly made up his mind that he needed one last fling of freedom before becoming an editorial slave for the rest of his life.

So he set out on a grand adventure with one of his college fraternity brothers. In a Model T Ford roadster, they started westward with the aim of "seeing the country" all the way to the Pacific Ocean. In 1922, when many rural roads were really only rutted dirt tracks, such an expedition was considered rather daring.

Although neither Andy nor his friend brought along much money, they lightheartedly looked for free hospitality on campuses along their route—or else unfolded the tent they had tied onto the car's running board with their luggage. To pay their other expenses, they worked a few days every so often at any odd jobs they could find.

Fortunately "the Model T was not a fussy car," White wrote years afterward. "It had clearance, it had guts, and it enjoyed wonderful health." Indeed, every-thing connected with his seven-month journey across the country acquired a sort of magical aura.

But when it formally ended in the state of Washington and White buckled down to work as a reporter for the *Seattle Times,* all of the magic evaporated. Covering businessmen's meetings bored him, covering crime stories horrified him—and yet he seemed to have such a lively mind that, after six months, the paper's editor decided to let him try conducting a small daily column of his own.

In that period many newspapers contained columns of brief humorous items collected from other publications or contributed by readers. A few of these stood out because they were presided over by talented writers whose own snippets of verse or prose provided a special flavor. White followed the pattern set by his favorite columnist back in New York City, and created regular departments with headings like "We Answer Hard Questions."

In addition, though, he veered off in a new direction by spinning lightly comic little tales out of his personal experiences, for instance a three-paragraph item starting, "Yesterday we encountered a salesman extraordinary. We told him we wanted to buy garters. 'Gray is your color,' he said, briskly handing us a set. We pocketed them in amazement."

Then Andy proceeded, tongue in cheek, to explain how this salesman's positive statement had vastly simplified his life.

Yet much as he enjoyed some aspects of column writing, he did not feel comfortable with the journalistic style of the era, which required him to refer to himself as *we* instead of *I*. And his editor set many restrictions limiting the topics he could write about, which upset him increasingly. So he actually felt relieved, after only three months as a columnist, when he got fired—especially because the blow was softened by assurances that his brand of wit would be better appreciated in New York than Seattle.

Not a bit prudently, White embarked on a cruise to Alaska just because he had always wanted to see it. Then, in the fall of 1923, at the age of twenty-four, he returned by train to New York. There he endured another few years of floundering, both personally and professionally, before his future finally turned bright.

Dutifully living with his parents again, White still shied away from forming any serious attachment to any young woman who attracted him. He spent many evenings alone, polishing bits of verse that he sent to his favorite columnist for the *New York World*—and every so often he thrilled at the sight of his own words in print. Otherwise, he earned a modest income from various dreary jobs writing advertising or publicity puffery.

Then during February of 1925 the first issue of a brand-new weekly magazine called *The New Yorker* went on sale. White had been keeping an eye out for it because somebody had told him it might welcome the sort of half-humorous, half-serious short pieces that he liked best to write. He would always remember snapping up a copy one evening as he "swung into Grand Central Terminal" after a boring day of work.

Just nine weeks later, his first contribution to the new magazine—a few paragraphs about the arrival of spring—appeared in print.

In years to come, it would sometimes be assumed that E. B. White and *The New Yorker* both achieved eminence as soon as they found each other. But the reality was more complicated. Even though White continued to send the magazine an occasional piece, he did not become a regular staff writer until the autumn of 1927. By then, the magazine's gifted editor, Harold Ross, had already put it on the track toward profitability.

Nevertheless White's agreement to take over writing "Notes and Comment" at the front of the magazine every week would soon give *The New Yorker* a very special stature. Instead of being regarded as just a source of clever humor, sometimes expressed rather snobbishly, it acquired a much broader appeal—along with genuine literary distinction.

All of this came to pass because the worldwide economic collapse that started in 1929, and then the outbreak of World War II a decade later, spurred White to a matchless eloquence. Unpretentiously, and yet with great power, he compressed complicated thoughts, sometimes into mere paragraphs. For instance, shortly after the war at last ended, in 1946 he wrote:

The subtlest sign in town is on an "L" pillar at Forty-eighth Street and Third Avenue. The sign reads, "UNITED NATIONS," and there is an arrow. The arrow is vertical—one of those conventional highway "straight ahead" indications. A harried motorist would probably interpret this without trouble and would keep going toward the East River Drive; but we were on foot, and far gone in meditation, and for us the arrow distinctly pointed straight up past the railroad tracks and on into Heaven.

Besides the hundreds of opinion pieces White wrote for *The New Yorker*, he also wrote numerous other articles reporting on whatever interested him. As these, too, made his own idealistic outlook an important part of the story, he would sometimes be credited with developing a new type of personal journalism. Yet most authorities placed him instead among the nation's outstanding essayists, often comparing him with his own literary hero, Henry David Thoreau.

Still, White himself refused to claim any literary grandeur, despite the many medals he received over the years from groups like the National Institute for Arts and Letters. Once he told an interviewer, "I read farm journals and boating magazines," and, except for Thoreau "my favorite authors are people nobody has ever heard of."

Shy as he always remained, White's personal happiness as well as his professional career owed much to his *New Yorker* connection. The first person he met there was an attractive woman with a mass of dark hair coiled at the back of her neck. Katharine Angell, the principal assistant to *The New Yorker*'s editor, was unhappily married then, and soon would be divorced. On November 13, 1929, Kay and Andy took the afternoon off and drove northward about fifty miles until they found a clergyman who would conduct a wedding ceremony for them.

Always at ease with children, White had no difficulty making friends with Kay's eleven-year-old daughter and nine-year-old son. Around a year afterward, she gave birth to another boy, whom they named Joel. When Kay's comfortable apartment began to seem too crowded, they bought a brownstone

E. B. White in his office at *The New Yorker* in 1954. *UPI/Bettmann Newsphotos.*

house near the East River with its own back garden, and in the same period they also bought a forty-acre farm on the Maine seacoast, not far from the town of North Brooklin, where they spent as much time as they could.

With a housekeeper as well as several other helpers, the Whites' living expenses kept increasing, but so did their income. Kay, holding what by then was considered one of New York's most important editorial jobs, earned a substan-

tial amount of money herself. However, her main contribution to the family finances came indirectly. One of her lesser tasks at *The New Yorker* was to prepare an annual feature reviewing the year's outstanding children's books, and great piles of possibilities grew on every available surface in their living room late every autumn.

So her husband inevitably started leafing through them, muttering about being able to do better himself without half trying. Having been the youngest in a large family, he had begun acquiring nieces and nephews at an early age—and, based on a dream of his in which he himself was a mouse, he had long ago made up a series of bedtime stories about a mouse named Stuart.

Over the years he had written down a few chapters containing Stuart's adventures. At Kay's prodding, not long after their marriage he had shown these chapters to a book publisher, who shook his head. Even so, late in 1944 he dug these out and during the next several months he added and polished until he felt fairly confident that he had created an acceptable children's book.

By then several volumes of E. B. White essays had won high praise from literary critics. His publisher decided to take a chance on *Stuart Little,* the mouse story White brought him, even though the retired head librarian in the children's department of the New York Public Library strongly objected. She claimed that children would be very upset by the fantastic notion that an ordinary human family could have a child who was a mouse.

But *Stuart Little* almost immediately became a best-seller and earned a lot of money for the Whites. White himself later noted that he had learned two things from the experience of writing it: "that a writer's own nose is the best guide and that children can sail easily over the fence that separates reality from make-believe. . . . A fence that can throw a librarian is as nothing to a child."

Several years afterward, spending a whole summer up at their Maine farm, White got an idea for another children's book while working in the barn. Without any advance notice, a few months later he gave his publisher the completed manuscript of a story about how a kindly spider named Charlotte saved the life of Wilbur, a pig doomed to be slaughtered. Upon its publication in 1951, *Charlotte's Web* received a marvelous welcome.

It was called "magical," "witty and wise," even "just about perfect." While professors proclaimed it a masterpiece on a par with *Alice in Wonderland,* many thousand parents bought copies for their children.

The third of White's trio of remarkable children's books, *The Trumpet of the Swan,* did not stir quite as much excitement, but ever since its publication in 1970 it has continued to rival the other two in popularity.

By 1957 both of the Whites were ready to give up New York's tensions and live all year round at their Maine farm. Andy loved taking care of assorted animals there, going out sailing, and playing with visiting grandchildren. Yet he continued sending contributions to *The New Yorker* for another several years.

Despite the many health problems that increasingly afflicted both Kay and Andy, they had twenty mostly happy years together in Maine before she died in 1977. By then, Andy was suffering frequent dizzy spells and his eyesight was failing. Nevertheless, watched over by relatives who had settled in the area, he still enjoyed some good days.

E. B. White was eighty-six when he died at his Maine home on October 1, 1985. In the literary world, about a dozen books of his essays are still widely read, and so is his much-admired small volume of advice about how to write correctly. *The Elements of Style*, his version of a text originally written by one of his Cornell professors, William Strunk, Jr., has sometimes been called a sort of bible for would-be authors on college campuses.

But most of all White is remembered for his three children's books, especially *Charlotte's Web*. Forty years after its original appearance, in 1992 it still held the number-one place on the publishing industry's annual list of best-selling paperbacks for young readers.

Tennessee Williams

1911–1983   Playwright from the South

When he was born on March 26, 1911, in Columbus, Mississippi, his parents named him Thomas Lanier Williams. But after he started to write he renamed himself Tennessee Williams. Under that name, he became one of America's foremost playwrights.

Why did he make the change? To him, his middle name of Lanier had the ring of bad poetry. And he felt that there were too many people named Thomas Williams already.

But why did he pick Tennessee as his new first name? One story was that his northern college friends knew from his accent that he came from the South and picked a Southern state they liked the sound of for his nickname. However, his mother once explained that some Williams ancestors had fought the Indi-

ans for control of Tennessee in the pioneer days. The playwright himself brushed aside questions on the subject by saying that he had made the choice because of his roots in Tennessee.

At any rate, one of his forebears was a Thomas Lanier Williams who had been an official of the territory that later became the state of Tennessee. Another was the John Williams who became the first senator from the new state of Tennessee. His grandfather, Thomas Lanier Williams II, ran unsuccessfully several times for the post of governor of Tennessee.

His father, Cornelius Williams, had studied law at the University of Tennessee before becoming a traveling shoe salesman. His mother, Edwina Dakin Williams, had grown up as the only child of a minister and his wife, living a sheltered life in the Episcopal rectory in Columbus. A beautiful young woman, she received many gentlemen callers—as portrayed in her son's first hit play, *The Glass Menagerie.*

Tom was the second child in his family. He had an older sister, Rose, then later a younger brother, Dakin. Because his father was away so often on selling trips, his mother and his sister were his main influences during his early years. He would later remember this period as rather ordinary—a peaceful time of playing with paper boats, keeping white rabbits, and collecting colored glass fragments from broken bottles.

But a serious case of diphtheria changed his life. Sick for a year, Tom was transformed from a robust, aggressive boy into a shy and solitary one, playing cards by himself for amusement. He later said that his mother's constant attention planted in him the makings of a sissy.

When Tom was seven years old, his father was promoted to a new job as a supervisor at the main offices of the shoe company he worked for, in St. Louis, Missouri. The family moved to St. Louis in 1918, and Tom went to school there.

One afternoon he heard a child screaming in back of the street where he lived. He ran toward an alley, where he found some hoods throwing rocks at a girl. Tom, then eleven years old, went to her defense and together they ran away to her house. The girl, Hazel Kramer, then nine years old, became his best friend.

They played together every afternoon in the attic of her house. Tom would make up stories and Hazel would draw pictures to illustrate them. As they grew older, they grew closer. Years later he would call her the greatest love of his life outside of his family.

Also when he was eleven, Tom's mother bought him a typewriter. He loved it and, as he said later, "I forgot to write longhand after that." He used his new typewriter when he started to compose poetry; his first known published works are two poems in his junior high school's newspaper signed "Thomas Williams, 9th Gr."

Throughout his high school days, Tom entered many writing contests. His first success was a five-dollar prize from a magazine for a story on a subject he knew nothing about: "Can a Good Wife Be a Good Sport?" But his biggest triumph was selling his first short story to a widely circulated magazine called *Weird Tales.* His contribution was "The Vengeance of Nitocris," a fanciful tale about a queen in ancient Egypt.

Tom did well academically at high school, graduating in 1929 with a B average. At the age of eighteen, he enrolled as a freshman at the University of Missouri. His first night there he wrote a letter to Hazel, who had gone to the University of Wisconsin, proposing marriage. Hazel, only sixteen, wrote back saying that they were too young to think of marriage.

After that rebuff from Hazel, Tom never asked another woman to marry him. He discovered that he was more interested in men than in women. Even though he had many women friends for the rest of his life, his intimate associations were with other men. He never hid the fact that he was an active homosexual.

At college Tom studied at the School of Journalism, with the aim of working on a newspaper. But he really was more interested in creative writing. He entered the university's dramatic arts contest, winning an honorable mention for his first play, *Beauty Is the Word.* His academic record, though, was undistinguished, apart from the good work he did in English.

After completing three years of college, Tom was forced to leave because of financial problems at home. His father found him a job as a clerk in a shoe company. Every day, Tom had to dust off hundreds of shoes in the sample room, then type out factory orders, and at four in the afternoon he delivered

Tennessee Williams in a high school photograph. *The Humanities Research Center, University of Texas at Austin.*

heavy boxes of shoes to the company's customers. He hated his job, but stayed with it for three years.

No matter how tired he was, every evening when he returned home he sat down at his typewriter. Drinking coffee and smoking cigarettes as he worked, he wrote verse during the week. On weekends he wrote short stories, trying to finish one a week. He sent off regular packets to *Story* magazine; all of them came back, rejected.

Meanwhile the family life of the

Williamses was falling apart. Tom's parents constantly quarreled and his sister Rose began to show signs of mental instability, for which she was later hospitalized. Tom, however, had an escape—his job and his writing.

In 1935, when he was twenty-four years old, he went for a summer to his grandparents in Memphis, Tennessee. Most of his time was spent reading, but he did write a short play in collaboration with a member of the local theater group. Called *Cairo, Shanghai, Bombay!* it was a one-act melodrama that the local group staged, making it his first produced play.

When Williams returned to St. Louis that fall, he was determined to be a playwright. After studying for a year at Washington University in St. Louis, he left in 1938 to take playwriting courses at the University of Iowa in Ames.

There, in addition to writing several short plays, he also wrote a short story, "The Field of Blue Children," about a poet at the state university who makes love to a girl in a field of wild blue flowers. It was published in *Story* magazine in 1939 under the byline of Tennessee Williams, the first recorded use of his new name. From then on, his new friends called him Tenn, while his old friends and family continued to call him Tom.

At the end of his year at Iowa, he sent off his work—four long plays and three short ones—to the Group Theater, a well-known theatrical company in New York City. Without a job and without money, Williams, now twenty-eight years old, moved to New Orleans, where he could live cheaply, and then to Los Angeles.

While there, he received a telegram from the Group Theater. With his Iowa plays, he had won a writing contest and an award of one hundred dollars, a respectable amount of money in those days. On the basis of that award, the theatrical agent Audrey Wood undertook to represent him. One of her first actions was to encourage him to apply for a foundation grant. He did, and received the impressive sum of one thousand dollars.

With that money he went to New York, the capital of the theatrical world. He enrolled in a playwriting course at the New School, went to the theater at nights, wrote plays in his spare time, and worked as an usher in a movie theater, an elevator operator, and a restaurant waiter to make money.

In 1940 one of his one-act plays, *The Long Goodbye,* was put on in a student production at the New School. Later that year, the Theater Guild, one of the leading Broadway producers, staged his full-length play *Battle of Angels.* It was a disaster. But he was not discouraged.

One day, Audrey Wood called him to her office to tell him that she had a job for him as a screenwriter in Hollywood.

"You are to get two-fifty," she said.

"Two-fifty a month!" he shouted. Two hundred and fifty dollars a month was far more money than he had ever earned.

"No," she replied. "Two-fifty a week."

In a daze, Williams went to Hollywood. He and the movie studio could not agree on what he would write about, so he spent most of his time working on his own plays. After six months he arrived back in New York with several plays in his suitcase, including a new one, *The Glass Menagerie.* It was a thinly disguised story about his own family—in particular, about his mother and sister and their gentlemen callers.

But in *The Glass Menagerie,* as in Williams's other plays, the atmosphere it conveyed of loneliness and unhappiness was far more important than the story it told. He once said that the main theme of all of his plays was the conflict between the Southern romantic attitude toward life and the down-to-earth elements of real life that tend to defeat it.

Everybody who read the script of *The Glass Menagerie* liked it. The play opened in Chicago late in 1944, and drama critics there gave it high praise. When it came to Broadway early in 1945, the opening-night audience applauded so vigorously that the actors took twenty curtain calls—and there were numerous shouts of "Author! Author!"

Williams climbed to the stage wearing a gray flannel suit with a missing coat button and a shirt of a strange shade of green. One observer wrote that "Mr. Williams appeared more like a farm boy in his Sunday best than the author of a Broadway success."

He sent a telegram to his mother: "REVIEWS ALL RAVE. INDICATE SMASH HIT. LINE BLOCK LONG AT BOX OFFICE. LOVE TOM." Not only was the play a financial success, but it was also praised by the critics. *The Glass Menagerie* won for him his first major playwriting prize—the best play of the year award from the New York Drama Critics Circle.

Throughout his career, Williams would maintain close relations with his family, except his father. He dedicated half of the money he earned from *The Glass Menagerie* to his mother, he paid for the support of his sister Rose in several different institutions, and he always kept in touch with his younger brother, Dakin. He often visited his grandparents, even taking his ailing grandfather on trips with him.

Although Williams seemed shy to strangers, he had many friends, both men and women. He had many ailments too. The one that bothered him the most was an injured left eye, damaged in a childhood game. He underwent many painful operations to restore his sight in that eye.

In 1946 Williams went to Dallas, where a regional theater was putting on his *Summer and Smoke.* Back in New York, he completed another play, *You Touched Me!,* with a collaborator. It received mixed notices and ran for only two weeks. But during those two weeks Williams had two plays—*The Glass Menagerie* and *You Touched Me!*—running on Broadway at the same time, most unusual for a young playwright.

Once again he traveled to New Orleans, one of his favorite cities. He got up early in the morning to begin working on two more plays, *Camino Real* and *A Streetcar Named Desire* (at that time streetcars in New Orleans were named according to the district they served, and Desire was one of them). Williams drove with his widowed and elderly grandfather to Key West in Florida, where he put the finishing touches on *Streetcar.*

When it opened on Broadway late in 1948, with Jessica Tandy and Marlon Brando playing the leading roles, it was an immediate hit. Set in New Orleans, it tells the story of two sisters, one a fading Southern belle, Blanche DuBois, and the other married to a crude former army sergeant, Stanley Kowalski. "A masterpiece," the influential critic Brooks Atkinson wrote in *The New York Times.*

That same newspaper years later would run an editorial commenting on the exceptional emotional power of *Streetcar's* final scene. "No one who saw it ever forgot it: a woman with a broken mind taking the arm of the man who is to escort her to an asylum and saying with exquisite courtesy, 'Whoever you are—I have always depended on the kindness of strangers.' "

With the production of a second hit play in three years, Williams became one of the most successful of American playwrights. *Streetcar* won many awards, including the Pulitzer Prize for the best play of the year and another Drama Critics Circle award. Many years after its first production, *Streetcar* is probably the best known of all Tennessee Williams's plays. It is still revived from time to time in the United States and many other countries.

Williams began to make large sums of money late in the 1940s, and gave some of it away to needy younger writers. He traveled widely—to England, France, Spain, Morocco, and Italy. In Rome he started to write his first novel, *The Roman Spring of Mrs. Stone,* and a play, *The Rose Tattoo,* for his new friend Anna Magnani, the well-known Italian movie star.

In 1949, Williams returned to the

Tennessee Williams in front of the door of his studio near his Key West, Florida home in 1957. *The Bettmann Archive.*

United States. First he rented a house in Key West, Florida, where he planned to stay and write. Then he visited Hollywood, where a film was being made of *A Streetcar Named Desire,* with Vivian Leigh as Blanche. He also finished *The Rose Tattoo,* which opened on Broadway in early 1951. It did not receive the enormously enthusiastic reviews that *Streetcar* did, and Williams was disappointed.

Now forty years old, he had become a celebrity who appeared frequently on radio and television talk shows. At home and abroad, he and his male companions moved easily in the world of film stars, directors, and writers at expensive hotels, restaurants, and resorts. But wherever he went, Williams carried his portable typewriter, and worked as well as played.

During the next ten years Williams wrote another six memorable plays. The first of these, *Camino Real* (The Royal Road), was produced in 1953. A departure from Williams's usual themes, it was a fantasy about famous characters from history and literature in their declining years—Don Quixote, Casanova, and Lord Byron among many others. It confused audiences as well as critics.

But his next play, *Cat on a Hot Tin Roof,* produced in 1955, was a smash hit, and remains one of his most admired plays. Like most of the others, it was set in the South, with unhappy characters trying to live in a world, as one of them puts it, filled with "mendacity," or lies.

Praised by the critics and the public, *Cat* ran longer on Broadway than any other of Williams's plays. It won for him his second Pulitzer Prize and his third New York Drama Critics Circle award for the best play of the year. Also, it was made into a movie with Elizabeth Taylor playing the leading role.

Instead of being elated by the critical and financial success of *Cat,* Williams became depressed. Worried about how he could write another play, he fled to Key West but felt himself blocked whenever he sat down at his typewriter there. Unable to write, he drank excessive amounts of coffee, then turned to pills, which he sometimes washed down with whiskey.

After a trip to Europe, Williams came out of his depression and began to write again. During the next five years, he completed four more plays that were successfully produced on Broadway. They were *Orpheus Descending, Suddenly Last Summer, Sweet Bird of Youth,* and *The Night of the Iguana.*

At the age of fifty, Williams appeared to be at the height of his powers. *The Night of the Iguana* won for him his fourth New York Drama Critics Circle award as the best play of the year. *Time* magazine put his picture on its cover and called him "the greatest living playwright in the English speaking world."

But his personal life was increasingly troubled. His lover of many years died. One of his new plays got terrible reviews. He lived in his New York apartment so uninterested in food that he boiled plain spaghetti for himself and ate it without any sauce at all. He began to take excessive amounts of pills to sleep and then others to keep himself awake. On top of that, he drank too much.

After being hospitalized for drug use, Williams began to write again with the help of a psychiatrist. During the next twenty years, he wrote about twenty new plays—but none of them reached the quality of his earlier work. He knew it, which depressed him greatly. He told one interviewer, "The wells of emotion that spring spontaneously from the mind and spirit do not flow with the power that produced 'The Glass Menagerie' and 'A Streetcar Named Desire.'"

In 1980 Williams, then sixty-nine years old, received the Presidential Medal of Freedom in a ceremony at the White House. In presenting the award, President Jimmy Carter said, "Tennessee Williams has shaped the history of American drama. From passionate tragedy to lyrical comedy, his masterpieces dramatize the eternal conflict of body and soul, youth and death, love and despair."

It was a fitting obituary, although Williams did not die until February 25, 1983, at the age of seventy-two.

Bibliography

For the factual foundation of each of our chapters we have relied mainly on two major biographical reference works—the multivolume *Dictionary of American Biography,* published by Charles Scribner's Sons starting in 1928; and *Notable American Women,* issued by the Belknap Press of Harvard University Press beginning in 1971.

In the case of writers from the comparatively recent past, not yet covered in supplements to the above authoritative compilations, we have sought birth dates and the like from such sources as *The New York Times* and *Current Biography,* published regularly by the H. W. Wilson Company of New York.

But our efforts to give each chapter the flavor of its subject's personality led us to read many other books. In addition to literary works by the authors we were writing about, we consulted numerous biographies and memoirs; in both categories, however, much of what we read would probably not appeal to many young readers.

For them we have prepared a separate list of suggestions for further reading, which contains examples of the most accessible writings of each of our subjects. This list will be found starting on page 301.

What follows here is an author-by-author compilation of just the biographical sources that were most useful to us in assembling each of our chapters.

Part I: Early Days

JAMES FENIMORE COOPER

Boynton, Henry Walcott. *James Fenimore Cooper.* New York: Century, 1931.

Brooks, Van Wyck. *The World of Washington Irving.* Philadelphia: Blakiston, 1944.

Ringe, Donald. *James Fenimore Cooper.* New Haven: Twayne, 1962.

RALPH WALDO EMERSON

Allen, Gay Wilson. *Waldo Emerson.* New York: Viking Press, 1981.

Brooks, Van Wyck. *The Flowering of New England.* New York: E. P. Dutton & Co., 1936.

McAleer, John. *Ralph Waldo Emerson.* Boston: Little, Brown & Co., 1984.

NATHANIEL HAWTHORNE

Mellow, James. *Nathaniel Hawthorne in His Times.* Boston: Houghton Mifflin Co., 1980.

Miller, Edwin Haviland. *Salem Is My Dwelling Place.* Iowa City: University of Iowa Press, 1992.

Turner, Arlin. *Nathaniel Hawthorne.* New York: Oxford University Press, 1980.

WASHINGTON IRVING

Brooks, Van Wyck. *The World of Washington Irving.* Philadelphia: Blakiston, 1944.

Myers, Andrew B., editor. *The Worlds of Washington Irving.* Tarrytown: Sleepy Hollow Press, 1974.

Williams, Stanley T. *The Life of Washington Irving.* New York: Oxford University Press, 1935.

HENRY WADSWORTH LONGFELLOW

Arvin, Newton. *Longfellow: His Life and His Work.* Boston: Little, Brown & Co., 1962.

Thompson, Lawrence. *Young Longfellow.* New York: Macmillan Co., 1938.

Williams, Cecil B. *Henry Wadsworth Longfellow.* Boston: Twayne, 1961.

HERMAN MELVILLE

Allen, Gay Wilson. *Melville and His World.* New York: Viking Press, 1971.

Arvin, Newton. *Herman Melville.* New York: William Sloan Associates, 1950.

Miller, Edwin Haviland. *Melville.* New York: George Braziller, 1965.

EDGAR ALLAN POE

Allen, Hervey. *Israfel: The Life and Times of Edgar Allan Poe.* New York: Farrar & Rinehart, 1934.

Buranelli, Vincent. *Edgar Allan Poe.* New York: Twayne, 1961.

Silverman, Kenneth. *Edgar A. Poe.* New York: HarperCollins, 1991.

HARRIET BEECHER STOWE

Gerson, Noel B. *Harriet Beecher Stowe.* New York: Praeger, 1976.

Rugoff, Milton. *The Beechers: An American Family in the Nineteenth Century.* New York: Harper & Row, 1981.

Stowe, Charles E. *The Life of Harriet Beecher Stowe.* Boston: Houghton Mifflin Co., 1890.

HENRY DAVID THOREAU

Harding, Walter. *The Days of Henry Thoreau.* New York: Alfred A. Knopf, 1967.

Krutch, Joseph Wood. *Henry David Thoreau.* New York: William Sloan Associates, 1948.

Schneider, Richard J. *Henry David Thoreau.* Boston: Twayne, 1981.

Part II: The Middle Period

LOUISA MAY ALCOTT

Cheney, Ednah D. *Louisa May Alcott: Her Life, Letters, and Journals.* Boston: Roberts Brothers, 1889.

Shepard, Odell. *Pedlar's Progress: The Life of Bronson Alcott.* New York: Greenwood, 1968.

Stern, Madeleine B. *Louisa May Alcott*. Norman: University of Oklahoma Press, 1950.

EMILY DICKINSON

Bingham, Millicent Todd. *Emily Dickinson's Home: Letters of Edward Dickinson and His Family*. New York: Harper & Brothers, 1955.
Leyda, Jay. *The Years and Hours of Emily Dickinson*. New Haven: Yale University Press, 1960.
Sewall, Richard B. *The Life of Emily Dickinson*. New York: Farrar, Straus and Giroux, 1980.

THEODORE DREISER

Elias, Pellham. *Theodore Dreiser*. New York: Alfred A. Knopf, 1949.
Matthiesen, F. O. *Theodore Dreiser*. London: Sloane, 1951.
Swanberg, W. A. *Dreiser*. New York: Charles Scribner's Sons, 1965.

O. HENRY

Current-Garcia, Eugene. *O. Henry*. New York: Twayne, 1965.
Langford, Gerald. *Alias O. Henry: A Biography of William Sydney Porter*. New York: Macmillan Co., 1957.
Snith, C. Alfonso. *O. Henry*. Garden City, N.Y.: Doubleday, Page & Co., 1916.

HENRY JAMES

Auchincloss, Louis. *Reading Henry James*. Minneapolis: University of Minnesota Press, 1975.
Edel, Leon. *Henry James*. 5 vols. New York: J. B. Lippincott & Co., 1954–1972.
James, Henry. *A Small Boy and Others*. New York: Charles Scribner's Sons, 1913.
———. *Notes of a Son and Brother*. New York: Charles Scribner's Sons, 1914.

JACK LONDON

Hedrick, John D. *Solitary Comrade: Jack London and His Work*. Chapel Hill: University of North Carolina Press, 1982.
Labor, Earle. *Jack London*. New York: Twayne, 1974.
O'Connor, Richard. *Jack London*. Boston: Little, Brown & Co., 1964.

MARK TWAIN

Kaplan, Justin. *Mark Twain and His World*. New York: Simon and Schuster, 1974.
Lauber, John. *The Making of Mark Twain*. New York: Farrar, Straus and Giroux, 1985.
Zall, Paul M. *Mark Twain Laughing*. Knoxville: University of Tennessee Press, 1985.

WALT WHITMAN

Allen, Gay Wilson. *The Solitary Singer*. New York: Macmillan Co., 1955.
Kaplan, Justin. *Walt Whitman*. New York: Simon and Schuster, 1980.
Miller, James E. *Walt Whitman*. Boston: Twayne, 1962.

Part III: Modern American Writers

PEARL S. BUCK

Buck, Pearl S. *My Several Worlds: A Personal Record*. New York: John Day Co., 1954.
Walsh, Richard J. *A Biographical Sketch of Pearl S. Buck*. New York: John Day Co., 1936.

WILLA CATHER

Lewis, Edith. *Willa Cather Living*. New York: Alfred A. Knopf, 1953.
O'Brien, Sharon. *Willa Cather*. New York: Oxford University Press, 1987.
Robinson, Phyllis C. *The Life of Willa Cather*. New York: Doubleday & Co., 1983.

WILLIAM FAULKNER

Blotner, Joseph. *William Faulkner.* New York: Random House, 1974.

Kreiswirth, Martin. *William Faulkner: The Making of a Novelist.* Athens: University of Georgia Press, 1983.

Oates, Stephen B. *William Faulkner: The Man and the Artist.* New York: Harper & Row, 1987.

F. SCOTT FITZGERALD

Mayfield, Sara. *Exiles from Paradise: Zelda and Scott Fitzgerald.* New York: Delacorte, 1971.

Mizener, Arthur. *The Far Side of Paradise.* Boston: Houghton Mifflin Co., 1951.

Turnbull, Arthur. *Scott Fitzgerald.* New York: Charles Scribner's Sons, 1962.

ROBERT FROST

Burnshaw, Stanley. *Robert Frost Himself.* New York: George Braziller, 1986.

Pritchard, William H. *Frost: A Literary Life Reconsidered.* New York: Oxford University Press, 1984.

Sergeant, Elizabeth S. *Robert Frost.* New York: Holt, Rinehart and Winston, 1960.

ERNEST HEMINGWAY

Baker, Carlos. *Ernest Hemingway.* New York: Charles Scribner's Sons, 1969.

Hemingway, Mary Walsh. *How It Was.* New York: Alfred A. Knopf, 1976.

Hotchner, A. E. *Papa Hemingway.* New York: Random House, 1966.

LANGSTON HUGHES

Berry, Faith. *Langston Hughes.* Westport, Conn.: Lawrence Hill, 1984.

Emanuel, James A. *Langston Hughes.* New York: Twayne, 1967.

Rampersad, Arnold. *The Life of Langston Hughes.* New York: Oxford University Press, 1986.

SINCLAIR LEWIS

Dooley, D. J. *The Art of Sinclair Lewis.* Lincoln: University of Nebraska Press, 1967.

Schorer, Mark. *Sinclair Lewis.* New York: McGraw-Hill Book Co., 1961.

EUGENE O'NEILL

Carpenter, Frederic I. *Eugene O'Neill.* Boston: Twayne, 1979.

Gelb, Arthur, and Barbara Gelb. *O'Neill.* New York: Harper & Brothers, 1962.

Sheaffer, Louis. *O'Neill.* Boston: Little, Brown & Co., 1973.

JOHN STEINBECK

Benson, Jackson J. *The True Adventures of John Steinbeck, Writer.* New York: Viking Press, 1984.

French, Warren. *John Steinbeck.* Boston: Twayne, 1989.

Valjohn, Nelson. *John Steinbeck, the Errant Knight.* San Francisco: Chronicle Books, 1975.

EDITH WHARTON

Auchincloss, Louis. *Edith Wharton.* Minneapolis: University of Minnesota Press, 1961.

Lewis, R. W. B. *Edith Wharton.* New York: Harper & Row, 1975.

Wharton, Edith. *A Backward Glance.* New York: D. Appleton-Century Co., 1936.

E. B. WHITE

Elledge, Scott. *E. B. White.* New York: W. W. Norton & Co., 1985.

Russell, Isabel. *Katharine and E. B. White.* New York: W. W. Norton & Co., 1988.

TENNESSEE WILLIAMS

Falk, Signi. *Tennessee Williams*. Boston: Twayne, 1978.

Williams, Dakin, and Sherman Mead. *Tennessee Williams*. New York: Arbor House, 1983.

Williams, Tennessee. *Memoirs*. New York: Doubleday & Co., 1975.

Suggested Further Reading

The following list contains works suggested for young readers written by the authors whose lives are the subject of this book.

Part I

JAMES FENIMORE COOPER

Cooper, James Fenimore. *The Deerslayer.* New York: Charles Scribner's Sons, 1929.
———. *The Last of the Mohicans.* New York: Charles Scribner's Sons, 1952.
———. *The Spy.* New York: Dodd, Mead & Company, 1946.

RALPH WALDO EMERSON

Atkinson, Bruce, ed. *The Selected Writings of Ralph Waldo Emerson.* New York: The Modern Library, 1992.

NATHANIEL HAWTHORNE

Hawthorne, Nathaniel. *Great Short Works of Nathaniel Hawthorne.* New York: Barnes & Noble, 1992.
———. *The House of the Seven Gables.* New York: Dodd, Mead & Company, 1979.
———. *The Scarlet Letter.* Columbus: Ohio State University Press, 1962.

WASHINGTON IRVING

Irving, Washington. *The Legend of Sleepy Hollow and Other Selections.* (paper) New York: Washington Square Press, 1962.
———. *Rip Van Winkle.* Tarrytown, NY: Sleepy Hollow Press, 1980.
———. *The Sketchbook of Geoffrey Crayon, Gent.* (paper) New York: Penguin, 1988.

HENRY WADSWORTH LONGFELLOW

Longfellow, Henry Wadsworth. *The Poetical Works of Henry Wadsworth Longfellow.* Boston: Houghton Mifflin, 1975.

HERMAN MELVILLE

Melville, Herman. *The Complete Stories of Herman Melville.* New York: Random House, 1949.

————. *Moby-Dick.* Berkeley: University of California Press, 1981.

————. *Typee.* New York: Dodd, Mead and Company, undated.

EDGAR ALLAN POE

Poe, Edgar Allan. *Complete Works of Edgar Allan Poe.* 2 vols. Cambridge: Belknap Press of Harvard University Press, 1969.

————. *The Pit and the Pendulum and Five Other Tales.* New York: Franklin Watts, 1967.

HARRIET BEECHER STOWE

Stowe, Harriet Beecher. *Three Novels: Uncle Tom's Cabin, The Minister's Wooing, Old-time Folks.* New York: Library of America, 1982.

————. *Uncle Tom's Cabin.* New York: Viking Penguin, 1981.

HENRY DAVID THOREAU

Thoreau, Henry David. *Walden and Other Writings.* New York: Modern Library, 1950.

Part II

LOUISA MAY ALCOTT

Alcott, Louisa May. *Eight Cousins.* Boston: Little, Brown & Co., 1927.

————. *Little Men.* Boston: Little, Brown & Co., 1913.

————. *Little Women.* Boston: Little, Brown & Co., 1968.

EMILY DICKINSON

Johnson, Thomas, ed. *The Complete Poems of Emily Dickinson.* Boston: Little, Brown & Co., 1960.

THEODORE DREISER

Dreiser, Theodore. *Dawn: A History of Myself.* New York: Horace Liveright, 1931.

————. *Sister Carrie, Jennie Gerhard, Twelve Men.* New York: Library of America, 1987.

O. HENRY

Henry, O. *Selected Stories.* (paper) New York: Viking, 1993.

————. *Tales of O. Henry.* New York: Barnes & Noble, 1993.

HENRY JAMES

James, Henry. *Daisy Miller.* Mattituck, NY: Amereon, 1987.

————. *The Turn of the Screw and The Aspern Papers.* London: J. M. Dent, 1952.

————. *Washington Square.* (paper) New York: Oxford University Press, 1982.

JACK LONDON

London, Jack. *The Call of the Wild.* New York: Macmillan, 1963.

————. *Short Stories.* New York: Macmillan, 1990.

————. *White Fang.* New York: Grosset and Dunlap, 1933.

MARK TWAIN

Twain, Mark. *The Adventures of Huckleberry Finn.* New York: Macmillan, 1962.

————. *The Adventures of Tom Sawyer.* Berkeley: University of California Press, 1982.

————. *The Celebrated Jumping Frog of Calavaras County.* New York: Franklin Watts, 1978.

————. *The Prince and the Pauper.* New York: World, 1948.

WALT WHITMAN

Whitman, Walt. *Complete Poetry and Collected Prose.* New York: Library of America, 1982.

Part III

PEARL S. BUCK

Buck, Pearl S. *The Good Earth.* New York: Harper & Row, 1949.

WILLA CATHER

Cather, Willa. *Great Short Works of Willa Cather.* New York: Harper & Row, 1989.
———. *My Antonia.* Boston: Houghton, Mifflin Company, 1954.
———. *O Pioneers!* Boston: Houghton, Mifflin Company, 1941.

WILLIAM FAULKNER

Faulkner, William. *Intruders in the Dust.* New York: Random House, 1948.
———. *Light in August.* New York: Modern Library, 1954.
———. *The Reivers.* New York: Random House, 1962.

F. SCOTT FITZGERALD

Fitzgerald, F. Scott. *The Great Gatsby.* New York: Charles Scribner's Sons, 1953.
———. *The Stories of F. Scott Fitzgerald.* New York: Charles Scribner's Sons, 1951.
———. *This Side of Paradise.* New York: Charles Scribner's Sons, 1920.

ROBERT FROST

Frost, Robert. *North of Boston.* Boston: Dodd, Mead & Company, 1977.
Lathem, Edward C., ed. *The Poetry of Robert Frost.* New York: Holt, Rinehart & Winston, 1969.

ERNEST HEMINGWAY

Hemingway, Ernest. *For Whom the Bell Tolls.* New York: Charles Scribner's Sons, 1940.
———. *The Nick Adams Stories.* New York: Charles Scribner's Sons, 1972.
———. *The Old Man and the Sea.* New York: Charles Scribner's Sons, 1952.

LANGSTON HUGHES

Hughes, Langston. *The Best of Simple.* New York: Hill and Wang, 1968.
———. *The Dream Keeper and Other Poems.* New York: Alfred A. Knopf, 1954.
———. *Not Without Laughter.* New York: Alfred A. Knopf, 1968.

SINCLAIR LEWIS

Lewis, Sinclair. *Arrowsmith.* (paper) New York: Signet, 1980.
———. *Babbitt.* New York: Harcourt, Brace & World, 1922.
———. *Main Street.* (paper) New York: Signet, 1980.

EUGENE O'NEILL

O'Neill, Eugene. *The Iceman Cometh.* New York: Random House, 1946.
———. *Long Day's Journey into Night.* New Haven: Yale University Press, 1956.

JOHN STEINBECK

Steinbeck, John. *The Grapes of Wrath.* New York: Viking, 1989.
———. *The Pearl.* New York: Viking, 1947.
———. *The Red Pony.* New York: Viking, 1945.
———. *Tortilla Flat.* New York: Covici Friede, 1945.

EDITH WHARTON

Wharton, Edith. *The Age of Innocence.* New York: Charles Scribner's Sons, 1968.
———. *Ethan Frome.* New York: Charles Scribner's Sons, 1939.
———. *The Old Maid.* New York: D. Appleton and Company, 1924.

E. B. WHITE

White, E. B. *Charlotte's Web.* New York: Harper & Row, 1952.
———. *Essays of E. B. White.* New York: Harper & Row, 1954.
———. *Stuart Little.* New York: Harper & Row, 1973.

———. *Trumpet of the Swan.* New York: Harper & Row, 1970.

TENNESSEE WILLIAMS

Williams, Tennessee. *The Theatre of Tennessee Williams.* 3 vols. New York: New Directions, 1971.

Index